ONCE WE WERE LIKE WOLVES

M. TODD GALLOWGLAS

ONCE WE WERE LIKE WOLVES
Copyright © 2024 M. Todd Gallowglas
Original edition published 2011

Cover design by Cody Parcell

ISBN:
979-8-89546-630-8

DEDICATION

For Sean Graethorne
He gave me the title and his song planted seeds deep in my imagination that
eventually grew into the Morigahnti.

ACKNOWLEDGMENTS

What's a guy to say the second time around? The landscape has changed so much since the last time I was here, I'm going to ramble a bit. First off, Cody Parcell has been my right hand man through thick and thin for over a decade now. He's put a good face on so many of my books and spent so much time listening to me talk about books and writing, that he's become an integral part of my process. I'm especially pleased with the new covers for *Tear of Rage*. He also designed the amazing script of *Galad'laman* you see on the covers. Robin helped shape Julianna and guided my initial forays into this world. Her fingerprints will forever be a part of this series. This reenvisioning of this story has been long overdue, years overdue, and I'd like to give my deepest thanks to those who have hung on with patience greater than a certain goddess waiting for one of the Greater Eldar to break free from the King of Order's prison. I hope it was worth the wait.

DRAMATIS PERSONÆ

The Komati Nobility

Julianna Taraen—A Duchess, and the Lord Morigahn.

Alyxandros Vivaen—A count. Julianna's uncle.

Allifar Thaedus—A Count

Parshyval "Parsh" Thaedus—a Baron. Allifar's younger brother.

High Blood of the Kingdom of the Sun

Octavio Salvatore—Kingdom Governor of Koma.

Dante Salvatore—Octavio's younger brother.

Hardin Thorinson—Adept of Old Uncle Night.

Carmine D'Mario—Half-blood noble both of the House Floraen and of Komati blood.

Luciano Salvatore—House Floraen Inquisitor.

Cadenza D'Mario—An Adept of All Father Sun. Carmine's cousin.

Vycktor Ilsaen—An Adept of Grandfather Shadow.

Luciano Salvatore—House Floraen Inquisitor.

Tamaz—An Adept of House Kaesiak.

Rosella—An Adept of House Floraen.

Ulfric—An Adept of House Swaenmarch.

Commoners

Colette—Julianna's maid.

Faelin vara'Traejyn—A bastard wanderer.

Jorgen—An acolyte of the Brotherhood of the Night.

Symond—An acolyte of the Brotherhood of the Night.\

Korrin Sontam—A Morigahnti in service to Count Allifar.

Nathan Sontam—A Morigahnti in service to Count Allifar.

Wyndolen "Wynd" Sontam—A Morigahnti. Nathan's Wife

Aurell—A Morigahnti in service to Count Allifar.

Taebor—A young Morigahnti.

Kaelyb—A farmer.

Isnia—Kaelyb's wife.

Erik Dressel—Mayor of Shadybrook township.

Gillaen Dressel—Erik's wife.

Jenise—A servant.

Kalla—A cook.

Ida—A wet nurse.

Novan—A young man in service to Erik Dressel.

Zephyer—A smuggler, among other callings.

Celestials, Infernals, and Others

Grandfather Shadow—Known also as Galad'Ysoysa. A Greater God.

Yrgaeshkil—The Mother of Daemyns, Goddess of Lies.

Kahddria—Goddess of Wind.

Muriel – A Seant of Yrgaeshkil, called "the Destroyer."

Galbra'thantalys—A Daemyn

Razka—A Stormseeker.

Morag—A Stormseeker

Maxian, also called "Smoke"

Kavala

PROLOGUE

Allifar scrambled through the underbrush. His hands bled from the scrapes and punctures he'd received from the jagged rocks and sharp thorns that covered the ground in Kyrtigaen Pass. Twigs and brambles caught on his clothes, especially his newly woven *Galad'fana*. His head pounded from a cacophony of gunfire, metal ringing on metal, the moans and cries of the wounded and dying, and howling wolves mixed. In a small blessing, the smell of gun smoke filled the pass, covering up all but the worst of blood, gore, and human waste. Given the choice, Allifar would suffer noise over stench. On the other side of the coin, the haze of smoke burned his eyes, nose, and throat. He was so thirsty, he might well give his title over for a healthy swallow of water.

How long had the fighting been going on? Was it even noon yet? This was supposed to be a decisive victory against the Kingdom of the Sun, the first of many on Koma's journey to freedom. This morning, Allifar had dreamed of glory and victory. Now, he just wanted to survive the day and return home to his wife and son.

Gods and goddesses, Allifar's throat burned. In that moment, if someone had offered, he'd give his entire inheritance for a bit of quiet and a cool drink. That thought made him wonder about his title. Was he still *Baron* Allifar Thaedus, or had this battle elevated him to being a count? He pushed that thought aside and continued on. If something had happened to Father, Allifar needed to survive, for the sake of his family and House.

A few moments later, Allifar came to a break in the brush. He regarded the open space, the earth blackened and scorched. What had caused this? A bolt of lighting? Possibly a sunflare? It didn't matter. He only cared about the twenty-or-so paces that lay between him and the brambles and thickets on the other side of the blackened ground. Taking seven slow breaths, Allifar steadied himself and tightened his grip on the two-shot pistol. He had one shot remaining. After he spent that, he could use the weapon as a club, but that wouldn't serve well against an enemy with a sword.

He exhaled the last bit of that seventh breath and dashed out of the brush.

Halfway across, a wave of vertigo crashed down like a physical blow. It wasn't a scorch mark. A blight. Likely comprised of some mix of Uncle Night's dominions of Death, Corruption, and Sickness.

Stomach churned; vision swam, wavering this way and that; the earth seemed to lurch to the side with each footfall; choking down bile; holding breath; closed eyes; take just one more step, one more step, one more step.

A few steps later, thorns and branches pierced and raked Allifar's hands and face. He dove forward into the thicket, little scrapes and cuts be damned, hoping and praying that he escape the effect of the miracle, *if,* that is, this was a localized effect. If not, he would soon be among the saents in Grandfather Shadow's hall. When he felt clear of the blight, in the full embrace of the thicket, Allifar collapsed to his hands and knees. He coughed, gagged, and then his sides heaved, purging bile from his body.

Sometime later, he lay on his side, panting, drenched in sweat, sides aching. How long had he been vomiting? It couldn't have been too long; the sounds of battle still echoed off the walls of Kyrtigaen Pass. A volley of gunfire followed by a chorus of screams urged Allifar to pull himself up and continue his way through the thicket. He needed to find other Morigahnti before any Kingdom forces found him.

A short time later, he came again to a break in his cover. This time the brush ended due to a creek bed, one of the many in the pass that saw torrents of water from the melting snowpack on the peaks above; however, this year's dry summer had diminished the torrent to a babbling brook. Still, Allifar pitched forward, almost diving for the brook. Desperate for a drink, at first he tried lapping the water up like a dog. After realizing that proved too slow a method, he cupped his hands and splashed water into his mouth, not caring that the water was slightly muddy with the faint taste of blood. After seven or so mouthfuls, Allifar stopped drinking. By that time, his rational mind had returned. If he kept guzzling, he'd make himself sick.

Reluctantly, he pulled his attention away from the creek and looked upstream. Even before looking away, Grandfather Shadow's Third Law came to the forefront of Allifar's mind: *A Morigahnti does not let a brother face danger alone.* Then, equally unbidden, came Father's words: *Make me proud. Make your son proud.* He'd spoken them just before heading off to join the Lord Morigahn, leaving Allifar with a Fist under the command of Duke Jaesyn Thaems. Within minutes of the conflict starting, the Fist had been scattered by members of the Brotherhood of the Night.

Allifar headed upstream, staying low as he made slow, steady progress. While he still flinched at every sound, now Allifar had a goal, a destination, rather than just wandering aimlessly around the battlefield just hoping not to die. Also, if he kept his head down, the creek bed provided better cover than the thicket.

Mid-stride, all the noise of the skirmishes — for it couldn't be called a battle any longer — seemed to quiet. It wasn't that the fighting stopped; rather, that the pace of the battle slowed to the point where each clash of swords, every gunshot, and the syllables of each miracle existed in a moment removed from all the others, with the space of time between those moments growing further and further apart. And, in that moment where the quiet seemed to permeate, a voice raised to echo across Kyrtigaen Pass.

"*Galad'thanya...*"

Allifar's heart quickened. Only one person could speak that miracle.

"*...kuiva aen...*"

Mostly on instinct, Allifar flung himself face-first to the ground.

"*...eva ruth!*"

A thunderclap *boomed*

A shockwave passed over Allifar, lifting him a few inches off the ground and carrying him back downstream a short way before dropping him back to the ground.

Pulling himself to his feet, Allifar started forward at a jog. The Lord Morigahn, the source of the miracle, was still alive. That meant Father likely was also. Unless, the Lord Morigahn had spoken the miracle of Shadow's Thunder as a last resort.

Casting stealth aside, Allifar rushed forward, feet sloshing in the creek bed. He kept his pistol up, gaze firmly fixed down the twin barrels as he shifted the weapon left and right. After about a hundred paces, the stream rose to weave through a relatively flat area about fifty paces across. Bodies littered the ground. Some in large jumbles of twisted limbs. Some in ones, twos, and threes. Scanning for movement, Allifar first noticed the large number of bodies wearing the black armor and skull helmets of the Brotherhood of the Night. Those remained unmoving, or if they did move, it was nothing more than a twitching hand or foot.

Out of the corner of his eye, Allifar caught something moving more than just a twitching limb. Turning, he aimed his pistol in that direction. Allifar saw a man in the Brotherhood of the Night armor trying to crawl out from a clump of bodies.

For just a moment, Allifar nearly squeezed the trigger to fire his pistol, but an uneasy quiet had descended on Kyrtigaen pass since the Lord Morigahn had spoken the miracle of Shadow's Thunder. No need to draw attention to himself. Also, with all the weapons laying around, why waste the precious bullets when he didn't have to?

As his enemy struggled to extricate himself from the pile of bodies, Allifar dashed forward, slowing just long enough to snatch a short sword off the ground before sprinting toward the Nightbrother. As Allifar closed the distance, water-soaked boots thumping and squelching on the bare and flattened earth, the skull-headed leather helm turned toward Allifar. The man tried to pull away but couldn't untangle himself from the other bodies. Allifar dropped his knee onto his enemy's chest. The Nightbrother flailed his arms and flopped about, a last struggle to keep Allifar from killing him. With three quick thrusts of the short sword, the Nightbrother stopped struggling.

Allifar released the sword, stood, and stepped away from the body. He'd killed before, maybe half a dozen men. He didn't know for sure. He'd never known for sure, as in the heat of battle, a man couldn't always tell the difference between a wound that killed or just incapacitated a man, keeping an enemy from fighting further. This was the first time that Allifar knew for certain that he'd sent a man to dance in Old Uncle Night's embrace.

A stray thought flittered through Allifar's mind. Why should a man who had dedicated himself to serving the god of death be so afraid to die?

"Morigahnti," a voice called.

Allifar spun and lifted his firearm.

In the center of this flattened area, a man wearing a *Galad'fana* around his head stood up from No. Not just a Man.

"Lord Morigahn!" Allifar cried.

All thoughts and worries of enemies and his father flew from Allifar's mind, and he rushed to the man who was Grandfather Shadow's voice in the physical realm. and examined his leader. The Lord Morigahn's left arm was soaked in blood from a deep gash on his shoulder, and a shaft of wood protruded from his left hip at an awkward angle. While the Galad'fana was still wrapped around Lord Morigahn's head, it had fallen away from his face. His pace was pale, and he sucked each breath through clenched teeth.

As Allifar spoke the words, "You're hurt," his ears grew warm.

Of course the Lord Morigan knew of his injuries. He didn't need some young Morigahnti, fresh to the gray, prattling on about the obvious.

Allifar considered both wounds. While the shaft in the Lord Morigahn's hip might be the more serious of the two, it wouldn't make sense to heal it without first removing the bolt. Allifar didn't want to gamble on the tip being barbed or not. So, instead, he placed his hands on the Lord Morigahn's shoulder and drew on the dominion of Balance through his Galad'fana. The words of a miracle came to the front of his mind. The cloth about Allifar's head hummed with the divine power of his god.

"Galad'Y soysa tsenki kin—"

Before Allifar could complete the miracle, the Lord Morigahn pulled away from Allifar's touch.

"No!"

Allifar stared at the Lord Morigahn Why would his leader pull away from a Morigahnti attempting to take some of the burden of his injuries?

"I am near death," the Lord Morigahn said. "If you try to balance my wounds, you will only weaken yourself. I have a task omore important than aiding me."

"I don't…" Allifar's thoughts just couldn't seem to come together.

"Understand?" the Lord Morigahn asked.

Allifar nodded.

"You don't see the knife wound in my lower back," the Lord Morigahn said. "Or all of my blood that soaks the ground around me. You can do nothing for me, Count Thaedus."

Allifar blinked at those words.

The Lord Morigahn would only refer to Allifar as *Count* Thaedus if… father had… had…

"I cannot do nothing, Lord Morigahn," Allifar said. "A Moriganti does not leave a brother to face danger alone."

Allifar knew that he'd misquoted the Third Law of Shadow. A Moraigahnti, a *true* Morigahnti must know, understand, and adhere to the Laws of Shadow at all times. Still, under the circumstances, the Lord Morigahn was unlikely to admonish Allifar for the slip.

"I would not have you sit idly by and do nothing, young Allifar," the Lord Morigahn said. "I am but a man with a title. A title other men will bear. This whole battle, this slaughter, was not intended for the Morigahnti. We are a pleasant collateral for the Brotherhood of the Night."

"Not us?" Allifar asked. "Then who?"

The Lord Morigahn coughed. A bit of blood dribbled from the corner of his mouth and his right nostril.

"The Stormseekers."

The Lord Morigahn pointed upward. High above them, on the mountains above Kyrtigaen Pass, Allifar saw a pillar of some silvery metal, glowing and emitting sparks. Looking about the high peaks he saw more of them scattered about. Tendrils of energy snaked and slithered through the air from one to another.

"What are those things?" Allifar asked.

"We know not," the Lord Morigahn said. "But since I first noticed those devices, the Stromseekers have been unable to use their gifts granted by Grandfather Shadow."

"How is—"

"The how matters not for the moment. Only that it is happening. You must save those Stormseekers still living. Have the Stormcrows spread the word. You must escape with as many of the Stormseekers as you can, above all other priorities." The Lord Morigahn gestured to his right. "Beyond the Night Brother corpses that way, you will find a Stormseeker female. Save her."

"Yes, Lord Morigahn. I will." Allifar saluted. Then, looking the high priest of Grandfather Shadow in the eye, Allifar added, *"Kun vaen ovat kuten makaesti."*

The Lord Morigan reach up with his right hand and placed it on Allifar's shoulder. His face softened into a wan smile.

"Medan kerta voida tas johta." The Lord Morigan squeezed Allifar's shoulder. "Go now, Count Thaedus. Spread the word. I will try to draw the Nightbrothers to me for as long as I am able. Tell my successor of my choice."

Allifar nodded. The Lord Morigahn released his shoulder. Without further comment, Allifar headed in the direction Lord Morigahn had indicated.

Roughly twenty paces up the stream, Allifar found a young woman sprawled on the bare earth. Her eyes were closed. Her breath came in fitful gasps. Dried blood from a gash in her forehead caked the left side of her face. Even with that, her stark and feral beauty stole Allifar's breath. He shook his head, clearing this sudden stupor of infatuation. He shoved his two-shot pistol into his belt. After a few moments of struggle, managed to get the Stormseeker maiden onto his shoulders.

Not having any idea which was the shortest way to get the Stormseeker clear of Kyrtigaen, Allifar returned to the stream. He looked first upstream and then downstream, back the way he'd come. Which way to go? After a moment, he realized that downstream was the only way that would lead him out of the pass. In the battle, Allifar had been turned around so much that he didn't know whether downstream would lead to Koma or the Dosahan lands. Had All Father Sun hung in at any point in the sky other than his zenith, Allifar could have used him to determine which way to go. However, since he had no better indication, he set off downstream.

After about a minute or so, when he reached the point where the creek bed walls were about even with his head, Allifar heard the Lord Morigahn's voice behind him...

"Galad'Thanya..."

"Shades!" Allifar snapped.

He pitched forward, twisting at the waist and shoulders so that the Stormseeker maiden came down on top of him. A small blessing that she didn't knock his breath away.

"…*kuiva aen*…"

With both of them in the stream, Allifar embraced the Stormseeker and rolled them to the side of the creek. He pinned the girl to the damp earth there, hoping to shield her at least a bit from the Lord Morigahn's miracle.

"…*eva ruth*!"

With the last word spoken, a thunderclap *boomed*, and a wave of force pulled them two of them downstream a few paces, but due to the extra weight of the girl in his embrace and being up against the creek bed wall, the miracle didn't affect them as much.

As Allifar lifted the Stormseeker back onto his shoulders and started off again, he gave a rueful laugh. By speaking the miracle of Shadow's Thunder a second time in such rapid succession, the Lord Morigahn would certainly draw the attention of every Nightbrother in Kyrtigaen pass. Hopefully, they would pay more attention to that than a lone Morigahnti carrying a young woman out of the pass.

Once on his feet and moving, Allifar made progress as quickly as he could without stumbling. He wanted to get far enough away so that he could be well past the affected area if the Lord Morigahn had the strength to speak the Miracle of Shadow's Thunder again.

Allifar pulled his pistol from his belt, gripping the barrel. After rolling about in the stream, he couldn't possibly expect the weapon to discharge. If it did, he couldn't know for certain it wouldn't do more harm to himself than it would to his target. He considered, for a brief moment, brandishing it like a pistol in order to intimidate and bluff his way past any enemies he might encounter; however, that would likely only work if he met with a solitary enemy. So, a cudgel it was.

From back the way he'd come, the sounds of battle returned, including now voices calling out in several divine languages. It seemed that the Lord Moirgahn's miracle had drawn the attention of more than just the Brotherhood of the Night. If Grandfather Shadow was in one of his rare, benevolent moods, that might just mean the way ahead was clear. On the other side of the coin, this might be one of those moments the god decided to test his followers to see which of them was worthy to wear the *Galad'fana*.

Allifar quickened his pace. After a few minutes, he had to slow. Allifar was no weakling, rather, broad-shouldered and strong. Still, the day and his burden wore upon him. After a short time, likely only a few minutes, he slogged his way through the stream, step after step, right foot then left foot then right foot then left foot, thoughts of yet another Lord Morigahn Fallen to the Kingdom weighed upon him.

The pattern had started with Maxian Taraen and had only gotten worse in the years since. Allifar's Father had been planning on taking him and Parsh to the gathering at Maxian Taraen's manor the night they'd lost the Taraens to the Brotherhood of the Night. Had the Thaedus family and their followers been there, the Taraens might very well still be a family of note. Maxian might still remain the lord Morigahn. Instead, that seemed to spark off events Then, six months after enduring Trial of Shadows, Hayden Collaen had been poisoned. Now, a year later, the Morigahnti were going to lose another Lord Morigahn. With each passing year, it seemed as though Kingdom Inquisitors and the Brotherhood of the Night killed the Morigahnti in greater and greater numbers, while more and more Komati turned from the old ways, seemingly content with Kingdom rule.

The echoes of battle fell further and further behind. Allifar's thoughts dwindled to a prayer, "Grandfather Shadow, send us a Lord Morigahn worthy of the mantle…" He whispered the prayer again and again as he placed one foot in front of the other, over and over and over…

Later — calves and thighs burning, stabbing pains lancing through his knees, and shoulders and lower back aching from the strain of carrying the Storm Seeker — Allifar placed his foot down, and his body refused to take the next step. Breathing deep breaths through his nose, Allifar stood straighter, despite the burden weighing upon his shoulders. He couldn't tell why he'd stopped, but in his exhaustion, he couldn't afford to ignore his instincts.

About twenty paces downstream, a man stepped out from the brush growing atop the creek bed. The furs and leathers he wore matched his wild and unkempt hair and beard, just as old and rugged as the man's wrinkled and cracked skin. Though this stranger seemed just a sigh away from venerably ancient, he moved with a strength of purpose and fluid grace few men, young or old, ever possessed.

Allifar drew in a deep breath and bent his knees, set to scramble out of the creek and into the brush. He might not be able to escape, but he would have to try. As the Lord Morigahn said, they had to save as many Stormseekers as possible.

"Once we were like wolves." The old man's voice sounded as old and weathered as his skin.

"Our time can come again," Allifar replied, then added. "You are not Morigahnti."

"No."

The man came toward Allifar. That he made no sound when stepping on the twigs and rocks of the creek bed sent a shiver through Allifar's stomach. He felt he'd rather face a Kingdom White Draqon than this man. With this dread tightening his chest, Allifar prepared to bolt.

"Relax boy," the man said. "I'm not here to harm you or her. I'm here to take her to safety, away from the Brotherhood, the Morigahnti," he waved his arm to encompass the whole of Kyrtigaen Pass, "all of this. We are done with this pathetic conflict that can't even seem to end even with the five trapped in their prison."

"What?"

Allifar felt as if he should understand that, but his fatigue seemed to keep his mind from putting the various pieces together.

"Stormseekers lad," the man said. "We are finished."

And then Allifar realized who stood before him.

"Razka?"

The leader of the Stormseekers nodded.

"I suppose the Stomcrows will continue to aid you. It's in their nature." Razka continued walking forward. "After this battle, we are too few in number to risk ourselves for your cause."

Allifar was too dumbfounded by being in the presence of this being who might as well have been a god to even consider challenging him or fleeing. Within the span of several heartbeats, Razka stood just beyond arm's reach. He stood nearly a head taller than Allifar and looked down at him, meeting his gaze.

"Give me my niece." The words came out as almost a growl.

Allifar nodded. He shifted his shoulders and passed the burden over to the Stormseeker. Razka eased the female Stormseeker onto his shoulders as if she were a child. The

Stormseeker moved away from the young Morigahnti, and with a clap of thunder and a small flash of lightning, he was gone.

Allifar dropped to his knees, the muddy water soaking him almost to his waist. His breath came in short gasps. First the loss of yet another Lord Morigahn, and now the Stormseekers were leaving the Morigahnti with only the Stormcrows. How were the Komati ever going to win their freedom from the Kingdom of the Sun? Had Grandfather Shadow truly forsaken his chosen people as the Adepts of House Kaesiack claimed?

TROUBLES COME TO A FARMSTEAD

You come to me, even as you prepare to end me, begging for answers. Don't bother lying. I know the look of men haunted by nightmares. You ask me which of them you have offended so you may make amends. Was it Aunt Moon, Uncle Night, or perhaps even Grandfather Shadow? And you all sneer at me for my blindness. Why do you assume these nighttime visions come from one of those three, especially when not a single one of them possesses the Dominion of Dreams? Ponder this: In your Pantheon of greater gods and goddesses, you acknowledge a Grandfather, yet ignore the existence of a Grandmother? If such a Grandmother exists, do you imagine she is pleased by this oversight?

  — The Blind Prophet, the night before his trial.

Of all those who have placed ink to page in this tome, I have the distinctions of being the first woman, and I am likely the least prepared to be Lord Morigahn. For the last fourteen years, memories of my family's allegiance to the old ways of the Komati and Grandfather Shadow had been hidden in the deep shadows of my mind. Despite lacking any knowledge of my ancestry or understanding of my people's ancient culture, Grandfather Shadow marked me as he has marked every Lord Morigahn since Kaeldyr the Gray. I should not have survived. Yet, thus far, I have overcome the elements, the Brotherhood of the Night, Kingdom Inquisitors, Daemyn Hounds, bouts of insanity, and my own naiveté and ignorance. Either I was truly destined to be the Lord Morigahn, or I'm also the most blessed person to ever bear this mantle. Neither side of that coin fills me with confidence.

  — Julianna Taraen, her first entry into *The Tome of Shadows*.

ONE

For the first time since Grandfather Shadow had marked her as the Lord Morigahn, Julianna felt she had achieved a true state of balance. She lay in a bed and managed to maintain that state just on the edge of sleep and wakefulness. The bed was more of a cot and the blankets were rough wool that scratched at her face and hand, but it had been so long since Julianna had slept on anything other than the ground and under the sky, she might as well have been sinking into a down mattress with the smoothest of linens. Her state of balance came from reveling in the warm and dry comfort of this small room and not allowing her to fall asleep and subjecting herself to the nightmares that awaited her there.

Julianna drew in a deep breath and shifted from her left side to her right. The musty air of the spare room filled her awareness for a moment. Dawn was sometime in the near future. Then Julianna would have to wake full. She and Faelin would have to decide their course of action. Where would they go while attempting to flee the Brotherhood of the Night and Kingdom Inquisitors; however, in that moment, Julianna settled down, content.

The door opened. A few weeks earlier, and Julianna wouldn't have even detected the soft brushing of the door as it slipped from the door frame and brushed across the floor. Events of the last fortnight, since her birthday, had made her keenly aware of those sounds that seemed innocuous.

Julianna opened her eyes. The light of a single candle filled her vision. As her eyes adjusted to this light, Julianna slid her hand under her pillow and grasped the hilt of her knife.

"Julianna," Faelin's voice came in a whisper, "are you awake."

"Yes," Julianna replied.

"Good," Faelin said. "We have to go."

"Now?" Julianna sat up. "Why?"

Her eyes grew accustomed to the new light, and she saw Faelin clearly. He had both his pack slung over his left shoulder and the saddlebags over his right.

He shook his head. "I cannot tell."

Julianna sat up, and her body protested. In their days of travel, she'd fought sleep so that she never fully recovered from the pace Faelin set each day. When they'd decided to seek a night of shelter at this farm rather than press on through the woods, they'd known it was a gamble. They also knew that they needed rest. While still weary, Julianna did not feel the ache of exhaustion that had pressed down upon her the last few days.

"Our hosts——?"

"Kaelyb and Isnia are still as they appear," Faelin replied. "It's not them. Something seems…off…wrong. As I said, I cannot put a name or a word to it. I just feel that we must go."

Along with the heightened awareness of sounds, in the last fortnight, Julianna had learned to trust Faelin's instincts. She'd accepted that Grandfather Shadow had sent Faelin as a guardian, and so she would heed such warnings.

"Very well."

Faelin crossed the room and pushed open the sole window. Cold, night air filled the room, nipping Julianna's nose, cheeks, and ears.

Julianna stood. She reached under the blankets for her *Galad'fana*, and wrapped it around her neck and shoulders like a scarf. Aside from the divine focus of her god, she still wore her clothes. They'd agreed to sleep dressed, on the off chance that they might need to flee upon a moment's warning.

"The window?" Julianna asked. "Truly?"

"Safest choice," Faelin said. "It's just before dawn. Kaelyb fell asleep in his chair in the sitting room."

"I think we are capable of sneaking past one old man asleep in a chair," Julianna said.

"Don't be so certain," Faelin said. "That old man has a canny awareness about him. He's wise and alert, like most folk who live isolated on the edge of the wilderness. If we wake him, we can hope the only thing we'll have to do is suffer through a parting meal, which will mean he'll wake his wife, they will fuss, and we won't be away until mid-morning at least. More likely he'll have questions about why we are being such poor guests. He may want to know what we're taking or hiding. Might even want to search our baggage."

"I won't let him," Julianna said. "We can't let him know who I am. Even in this remote place."

"Indeed," Faelin said. "But then that will lead to other problems and other questions. How far are you willing to go in order to keep your secrets?"

Julianna opened her mouth, mind searching for a response. She closed her mouth when she realized she didn't know the answer to his question."

"Right," Faelin said. "I don't know either. So, better to just climb out the window and lead Vendyr quietly away."

Glancing at the window, Julianna wanted to protest. She was a Duchess of House Kolmonen. More than that, she was the Lord Morigahn, first chosen of Grandfather Shadow. She should not be forced to climb about through a window like some thief in the night. Then, Julianna looked at the bed, with its lumpy mattress and worn wool sheets. A part of her also didn't want to believe that she had come to consider such sparse accommodations as luxurious; however, that changed when she accepted Grandfather Shadow's offer and become the Lord Morigahn.

"I understand it's not particularly dignified," Faelin said. "But it's the best option."

Julianna sighed. "I wouldn't go so far as to say it's the best option. However, it's the practical choice. Give me a lift up."

As she sheathed her knife and set to climb out the window, Julianna had two thoughts.

First, at least it wasn't raining. She could tolerate cold. As the day went on, she would warm, which wouldn't be the case with rain. Cold and wet would define her existence. And while Grandfather Shadow was the god of storms, Julianna could do with a bit of balance in being wet and dry.

Second, it pleased Julianna that whatever danger Faelin sensed coming would not take them unaware. Perhaps they might avoid the dangers altogether, though she didn't really believe that. She'd be dealing with danger for the rest of her life. She had come to accept that. However, she could force those dangers to come on her terms, taking at least some of their advantages away.

Even with her aching joints, crawling through the window hadn't been nearly as challenging as Julianna had expected. Once through, she turned back and took the pack and saddlebags from

Faelin. A few moments later, Faelin stood with her outside of the farm cottage.

Julianna slung the saddlebags over her shoulder and drew her knife. Faelin slid his arms through the straps of the backpack and drew his dagger. Those were the only weapons they had brought to the farm cottage after they'd decided to approach the place. After much discussion about what to do with the other weapons, they'd decided to wrap them in blankets and bury them beyond the tree line. That seemed less dangerous than having to explain why a young couple was traveling the wilds of Koma with a collection of swords and firearms.

Together they walked toward the barn which was about fifty paces from the farm cottage. A small sliver of light shown at the edge of the eastern horizon. This set the darkness and shadows to intertwine across the farm.

"Keep us safe, brothers and sisters," Julianna whispered to the shadows being born of the first interactions between night and day. "And hide us from our enemies."

Even knowing that when Grandfather Shadow had cut her face, scarring her with a mark declaring her his high priest, Julianna still found it strange to pray to one of the five greater gods and to speak to the shadows.

When they reached halfway between the farm cottage and the barn, Faelin stopped. It took Julianna two steps before she realized that Faelin was no longer beside her. She turned to find Faelin facing away from her, staring back at the cottage, head cocked slightly to the side.

"What—?"

Faelin held up his hand.

Julianna held her voice. She shifted her grip on her knife, scanned the fields for movement, and brought the words of several miracles to the front of her mind. The *Galad'fana* tingled with Grandfather Shadow's dominions, almost as if the divine focus was whispering the names of those dominions into Julianna's skin.

When she saw nothing, Julianna stepped just behind Faelin.

"What is it?" Julianna whispered.

Faelin shook his head. "Don't know. Can't place it. Something between my shoulder blades. Best we get to the barn and out of sight. Don't run, but don't dawdle."

They headed for the barn once again, this time at a brisk walk.

Faelin went through the small door first, and Julianna followed seven heartbeats later. That was long enough for Faelin to determine if any enemies or danger lurked within but not so long that Julianna would remain exposed outside. After Julianna entered, Faelin stood at the door, head moving side to side as he searched for the source of his uneasiness.

After a few moments, he muttered, "There."

Julianna moved next to him, peering just over his shoulder. A dark figure strode across the field in front of the farm cottage. Where had it come from? Not from the woods. The space between the treeline and the cottage was too great for this newcomer to have come from the trees. The light growing in the east showed just brightly enough for Julianna to make out the leathery wings sprouting from its shoulder blades.

"Daemyn," Julianna gasped.

Not just a Daemyn hound, a fully formed Daemyn wandering about the physical world. Even with their faerii steel knives, how could they hope to fight such a creature?

"Hush," Faelin whispered. "It doesn't seem to know we're here. Let's not change that."

Julianna held her breath and sent silent prayers to the shadows of early morning as the Daemyn walked up to the cottage, ascended the steps to the porch, and crouched down. Then, the otherworldly creature stood, turned, and headed back the way it had come. About halfway between the cottage and the treeline, the Daemyn faded slowly from sight, vanishing altogether as the light of dawn grew more and more steadily.

"We should go before any other strangeness decides to pay this farm a visit," Faelin said.

He went to where Vendyr's tack and saddle hung on the barn wall. The white and black horse had free reign of the barn, as this small farm had goats, sheep, and an ox, but no room to stable a horse. When Vendyr saw Faelin lift the saddle blanket, the horse walked over and nuzzled Faelin's shoulder.

Faelin went about putting the saddle and tack on Vendyr.

Julianna asked, "Is it safe to wander while a Daemyn might be about?".

"Safer than staying," Faelin replied without looking at her. He added softly, "Besides, I doubt that was merely a Daemyn."

Julianna's mouth went dry with that implication. "What?"

"Under the Ykthae Accords," Faelin replied, "normal Daemyns are not usually able to enter the physical realm in their natural form."

Julianna shuddered at the thought that her life had come to a point where they were so casual in their discussion of normal and abnormal Daemyns. Then her stomach clenched as the weight of what Faelin had revealed settled into her mind.

"Then what did we see?"

"I don't know," Faelin said. "I'm not sure I want to. I just want to be on our way and hope we don't get wrapped up in whatever plot that thing is scheming."

Julianna found herself in agreement. A part of her was curious, but she now knew better than to go looking into matters that concerned the celestial and infernal realms. She joined Faelin in preparing Vendyr for travel. In moments, they completed the task and led Vendyr out of the back door of the barn.

"Should we check on—?"

"No," Faelin cut off her question. "We should not. With Grandfather Shadow's return to the world, other celestial and infernal powers will seek to assert influence over the physical realm. We must choose our battles with care and avoid every conflict with them whenever possible."

With a glance over her shoulder, Julianna let out a long sigh. She couldn't see the farm beyond the walls and closed doors, but the image of it in the growing morning light came to her mind. Kaelyb and Isnia deserved better than to get wrapped up in the machinations of the higher realms. They were curt, occasionally abrasive, but they were good, honest Komati folk.

Faelin led Vendyr out of the barn. Julianna followed and tried not to hate herself for thinking about how much she was going to miss that bed with the same conviction as her concern for the farm folk they left in danger.

Two

Kaelyb sat at the table watching his wife prepare breakfast. The young couple had snuck away before like a pair of thieves. Only, they hadn't taken anything. He sipped his tea and wondered about their story, suspecting he would be imagining wondrous and strange explanations for their sudden arrival and departure for the rest of his days.

"What are you about?" Isnia asked. "Get up off your backside and get to the door."

Kaelyb looked up from his tea and blinked. "What my love?"

"A cry came from the door," Isnia said. "Sounded like a baby or a child. Go see about it."

While he was surprised that some child might be crying at their door, it didn't surprise Kaelybe that he hadn't heard it. Over the last few years, his hearing wasn't what it had been in his youth, especially as his mind went wandering.

Kaelyb stood from his chair and gave a little bow. "Your will is my deed, my heart."

He always answered her with those words when she asked him to do something. He'd started back when they'd first married because he thought those words sounded special, fancy. He wanted to make her feel as special as he did by her marrying him. Even after all these years, after all their hardships, Kaelyb wanted his darling Isnia to feel like a newly wed wife. He didn't know if he succeeded all the time, but every now and then, she gave him that coy little smirk she'd flashed again and again while they were courting. That was enough for Kaelyb to keep saying it.

When Kaelyb reached the door, he picked up his ax, really no more than a hatchet, but it had made more than a handful of rogues and ruffians reconsider any amount of mischief they planned for this farm and this house. Kaelyb was by no means a small man, and though streaks of gray shot through his hair and beard, his work about the farm kept him sturdy and strong.

"Who comes to call?" Kaelyb said with a slightly raised voice.

No answer came from beyond the door.

Kaelyb waited a few moments, and then he called out, "Name yourself and your business."

Again, no one answered.

Kaelyb lifted the latch and opened the door. He saw no one. At first, he feared some wee spirit creature of the wood had grown bold enough to bring its tricks out into the fields and to the houses. The absolute last thing he needed was a spirit thinking to play old Kaelyb for the buffoon.

Shaking his head, Kaelyb began to shut the door when he heard a soft whimpering below him.

"What's about at the door?" Isnia asked.

Kaelyb stared, struck nearly dumb before he managed to sort his wits out enough to answer.

"It's a baby."

"What now?" Isnia called from the kitchen nook.

Kaelyb had spoken lower than he intended, still a bit unsure of what he was seeing. In truth, a babe lay in a basket, wrapped in swaddling cloths, so small it couldn't have been more than a few weeks old, a few months at the most.

"A baby." Kaelyb managed to find his voice and raise it enough for his wife to hear. "Someone left a baby on our doorstep."

"Like in a story?" Isnia called. "Such a thing actually happen?"

"Seems so," Kaelyb said. "Come see after the child."

Stepping over the child, Kaelyb moved about the porch, peering this way and that, out into the fields, looking for whoever might have left the child. Seeing no one, he walked out behind the house, around and through the barn, and, just to be sure, he looked under the chicken coop and inside the pig stall. Not only did Kaelyb not find anyone, he found no trace of anyone's passage. He wasn't the best tracker in Koma, but he knew his farm well enough to know when someone had been through. The lack of any signs pointing to someone having been there, along with the sudden and odd appearance of the babe, made Kaelyb grip on his ax a little tighter as he kept making furtive glances to the tree line beyond his fields. While such an oddness as this put Kaelyb ill at ease, he also knew better than to go wasting time on impossible tasks.

By the time Kaelyb returned to the porch, the child no longer lay there. The farmhouse's door swung slightly ajar, and Kaelyb heard Isnia singing softly. This more than anything worried Kaelyb beyond his mind's ability to comprehend.

"Dearest of my heart," Kaelyb said as he walked in the house, "I don't know that...we...should..."

He saw how she cradled the child, gently swaying side to side, humming and singing to it as she had their children when their children had still been about. In this moment, protesting taking the child in would prove futile. Kaelyb knew how much his wife missed being a mother, and they had grown well beyond the years when either would be producing further offspring. Instead of arguing, Kaelyb walked over to his wife and the child, placed his hand on her shoulder, and began stroking her neck, just under the ear, where he knew she really liked it. Isnia leaned into his hand and craned her neck toward his palm.

Even after all these years, Kaelyb still thought his wife beautiful. However, looking at her looking down on the child with the same amount of love and adoration she would have had she carried the child herself, Kaelyb longed for her in a way he hadn't since he was much, much younger. Then, as he looked down at the babe, barely a few weeks old, if that, the dread Kaelyb had felt while he searched for signs of who had left this tiny creature returned.

The baby looked first at Kaelyb, then at where Kaelyb affectionately caressed his wife. It *knew* what was happening there, and then the baby looked directly into Kaelyb's eyes and he say jealousy, the same sort of jealousy he'd seen so many decades ago in the eyes of his best friend on the day Kaelyb married Isnia. That look, that *knowing* look of unbridled jealousy convinced Kaelyb that this child could have only come from the folk of the wood, and those stranger folk had not given this child over out of any sense of benevolence. Still, perhaps if Kaelyb and Isnia could love it enough, care for it, and raise it as a true human child as they had their own children, perhaps their love could wipe away whatever darkness lurked within it.

"What shall we call the child?" Kaelyb asked.

"Muriel," Isnia answered. "I feel that she's a Muriel."

"Well, sweet and darling Muriel," Kaelyb said, "welcome to the family."

He leaned down and kissed his new daughter. If anything else, that made the baby's gaze upon him turn even darker.

Kaelyb sighed. He felt that even with all the love that both he and his wife had to give this child, raising little Muriel was going to be the greatest challenge of his life.

THREE

Symond walked across the fields toward the farm house, and the great dilemma of his life plagued him once again. who should he beseech for aid when he wished for some influence from the higher or lower realms? If he asked the celestial realms, would any there look favorably upon the blood of his grandfather while ignoring his father's infernal origins? Considering his experience with daemyn hounds and other such possessed creatures who detected his mixed blood, Symond felt he could make a fairly accurate educated guess as to what he might expect from seeking aid from the infernal, despite his father being daemyn born. As the light of false dawn rose about him, Symond did what he always did when he faced this inner turmoil; he pushed aside all thoughts of asking any realm for assistance. Let fate and fortune decide the outcome of his errand.

When Symond reached a point of about twenty paces from the porch, the door opened. A man stepped out onto the porch. Symond's gaze fell upon the ax resting on the man's broad shoulder. Symond took in the clean and cared for, yet patched, clothes as well as the man's clean and combed hair and beard and suspected the ax a precaution rather than a threat.

"A strange time you be coming about," the man said, his voice the rough and gravelly accent of rural Koma. "Just at the balance between night and day."

"Sometimes things happen according to no greater plan than chance," Symond said.

"And sometimes things happen as they do by way of the cycle of the worlds above and below," the man said. "What do you want, stranger who comes at a strange time?"

Symond couldn't very well blame the man for his suspicions and superstitions. The celestial and infernal realms held great sway over the physical realm, much to Symond's chagrin and dismay. If the powers above and below left the world and the people in it to live their lives as they would, without interference, the world would likely be a less-troubled place, and Symond mightn't need to remain a drunkard.

"Pardon my manners. I am Symond. Good morning, goodman...?"

The question hung in the silence between them for several long moments as the man stroked his beard with his free hand while looking Symond over as a man might be sizing up some animal at a country market.

"Kaelyb," the man said. "No family of note. And again, what brings you here at such strange a time?"

Symond gave Kaelyb as warm a smile as he could manage.

"Well, Goodman Kaelyb, I seek spirits." Symond replied.

"We have no spirits here," the man said. He pointed his ax out toward the field. "We have the old guardians keeping them at bay."

Symond glanced over his shoulder. In the goring light, he could now see sticks rising up out of the crops, each one had a replica of a crow atop it. Lords and Princes! Had the Adepts, Hardin and Carmine, led this band of Brotherhood of the Night so far into the reaches of Koma that they practiced the old ways of the Morigahnti so brazenly as this?

"What sort of man are you that you would seek to traffic with spirits?"

"You misunderstand me." Symond considered his words with the greatest of care. "I misspoke, using terms familiar to me from Koma City. I meant drink. Wine. Ale. Mead. Brandy. Whatever you can spare. I have coin."

Again, Kaelyb appraised Symond.

"You are not from about near," Kaelyb said. "You speak oddly."

It took Symond a moment to decipher Kaelyb's meaning.

"My mother was Bestrian," Symond said. "My father from Heidenmarch. I suppose that's why my speech sounds odd."

"Why all the black?"

"My service to my master requires me to travel frequently. I have discovered that black cloths shows the dust and dirt of the road far less than other colors. Not that I am slovenly, mind you. Just that I don't have to be quite as careful."

"Sense in that," Kaelyb replied. "Why the drink?"

"Traveling is thirsty work," Symond said. "I have a dislike for water. You never know what animals are doing in streams and rivers. Besides, the drink makes the road seem shorter."

"Sense in that as well." Kaelyb set the head of the ax on his porch and leaned on it. "Show me your color."

"I'm sorry. My color?"

Looking at Symond as if he were a simpleton, the man nodded. "You mentioned you have coin."

"Oh. Right."

Symond pulled his coin purse from his pocket. The purse had grown light, much lighter than he liked bribing the other Nightbrothers for their allotment of drink and not knowing when he'd next see a bank. Normally, Symond's dwindling coin wouldn't cause such worry; however, he had never spent so much prolonged time in the presence of Daemyn hounds.

Kaelyb came down the steps with a slight limp on his left leg. His face tightened a bit with each step, indicating it was a likely recent injury. When Kaelyb reached the bottom step, Symond handed the farmer one of the silver coins.

"You all right there?" Symond asked, nodding at the older man's leg.

"Hhhmmm? Oh, that," Kaelyb said. "It's nothing. Wife's just got a testy since the baby come."

"You seem a bit old to have a baby," Symond said.

"Truth in that," Kaelyb said. "It's not our true-born child. Found the girl left on the doorstep a few days back. Being of a decent sort, we take the child in. Little sleep is making for short tempers, and never was I the sensitive sort." He examined the coin. "Strange looking color."

"It's a Hiedenmarch coin," Symond said. "Weighs a little more than a Komati mark, but as we are in Koma, I'll treat it as a mark for trading purposes."

"Right nature of you," Kaelyb said. "How much drink you want?"

"As much as this will buy me." Symond held out his hand, showing another four of the coins.

"Well. I haven't drink such as that, but I got some such as will make the road seem shorter. Come be welcome and meet the wife."

Symond followed Kaelyb up the stairs to the porch, willing the old farmer to limp a little faster. If Symond didn't return to the camp soon, someone would notice he was missing, and explaining his absence grew more and more difficult by the minute. Still, badgering this man would likely cause prolong this interaction and possibly bring an end to the bartering.

The scent of frying bacon filled the house. Symond was surprised to see it cluttered with clothes and dishes. Most Komati kept their homes clean, the meticulousness of their culture being a reflection of their self-respect. A plump woman who was just a slight bit shorter than Kaelyb stood in the center of the room. She held a baby in the crook of her left arm and a long cooking knife in her right hand. Symond considered commenting on the knife, but, seeing Kaelyb limping across the room, he reconsidered. Something about this place had Symond clenching his teeth from an unseen tension. He just wanted to get his drink and get back to the camp.

"We have a guest, Isnia dear," Kaelyb said. "Symond, my wife, Isnia."

"What's the likes of this stranger coming about at this time?" Isnia asked.

Symond tugged his forelock in the Komati way of greeting as he bowed. "Good morning."

"He wants to buy our mead," Kaelyb said.

Isnia's gaze shifted between her husband and Symond several times. "Oh, does he now?"

"He does." Kaelyb held up the coin Symond had given him. "And his color suits me just fine."

"And when the babe's teeth start coming in, and the wails are enough to drive our minds out our heads, what'll we do then to easy the wee girl's suffering?"

"Her teeth won't be cutting out for months," Kaelyb said. "I got plenty of time to brew us more. The money may do us good. Might even be such as to provide a horse or a cow."

"Oh, shades," Isnia cried. She lifted the knife and pointed it at her husband as he went into another room. "You and your grand dreaming of horses and cows. You have trouble enough with pigs and chickens."

"Well," Kaelyb's voice came rolling in from the room he'd entered, "chance might favor me with the pigs and chickens if I had a horse to help with the work, or perhaps a cow for milking and making cheeses and butter, and creams and such." His speech devolved into incoherent mutterings and grumblings as a crash came from somewhere out of sight.

Symond turned to the woman. "Mistress. If it would be too much of a strain on your household, I'll look elsewhere for my drink. If you'll point me to your nearest neighbor, I'll happily be on my way."

The farmer's wife shook her head. "Won't do any good, that. Once Kaelyb gets some idea or scheme taken to root in his mind, he's about nothing else until he either succeeds or fails or gets his mind set on some other fool task or scheme. He comes out here and sees you off and away, he's more likely to chase you down so that he can honor whatever bargain you two met upon. Might as well stay and see it done. The least waste of his time you make, the better."

"I'll trust your word on it, goodlady," Symond said. "I don't want to be any bother."

She looked him up and down again.

"Too late on that, don't you think? No. Don't bother answering. You wouldn't understand."

While Isnia was only a farmer's wife, she spoke with the complete confidence of someone who understood that they were at the center of their realm of power. She may have well been an Adept or High Blood in using that tone that indicated that she really didn't want to hear any more from this lowly creature who had dared bring itself uninvited into her life.

The baby began fussing. Isnia turned her attention to the infant, going so far as to put the knife down on a table. That made Symond relax from a tension in his shoulders, arms, and hands that he hadn't realized he'd been feeling.

I few more crashes came from the room where Kaelyb had gone, followed by a few creative comments on just what exactly which gods could go and do to other gods. Isnia gave an exasperated, groaning sigh.

Symond kept his mouth firmly closed when he noticed a slight shimmering about the child. The next moment, the tension returned to his body just as Isnia picked up the knife again and began pacing back and forth across the room. Remembering a bit of a saying about discretion and survival, or some such thing, Symond slowly shuffled back toward the farmhouse door. He wanted to ask about the baby. *Where did it come from? How long has it been here? Have they noticed any strange occurrences since the child came to them?* However, such questions might raise questions of their own. Aside from that, Symond had no way to judge if the child had any close connection with its celestial or infernal parent, and considering the tension and Isnia's underlying anger, Symond suspected the child was Daemyn born.

A few more crashes and Kaelyb called from the other room, "Ah, there we are."

A moment later, the old farmer limped through the doorway, carrying an armload of hard leather bottles and a small cask. Symond nearly took a step forward to help Kaelyb, but Isnia's stalking back and forth across the room, knife gripped firmly in her hand stopped him short. He just wanted to get the spirits and be on his way with as little trouble as possible.

Kaelyb spoke as he carried the bundle toward Symond. "I've already got one of your fancy heavy foreign coins. Give me one more, and all this is yours."

"Seems a fair trade to me," Symond said. "What's the likelihood of a sack or bag of some sort to carry these? I have a long way to journey, and having a sack would make carrying those so much easier."

"Of course," Kaelyb said, and headed back toward the back room.

"Don't you dare give that man anything of my making." Isnia's voice rose to nearly a screech.

"Hush woman," Kaelyb snapped, as he came back into the main room. He held a rough cloth sack. "We've nothing here, made by your hand that didn't come first by the work of mine."

Isnia opened and closed her mouth several times as her husband limped across the room, placed the bottles and cask into the sack, and then handed them to Symond; whereupon, Symond handed Kaelyb the other Heidenmark coin.

"Good custom as yours is welcome," Kaelyb said. "Stay for breakfast?"

"Sadly, I cannot. I've spent too much time minding my own concerns," Symond lifted the sack, "now I must pick up my feet so I might mind my master's concerns."

Normally, a meal cooked in an actual home with an actual kitchen would have had Symond trying to concoct some sort of story for his absence, for he truly a loved well-cooked meal even more than he loved drink. However, his concern about how the lady of the house held that knife and the other-worldly baby cradled in her arm far overshadowed his concern for the Adepts back at the Brotherhood's camp.

"I thank you muchly for the drink." Again, Symond tugged his forelock. "If my master's concerns bring me back this way, I'll be sure to bring my greetings again."

"Wind at your back, friend," Kaelyb said.

And with that, Symond left the farmhouse. He skipped down the steps and began his journey back toward the Nightbrother's camp.

Symond took a total of four strides away from the steps up to the porch when he heard both Kaelyb and Isnia shouting from inside the house. He couldn't make out the actual words, but it surely did not sound like the normal bickering of a couple that had spent several decades becoming overly familiar with each other. Those voices sounded as if they were full of rage and hatred. When he heard the crash, Symond turned around.

"Gods and goddesses be damned," he muttered as he went back up the stairs.

He knew deep in his joints that this would be yet another day that he would likely curse his mother's father for the streak of good nature that flowed through him.

Just as he reached the door, the baby started wailing from within. Taking a deep breath in preparation to have both Kealyb and Isnia turn on him—involving one's self in a marital squabble was dangerous enough, never mind when some other-worldly creature might be exerting influence over the situation—Symond pushed the door open.

"No!" he cried. "Stop!"

Kaelyb and Isnia stood over the babe, who lay wailing on the floor in the center of the room. Blood spurted from a deep gash in Kaelyb's neck. Isnia held the knife high above her head. The weapon dripped blood onto the woman's shoulder and into her hair. The air around the child seemed to shimmer and waver in time with its wailing and crying.

Symond's skin prickled and his breath quickened as he took in the sight before him. He moved to step between the old, married farmer fold, but the distance was too great.

Kaelyb swung the ax in a wide arc. Isnia's arm came down. The ax caught the woman full in the head just as the knife stabbed into the man's stomach. Isnia screamed. Kaelyb could only manage a gurgling cough. Blood spilled down their bodies and on the floor. First, they wavered. Then, they fell.

Symond stared at them as they died. He had some knowledge of healing, but not nearly enough to save them.

With nothing to do for the old couple, Symond choked down the swell of feelings threatening to rampage his mind and spirit. He turned his attention to the child. The baby, a girl by the look of her, had stopped crying. She looked up at Symond with eyes full of intelligence far greater than any infant should have. This was no Daemyn spawn or Angel born. This child was something more, and that churned Symond's stomach.

He wanted nothing more than to walk away but knew with a certainty that came from his grandfather's bloodline that in doing so, the babe would somehow find its way to other people and destroy their lives as well.

Letting out a sound that came out partly between an exasperated sigh and a pained groan, Symond set the sack of spirits down and went into the cooking area. A pan full of bacon was sizzling away. More than that, the pan had a thick layer of grease. Symond took the pan off the stove and put it under the table. He built up some kindling and logs on top of the pan. When he was satisfied that it would catch well, Symond went back to the baby with a pair of fire tongs.

"I don't know what you are, little creature," Symond spoke through gritted teeth, "but seeing that," he waved the tongs at the farmer and his wife, "I'm not about to touch you myself."

He used the fire tongs to pick the child up by the middle and took it over to the table. All the while, the child glared at him with those too-knowing eyes. Symond had never known fear of this kind, a fear so deep that all his senses seemed dull and muted, while his thoughts kept turning back to fleeing this place to escape this creature's influence. After Symond set the babe on the table, right above the place where he'd piled the kindling and wood above the pan of grease, he took the tongs to the stove, but before pulling out a log, he put the tongs aside.

Picking up the sack of spirits, Symond walked to the other room, the one where Kaelyb had first gone to get the spirits. There in the room, Symond found three more of the leather bottles and a cask. He found two more sacks. He put those new treasures into the sack, making it bulge, and returned to his task of destroying the foul creature that had taken a babe's form.

Taking up the tongs once again, Symond pulled out a burning bit of wood and took it over to the table. Seeing the flames jumping along the length of the small log, the child started to cry again. For a brief moment, maybe three or four heartbeats, Symond hesitated. Then, he saw the air around the child shimmer, and he placed the burning log into the pan of grease. Instantly flames leaped up from the pan, and the grease popped and sizzled onto the kindling and the logs, spreading the flames much faster than they might have otherwise.

Without a shred of remorse or shame, Symond turned his back on the fire and strode quickly, not quite as a jog but almost, across the farmhouse, past the bodies of Kaelyb and Isnia picked up his sack of spirits, and left, hoping that the fire would spread to engulf the house, ending the other-worldly babe's destructive influence in the physical world.

Making a circle around the farmhouse before the blaze took the whole thing, Symond saw several pigs and some chickens, just as he thought he might after Isnia chided her husband. He took one of the spare sacks and put three chickens in it. Then, after finding a rope, Symond tied it around the neck of one of the pigs and led it away. He considered trying for more than one pig but thought better of it. That might be a bit much for him to manage. It took him to the other side of the field until he managed a balance of the sack of spirits, the squirming chickens, and the somewhat stubborn pig, but once there, he felt he could make good time back to the camp, all with and even greater justification as to why he hadn't been in camp.

By the time Symond approached the camp, his feet ached to the point where he did not relish the thought of pursuing the Morigahnti woman and her protector, much less the chance of actually overtaking them. The last two encounters had been just this side of disastrous, with many of the Nightbrothers having gone to Old Uncle Night's embrace.

By the time Symond smelled the smoke of the campfires, All Father Sun had journeyed well above the eastern horizon. By now, his absence would be noticed for certain.

"Symond," a voice cried.

He hadn't realized how tired he was, until he saw Jorgen coming toward him, dark hair unruly and unkempt. Symond should have seen his fellow Nightbrother well before this. Drinking a third of one of the bottles of mead likely hadn't helped much, but he had to make sure the Daemyn hounds wouldn't detect the infernal and celestial nature of his various bloodlines.

"Where have you been?" Jorgen asked. "Adept Carmine has been searching for you. Whispers about the camp are that you deserted us."

"Not so, Brother Jorgen," Symond said with as wide a smile as he could manage. The mead warming his belly certainly helped in that regard. "I've been plundering the countryside and sending some Komati farmers to the Uncle's embrace." He silently added, *And hopefully, if Old Uncle Night is kind, a dark creature back to the dark realm below,* but didn't feel the need to share that thought with Jorgen. "What does Adept Carmine want with me?"

"I don't know for certain," Jorgen said. "But I've heard whispers of splitting into two groups."

"That's interesting," Symond said. "Any idea why?"

"No," Jorgen said. "But the Adept has been looking for you for some time. He's near to getting angry."

"Well," Symond said, handing the sack of chickens to Jorgen, "let's hope some fresh meat will brighten the Adepts' moods."

Jorgen smiled. "Adept Carmine, perhaps. I don't think anything ever brightens Adept Hardin's mood, ever."

"You speak no lie in that," Symond said. "Let's deliver my bounty and see why the Adept has such urgent need of me."

In truth, Symond would prefer to stay far beneath the notice of either Adept, but it seemed that fate smothered and killed that little piece of hope. Now, Symond's best course was to present himself as the dutiful and loyal Nightbrother, ready and eager to help in any way, turning his hope toward duties that would keep him as far from the Daemyn hounds as possible and allow him to sneak away to forage for more spirits in order to stave off the hounds picking up the scent of his true nature as long as possible.

With that thought, Symond said, "Hold a moment."

Without stopping to see if Jorgen had heeded him, Symond opened his sack of spirits. First, he took out the third and final sack. Then, he placed the two casks into that one, leaving the leather bottles in the other. It would be easier to keep those for himself if they were already separated before Symond handed the spoils over to the Adepts. Having completed that, Symond hurried to catch up with Jorgen.

As the two of them made their way through the camp, the pig and occasionally squawking chicken elicited quiet comments from many of the Nightbrothers. The appearance of this amount of fresh food should have been a cause for barely-contained excitement, but this strained, subdued reaction gave Symond cause for concern. He didn't think this was all because he had been absent from camp this morning. Seeing no looks of either pity or smugness from his fellow Nightbrothers at not having to suffer as Symond convinced him that something else was going on. Well, he might as well find one of the Adepts and find out.

"Symond!" Carmine called out.

Symond turned to his left, encouraged that the Adept seemed relieved and angry to see Symond.

"Adept Carmine," Symond said. "I went foraging. I found a pig," he pointed to the sack Jorgen carried, "three chickens," he handed Carmine the sack with the two casks, "and drink."

This seemed to take Adept Carmine aback. He blinked a few times, and then he smiled.

"Well done," Carmine said. "It's just the thing we need to lift our spirits. You see, I sent my nightbat to scout, and the two Adepts the First Adept sent to join us will be upon us by this afternoon. Only, they are not Adepts of Old Uncle Night. One follows All Father Sun, the other Grandfather Shadow."

"I don't understand," Symond said. "Why would... No. My place is not to question the First Adept. My place is so obey. How may I serve?"

"We must split the camps. With these numbers and the Daemyn hounds, we cannot hope to hide our true master. Since the First Adept did not send these Adepts to us for us to send them to the Uncle's embrace, we must obfuscate ourselves."

"It seems the wise choice," Symond said. "What do you require of me?"

"We will be putting the majority of the Nightbrothers in the other camp. Unfortunately, Adept Hardin and I must stay with the other Adepts." Carmine placed his hand on Symond's shoulder. "We have decided to have you lead the other camp, to keep the Nightbrothers hidden, and care for the Daemyn hounds."

Symond looked across the camp to where the Daemyn hounds were tied. Their sleek, muscled bodies rippled as they moved about as well as they could being bound to a tree. A chill settled over him and he swallowed. He did not have nearly enough spirits to keep the stench of his grandfather's bloodline hidden from the amount of interaction with the hounds such a post would require. Symond also doubted further attempts at foraging would be as successful as this morning's venture had been. Kaelyb and Isnia's faces came unbidden to Symond's mind, and perhaps successful was not a completely applicable description.

"Symond?" asked Carmine. "Are you all right?"

Symond shook his head in an attempt to clear away the cold dread settling over him.

"Apologies Adept," Symond said. "Your confidence left me speechless and stunned for a moment."

"I can imagine," Carmine said. "I'm placing a great trust in you. Sylvie and the servant girl will be under your care. I trust that you will not allow them to escape, nor will the men spoil either of them."

"I am your man, Adept."

"Excellent." Carmine nodded and gave Symond's shoulder a squeeze. "Now, let's see about transforming your spoils into breakfast. Jorgen?"

"Coming, Adept Carmine," Jorgen said.

Adept Carmin and Brother Jorgen headed over toward the fire. Symond stood wondering how he was going to manage to lead a camp of Nightborthers while caring for the girls and the Daemyn hounds, all without revealing his infernal or celestial birthrights.

FOUR

Yrgaeshkyl, the Goddess of Lies and Mother of Daemyns walked through the smoke and ash of the burned farmhouse.

"Muriel," she called. "Little destroyer, where are you?"

A bit to her left and ahead, Yrgeashkil heard a baby begin crying. She pushed a red-hot cooking stove out of her way and went to the little saent. Yrgaeshkil found Muriel the Destroyer laying in a cast iron pan that had also glowed a deep red from the heat of being trapped in the flames. The little Saent's skin popped and charred from the heat of the pan, and her screams and cries were raspy and pitiful from her having breathed so much smoke. Temporary conditions, due to the bit of infernal power Yrgaeshki had infused into the child upon its death. Still, the whimpers tugged at Yrgaeshkil.

Many beings in both the celestial and infernal realms considered the Mother of Daemyns to be cold, cruel, and unfeeling. Over the last thousand years, these whispered opinions reach her ears, again and again and again. Each whisper had planted a seed within a vast garden of bitterness with Yrgaeshkil's spirit. In fact, she'd heard one such whisper just a bit over seven years ago, when she'd sacrificed one of her children to create the sickness that was supposed to have Julianna call Grandfather Shadow from his prison seven years early.

Yrgaeshkil walked from the burning house and said, "Galbra'thantalysI require you."

As she was the mother of all Daemyns born between her and Old Uncle Night, Yrgaeshkil knew each Daemyn's full and true name and could summon them at will without needing to bargain, plead, or bribe them as other creatures did. She sighed at a memory from so many long years ago when she had commanded the Dominions of Lies and Daemyns so briefly during the Second War of the Gods.

A moment later, the air next to Yrgaeshkil shimmered like a heat mirage. A stubby, reddish-orange creature with arms longer than its body and wings that wrapped around its waist so as not to tangle up in its arms or legs. Its oddly shaped face resembled what might have been an unfortunate paring between a cow and a crow, with spiny feathers, all over its body and deer-like antlers sprouting up from behind gangly, floppy ears.

"Mother." The thing prostrated itself at her feet.

"Oh get up," Yrgaeshkil snarled. "I'm perfectly capable of telling you when to grovel and when to serve. For now, I require you to serve by caring for Saent Muriel."

Yrgaeshkil thrust the baby into Galbra'thantalys's arms. Once Saent Muriel was out of her arms, Yrgaeshkil turned in a slow circle to observe the Destroyer's handiwork. The whole of the farmhouse had burnt near to the ground. In the wreckage, she saw two human skeletons amongst the ash and smoking timbers. All in all, this amount of destruction pleased Yrgaeshkil greatly. In truth, she'd have been pleased if Muriel had managed to cause the death of either the farmer or his wife.

"What are you doing with that baby, you nasty creature?" a voice cried out behind Yrgaeshkil.

The goddess spun about to find a lovely young woman wagging her finger at Galbra'thantalys as if the Daemyn were a misbehaving servant. The new arrival wore a tasteful riding dress of greens, grays, and blacks, both far more tasteful and functional than she might normally wear.

"What do you want, Hope?" Yrgaeshkil asked.

"To see what you were about," the lady said. "I felt a complete lack of hope in this place, and to my surprise, I find it covered in the scent of both Lies and Fear. The troubling thing is that the Fear I smell doesn't have your husband's tell-tale stink, but rather yours. Curios. Especially since recent rumors speak of your death."

"Is that what rumor says?" Yrgeashikl asked.

"Indeed," Hope replied. "Killed by Grandfather Shadow himself, using the weapon *Thanya'taen.*"

"Do you always listen to rumors?" Yrgaeshkil asked.

"Not always," Hope said. "What is that baby doing to that Daemyn?"

The Mother of Lies glanced over toward her Saent and her child. It was missing a wing, an antler, and an ear.

"Oh, she's devouring his essence to heal."

"What?" Galbra'thantalys moved to put the baby down.

"Do not do that, pathetic whelp," Yrgaeshkil snapped. "If you do…" She drew on her newest Dominion of Fear, and unleashed a wave of it at the Daemyn with such force and power that the creature stood ridged in terror. "Well. I suppose I won't have to do anything now. Muriel, please take all you need."

The baby cooed and burbled happily as more and more bits of the Daemyn faded, all while this happened, the burns healed faster and faster.

"You're letting that Saent eat one of your children?" Hope asked.

"Yes," Yrgaeskil replied.

"Truly?"

"You make it sound like some terrible thing. I have lots of children. Many of whom do not disparage me when they believe I can't hear them."

Hope gave Yrgaeshkil a puzzled look. "You're odd. Possibly the oddest of all of us."

The Goddess of Lies shrugged. "I'm the only one of us who managed to become a Greater Eldar and then became Lesser again."

"Not entirely true," another voice said. "Some of us chose *not* to be Greater Eldar, rather than have that distinction ripped from us by our husbands."

Yrgaeshkil turned to her right and saw a willowy young woman with wispy hair the color of lilacs and eyes that shown like emeralds. She wore an outfit several centuries out of date, which was a change from the last time Yrgeashkil had seen her a few decades ago, maybe a century. Back then, the young lady's dress had been out of fashion for over a thousand years.

"Imagination," Yrgaeshkil sneered in response to the self-righteous smirk Hope gave her. "Where is your third sister?"

"Off doing this," Imagination replied.

"Or that," Hope said.

"Hard to tell with her," they said together, "but probably something necessary."

Both of the infuriating goddesses snickered, likely overly proud of their own cleverness.

"What do you two, or should I say three, or is it one now?" Yrgaeshkil looked back and forth between the goddesses Hope and Imagination. "Will you be rejoining together now that it is safe for Greater Eldar to roam the world?"

"We aren't the ones to determine that," Hope said.

"Either of us," Imagination said. "We can suggest."

"It will come done to Necessity," Hope said. "She's the one who decides when that time will be."

Yrgaeshkil couldn't resist sharing a slight smirk with the two Lesser Eldar. She reveled in the *Lesser* part of their essence in comparison to the *Greater* part of her essence.

"Well." Yrgaeshkil took a step toward Imagination. "I have little interest in Hope. "However," she took another step toward the lesser goddess, "the Dominion of Imagination would go quite nicely with the Dominion of Lies."

"Careful." Imagination stepped back. "I understand my Dominion is tempting. It holds more power than many realize. However, attacking me might cause our sister to realize it's necessary for her to appear."

"Oh, I hope she does," Hope said with a wry little smile.

"Fine," Yrgaeshkil snapped. "You've had a bit of fun. You've determined I'm still alive. Begone before you make me angry enough to summon enough children to deal with the three of you combined."

Hope and Imagination vanished.

Yrgaeshkil turned back to where she'd left Saent Muriel with Galbra'thantalys. Muriel lay in the grass, kicking and cooing happily. The daemyn was nowhere to be seen. Yrgaeshkil picked the infant Saent up and cradled her gently in the crook of her arm.

"I thought that Saent Raena the Sacrificial would have earned me a little more time," Yrgaeshkil said in a sing-song tone. "However, I shouldn't be terribly surprised that Grandfather Shadow sought to eliminate any other Greater Eldar. He was always a jealous one. But now, what to do with you? You're living up to your word quite nicely, my little Destroyer. Perhaps a little too nicely. Where shall we take you next?"

AUTUMN'S FIRST STORM

louds turn noon to midnight.
Lightning brings noon to midnight.

Each storm reminds,
just as with the coin,
* all things possess two sides.*

The storms of Spring brings life;
the storms of Autumn herald
cold death for the unwary.
In this way, Grandfather Shadow
shows the Balance in all things.

How is this not unlike
the truth and lies
of each human soul?
How does this not reflect
the ripples in our minds
with every choice we make?

- Archer

ONE

Storm clouds blocked the moon and stars, and the night seemed to press down on Julianna. This added to the weight of her waterlogged cloak. Julianna shivered weakly as she struggled to remain in Vendyr's saddle. Faelin kept insisting that their destination was not far off. Now, several hours beyond when he'd first assured her the township was just a little further, with the wind biting her cheek and nose, Julianna spied the flicker of lights in the distance. She sat a little straighter. For this first time since receiving the *honor* of being marked the Lord Morigahn, Grandfather Shadow's high priest, Julianna might possibly get to sleep in a bed—a real bed, not like that cot thing in a farmhouse's stuffy storeroom.

Faelin walked a few paces ahead, making sure the way was clear for Vendyr. Since Smoke's visit, Faelin had taken to leading Vendyr more and more often to give Julianna as much time as possible to read from the *Galad'parma*. The first morning, they had argued, mostly due to Smoke's accusations that she still thought too much like a noble, but Faelin had used the logic of Julianna's time being better spent riding and studying to end the argument. She didn't bother fighting with Faelin about keeping the book from her. She hadn't been in any state to actually make use of it as she recovered from her experiences with Grandfather Shadow and the Lords of Judgment.

In the days since Smoke had come to them, Faelin had set a grueling pace, stopping only for short rests during the day and a few hours of sleep in the darkest hours of the night. Julianna suspected these respites were more for Vendyr than for either of them. Well, for Julianna anyway. Faelin seemed tireless and unrelenting. By the time the sun had set on the second day, both Julianna and Vendyr were near the point of collapsing; however, no matter how hard and far they traveled, Faelin was still awake and alert as if he'd just gotten a full night's sleep. Julianna also noticed that the injuries he'd taken from the Brotherhood of the Night and the Inquisitors, as well as the more serious ones from the Daemyn hound, were almost completely healed.

Julianna wondered how Faelin maintained his awareness and strength despite the exhausting pace he set. So many questions danced at the tip of her tongue, and several times, curiosity almost overcame her, but she remained silent. She respected Faelin's privacy, and that he would tell her his secrets in time. Or perhaps he wouldn't—according to those who had borne the title of Lord Morigahn before her, shadows never lied to each other, but Grandfather Shadow held nothing against his followers keeping their secrets safe. Julianna understood the distinction between secrets and lies. She might not have a week ago, but that was before Grandfather Shadow had marked her face and whispered *Galad'laman* into her ear, so that now the language called to her from within her own mind, pleading to be spoken into miracles.

Now, so tired that even *Galad'laman* had remained quiet in her mind, water soaking through her cloak and running down her back, Julianna followed Faelin into the town of Shadybrook.

Like most small Komati farming communities, Shadybrook's buildings were separated from each other to make controlling fires easier and to make it harder for enemies to use them as cover for very long. Of course, this hearkened back to the time when Koma was its own nation and the center of an empire, before becoming a protectorate of the Kingdom of the Sun. The buildings at the center of the community were the exception. Seven structures lined the cobbled road, making a small fortress, or at least what would have been a small fortress if the walls hadn't fallen into disrepair after decades of neglect: the mayor's manor house, the smithy, the mercantile shop, the stable, the warehouse, the public house, and the small shrine adorned with depictions of the lesser gods. Julianna knew all these buildings, for close to all the small towns like these across Koma, from the ocean in the east to the mountains in the west, had these buildings laid out in this fashion.

Around the shrine, fires burned in specially constructed iron drums. These stone and iron structures gave light at all times and during any weather and kept the shrine warm when people came to pray. In the gloomy edges of the firelight, Julianna saw other houses. Before Koma fell under Kingdom rule, the shrine would have been to Grandfather Shadow, but now it was dedicated to the four lesser gods of the seasons. With memories of her childhood returned when she'd freed Grandfather Shadow,

Julianna recalled Father and Mother taking her to see an unmarred shrine to their true god deep in the hills outside their estates. They passed the shrine, and Julianna's scar began to ache. It wasn't the flaring pain she usually felt after doing something that displeased Grandfather Shadow, but it hurt enough to cause her a sharp intake of breath.

At the sound, Faelin stopped the horses and turned to her. "Are you alright?"

"Fine," Julianna said through clenched teeth. "I think Grandfather Shadow is just reminding me how much things have changed. And how much he expects of me. For now, I want to wash and rest."

She also hoped for some time to herself in order to practice more miracles. Faelin had given her little time alone, and so she hadn't had any opportunities to channel Grandfather Shadow's Dominions. Doing so purged the feelings of weakness and uncertainty that had plagued her since the Lords of Judgment had remade her soul, taking away the birthright of her mother's people.

They neared the manor. People dancing in the windows. It reminded Julianna of the last time she'd been to a country manor like this. Her cousin, Marcus, had just received a small portion of his father's lands to govern. The local people welcomed him with a celebration of feasting and dancing.

Seven years later, and Julianna still missed Marcus. Rachel too. Would that she could have them here now. It was not to be. He was dead and gone, taken by the same sickness.

Faelin stopped Vendyr when they reached the mayor's house. He helped Julianna dismount and led her up the steps to the porch out of the rain. The building even blocked some of the wind.

Faelin pounded his fist on the door.

After a few moments, the door opened and light poured out, illuminating the rainwater draining off the porch. The music, laughter, and cheers grew louder. A youth of fourteen or fifteen winters peered out, wearing a grin that shone almost as much as his eyes.

"Greetings," the boy said. "Be welcome here."

Julianna pulled the hood of her cloak tighter around her face. The fewer people who saw her scar, the better. Even if no one recognized what it meant, it was a distinctive feature and easily remembered, especially on a woman.

"Is Erik Dressel still mayor?" Faelin asked.

"He is," the lad replied. "But he is at our lord's manor."

"Does Count Allifar Thaedus still govern these lands?"

"He does." The youth looked Faelin up and down. "Why?"

"Go and fetch Mistress Dressel. I must speak with her."

"Would you like to come in? This house is welcome to all tonight."

"I will speak with her before entering," Faelin said. "Tell her it concerns some unfinished business with Raelian and Branton."

The boy's brow furrowed, and he chewed on his lower lip for a moment. His gaze shifted from Faelin, to Julianna, and back again. Finally, he nodded and went back inside.

Julianna turned to Faelin. "Why couldn't we go inside? I'm freezing."

"I remember the Dressels as good, honest people," Faelin replied. "I suspect they will take us in, but they may have turned from the old ways. It's happened before and created awkward moments."

"Awkward?" Julianna asked.

"Sometimes they turn traitor and work for the High Blood, sometimes the Inquisitors," Faelin said. "It's best to know out here. It will be easier to retreat from this porch than it would be from inside the house."

The door opened again. A woman came out onto the porch and shut the door behind her. She was tall for a woman, taller even than Faelin. Her party attire gave her little protection from the biting wind, but she didn't show it. Her gray hair shone even in the darkness of the storm, and her hard eyes fixed on them. This woman would suffer little nonsense.

"I am Gillaen Dressel," the lady said. "Who are you to not accept my hospitality?"

Faelin stepped into the light pouring out from the door and removed his hood.

"We wish to accept the comfort of your home," Faelin said, "but you should know who you're inviting in."

Mistress Dressel's eyes grew wide. "Faelin?"

Faelin nodded, his face splitting into an embarrassed grin.

"Shadow be praised! You're alive!"

Mistress Dressel scooped him into her arms and hugged him with such force that he groaned. When she put him down, Faelin gasped for air.

Julianna didn't know what to think about the woman thanking Grandfather Shadow. As memories of her early childhood returned to her, she recalled people worshiping the greater god — Mother and Father even had a secret shrine to Grandfather Shadow in their manor. However, seeing someone breaking one of the very foundation laws of the Kingdom of the Sun right before her eyes shocked her. She'd grown up in her Aunt and Uncle's care, hearing whispered tales of people being caught worshiping above their station, with the punishments worse than for people caught possessing firearms. Julianna had never imagined people actually committing those crimes, but that had all changed on her birthday, when she'd freed Grandfather Shadow.

"Did any of my family survive?" Faelin asked after regaining his breath.

"I'm sorry lad. You're the last."

Faelin's head dropped. Julianna reached out and gripped his shoulder.

"And who is this?" Mistress Dressel asked, facing Julianna.

Faelin's head came up as he stepped in front of Julianna. "Does Count Allifar still follow the old ways?"

"What do you think we're doing, lad?" Her voice carried a healthy dose of indignation. "We're celebrating the first of the autumn storms. Come in. Eat and drink with us. Bring your guest. I trust she…" Mistress Dressel looked Julianna over, "yes, she, definitely she, follows the old ways or you wouldn't have brought her."

"It's not as simple as that," Faelin said.

Mistress Dressel turned from Faelin to Julianna. "Why not?"

"Show her," Faelin said.

Julianna pulled her hood back and stepped next to Faelin in the light. Mistress Dressel squinted and then blinked in rapid succession. She looked at Faelin. Her mouth opened and closed a few times until she managed to speak.

"Is she?" Dressel asked.

Faelin nodded.

"But Khellan Dubhan?"

At the mention of Khellan's name, Julianna's chest seemed to get smaller, so small that it couldn't hold enough air.

"Khellan is gone," Faelin said. "This is the new Lord Morigahn."

Tears welled in Dressel's eyes.

"But how can she have been named so soon, and without the trials?" She spoke the words softly, asking the question, and knowing the truth of them, but not daring to hope.

"Look at her mark again," Faelin said.

Mistress Dressel stared even harder at Julianna's face, then her eyes went from squinting in the dark of night to opening wide in surprise.

"The right side?" Dressel spoke barely above a whisper. "You mean——?"

"*Galad'Ysoysa*——," Faelin started, but Julianna placed her hand on his shoulder.

As a true Lord Morigahn, Julianna could allow someone else to speak for her only so long.

"*Galad'Ysoysa* is free," Julianna said. She drew the Faerii steel blade from its sheath on her belt and held it toward Dressel so the mayor's wife could see the word *kostota* etched into the blade in the light coming from the windows. "He marked me with this blade by his own hand."

Dressel looked at the blade, at Julianna, and then past the two travelers. Her eyes scanned the darkness. "Bring her inside."

"No one can know who she is," Faelin said. "The Brotherhood of the Night and Floraen Inquisitors are hunting us."

"Everyone here is loyal to the old ways." Indignation saturated Mistress Dressel's tone. "None here will betray her."

"Not willingly," Faelin replied. "But can they hold the secret if asked by a House Floraen Inquisitor, or tortured by the Brotherhood of the Night?"

"You speak true." Mistress Dressel turned to Julianna and curtsied. "Lady Morigahn——"

"Lord Morigahn," Julianna said.

"Excuse me?" Mistress Dressel asked.

"I am the *Lord* Morigahn," Julianna said. "That is the title Grandfather Shadow gave me. That is the title I expect other to use."

"Aah, yes, aah, Lord Morigahn," Mistress Dressel said. "Please, be welcome to my home. We will comfort you, fight for you, and die for you. But before you come inside, I must ask you to raise your hood."

Julianna took in Mistress Dressel's words. A vow. Mistress Dressel had given Julianna a vow, and not just for herself, but for all the people of Shadybrook. The people of Shadybrook would look to her as what she was now, the voice and presence of Grandfather Shadow, and if it came down to it, yes, they *would,* in fact, die for her.

"I'm not ready for this, Faelin," Julianna said.

"If what Faelin says is true," Mistress Dressel said, "and Faelin vara'Traejyn would not lie about such things, you have been granted a great honor. You may not understand it at the moment, but you will in time. Now, enter and receive the hospitality of my home."

Julianna raised her hood. Faelin went to Vendyr and collected the satchel that contained the *Galad'parma.* That was something they did not just leave about anywhere. Mistress Dressel opened the door and ushered them inside. As they entered, she waved a young man toward Vendyr and then to the stable.

The place resembled an inn.

A fire roared in each of the fireplaces, one on the north wall and another on the south. Candles and lamps were set about the room, casting light everywhere. Two windows on the east and west walls were each open a crack, allowing the wind from the storm to blow through, causing flames of the lamps, candles, and fires to flutter and dance. Shadows danced across the walls and under the tables and chairs as the wind whistled through the room. A row of tables laden with food dominated the west wall. The smell of cooked meat and fresh bread stirred Julianna's stomach. Still, as much as she wanted to find a plate and smother it with a helping of every dish, Julianna yearned to bathe even more. The filth of her molesters had clung to her for days, and she wanted it gone. It looked as though the guests were half locals and half travelers. Some were wetter and muddier than others, though none so much as Julianna and Faelin. Everyone met them with welcoming smiles.

In the southwest corner, a man stood in the one gloomy part of the room. It was as if the light of the fires refused to touch that corner. Even in that patch of semidarkness, she could see his eyes. They seemed to pierce the shadows in her hood and meet her own gaze.

"Who is that?" Julianna asked, gesturing toward the man.

Mistress Dressel looked into the darkened corner. "That? That, is Baron Parshyval Thaedus, brother and right hand of Count Allifar Thaedus. Pay him no mind, my lady. He is merely here to observe the celebration."

Understanding came from that corner of Julianna's mind that held Grandfather Shadow's voice. Everything must have a balance. The baron was starkly alone and stoic to remind these people that, even in their celebration, winter crept ever closer, and moments of revelry would be in short supply as they sought to survive. As winter deepened, someone in the community would take up the task of creating joy and mirth, to remind everyone that no matter how harsh and cold Sister Winter treated them, Sister Spring would eventually arrive to chase her off.

While Julianna had been looking at Baron Parshyval, someone had come up to them, a young man, no more than a handful of years older than Julianna at most. The blond hair that fell into his blue-green eyes framed his face.

"Faelin?" the young man said. "I thought you were dead!"

Faelin's face broke into a huge smile. Then, both of them started laughing and threw their arms around each other, spinning in a joyous circle and pounding on each other's backs. Many of the celebrants noticed this and smiled at the display. Finally, Faelin and his friend separated.

"Me?" Faelin asked. "I'm not the one that decided to follow in his fath—"

The young man coughed, loudly, deliberately, and interruptingly.

"Ah, yes," Faelin said. "Still, I thought *you* would be dead by now. In truth, I should have known the Kingdom would never be able to catch you."

Julianna took in the sight of Faelin's friend. He wore a black frock coat of polished leather, perfect for keeping the rain off, and baggy trousers with pleats of midnight blue with saffron yellow in the style of the Inis O'lean islanders. His black riding boots were well worn, but cost more coin than most of the citizens of Shadybrook would see in a year, possibly three years.

Faelin turned to Julianna. He bit his lip in that idiotic way he always did when trying to suppress the lopsided grin he claimed to hate.

"This is my friend…uh…" Faelin glanced to his friend.

"You forgot his name?" Julianna asked.

"Zephyr," Faelin's friend said, with a perfect courtier's bow.

"Zephyr?" Faelin asked. "Truly?"

"What?" Zephyr replied. "You don't like it?"

"Not for me to say one way or the other?" Faelin said. "Does she know?"

"She who?" Julianna asked.

A look of two men sharing a conspiracy passed between Faelin and Zephyr.

"A mutual acquaintance," Faelin said.

"A lady," Zephyr added. "One of some influence, and I doubt she would be overly fond of either of us babbling about our mutual acquaintance. But as for recalling my name, don't judge Faelin too harshly. I use different names in different company. He knows several of them, but not all." Zephyr's grin grew wider. "And you are?"

"I am Julianna."

Faelin blinked several times in rapid succession but said nothing.

"Well, this reunion is touching," Mistress Dressel said, "and it warms my heart, but the lady is tired, and, I imagine, chilled to the heart. You two can stay here and plot all the mischief you wish while you eat and drink. The lady needs a bath."

"Don't go to the trouble of a bath for me," Julianna said. "I only need a bucket of hot water and some soap."

"Nonsense," said Mistress Dressel. "We have a heating pump in the cellar that runs into the kitchen and the upstairs washroom. We keep it concealed when representatives from the Kingdom come to call, but most times it's just a precaution. Most of them wouldn't even know what they were looking at. So, drawing you a bath is only as difficult as lifting and dropping the handle."

Mistress Dressel waved a woman in her middle years over. Two girls, younger than Julianna, followed in the woman's wake. All three wore matching dresses of gray and green, which Julianna guessed were the Thaedus family colors. For the first time, she wished she'd paid closer attention during Aunt Maerie's lessons of Koma heraldry.

"We have new guests," Mistress Dressel said. "Take her upstairs and draw her a hot bath. Then set out fresh clothes for her. One of Lauri's old riding dresses should fit her nicely."

All three curtsied and headed for the stairs next to the fireplace on the north wall.

"I am grateful and honored to accept your hospitality."

"It is you who honor us," her hostess said. "Now, up the stairs with you."

Dressel's tone declared that she would accept no argument. A bath was more than Julianna could have hoped for. Julianna followed the servants, and partway up the stairs, she saw Baron Parshyval Thaedus leave the shadowy corner and approach Faelin and Zephyr. The baron stepped forward, fully into the light, and Julianna saw a *Galad'fana* draped around his neck and shoulders.

Two

Once Julianna was out of sight up the stairs, Faelin turned to his friend.

"Zephyr?" Faelin knew Damian used aliases as he traveled, but the ridiculous audacity of that particular nickname baffled him. "Are you mad?"

Damian stilled his face, but the smirk remained in his eyes as he shrugged. "I adopted it after the last time we parted ways."

"Don't you think she's angry enough at you already?" Faelin asked.

"Who? Kahddria?" Damian asked.

Faelin nodded.

"I have no idea." Damian shrugged. "I don't care much either." Damian stepped back and looked Faelin over. "You look like Old Uncle Night has a firm grasp of at least one of your feet. Get warmed by the fire. I'll get you a plate of food and something to drink."

"May all the gods and goddesses bless you." For the first time since waking up in the apple orchard, Faelin felt able to relax, if not be content.

"No thank you," Damian said. "The gods can keep to themselves. I'll keep to myself. Then, the world will remain well."

Damian went to the tables with the food, and Faelin headed to the fire.

Baron Parshyval walked over, his *Galad'fana* hanging about his neck and shoulders. Faelin's mood dropped just as quickly as it rose. Count Allifar and Baron Parshyval had been close friends to Father's family. The last time Faelin attended a Morigahnti celebration of any kind had been right before Kingdom Inquisitors had killed his family.

Another person came out of the darkened corner from behind Parshyval, having been hidden by the baron's stocky frame. This second man also wore a *Galad'fana* draped about his shoulders. Both men had rapiers belted around their waists. The baron looked to be maybe ten years older than Faelin. The second man was tall and wiry, and he looked to be of an age with Faelin's, about twenty-and-four winters. The baron eyed Faelin with some slight suspicion. The second man looked as if he were sharing some private joke with himself.

"*Kun vaen ovat kuten makaesti,*" Faelin said, speaking the same greeting he'd used with Razka, only this time speaking in *Galad'laman.*

"*Medan kerta voida tas johta,*" Baron Parshyval replied, extending his hand.

Faelin took the baron's hand and gripped it firmly. He hadn't expected such a warm reception from any noble. With his father's line gone, Faelin feared they would see him as a reminder that one of the great Komati families was gone, not embracing him as his father's true-born son.

"We are well met, Faelin vara'Traejyn," Parshyval said. "My family loved your father and uncles well. It is good to see their blood lives on."

"I am well received by Thaedus hospitality, my lord," Faelin replied.

"Call me Parsh. I dislike standing on ceremony." Parsh released Faelin's hand and gestured at the man standing behind him. "This is Korrin. He serves my brother."

"We are well met," Faelin said, reaching out.

Korrin took Faelin's hand, but his eyes focused on something beyond Faelin's shoulder.

"That was a happy reunion," Korrin said. "Oh, but allow me to remember my manners. Anyone who travels in such company," Korrin's paused; his eyes looked to the ceiling, and his hand squeezed a little tighter, "is definitely well met here."

The man's dark eyes lowered to meet Faelin's gaze and danced with private humor.

Faelin gripped Korrin's hand a little harder, and said, "What do you mean by that?"

Korrin squeezed back and his lips curved into a smirk. "I have a little friend named Raze that whispers all sorts of secrets to me." Korrin wiggled the fingers of his free hand next to his ear. "My friend knew that you and," again, he cast his eyes toward the ceiling, "*she* were coming over an hour ago."

Faelin released Korrin's hand. "You're bound to a Stormcrow?"

"And my brother Nathan." Korrin's voice filled with pride. "As soon as Raze told me you were coming, I sent him to take word to Count Allifar. One man does not make the best protection for someone as important as herself. Even we three, you, Parsh, and myself, while formidable, are a paltry honor guard. She should have seven, at the very least. Don't you think?"

"Yes." Faelin nodded. "At least."

At that point, he was only half-listening to Korrin. Instead, Faelin considered his claim that he was bound to a Stormcrow. So few Morigahnti were bound to Stormcrows these days that Faelin hadn't considered that possibility. In the old stories, Grandfather Shadow spoke directly to the Stormcrows. If the old stories held any truth, any Morigahnti bound to a Stormcrow was more likely to accept Julianna as the Lord Morigahn. This made Faelin feel so much better about bringing Julianna here.

"But enough of religion and politics," Korrin said.

"Yes." Damian returned with a plate piled high with food and a mug of something that would hopefully ease much of Faelin's tensions. "This is a party, and those subjects have done more to end decent parties than anything else I know. Wouldn't you agree?"

"Indeed, friend Zephyr," Korrin said.

"Parsh?" Damian asked. "Save it for later and let us enjoy the party?"

"I will," Parsh said. "I'll also save my questions for how you are acquainted with Faelin vara'Traejyn and some of these other names you go by."

"You'll be waiting for those answers a long while," Damian replied. "I sell you guns, just as I sell other people guns, all over this continent. That's all you need to know. Yes, I have my secrets, just as you do."

Parsh stiffened and his gaze grew more intense.

Damian snickered a bit. "My dear, Baron. How could you possibly imagine it otherwise? I make my profession violating the Kingdom's second highest law? At least I have the good sense not to worship one of the five greater gods above my station."

Parsh stiffened at that. Korrin placed his hand on the baron's shoulder and whispered something in his ear.

Faelin sighed. He'd forgotten how Damian sometimes couldn't help but pick at the tender spots people tried to keep guarded.

"My brother will be here soon enough," Parsh said to Faeline, "and then we can speak of Morigahnti matters until we lose our breath. For now, the celebration continues. Enjoy our food and drink. Be merry, for winter comes."

"But spring will follow," Faelin said. "And so balance is maintained."

Parsh and Korrin nodded and retreated back to their shadowy corner.

Faelin smiled, partly because he was pleased to be among Morigahnti ritual again, but also because he hadn't realized how much he'd missed Damian. They'd seen each other only twice since the Kingdom attacked and killed Faelin's family and Damian's father had been executed after being caught with an extensive collection of firearms. Still, even with these little joys, Faelin could not forget that the Brotherhood of the Night and a Kingdom Inquisitor still hunted Julianna. No matter how pleasant things seemed inside these walls, those dangers remained a harsh truth. In some ways, he had hoped to find a few more Morigahnti here to help confuse Julianna's pursuers. On the other side of the coin, the more Morigahnti they found in a place, here or elsewhere, the more expectations they would have. Was Julianna ready to live up to that?

"Why the melancholy face?" Before Faelin could reply, Damian continued, "Oh, it must be due to hunger and cold. Come sit by the fire and tell me about the last few years."

Faelin allowed Damian to lead him over to a bench by the fireplace on the south wall. The fire was smaller there, and it was further from the food and drink thereby making it further from the other celebrants. They sat, and Faelin ate for a few minutes. He hadn't realized how hungry he was until that first mouthful of ham. Salty enough for flavor, but not enough to be too dry, and the honey and cloves warmed his tongue. Once he swallowed that first bite, his stomach demanded more, and the shoveling began.

At one point, just to get Damian to do something other than grin at him while he ate, Faelin said, "So, gunrunning?" in between bites.

Damian nodded. "Seemed like the thing to do. The Kingdom's been hunting me ever since my father's execution. When I figured out where he actually made the guns, I sort of took over his personal crusade. Not because of any self-righteous call to free Koma, but rather mostly because if the Kingdom is going to catch me and execute me for my father's crimes, I figured I might as well earn it." Damian's smile faded, and he took a long swallow off his mug. "Isn't it odd how we've each tried to deal with our fathers' deaths? I followed in my father's footsteps. Xander actually betrayed Vincent Adryck's memory and joined the very people my father despised. And you, well, I have no bloody idea what you've been up to."

"Wandering," Faelin said around a mouthful of biscuit and ham. "And learning. Studying any bit of the old knowledge that I can find."

"I've been doing a bit of that, too. Mostly maps. I found a map in my father's study that shows the location of quite a few Morigahnti storehouses and hidey-holes."

"The Kingdom left his study alone?" Faelin asked.

"Oh, not the one in Mother's estate," Damian replied. "They had a trio of House Floraen Inquisitors go through that. I meant the one above his gunsmith workshop."

"Do any of the Morigahnti know about this place?"

"I'm sure some know about some of the places. They aren't as chatty with each other as they used to be. Not since Kyrtigaen Pass. At least that's what my father said. I may have told one of two Morigahnti that I like about one or two of Father's hideaways. However, I hardly want them knowing about *all* of them." Damian took another drink. "If the Morigahnti start using them again, they won't be any good for me. After all, I have a business to run."

"I'm going to reach for something here," Faelin said, "and tell me if I'm wrong, but wouldn't the Morigahnti be your biggest customers? And wait…if you are selling guns to the Morigahnti, why are they letting you roam free?"

"First, the Morigahnti I deal with have no idea who I am. Why do you think my contact is Baron Parshyval over there and not his brother Count Allifar? Because the Count leaves his brother, the baron, to handle the estates when the Count goes to court. Makes things simple because the old grouch doesn't bother to recognize me as me. Doesn't pay too much attention, as I'm not a pretty young thing in a flowing skirt. Second, the Morigahnti are my best customers in Koma. I've got two sultans in the Lands of Endless Summer who love firearms, and Heidenmarch is getting ready for something big. Possibly huge. The deposed nobles there are spending the last of their fortunes on any firearms they can get. Even still, they don't stand a chance against an amassed Red Draqon army, which is what they'll be facing the instant they win a single decisive victory."

While Damian drank again, Faelin said, "Speaking of Heidenmarch, I saw your brother."

Damian looked at Faelin over the rim of his mug. He blinked three times. When Damian gave no other response, Faelin continued.

"I saw him on a battlefield. He was fighting in a Red uniform in the ranks of the Draqons."

Damian looked into his mug. "I'm empty. Let me refill yours, too."

Damian took Faelin's mug, got up, and went back to the food and drink. Faelin's face scrunched up, and he kicked himself for being a fool. He hadn't needed to bring up Xander. Yes, Damian had mentioned his half-brother's choice to become a soldier in the Kingdom armies; however, Faelin didn't need to pour salt on that wound.

A few moments later, Damian returned with a pair of full mugs. He handed one to Faelin.

"So…" Damian said, smirking at Faelin, "tell me about this lady you arrived with, in a small little village, in the middle of Autumn's first storm."

Faelin took a long drink. The beer was good, dark and rich, spiced with cloves. It went well with the ham he'd eaten earlier. He let the warmth of it slide down his throat into his stomach and settle there before he answered.

After a moment, he replied. "You don't want to know about her."

"Oh, but I do." Damian's smirk grew into a grin. "She intrigues me in ways you cannot begin to comprehend."

Faelin put his mug down and looked at Damian eye to eye. He held the gaze long enough for the grin to falter.

"I know you, Damian Adryck. That woman is more trouble than all your father's guns combined." Faelin gripped Damian's shoulder. "As a friend, I suggest you be about your business and be away from Koma. Perhaps visit one of your sultans in the Lands of Endless Summer for a time. In a very short while, Koma is going to be a place none of us want to be. And don't ask. The less you know of it at this point, the better."

Faelin released Damian's arm, picked up his beer, and took another swallow. As good as it was, he set it aside again. He couldn't afford to addle his wits even the slightest bit.

Damian looked first up at the top of the stairs where Julianna had gone, down at the still mostly full mug, then back at Faelin.

"It's like that?"

Faelin shook his head. "It's worse."

Damian took one last drink in a single swallow and put his mug next to Faelin's. They sat together in silence as the celebration of Autumn's First Storm grew to match the fervor of winds and rain outside.

One servant helped Julianna out of her clothes. Another servant poured steaming water into the bathtub. Once Julianna stood in nothing but her shift and the *Galad'fana*, which she'd wrapped about her head as a shawl to hide her scar, she shooed the servants away.

"But my lady," the older said, "Mistress Dressel instructed us to help wash you."

Julianna stood straight and looked the servant girl right in the eye, knowing full well what kind of effect her pale, steel-gray eyes had on people.

"Sometimes, a lady wishes a bit of privacy, no matter what the mistress of the house says. Please respect my wishes. If Mistress Dressel has any issues with it, I will correct the matter. I'm sure, the lady of the house has no wish to earn the disfavor of my family."

Both servants curtsied and left.

By the twittering and stifled giggles from the other side of the door, Julianna was fairly certain that the servants had decided she hid her face because she was Faelin's mistress. Julianna accepted that. In truth, people thinking of Faelin as her lover would make it traveling much easier. It gave them a reason for hiding Julianna's identity that wouldn't arouse too much suspicion.

Now alone, Julianna turned to the bathtub and lost herself for a few moments watching wisps of steam rise from the surface of the water.

She sighed and unwrapped the *Galad'fana* from her head and lay it next to the tub where she could reach it. She slipped out of her shift and eased her body into the near-scalding water. Once it came up to her neck, Julianna wrapped her arms around her chest and let the tears flow.

She wept for those killed by the Brotherhood of the Night. Khellan, hung by *Galad'fana*, and for the children they would never have together. Perrine, trampled under the charging horses. She wept for her maid Collette and Perrine's sister, Sylvie, taken by the Nightbrothers and subjected to Shadow only knew what tortures. Lastly, Julianna wept for her mother, because when the Lords of Judgment came, Julianna had chosen to reject her mother's heritage, and Julianna couldn't help but think of that as the ultimate betrayal of her mother's memory.

Her body shook in rhythm with her sobbing, and some of the water splashed onto the tiled floor. *Let the servants clean it.* This was the first moment when Julianna could be alone, truly alone, with her grief. She had slipped once with Faelin and hated herself for it. She could not let herself show weakness in front of anyone ever again, not if she expected anyone to respect her as the Lord Morigahn.

Time lost its meaning.

Eventually, Julianna recovered. While this mountain of grief might never fade completely, for now, life must move on. Even in the darkest part of winter, spring was waiting to brighten the world. By the time Julianna pushed her grief to the back of her mind, the water had cooled considerably.

Julianna almost got out of the bath to dress but decided she wasn't ready. This might be her last bath in quite some while. Also, this was a perfect way to begin to practice speaking miracles again.

With the pace Faelin had set in his attempt to keep ahead of the Brotherhood of the Night, they'd rarely stopped. So as they traveled, Julianna had contented herself in imagining what words she would speak and what Dominions she would draw upon to channel Grandfather Shadow's power into the world. Understanding that she possessed this ability had kept her from falling completely into despair. Now, with the Morigahnti downstairs, she could practice a bit. Their presence would muddle the scent of any miracles she would speak to anyone pursuing them.

She reached her arm over the side of the tub, touched the *Galad'fana,* and focused on the Dominion of Shadow. She smiled when she touched even that small bit of power.

"*Tuoda nina minul,*" Julianna spoke in *Galad'laman,* addressing the shadows in the room.

Power surged through the *Galad'fana.* Shadows jumped to life. They stretched out from under the table and the bathtub and carried the brush, cloth, and soap across the room to her. Once they delivered the desired items to Julianna, the shadows returned to their natural places. Julianna slumped into the water, even more tired now, but the exertion satisfied her. With time and practice, she would build up her endurance against the rigors of channeling divine energy through her body and soul.

She touched the *Galad'fana* again. This time she looked at the small fireplace in the far corner of the room. She drew on the Dominion Balance, and spoke, "*Sadela aen era seurasa aegni ja enkii.*"

For a brief moment, the connection between the fire and the water danced along her skin and surged through her blood. Then the fire snuffed out. The bathwater came near to boiling. Despite the wave of exhaustion that washed over her, Julianna scrambled out of the tub. Most of her skin was bright red from the scalding water, and a few places had started to blister.

Julianna picked up the *Galad'fana*.

Weariness made her arms heavy and her legs threatened to buckle beneath her. The burns covering most of her body did not help either. She just wanted to sleep. However, before sleep, she had to fix what she'd done to herself. Now, what words and what Dominions should she call upon to heal her burned skin?

FOUR

Faelin stared into the fire.

Damian had excused himself to attend to some task outside, most likely preparing any necessary details to leave upon a moment's notice. Those who found themselves hunted by the Kingdom of the Sun developed such traits, or they died.

Faelin tapped his foot in time to the music as the celebrants danced Saerynjyr's Round in the center of the room behind him. He had allowed them to pull him into one dance. However, with so many worries nagging at him, his performance in the dance had been rather dismal. After that dance, Faelin declined the next, deciding that no one should suffer through anything like that. Instead, he sat by the fire and soaked in the warmth. He suspected in the months to come, he'd look back longingly at the pleasure of this moment of a warm fire and good drink.

Every so often, Faelin glanced over at Parsh and Korrin. Most times the two Morigahnti simply stood in their place, acting in their roles as reminders of the bleakness of winter. Occasionally, they had their heads together, speaking softly. However, on this occasion, Korrin knelt down and spoke with a child, a boy perhaps ten years old with dark hair, wild and unkempt. Parsh stood over them. Faelin couldn't hear the boy, but the child's lips moved quickly. He pointed to the ceiling and then to the door. Korrin looked up to Parsh. Parsh said something, and Korrin nodded and walked over to Faelin. The young Morigahnti stopped two paces away, his eyes sparkling with that same I-know-something-that-you-don't-know humor that Faelin had seen earlier.

"What?" Faelin spoke with more harshness than he had intended. That didn't seem to distress Korrin. If anything, his smile grew wider. This made Faelin's mood match the tone his voice had just taken. "Is there something you want of me?"

"Yes," Korrin replied. "The Lord Morigahn is channeling enough divine energy that she's either going to alert the Kingdom to her presence, or she's going to burn her soul away. Perhaps both. As Morigahnti, it is not our place to question the Lord Morigahn. However, Parsh tells me that you are not Morigahnti, and you seem to have a relationship with the Lord Morigahn that might allow you to suggest she might choose to temper her actions."

Faelin sighed and forced his voice to remain even. "I'll see what I can do."

He didn't know which he liked least: that Julianna was speaking miracles while she should be resting, with the added danger of calling to their enemies, or that the Morigahnti saw him as having any influence over her. The first might lead to her death, the second, to his.

Faelin felt eyes on him as he crossed the room. Despite the sensation of his stomach sliding toward his feet, Faelin must maintain a calm demeanor. With the nearly constant infighting among the Morigahnti, any one of them might seek to further themselves by exploiting any perceived weakness in Julianna.

Faelin ascended the stairs and met one of the servant girls who had taken Julianna to her bath.

"Would you show me to my ladyship's room?" Faelin asked.

The girl dropped into a curtsy. "Yes, sir."

Faelin tried to ignore the young servant's sideways glances. When they reached the door, she curtsied and scurried off. Faelin sighed when he heard her giggling in the distance. Part of him wanted to laugh at the ridiculousness of him and Julianna being lovers, but most of him knew how dangerous those rumors could become.

He ran his hand through his hair and scratched the back of his head, truly reconsidering the wisdom of coming here. Well, it was far too late to worry about that now.

Without knocking, Faelin opened the door and entered.

Julianna stood on the far side of the room, naked, aside from the *Galad'fana* wrapped around her shoulders. Her eyes were closed. Her left hand rested on the room's single window. Fresh, red-and-blistering burns covered her body as if someone had poured a kettle of boiling water over her.

Faelin glanced at the bathtub. Steam rose from the surface. Enough time had passed since Julianna had come up here that the water should be tepid, if not chilled.

Julianna whispered in *Galad'laman*.

For a few heartbeats, Faelin watched the blisters and burns fade from Julianna's skin. The circles under her eyes darkened. Her knees shook, almost ready to buckle underneath her.

Faelin reached into the special pocket he had sewn into his boot and brought out his small journal. He ran his finger over the sentence he wanted, making sure of the pronunciation in his mind before speaking the words of *fyrmest spaeg geoda*.

"*Aeteowian ic seo wat sodlis ikona.*"

A slight humming echoed through the chamber.

Words in *Galad'laman* appeared in the air. Julianna had spoken three distinct miracles in the room.

Faelin easily deciphered the miracle to control shadows. The words that stretched from the bathtub to the fire were a bit more of a challenge; however, considering the logs in the fire had gone out and the steam rising from the bathtub, Faelin suspected the effect of that second miracle. The last, with the words floating right next to Julianna and the window, Faelin wouldn't have deciphered that one if it hadn't been for the similar wording of the miracle directed at the fire and the obvious effect it had on Julianna.

What did the girl bloody well think she was doing? She didn't have enough control to be speaking miracles based on the Dominion of Balance, not yet, and at this rate, not ever. If Faelin let her keep on like this, she'd kill herself from taking in the cold or heat or something equally stupid. As it was, the storm outside the window would keep pulling warmth from Julianna while at the same time pushing cold into her until she froze to death.

Faelin dashed across the room and banished the words floating in the air. No need to leave those visible to raise even more uncomfortable questions.

Faelin reached Julianna and pulled her arm away from the window. She shook her head, and her eyes fluttered open.

"I told you to be careful," Faelin snapped. "The Morigahnti downstairs can feel your miracles through their *Galad'jana*. As might any Adepts in this area who might be tracking us. Which is likely because we didn't kill them all. Beyond that, you haven't built up enough strength to be speaking so many miracles at one time."

Julianna yanked her arm out of Faelin's grip.

"I don't have time to be careful. Isn't that why you brought us here? So the Morigahnti could mask our passing? I'm taking the opportunity to practice while I can." Her skin began to lose the hint of blue, and life returned to her features. "How many enemies do I have now? How much stronger are they? Can you truly tell between friend and foe before we get attacked again? I must learn. I must learn, quickly. If I don't, I might not be ready before my enemies find me again."

"The Morigahnti will only mask you if they speak miracles as well. Stop being foolish and making assumptions about things you have little or no knowledge of. If you push too hard, you'll be dead long before you have to worry about anyone else."

Julianna stiffened, standing straight up. This pushed her breasts out enough to remind Faelin of her nakedness. Faelin blinked, drew in a deep breath, and very deliberately met Julianna's gaze, eye to eye. This was more for her sake than his. He didn't know her feelings on modesty and such. The last thing they needed was one more barrier between them. Her chin rose up a bit as she glared back at him. The Lord Morigahn's scar glistened in the lamp and candlelight.

"Better that than suffer the Ritual of Undoing," Julianna said. "I'm not going to spend the rest of eternity as a prisoner in the Realm of the Godless Dead."

"Is that what this is about?" Faelin's voice softened, anger giving way to concern. His face grew warmer and warmer as he struggled to continue looking into her eyes and only into her eyes. "You're afraid of being undone?"

Julianna nodded.

"That is one thing you needn't fear," Faelin said. "By being named the Lord Morigahn, your soul is protected by the Ykthae Accord."

"The what?" Julianna asked.

The last of his anger faded. She knew so about the ways of the Morigahnti or any of the bargains and pacts governing interactions between the Celestial and Infernal power. This must be one of the reasons Grandfather Shadow had chosen Faelin to be her guardian — for the knowledge that he possessed that few, even among the Morigahnti, would have. Once they rode away from this place, hopefully soon, Faelin would make a list of the very basic and most important things Julianna needed to know.

Faelin turned away from her. "Perhaps we should wait until after you finish your bath."

"Yes, that might be best."

"Please stop the miracles. I promise you, you have nothing to fear from the Rite of Undoing."

Faelin hurried from the room. Once outside, he rested his forehead against the wall. He could not cast her naked body out of his mind. While he had no interest or desire in Julianna, he could not deny her beauty.

A creaking of the floorboards down the hall drew Faelin's attention. He glanced up and saw Parsh at the top of the stairs. The Morigahnti's face was devoid of expression.

"Is all well with the Lord Morigahn?" Parsh asked.

"Yes," Faelin answered. "She will stop speaking miracles."

"Excellent. It would be a tragedy to lose another Lord Morigahn so quickly."

Without waiting for a reply, Parsh turned and went back down the stairs.

Faelin tried to decipher his last statement. Had the baron spoken out of concern, or had he offered a veiled threat?

FIVE

After wrapping herself and her companion in a Lie that covered all the senses, Yrgaeshkil and Alyxandros Vivaen entered Shadybrook's stable. Yrgaeshkil carried Saent Muriel the Destroyer in her left arm and a sword of Faerii steel in her right hand. The blade was as thin, though only half as long, as Thanya'taen. While her weapon might not possess the same weight of history and intimidation as Grandfather Shadow's ancient sword, hers could be just as deadly to any celestial or infernal being. Yrgaeshkil decided carrying such a weapon was prudent after witnessing Grandfather Shadow kill Saent Raena the Sacrificial right after Yrgaeshkil herself had dispatched the goddess, Innaya.

Yrgaeshkil walked past the wagon in the center of the barn and took Saent Muriel to a middle stall, halfway between the large, double doors at the front of the stable and the single door at the back. She made a little nest out of straw and placed the Destroyer within it. Muriel fussed a bit but made no other sounds. As a Saent, the infant had no need for mortal nourishment.

"And you're just going to leave her there?" Alyxandros asked.

"That is my intent," Yrgaeshkil said.

"Is that wise?"

Yrgaeshkil fixed Alyxandros with her most disapproving stare. The mortal didn't even have the decency to look away. She sighed. So much would change once she grew fully into her power as a Greater Eldar.

"Perhaps," Yrgaeshkil replied. "Perhaps not. However, if you plan to be my first high priest, you should probably learn to trust that I have a reason for everything I do, considering how long I spent planning and implementing Grandfather Shadow's release."

"I did not mean to speak out of turn," Alyxandros said with a bow. "I only wish to aid you, which I can do better if I know your plans and intentions. My question was poorly worded. Forgive me, goddess."

"This once." Yrgaeshkil arranged the straw to look less like someone had made a bed for the child. "But I will answer, as your reason for asking shows merit.

"Kingdom forces are converging on this village. Two separate Inquisitors, and a band of the Brotherhood of the Night. Oh, and one of the inquisitors has a squad of Draqons. A fist of Moriganti also rides here. When these forces descend on the village, fighting is nearly assured. If Julianna survives long enough to escape, she and her protector will need horses. When they come for the horses, they will find this darling child. I do not believe that Julianna has yet grown as harsh as my husband's followers or any number of her predecessors. She may one day, perhaps, but not yet. And even if she has, I doubt her protector has. At least one of them should have compassion enough to care for the baby. That will be their undoing."

"And if you are wrong, and they leave the child behind?" Alyxandros asked. "Or if someone else takes the child?"

"She will live up to her word," Yrgaeshkil replied. "No matter who finds her, she will serve my ends. Destruction can come in many ways.".

SIX

Julianna rifled through the pile of clothes the servants had left for her. She found a robe and pulled it on. Gods and goddesses, she was cold. She looked down at her hands which clutched the robe closed. The tips of her fingers were pale, almost to the point of being blue. She brought her hands to her face and breathed on them as she rubbed them together.

She hated to admit that Faelin wasn't completely wrong. On the other side of the coin, he wasn't completely right either. She needed to determine a way to balance practice with caution.

The bathtub, still full of steaming water, gave Julianna an idea. She stood by it and held her hands a finger's length above the surface. Soon, the steam warmed her. Her skin returned to a more normal shade, and the shivers left her.

Julianna opened the door and let Faelin back into the room. Even though he wasn't blushing any longer, he couldn't quite meet her eyes. She couldn't help but smile at the sweetness of it. She doubted most men would have looked away, much less have had the decency to be embarrassed. However, even with all they'd been through together since Faelin had found Julianna lying among a field of corpses – mostly Nightbrothers, but also some of her closest friends – he was still, at his core, a decent man.

Julianna closed the door, picked up the bundle of clothes and toiletries, and led Faelin into the bedroom attached to the bathroom. She sat on the bed while Faelin leaned against the wall looking at the floor between them.

Julianna broke the silence. "What is the Ykthae Accord?"

Faelin flinched at the sound of her voice. He would not meet her eyes.

"This is stupid," Julianna said. "You saw me naked. Fine. I'm sure you've seen other women naked. I'm still Julianna. You're still Faelin. Shall we proceed now that we've gotten beyond that bit of awkwardness?"

At that, Faelin met her gaze.

"This has nothing to do with seeing you naked. Please, allow that... You know... I mean... We've seen each other squat enough times traveling that a bit of unclothed skin—"

"It was quite more than a *bit*, Faelin."

Faelin shook his head and chuckled.

"What?" Julianna asked.

"It's surprising you think this is about me seeing you without any clothes on.:"

"Very well," Julianna said. "If not that, what then?

Faelin's mouth opened and closed. He looked past her to the window.

"Ah," Julianna said. "I think I have it. You think I'm not going to like what you have to tell me."

Faelin shrugged. "Perhaps."

Julianna sighed. "I'll be all right with hearing about unpleasant things. I have a slightly different perspective now. Now, the Ykthae Accord?"

"It's an agreement," Faelin said, "made between the gods and the Incarnates that ended the Second War of the Gods. It was meant to regulate the influence of the greater and lesser gods and goddesses over the physical realm."

"I've never heard of the Incarnates," Julianna said. "What are they?"

"I'm not sure," Faelin replied. "Perhaps no one really is. I've read about them in ancient texts and heard stories. The only thing any sources seem to agree on is that the Incarnates are even more powerful than the gods."

"More powerful than the gods? How is that possible?"

"The heavenly spheres are vast and mysterious," Faelin replied. "Who knows what wonders lie beyond our understanding? However, because of the Incarnates and the Ykthae Accord, you have no reason to fear the Rite of Undoing. Part of the Ykthae Accord states that when the high priest of any greater god dies, the high priest becomes a Saent. Since you are the Lord Morigahn, your soul will rise up to Grandfather Shadow's celestial realm. To my knowledge, no power can change that."

"So when I die, I'll become even more powerful?"

"Except if you die by channeling too much divine energy. Every time you speak a miracle, you are damaging your soul. Kill yourself that way, and you burn yourself out of the Cycle of Life, Death, and Rebirth."

"Those cloaked figures, the Lords of Judgment, they remade my soul. They are Incarnates."

Faelin nodded. "We may be the only mortals since the Ykthae Accord to interact with an Incarnate. We might want to keep that to ourselves. Some people would like nothing better than to study us just for being in close proximity to an Incarnate, much less having them affect your very soul."

"House Floraen Inquisitors," Julianna said.

"Among others," Faelin agreed.

"Well," Julianna said, "that detail about becoming a Saent does take some of the fear out of dying."

"Don't let this be an excuse to act rashly.' Faelin looked Julianna directly eye to eye for the first time since he entered the room. "Many people are going to swear their lives to you, Julianna, many of them willing to die so that you may live. Do not waste their lives by taking foolish risks because death doesn't hold the same fear for you as for them. Grandfather Shadow may hold you accountable if you waste his followers' lives needlessly."

"I'll think upon this," Julianna said. "What do you have planned next?"

"I think we should ride out just before first light," Faelin replied.

"Where will we go?"

"We should flee any Kingdom-controlled lands," Faelin said. "I'd like to get to a ship, but heading to the coast would be far too dangerous considering most of the Kingdom presence in Koma is concentrated by the coast, so we'll go to the Dosahan. I know some of the tribes who wander near Koma. We should be able to find shelter while we decide where to go after that."

"That sounds well-planned," Julianna said. "Should we go now?"

"No. The celebration continues. Leaving now would draw too much attention. Besides, both you and Vendyr need rest. We'll slip away once the festivities wane and most everyone is asleep."

Julianna chuckled. "It will be just like our childhood."

Faelin smiled his warm, older-brother smile. "You're right. Nobody ever caught us then, and nobody will catch us now. We'll be fine."

Looking into his eyes, she believed him.

"Thank you," Julianna said.

Faelin nodded and left.

Glancing at the table on the other side of the room, Julianna's gaze fell on the pitcher of wine. Remembering her dreams and nightmares, the thought of rest became less of a comfort, unless she could find a way to keep the dreams at bay.

She almost reached out through the *Galad'fana* and drew on the Dominion of Shadows, but thought better of it.

Instead of speaking a miracle, Julianna walked over to the pitcher, placed the vessel to her lips, and drank. When she finished the pitcher, Julianna crawled into the bed, thinking, *Let the nightmares come if they will. They can't be any worse than what I've already lived through.*

SEVEN

Several leagues north of Shadybrook, five Morigahnti rode through the storm toward the town. Wynd Sontam rode beside her husband, Nathan, Korrin's twin Brother. Unlike the others, she did not wear a hood to protect herself from the rain. The storm was a blessing sent by Grandfather Shadow, and she refused to hide from it. Why would she hide from the raindrops? She smiled as the rain kissed her face and soaked her dark hair.

Glancing to her left, she saw Nathan's half-amused smile barely visible in the shadows of his cloak. He only made that smile for her, and it sent her heart fluttering.

"I love you, too," she mouthed.

She considered leaning over and kissing him when a shape just a bit darker than the night descended out of the sky. She and Nathan reined their horses to a stop. Nathan raised his arm, allowing his Stormcrow, Thyr, to land on his forearm. Wynd heard the other Morigahnti come to a stop behind them.

The bird was slightly bigger than a normal crow but smaller than the average Stormcrow. Nathan and Thyr locked eyes, speaking from mind to mind, and Wynd reached out and scratched Thyr behind his wings.

After two years of marriage without children, Wynd and Nathan thought of Thyr as their child, despite Thyr likely being decades older than either of them. Stormcrows were strange beings that embodied all the wonder and wisdom and wit of childhood. Yet, as far as Wynd could determine, each and every Stormcrow understood the dark and grim truths of the world; they just seemed to be immune to the corruption that humans succumbed to as they lived through those dark and grim truths.

Nathan's eyes went wide. He blinked away the mind-to-mind link and sent Thyr back into the air.

"What is it?" Count Allifar's voice boomed from behind them.

"Thyr just spoke to Raze," Nathan called back. "The Lord Morigahn is speaking miracles, powerful miracles, and is using them to perform menial tasks."

"Damn," Wynd said, voice quiet with shock. "That's not good."

"No," Nathan replied, matching her tone. "Not good at all."

Questioning the Lord Morigahn any louder than that was simply not done. At least, not by rank-and-file Morigahnti such as themselves. Still, Wynd tried to fathom why the Lord Morigahn would jeopardize himself like that. Every Morigahnti with a *Galad'fana* knew that they could not use its gift for any little whim. Each time one of them spoke a miracle, it invited Kingdom wrath down on all their heads.

"Morigahnti," Count Allifar boomed again. "We must reach Shadybrook. Now."

Wynd kicked her heels into her horse's flanks. She normally

loved riding through the rain, but tonight she no longer took joy in it. How could the new Lord Morigahn place them all in this much danger? Wynd prayed to Grandfather Shadow that there were no Kingdom Adepts about..

EIGHT

Damian went about checking his horse's tack. In weather like this, he wanted to make sure he'd perfectly hitched Stamper to the wagon.

The stable door opened, and a gust of cold wind ripped through the barn. Damian grabbed the two-shot pistol from beneath the seat and aimed the weapon at the figure standing in the doorway. The lanky Morigahnti, Korrin, smiled at Damian and waved.

Damian had hoped to depart before being discovered. Many of his customers grew touchy when the details of an arrangement changed. In such instances, Damian found heated arguments were more pleasant than most outcomes.

"It is a beastly night for traveling," Korrin said. "While Grandfather Shadow blesses us with his storm, he also blesses those with the knowledge to stay indoors on a night like this."

Damian kept his aim on Korrin. "You know how I feel about signs and portents of the gods,"

Korrin shrugged. It was his way of politely saying, "Yes, Zephyr, and I still think you're an idiot for not believing."

Damian was happy to leave Korrin and all others who dedicated themselves to any religion and the delusion that the gods controlled all aspects of the world. On the other side of the coin, Damian had actually met one of the gods. Well, a goddess. The experience was not what he'd always been led to believe it would be. Thinking of that brought other memories of times spent with Faelin, and Damian couldn't help but grin. That grin seemed to confuse Korrin, who stopped smiling.

"As you would, Zephyr," Korrin said. "Where does that leave our business, with you leaving so suddenly?"

"You also know how I feel about too many of you around when we do business," Damian said. "I deal with you and Parsh. I know you, and despite Parsh's peculiar tastes, I like you both. I don't know Count Allifar or anyone else in your Fist." The Allifar bit was a lie, but Damian would wager Korrin didn't know that. "I've managed to elude Kingdom justice for so long because I'm careful. This won't be the first time I've been rained on. Three days from now, have Parsh meet me down by my boat with the coin. I'll have all your guns there. You can have this horse and cart at no extra cost. That should give you all the time you need to handle whatever business Count Allifar has with that lady."

Korrin nodded. "That's all Parsh wanted to know. He has plans for…"

"No." Damian held up his right hand, the hand not aiming a gun at Korrin. "I'm not your confidant. As much as we enjoy each other's company, we're not friends. I don't want to know a bloody thing about your plans, plots, schemes, agendas, or anything else remotely resembling information about courses of action you intend to engage in with these guns. I sell. You buy. Well, Parsh buys. That's it."

"Very well," Korrin said. "We meet in three days in the cove where you land. All other details of the arrangement remain the same?"

For the briefest moment, Damian considered making a point of the time he'd be spending in the woods rather than a bed in the Dressels' house and the time lost traveling waiting for the Morigahnti to complete whatever Morigahnti business they had brewing in this small little town. But, he left it alone. In truth, this was one of his last deliveries before the winter snows trapped him in his father's workshop in Koma city. His last sales were in that city. A delay of three days wouldn't make much difference.

"Agreed," Damian replied.

"Then, let me help you finish," Korrin said.

"Gladly that," Damian said.

They worked to hitch the horses, Damian said, "Do you hear that?"

"The tapping at the back door, just above the wind?" Korrin asked.

"Yes, that."

"I hear it."

With a sigh, Damian picked up the two-shot pistol again.

"Don't bother," Korrin said.

The Morigahnti went over to the door and yanked it open. A cloaked figure fell into the barn.

After a moment of scrambling, the figure under the cloak turned out to be a young lady. Damian recognized her as one of the servant girls from up at the manor house. She was a pretty thing, despite her youth, fourteen perhaps fifteen winters. Had Damian been a few years younger, or she a few years older, he might have had some interest in her. And if Baron Parsh and Korrin weren't some of his best customers. And if Damian hadn't been a fugitive of Kingdom Inquisitors.

A moment later, a large crow hopped in through the door behind the young lady.

"Jenise." Korrin sighed and shook his head. "Jenise, Jenise, Jenise. You're supposed to be attending to Mistress Dressel's guest."

"The guest lady dismissed me," the young lady answered. "I tried to argue, but she was adamant about being left alone."

"Fair enough," Korrin said. "I've heard that some ladies are like that. But that doesn't explain why you are here."

"I... uh..." Jenise stammered, glancing back and forth between Korrin and Damian. Her deep blush showed even in the dim lights from the lanterns.

Damian wished he didn't remember the shy smiles she gave him and the way she seemed to keep finding excuses to be around him.

Damian sighed and rolled his eyes. "I want no part of this. I encouraged none of it."

"Oh, I don't think you did," Korrin said. "And I don't find you at fault. You're far too careful to make that kind of mistake. Besides, this one has an eye for a handsome face. Any handsome face. She'll likely try to sidle up to Faelin before the night is done."

Damian laughed. "I'll wish her all of Sister Wind's luck with catching his eye."

"A hard one to catch is he?" Korrin asked.

Damian laughed even harder. "It depends on who is doing the hunting." He wiped his eyes, worked to calm his breathing, and bowed to Jenise. "Thank you for the much-needed amusement. Now, if you will excuse me."

Korrin looked at Damian with that not-quite-mocking grin.

"Be well, friend." Korrin's smile faded and he fixed an expressionless gaze on Jenise. "You. Come away from the door and stay as warm as you can. Once I'm done helping Zephyr here, we'll be back up to the manor."

With Korrin's help, they completed hitching the horse to the wagon in short order. The girl, Jenise, watched them with wide-eyed attention the whole time.

Once they finished, Damian climbed into the wagon, made sure his scattergun was in its proper place, reached into the back of the wagon, pulled out his leather, fur-lined cloak, wrapped it around his shoulders, and then put on his wide-brimmed hat. It was made of deep brown leather, hard and stiff, and the brim stretched out past his shoulders. He cinched the leather cord tight under his chin.

"I've never seen a hat like that," Jenise said.

"It's popular among the Komati and Heidenmarchs who have formed communities in the Dosahan lands," Damian said. "It keeps the sun off in summer and the wind and rain off in autumn and winter. I'll see you in three days."

"Indeed." Korrin reached up, offering Damian his hand.

Damian grasped the young zealot's hand, wondering not for the first time if, in another world where men might worship as they wished, arm themselves how they wished, and with no order of precedence separating noble from common, he and Korrin might have been friends. Ah well. As Damian's father had said time and time again, wondering is a pastime for dreamers, lovers, and philosophers—fools one and all. Damian's father had been a bit of all three, and all fool.

Whipping the reins and clicking his tongue, Damian urged the horse to move, heading into the storm.

Korrin walked beside the wagon. "I don't understand how it is that you seem able to get any beast you wish to accomplish any task you wish."

"I've always had a way with animals," Damian replied. "When I was younger, I spent more time in the pasture than I did with other children."

Damian missed those simpler times, but those were gone, never to be had again.

Stamper trod onto the cobbled street between the buildings. Damian spared one last glance at a magnificent black and white gelding, a mix of Saifreni and Nibara breeds. A rare animal to be sure, and one Damian would have loved to have had the opportunity to ride.

Ah well, Damian thought, as the rain pelted his hat and leather cloak, *perhaps Father wasn't the only foolish dreamer in the family. At least I have the sense not to get trapped up in my dreams.*

NINE

Jenise watched Zephyr's wagon fade into the gloom of the stormy night and sighed.

"None of that," Korrin said. "I understand you're at the age where…"

Even though Jenise knew it was rude to ignore one of the Morigahnti when they spoke to her, she thought she heard something else in the barn.

"Jenise," Korrin spoke in a forceful tone, meant to draw her attention back.

She raised a hand. "Hush."

"Excuse—"

"*Hush*," Jenise said again.

That time Korrin did listen to her. He fixed her with a look equal parts intrigued, amused, and irritated, bordering on upset.

For a few moments, perhaps fifteen or so heartbeats, Jenise strained to hear the sound again, something that wasn't the rain pelting the barn's roof, the whine of the wind as it beat against the barn, or any of the horses shuffling or nickering. She couldn't be sure, but she thought she heard the sound again.

"Did you hear that?" Jenise asked.

"I think I did," Korrin said.

Jenise swallowed, and her heart quickened when Korrin drew his rapier.

"What—?"

"Hush, girl," Korrin snapped.

He crept around the stable, craning his neck to look into the stalls. Not knowing what else to do, Jenise followed close behind him. If someone or something that meant harm jumped out at them, Jenise wanted to be as close as possible to the Morigahnti.

When Korrin reached the third stall, he stopped. His head cocked first to the right and then to the left.

"Well," he said, "I'll be damned."

"What is it?"

"Stay there," Korrin said. "And stay quiet."

Jenise was already ignoring him. She knew the constant draw of her curiosity was her curse. Sometimes she should leave well enough alone, do what she was told, and she'd just stay out of trouble. Like tonight. She knew she shouldn't have followed Zephyr to the stable, but she couldn't resist the air of mystery and danger that seemed to cling to him — not to mention that fiendish smirk and the mischievous glint in his eyes.

"Stop!" Korrin's word cracked like a whip. "Stay still. Stay quiet. I'm thinking and waiting."

Staying still, Jenise heard what she thought was a soft sigh followed by a cooing sound.

"Is that—?"

"Quiet," Korrin said, though not quite so harshly. "For once, girl, do as you're told. This night has already been strange enough. Those of us who follow the old ways only survive with our souls intact when we mistrust anything overly strange."

Waiting for what? Jenise wanted to ask, but she did as Korrin said. She stood, barely daring to breathe.

Korrin stood in the middle of the barn, turning in slow circles with his mouth hanging slightly open. He clicked his teeth together seven times. She knew because most Morigahnti did things in repetitions of seven. That's how Grandfather Shadow wanted it. Or, at least that was what everyone said. For herself, Jenise felt worshiping the old ways was all well and fine, but she wanted to learn of the other ways and hear the words of the other gods. Her mother and especially her father kept hoping she'd wake from that particular fantasy. All while these thoughts ran through her head and Korrin turned about, Jenise continued hearing that cooing and sighing child.

"Well then," Korrin said. "I suppose we're going to have to take it on face value that someone abandoned a baby in our stable. You might as well go fetch it," Korrin waved toward the middle stall on the north side of the stable, "and go see what Mistress Dressel wants us to do with it."

"It?" Jenise shook her head moving into the stall. "Don't call the little thing an it. It's a baby."

There, in the back corner, she saw the baby, mostly covered in straw, kicking and squirming.

"You just called it an it," Korrin said.

"I did not" Jenise picked the baby up and cradled it.

The baby — a she, if Jenise guessed right by looking into her lovely face — looked up at Jenise and gave a half-smile before sneezing. The raggedy blanket wasn't nearly enough to keep the chill and cold from biting into the little miss's bones.

"It's a baby," Korrin said, repeating Jenise's words back at her. "Your words. You called it an it."

"You know what I meant."

Jenise pulled her baby close and tucked it between her arm and breast. Even after wrapping her cloak around them, Jenise wasn't satisfied the sweet little thing would catch a chill between here and the manor. Not on a night like this.

"Now," Jenise turned to Korrin, "Master Morigahnti, if you will kindly lend me your cloak, I'll be on my way."

"My cloak?" Korrin said. "Why in the name of anything would I do that? It's cold and wet out there."

"And this is a baby," Jenise said. "You are a big strong Morigahnti. This baby needs to stay warm and dry between here and there. I'm not about to ask for your *Galad'fana*, unless…"

Korrin pulled his cloak from his shoulders and tossed it to Jenise. "Go."

Jenise bundled herself and the baby into both the cloaks and ventured out into the glory of Grandfather Shadow's first storm of Autumn. The wind and rain pelted her. Jenise wondered why Grandfather Shadow couldn't start with something gentler, perhaps a slight drizzling so that his loyal followers could grow accustomed to the coming change in the weather. Still, with the addition of Korrin's cloak, Jenise and the child stayed mostly dry, except for Jenis's feet, which she hated. For Jenise, cold feet were the absolute worst. Still, after a short walk, she'd be in the manor house kitchen where she could kick her shoes and stockings off by the fire.

When she pushed the kitchen door open and stepped across the threshold, Jenise drew in a deep breath of warm, soothing air, before closing the door with her foot. It would take a few minutes for the chill to fade completely, but this was a good start.

"And just where have you been, young lady?" Kalla the cook demanded.

"Out," Jenise said, making her way across the kitchen. "Not that it's any of a mind to you."

The massive woman who ran the Dressel's kitchen tried to get between Jenise and the door to the main dining room. However, even at her fastest, the old, rotund woman couldn't manage anything greater than a waddle. Jenise, having years of practice at avoiding Kalla, easily danced around the cook and made it to the door.

"It's plenty of a mind to Mistress Dressel," Kalla called even as Jenise left the kitchen, kicking the door shut behind her.

Behind the closed door, Jenise heard Kalla continue ranting and raving in the kitchen, as she would likely do for some time. Jenise paid no mind to it. Instead, she wove through the crowd of celebrants toward Mistress Dressel. Jenise knew, and had known for many years, that Kalla was all shade and bluster, so much so that the cook hadn't intimidated Jenise for a long, long time. Now, Mistress Dressel, on the other side of the coin, could intimidate anyone in Shadybrook Township. Once, on an equinox celebration, Jenise had seen Mistress Dressel stare down both Count Allifar and Baron Parshyval to the point where both noblemen sat meek and cowed for neglecting their manners. While Mistress Dressel was not regarding Jenise with as severe a glare as she had that spring day so many years ago, the gaze the mayor's wife did fix upon the servant girl who was supposed to be upstairs seeing to the guest caused Jenise to slow a bit in an attempt to forestall the inevitable.

When Jenise finally stood before Mistress Dressel, she curtsied. Mistress Dressel stood silent, fists on her hips and glaring down a Jenise.

"I don't believe both of those cloaks are yours," Mistress Dressel said.

"No, madam," Jenise said. "The second is Korrin's. He gave it to me in the stable."

"Well, I don't need to know why you were in the stable," Mistress Dressel said. "What with how you couldn't keep from looking at Zephyr like Aunt Moon herself had introduced the pair of you. I'm more interested to know why Korrin gave you his cloak."

Jenise shrugged Korrin's cloak from around her shoulders. It slid to the floor, and Jenise held out the baby.

"Shades and damnation," Mistress Dressel said. "Where did that come from?"

"We found her in the barn," Jenise said. "Hidden under a pile of straw. Korrin stayed to see if he could find out anything. I made him give me his cloak so I could keep the baby warm."

"Well." Mistress Dressel looked the baby over. "Well…well… Whatever are we going to do with you?" Then she looked back to Jenise. "No sign of the mother anywhere?"

"No, Madam," Jenise said. "I think that's why Korrin stayed out there. Said we shouldn't trust any oddness that comes, especially on a night like this."

"Always been a bright one," Mistress Dressel said.

Again, she looked down at the baby, chewed her upper lip, and tilted her head from side to side for a few long moments. At last, she drew in a deep, long breath, held it for a few heartbeats, and then released it even more slowly than she'd drawn it in. She'd come to a decision.

"It's a wonder the thing is as good-natured as it is," Mistress Dressel said. "It must be near to starved. Take it upstairs to Ida. Having a baby of her own, she's watching some of the other children and playing nurse made to Lazar, whose wife got herself claimed by Old Uncle Night during childbirth. And since I can't seem to think of any other way to keep you from trouble, you can stay up there and help her mind the children. The Grandfather knows with three babies alone, she'll need at least one extra pair of hands."

Jenise didn't bother arguing. Arguing with Mistress Dressel never led to anything good. Instead, Jenise curtsied and headed for the stairs. Once she was out of Mistress Dressel's immediate presence, Jenise sighed. This evening had gone far and wide away from anywhere she'd hoped it might. She reached the top of the stairs and sighed again.

Novan stood between Jenise and the door at the far end of the hall where the children would be. The young man's shoulders were slumped, and from the look of the puffy redness around his eyes, it didn't take an abundance of intellect to surmise he'd been crying. The flush of his face made his pimples stand out even more than usual.

"That dashing Zypher rejected you?" Novan's voice cracked.

"I'm free to speak with whom I wish," Jenise said.

"But..." Novan said. "But... our fathers... mine... yours... they..."

"Yes," Jenise said. "They met. They talked. Then my father came and talked to me. I told him that I'm not going to marry you."

"I'll grow beyond this." Novan waved his hand around his face.

"It's not that," Jenise said. "It isn't anything other than we would be miserable together. Haven't you listened to what Count Allifar and the Morigahnti tell us? We need balance within ourselves before we can find balance with another. You have no balance, Novan. None." Then she added, hoping to take a little of that sting away. "I'm not much better. Now, please move. Mistress Dressel sent me to help with the children."

Without waiting for a response, or to see if Novan was going to move even a little, Jenise started for the other end of the hall. As she suspected, Novan turned and backed against the wall, making way. Jenise did not look back. She walked to the door that led into the nursery, opened it as quietly as she could, stepped inside, and closed the door just as quietly.

The willowy nursemaid, Ida sat with a baby in her arms, another in her lap, and a small crowd of children sitting around her, staring in rapt attention. Her raspy voice held them as she spoke.

"And so Grandfather Shadow taught Kaeldyr to put markings of his language upon the stones. Then, the first Lord Morigahn taught his followers how to read the markings. They would give each other information about the enemy in this way, location, and numbers. Soon, once the early Morigahnti realized that sharing this information gave them a great advantage over the followers of the sun and the night, they began devising other ways to share what they knew. Eventually, the Morigahnti developed paper and ink, which gave us books, where men could keep all the knowledge of the world. And that, children, is why you should pay close attention to your studies. To read is to honor Grandfather Shadow's Dominion of Knowledge."

Most of the children nodded. A few, the younger ones, seemed less than impressed, mostly because they were too young to have begun their studies.

"Found a baby in the stables," Jenise said. "Mistress Dressel told me to bring her up and to help you with anything you need."

Ida's dark eyes took in the little thing in Jenise's arms.

"Bring the dear thing here," Ida said. "I'm a bit dry after the feast these two just had, but we'll see what we can do. You take this one in my arms. Just got it to sleep. The rest of you scamps and rascals, be about your games. But mind you keep quiet. Any of you wake either of these babies, and it's to sleep with the lot of you. *Ymarta?*"

The children muttered that they did indeed understand. They moved away from Ida, the large crowd dividing into smaller groups.

Jenise went over to Ida. With slow and careful movements, they managed to trade infants. Ida took the stable baby, put the little thing to her breast, and worked to get a nipple into its mouth. Jenise thought she saw a shimmering around the baby. Blinking, in surprise, Jenise looked again, but it had stopped.

"Give it back!" one of the children cried.

"No!" another said.

Jenise heard the sound of a slap behind her. The baby in her arms began to wail. She turned around just in time to see several of the children begin flinging toys at each other.

Sighing, Jenise knew that she shouldn't tempt fate by saying it out loud, but she couldn't help thinking that this night could not possibly get any worse.

TEN

Wynd and the other Morigahnti rode into Shadybrook proper. Seeing the stable doors open this late at night, in this weather surprised her. Count Allifar raised his hand for them to slow. Wynd's horse slowed immediately and nickered. The gelding wanted to stop completely. Wynd understood the beast. She also the need for caution in such circumstances. In truth, caution could damn itself to the dark realm of the godless dead so long as Wynd could get out of the rain for a few minutes. Usually, the first storm of autumn was warmer than this, but this year, Grandfather Shadow seemed in a spiteful mood. If this storm was any forecast, the winter that followed would be long and bitterly cold.

Inside the stable, Korrin wandered about, looking into every stall.

"Isn't your weapon smith supposed to be here?" Allifar asked.

"He was," Korrin said. "He left. Decided to depart shortly after the Lord Morigahn arrived."

"That's not disconcerting," Nathan said.

"Perhaps," Korrin continued searching the stable. "Perhaps not. He's cautious as a habit, a necessity of his profession. I'm less curious about his departure than I am about the baby."

"Baby?" Allifar asked.

Aurel, Nathan, and Wynd looked back and forth at each other, the same question hanging on their glances.

"Indeed," Korrin said. "Little Jenise came down to give Zephyr a send-off. She's taken quite a liking to the smuggler. Relax, I interceded and will ensure that any future business takes place away from the village. After Zephyr left, she found a child in that stall. I told her to take it to Mistress Dressel. I've been looking about, to see if I can discern anything else about this situation."

"And?" Allifar asked.

"It's odd," Korrin replied.

"Odd?" Allifar asked.

"Indeed," Korrin replied.

"That's all you have concluded?" Allifar asked.

"I could add perplexing," Korrin said. "However, that might be premature, as I've not been investigating overly long."

Allifar sighed. Wynd disguised a little laugh with a cough. The Count should be used to this by now, but somehow, he never grew accustomed to Korrin's ways. Perhaps if Count Allifar didn't spend so much time at court, he would better know the Morigahnti who served him.

"Has your talent given you any insight?" Allifar asked.

"If it had, your Excellency," Korrin said, "I would have mentioned that right off."

Allifar looked about the stables for a few moments. "I do not like a situation with so many questions without any answers."

"Should you like any of us to bring the smuggler back?" Nathan asked.

Wynd suppressed a sigh. Of course, her husband volunteered for such duty. Of course, Wynd would go with him if Count Allifaf gave that order. She did like the feel of the elements upon her face, but the rain had soaked her every garment. Both the wind and rain had softened, but on this night, that did not mean much with the chill settled into all of her joints. Now she only wanted a warm fire and a warmer drink.

Allifar stared into the night.

Wynd held her breath and shivered. She also decidedly did not look at her husband.

"You truly believe this weapon smith is not a danger?" Allifar asked Korrin.

"He can be dangerous when he needs to be," Korrin said. "But he is first and foremost a survivor, and, secondly, he's a businessman. He'll not be dangerous to us unless we give him reason to be."

"Good," Allifar said. "I do not like the idea of splitting the fist. Not on a night like this, with so many... oddities." he looked at Nathan. "No need to fetch Korrin's contact. It is best we remain together. Let's care for the horses. Then, we'll head to the manor where we can get warm and make ourselves presentable for the Lord Morigahn."

Wynd led her horse to an empty stall. She hadn't followed the old ways all her life, unlike her husband's family and those they served. The others had all met at least one man who had born the title of Lord Morigahn and seemed to be taking all this in stride. Despite privately rebuking the Lord Morigahn for being a fool with miracles during the journey here, Wynd's heart fluttered down into her stomach and danced a nervous little jig.

ELEVEN

Carmine's insides turned into knots. Despite the damp weather, the inside of his mouth had the dry, tacky feeling of being wine-sick.

Two days—thus far, Hardin and he had suffered through two days with these Adepts sent by the First Adept, Adept Vycktor Ilsaen of House Kaesiak, and Adept Cadenza D'Mario of House Floraen. Cadenza was Carmine's cousin on his father's side. They made an odd pair, Vycktor being tall and lanky while Cadenza was short and fat. Carmine considered that some might find a more polite term to describe Cadenza, perhaps plump, fleshy, or if they were being very generous, curvy. However, Carmine's disdain for Cadenza would not allow her to be anything fat in his mind.

All four of them sat on horseback just inside the edge of an apple orchard, disguised by Vycktor speaking a subtle miracle using the Dominions of Shadows, Secrets, and Illusions. From this hiding place, they watched five people ride into the town, just as they had watched the sole wagon leave the town only a few minutes before the riders arrived. Those riders were likely Morigahnti, and who knew about the wagoneer? He might be just a local farmer heading back to his home after a night of celebrating, or he might be carrying a message. The riders might have been normal travelers; however, the trail of miracles that led to this township and the fact that their leader wore the tell-tale *Galad'fana*, as the Morigahnti called it, wrapped around his head made it clear who they were.

Vycktor was the furthest from Carmine said something. Between the wind and Vycktor's thick, Kaesiack accent, and the mask that muffled his voice, it took a moment for Carmine to decipher the words, *how shall we proceed?*

All Adepts and High Blood of House Kaesiak wore masks as symbols of their devotion to Grandfather Shadow. In the case of Kaesiak Adepts, those masks also served as the divine focus they used to channel miracles, but in most cases, High Blood and Adepts had moved beyond the archaic, full-face-covering mask that Vycktor seemed to prefer.

"We should wait," Cadenza's nasally voice replied. "Right now, they will be alert and ready for their ride. Let them join the celebration. They'll settle and relax. Once the festivities have concluded, we will strike. When that time comes, Vycktor and I will take our squad of Red Draqons into the village, capture the blasphemers, and prepare for the Ritual of Undoing. Hardin, you and Carmine will wait outside the village in case any of the townsfolk slip through."

"An excellent plan," Hardin said.

Vycktor voiced something that sounded like an agreement.

Carmine's nerves grated at Hardin's subservience to these two Adepts. The decrepit Swaenmarch was twice the Adept these two were, combined. Unfortunately, Hardin had spent most of his studies on the teachings of Old Uncle Night and not Aunt Moon, the traditional patron of House Swaenmarch. Because of this, he did not possess the same perceived level of talent and was forced to defer to Adepts who served lesser gods.

Neither Cadenza nor Vyktor were Adepts of Old Uncle Night, requiring Carmine and Hardin to constantly be aware of what they said and subtly speak miracles using the Dominion of Lies in order to keep their identities as the Brotherhood of the Night hidden. Most of the Nightbrothers, the girls, and the Daemyn hounds did not actually ride with them but rather rode a short way off, hidden by subtle Lies spoken by Carmine and Hardin together.

"Do you think you can handle that much responsibility, Marquis Carmine?" Cadenza asked.

"Of course, Adept Cadenza." Carmine lied so well he almost convinced even himself of the humble subservience in his voice.

The hardest thing for Carmine to stomach was that he was not an Adept outside of the Brotherhood of the Night. Half-bloods and low blood needed special dispensation from the First Seat and First Adept of their House in order to train as an Adept. Carmine's father had burned several political bridges when he married a Komati girl. Father had originally been betrothed to the Sun King's cousin, who now sat as First Adept of All Father Sun. After such an offense, Carmine would never be allowed to train at the Academy of the Sun, a fact that Cadenza never allowed him to forget.

"Good," Cadenza sneered. "You may return to your men and prepare them however you see fit; however, I doubt we'll require you."

"With two Adepts of your power and a squad of Reds, you are sure to succeed," Hardin said. "Carmine's and my presence here is a mere formality, mostly redundant."

"You don't need to overdo it, Hardin," Cadenza said. "I'll be sure to speak of you in the most favorable light when next I meet with His Radiant Majesty."

"Long may he shine," Carmine and Hardin said, together. Vycktor said something as well. Carmine presumed it was the same but couldn't tell for sure.

But not too much longer, Carmine thought. *Always, the sun must eventually set.*

Soon the Zenith would shift, and darkness would blanket the Kingdom when the Night King sat upon the throne. This time, the Brotherhood would dominate the Kingdom for generations. All the proper marriages had been arranged; all but one of the proper heirs had been conceived. As it was, the future Night King had married a young woman, proclaimed by prophecy to be a fertile field once true night came over all the lands the Kingdom touched.

"My thanks to you, Adept Cadenza." Hardin bowed in his saddle and turned his horse. "Come along Carmine, we mustn't be underfoot."

Carmine bowed only as deep as he needed to without causing offense, then followed.

Once out of earshot, Hardin leaned over and whispered, "Once they start for the town, I want you to send out your pet and keep a close eye on things. Once they finish with the Morigahnti, we'll attack and be rid of two people in the order of precedence a bit earlier than expected."

"What about the Draqons?" Carmine asked.

"It wouldn't be the first time we sacrificed a few Brothers for the cause," Hardin replied. "Pick out the six who are the least worthy. Have them attack the Adepts with the Daemyn hounds. If any of the Draqons actually survive an encounter with the hounds, they should still be easy prey if the Brothers swarm them. After that, you and I will deal with any final survivors."

"Has the First Adept sanctioned this?" Carmine asked.

"No, but neither has he ordered us *not* to harm these two."

Hardin's face grew grim, but a light shone in his eyes. It was the gleam of hungry ambition that comes only from youth.

Carmine suspected he was, at last, glimpsing the man Hardin had been before bargaining his youth to a Daemyn.

"One way or another, every person in this town who is not of the Brotherhood of the Night will die. If the Daemyn hounds don't devour their souls, we'll send them back into the cycle of Life, Death, and Rebirth."

"All except Julianna," Carmine said. "I have special plans for her."

"Oh?" Hardin asked.

Carmine explained his plan to use Julianna as a broodmare for Daemyn spawn for the rest of her life.

"You're learning to think like a true Adept of the Night," Hardin said. "This scheme of yours eliminates the leader of an enemy faction and repays her for killing one of Uncle Night's faithful."

"And as long as she lives, the Morigahnti cannot name a new Lord Morigahn," Carming said.

Hardin looked at Carmine for a long moment, as if re-appraising some family bauble that he'd learned was a rare antique. Smiling, Hardin clapped Carmine on the shoulder.

"Perhaps the First Adept did choose well with you. I know just the Daemyn to breed her too. The one that should have had her on her birthday. Once the Daemyn is done with her, we'll share the Morigahnti bitch with the rest of the Nightbrothers, just so she can learn her true place in the world. Perhaps you might like a go at her yourself."

Carmine laughed. As beautiful as she was, he would never soil himself on such a woman as Julianna Taraen. He would let each of the Brothers take a turn with her, but only after Hardin's Daemyn made her a mother. Tonight would only be a small taste of the suffering Carmine would visit upon her. And even with everything he had planned for Julianna, it would never be enough to repay Julianna for killing Nicco.

And suddenly, a thought came to Carmine.

"Might I suggest we send twelve brothers after the wagon?" Carmine asked. "It would not pay to leave a single loose end from this village wandering about ."

"An excellent thought," Hardin said. "But a full twelve? Isn't that a bit much for one man?"

"One man that we can see," Carmine said. "I've not been fighting Morigahnti as long as you have, but I've learned how cunning they can be. Can we be sure that one man is the only man with the cart?"

"Indeed," Hardin replied. "You are showing greater and greater insight. Send eighteen, and one of the hounds, for caution's sake. Then they can come in from the other side of the town when we are ready to strike."

"It shall be done." Carmine rode off to where the Nightbrothers waited.

TWELVE

Novan paced back and forth from wall to wall in the front room of his parents' house. Each time he reached a wall, he took a long drink off the bottle of brandy that Mother didn't know Father kept hidden away. That way, even if Father got angry, he couldn't do anything to Novan. Well, not without first explaining to Mother exactly where the brandy had come from, which would likely wind up being far worse for Father. Mother felt he drank too much, and that was only the drinking that she knew about. More than a few times while she'd nagged Father, Mother had mentioned that Novan's grandfather had drunk too much as well. Novan didn't understand why Mother thought drinking was such a terrible thing. He loved the way spirit made his arms and legs a little heavy, in a pleasant, lazy kind of way. He also loved the way his thoughts slowed down so they could overwhelm him, especially when he was upset like this. When his head swam and his thoughts came slowly, he could ask himself questions and take all the time he needed to find the answers. Soon, he'd reach the point where he didn't care about the answers.

Why would Jenise go chasing after that Zephyr like some...?

Novan didn't have to think too long on that question. Zephyr was handsome, dashing, and mysterious — the kind of man a young woman who wished she was the maiden in a story would long for.

Why couldn't Jenise see that Novan was a better man for her?

Because Zephyr came to sell the Morigahnti firearms every several months, just often enough so that she wouldn't forget him.

Novan wasn't supposed to know Zephyr's business here, but Novan paid close attention to the Moriganti. After all, what better way to become a Morigahnti than to know what the Morigahnti were about?

But he wasn't a Morigahnti yet. Without that, what was Novan compared to Zephyr?

Nothing. Nothing at all.

What could Novan ever hope to offer a beautiful woman like Jenise?

Nothing. At least not as he was now.

What was Novan going to do about it?

Likely nothing. He was nothing more than a small country lad, not even really a man. As it was, trapped in Shadybrook, Novan had little prospects for becoming anything like what Jenise might want for her man.

No. Wait.

Novan had a thought, but his head swam around and away from it and around it again. He rubbed his face, trying to get some feeling back into his brain. It took a moment for his hand to comply with his mind's desire. In his bit of drunken confusion, he wound up rubbing the brandy bottle on his cheek. The cool glass on his flushing warm face actually helped him focus and realize why he couldn't catch the thought. He was pacing back and forth. The thought was moving willy-nilly about the room.

That was easier to fix than he thought it would be. Upon that realization, Novan changed course. Instead of pacing in a relatively straight line, Novan began walking in a circle. That should eventually allow him to cross paths with the stray thought. Until then, he kept circling, doing his best not to let any other thoughts into his mind, as they would likely distract him from catching the one he let get away. Fortunately, the brandy swirling in his stomach and mind made it fairly easy not to have other thoughts.

Walking and drinking. Drinking and walking.

Eventually, Novam stopped. A thought came into his mind. Before allowing himself to think the thought, he had to make sure that it was the thought that had gotten away and not some new thought. Novan looked it over, that thought, and realized that it was, in fact, the thought that had gotten away from him. He stopped walking and concentrated really hard on that thought in order to think the thought again.

Yes!

It was a brilliant thought!

A thought so brilliant that it might even work to turn Jenise's eye away from that Zephyr man.

Novan turned to the door and set himself to head back to the manor house and ask that Baron Parshyval take him to train as a Morigahnti. No. He wouldn't ask. Moriganti didn't ask. Morigahnti were strong. Novan would go and tell Baron Parshyval that he wanted to be a Morigahnti. Novan was ready to give his life and soul to Grandfather Shadow and the old ways of Koma.

Two steps later, Novan stumbled. That would not do. This was no way for a Morigahnti to begin his discipleship.

Bed. Rest.

The morning would be better. Yes, especially with that fancy and secretive lady that came to the celebration. She would definitely be the center of everyone's attention for this evening, possibly even in the morning.

Sleep for now. Tomorrow, he would take his first steps to becoming a Morigahnti.

Again, Novan altered his course, heading now toward the stairs up to his small room. His mind thought about his bed, about how comforting and warm and wonderful his downy mattress would feel as he sank into it. Back when he'd been collecting the down and stuffing the thing all by himself, on more than one occasion Novan had questioned whether it would be worth the effort. The first night he lay in it, he realized it was worth every shoulder-aching moment. How many nights had he imagined and dreamed of what it would be like to have Jenise sharing that heavenly mattress with him?

The more Novan thought about his bed, the more his eyes drooped. How he just wanted to lay down, to stand facing away from the bed, and fall backward into it. He'd done that often enough without the brandy. Falling into the softness of the mattress might be the closest thing he might come to falling into a woman, not that he would know that, but still, that is what Novan imagined it would be like.

Novan imagined Jenise and himself standing at the foot of his bed without any clothes on and falling onto the bed and into each other. It was possibly the finest thing he'd ever imagined. He imagined it so hard, with so much of the brandy swirling around in his head, that Novan forgot how to walk, especially how to walk upstairs.

The next moment, Novan couldn't feel the stairs beneath his feet. The ceiling filled his view, falling away from him. Wind rushed pasted him.

That's when the brandy faded from Novan's mind as he realized he was falling backward down the stairs. From the very top of the stairs.

Novan would never be a Morigahnti now, even if he somehow managed to survive the fall, which would only happen by the blessing and intervention of some god or goddess, in other words, a miracle. Unfortunately, that would never happen. Novan knew he wasn't important enough for any god or goddess to intercede against fate on his behalf. Especially not when Novan was about to die, or at best be crippled, due to his own self-loathing.

After a few moments of looking up at the ceiling and not feeling himself colliding with the floor or the stairs, Novan realized quite a bit of time had passed since he'd slipped. He looked about, craning his neck and blinking in surprise.

The face of a beautiful lady filled his vision. She wasn't old, nor was she young. Yet, she had the loveliest face Novan had ever seen. Framed by her dark hair and skin so pale it seemed to shine in the faint candlelight, she was so lovely that he might have fallen instantly in love with her, except his mind reveled in the realization that he was not going to die. In that realization, the brandy came crashing back into his head, making it and his stomach swim.

"It's quite a thing to suffer the curse of a Saent's word," the lady said as she placed Novan on the floor. "But nothing a deity can't overcome. Rest. Dream. This was not your time to pass on. You, like all the people of Shadybrook, are necessary. If I can, I will help you all to play your proper parts at the proper time."

"How can you know what those are?"

She knelt next to him and smiled. Novan had never had anyone smile at him as lovingly and sweetly as she did.

"I know when everyone and everything is necessary," she said. "It's in my nature. Now sleep."

The goddess Necessity leaned over and kissed Novan on the forehead, placing just the slightest bit of her divine power into him. The threads of so many lives wove together on this night in this small little township, she might not be able to keep them all aligned to their purposes. This young man would wake when he needed to, and he would do what needed to be done.

Thirteen

Watching Julianna escape down the dumbwaiter made Yrgaeshkil want to scream. She paced back and forth in the darkness of a copse of trees, watching the battle raging around the manor house. Morigahnti, the followers of Grandfather Shadow, fought against the Brotherhood of the Night. Even though the Brotherhood warriors outnumbered the Morigahnti more than three to one, the battle was going against the Brotherhood. They did not have the advantage of firearms, and only one in six or so of the Brotherhood could channel divine power as miracles, whereas nearly half of the Morigahnti could.

She wanted to kill someone. No. She specifically wanted to kill the scarred-faced man standing next to her. But she couldn't. Kavala was a necessary component of too many of her schemes. Even if she didn't need him, Yrgaeshkil wasn't sure she could contain her power in her current mood. Getting noticed while wandering around the physical realm was the last thing she wanted.

Somehow, Julianna had managed to escape the initial attack. The girl had gotten out of the building and her grandfather had spirited her away to who knew where or even when. It couldn't be too far. The girl's human blood would make shifting her over too great a distance impossible, but a Stormseeker could still travel beyond reach very quickly in a series of short, rapid jumps.

The only consolation to this failure was the Morigahnti corpses that littered the ground outside the manor. Unfortunately, this was countered by an even greater number of her husband's followers. While Yrgaeshkil didn't actually care about these mortals in the greater scheme, she needed them for the time being, as she built her own powerbase.

Yrgaeshkil turned to the man known as Kavala. "You

promised me it would happen."

Even though the right side of his face was a mangled mass of cuts and scars, she could see boredom in the way his gaze would not quite meet hers and how his shoulders rocked slightly back and forth.

"It should have," he replied, looking past her to the house. "I cannot be blamed if the men attack the wrong person, especially from out here. I recall wanting to lead the attack myself."

It matters not," Yrgaeshkil snarled through her teeth. "In seven years, I will ensure that she calls him forth."

FOURTEEN

Symond put the drinking skin to his lips and took three large swallows. Even with careful rationing, his supply of spirits was dwindling to the point of worry. Between the weather and those other two Adepts that had joined with Adepts Hardin and Carmine, Symond hadn't been able to get away from the camp to scavenge for more. Not that he particularly wanted to after his interaction with the farmers, Kaelyb and Isnia. Still, he needed to find some kind of spirits, or he would have to deal with the Daemyn hounds being able to sniff out his grandfather's lineage. At that thought, he glanced to the other side of the camp, where the hounds were penned. Luckily, most of the Nightbrothers feared and avoided the hounds, so Symond's own reluctance to go near them hadn't been noticed, or if it had, it wouldn't be seen as an oddity.

Gods and goddesses, Symond wanted a drink, but he dared not. Perhaps if fate, luck, or both smiled upon him, Symond would find more spirits in that township once the fighting was over. If they won, that is. A double-edged sword that victory would be, creating even more challenges for him.

Fe glanced at the two young ladies, one noble and one common, who helped serve the Nightbrothers. Symond's entire purpose in being among the Brotherhood of the Night was to keep ladies like those from mothering children like Symond, sired by fathers from the celestial or infernal realms. The noble, Countess Sylvie, had likely ensured she would escape that fate by seducing her way into Adept Carmine's bed. The commoner girl, Colette, had no such recourse. At some point, likely in the near future, one of the Adepts would seek to bargain with a Daemyn, and should the price be high enough, they would offer up the girl as a mother for the Daemyn's offspring, giving the infernal creature a foothold in the physical realm for as long as the child lived. Symond would do everything he could to spare Colette from that fate.

As if summoned by Symond's thoughts, Adept Carmine rode into the camp.

"Symond!" Adept Carmine called. "Put that skin away. Light a fire under the brothers. The Uncle is hungry."

"Of course, Adept!" Symond said. "Brothers! See you your arms and armor! Tonight we will send our enemies to dance in Uncle Night's embrace."

A cheer went up through the camp. Nightbrothers gathered their weapons and helped each other into their black armor and skull-shaped helmets.

Symond walked over to Adept Carmine.

"Any special commands, Adept?" Symond asked.

"Yes," Adept Carmine said. "I want you to take eighteen brothers and one of the hounds to the far side of the township and intercept a wagon we saw leaving not too long ago. You'll need to hurry to catch it. Adept Hardin has ordered that we leave no loose ends. Send anyone you find with the wagon to Uncle Night's embrace. Then, ride down to the township and help us kill anyone you find, except one. If you see a young woman, perhaps a year or two younger than me, with a scar on her face—"

"The Lord Morigahn?" Symond asked.

"Indeed," Adept Carmine said. "The Lord Morigahn. Spare her. Bring her to me. I have plans for that one."

Symond nodded and made the appropriate, "Of course," and, "Your will is my action, Adept." However, Symond had no intention of turning over the Lord Morigahn to either Adept Hardin or Adept Carmine. They would breed her to a Daemyn before the All Father Sun rose in the east.

Even before Symond completed his near-to-groveling response, Adept Carmine had turned away from him and was bellowing orders to other Nightbrothers.

"Jorgen! You see to the girls. They escape, or any harm comes to them. I will personally feed your soul to the hounds."

"Yes, Adept Carmine," Jorgen called back.

Symond shook his head. He didn't know if it was a terror or a relief that Adept Carmine had set Jorgen watching the girls. On one side of the coin, Jorgen was an incompetent boob. On the other side of the coin, Sylvie had a firm hold on both Jorgen's loins and his heartstrings. Who could tell how that little mixture would play out, especially once Adept Carmine discovered the extent to which Sylvie had entwined the poor, foolish Jorgen? Regardless of any other factors, sooner or later, Jorgen was likely fated to feed the house.

Sighing and pushing the lines and webs of plots and schemes and loyalties and betrayals within the camp out of his mind, Symond lifted the skin to his lips and took another long, healthy swallow from his skin. The brandy warmed him as it hit his stomach. Even though he was running low on spirits, if he was going to be leading a hunting party alongside a Daemyn hound, Symond would need the extra spirits flowing through his blood to mask the scent of his mother's father. He would have to trust fate or luck, or perhaps both, to provide him with more spirits soon.

For now, Symond needed to get his armor on and lead a group of Nightbrothers in search of a wagon. At least it would likely be on the road, if fate was kind.

It was going to be a long hard night.

FIFTEEN

Octavio Salvatore paced across the length of the Temple of Night, a secret room hidden deep within the Governor's Palace in Koma city. The bubbling cauldron to his right showed him the newest Lord Morigahn, Duchess Julianna Taraen, tossing and turning in her bed. A hastily drawn map of the Shadybrook Township lay spread out on the table to his left. Other hastily-drawn scraps of paper littered the map, representing the various forces within and converging on Shadybrook. Well, except for the wagon, which was leaving.

Four Night Adpets stood around the table, each in touch with one of the nightbats which patrolled the skies around Shadybrook. Octavio's brother, Dante currently had his nightbat watching over Cadenza, Vyktor, and their Squad of Draqons. Tamaz Aegotha, focused his nightbat's attention on the Nightbrothers heading to intercept the wagon currently leaving Shadybrook. Ulfric Svornson had volunteered to watch the Morigahnti movements in the township proper. Finally, Rosella Andres had her nightbat on a tree in the apple orchard not far behind Hardin.

"I still don't understand why we're going to all this trouble over this girl," Dante said. "We could have easily herded her toward an ambush of Nightbrothers, Adepts, and Daemyn-possessed such as that she wouldn't possibly be able to escape."

Octavio paused his pacing and turned to the table. However, before he could speak to admonish his impulsive younger brother, Rosella reached out and smacked Dante in the back of the head.

Dante spun on Rosella, his face flushing.

"How dare you strike me?" Dante hissed. "I am the Whisperer of Lies, proclaimer of the Night King."

Both Tamaz and Ulfric subtly shuffled away from the quarrel. However, unlike so many other Night Adepts, Rosella did not cower just because Dante had the fortune of being less ambitious than Lidia, their sister who had been born three years younger than Octavio and seven years older than Dante.

"Then act like you deserve your position and the powers that come with it." Rosella's face flushed as well, but Octavio suspected not from shame as Dante's had. She had the reputation for not suffering fools even the slightest bit. "For someone who can pluck upon the very fabric of fate, you have such a small grasp of the scope of the conflicts between the Great Houses, the Kingdom Protectorates, and those who follow the gods."

"Octavio," Dante said, "are you going to—"

"To what?" Octavio asked. "Let her speak to you like that? So long as you refuse to think beyond your next social engagement, I will allow any Night Adept to speak to you in any such manner. Why do you think I'm letting this play out in such a manner? What's different?"

"Uuum." Dante's face tightened as he looked from Octavio to the map to the cauldron and back to Octavio. "The Lord Morigahn is a woman?"

Rosella's mouth tightened as she glared at Dante. "Why would that make such a difference?"

"He's not entirely wrong," Octavio said. "But not for the reason that he thinks, which is the reason you are upset. Yes, Julianna Taraen being a woman plays into my decisions in this matter, but tell me, brother dear, what about Julianna being a woman and the Lord Morigahn is special."

Dante's face went through a series of contortions as he considered. After a moment, Dante's face brightened.

"Grandfather Shadow marked her with his own hand," Dante said. "Right after she freed him. You want to see how directly Grandfather Shadow will defend this new Lord Morigahn. That's why you sent the other two Adepts with the Draqons, to add more threats and dangers to better gauge what will and will not entice the god to intercede."

Octavio gave his brother a warm smile.

"Indeed. You are smarter than you allow yourself to be in most moments. This is the man I hope you will be when I kill the Sun King in the courtyard of this very palace and rise to become the Night King."

"I know, brother," Dante said. "I am trying."

"In every sense of that word," Tamaz said.

Dante spun and glared at the Kaesiak Adept.

"Enough," Octavio said. "We should not admonish each other after learning a successful lesson."

"Apologies, First Adept." Tamaz bowed to Octavio. Then, nodding to Dante, the Kaesiak Adept added, "Whisperer, forgive me?"

Dante glanced at Octavio. Octavio kept his face smooth. Dante would have to forge his own path in this instance. While Octavio could step in, he felt it better to allow Dante to continue learning in this moment.

Without getting any direction from his brother, Dante looked back at Tamaz. Tamaz looked back at Dante, face nearly as smooth as Octavio's.

"Apology accepted," Dante said. "It has been a stressful night. It's only going to get worse. If I behave as Rosella said, not thinking things through, by all means, admonish me. However, do not belittle me again for nothing more than the sake of being spiteful." He took a deep breath. "We have enemies enough seeking to destroy us. We don't need to aid them by undermining each other."

"Yes, Whisperer." Tamaz gave Dante a bow.

Rosella also bowed to Dante. "Well said, Whisperer."

Dante glanced at Octavio. Octavio nodded at his brother with approval.

"The Morigahnti have moved from the stable to the manor house," Ulfric said from across the table, eyes closed as he concentrated on seeing through his nightbat's eyes.

The other three Adepts closed their eyes as well.

"Cadenza and Vyktor are waiting on the edge of the town with their Draqons," Dante reported. "They are discussing how much longer they are going to wait before heading in to fight the Morigahnti."

"Rosella?" Octavio asked.

"Hardin is still in the apple orchard," she replied. "Carmine just rejoined him. He's got about half of the Nightbrothers with him, as well as those two girls."

Not for the first time, Octavio hoped that those two Komati girls would not prove too much of a distraction for Carmine or the brothers.

"Brother," Dante said, "may I ask a question about Carmine D'Mario and the situation you've put him in?"

"You may," Octavio said.

"I thought he was a protege, that you were grooming him to assume some high-ranking position when the Brotherhood of the Night assumes the Zenith."

"He is," Octavio said. "And I am."

"Then why have you placed him in the midst of that?" Dante waved at the map.

"I put him in the middle of that," Octavio also waved at the map, "because once we take the Zenith, that is something we will wish is all we had to deal with. From the moment we take the Zenith, every member of each of the Great Houses will be working to pull us down, and not just with influence and marriage. We will be living in a constant battle for survival. If Carmine cannot handle himself in that situation and survive, he has no place in ruling the Kingdom of the Night."

"First Adept," Tamaz said. "We may have an issue. I took the liberty of sending my nightbat to watch the wagon. On its way, it found something that may be a problem. An Inquisitor is riding toward the town and will intercept the wagon in just a few minutes."

"Well now," Octavio said. "This does make things interesting."

"Hopefully the Daemyn hound will devour the Inquisitor's soul," Dante said.

Everyone in the room echoed that opinion.

Night Adepts celebrated every time a Daemyn hound managed to devour an Inquisitor's soul, thus removing it from the cycle of Life, Death, and Rebirth. It was said that once a soul became an Inquisitor, it would seek out that path in every life following. Destroying those souls was the only way to end that cycle.

For Octavio, part of him hoped that somehow the Inquisitor made it past the Nightbothers converging on the wagon and down to join the chaos that would soon engulf Shadybrook. His presence would be one more potential catalyst to see how blatantly Grandfather Shadow would come to this new Lord Morigan's aid.

As much as Octavio wanted to change the location his cauldron viewed, he dared not take it away from Julianna, even for a moment. She was the crux of everything. The unknowns surrounding her terrified Octavio right to his joints. He'd spent the better part of two decades planning to take the Zenith, going even so far as to sabotage the Brotherhood's previous attempt nearly ten years before. Now, despite his plots, schemes, alliances, and machinations, this young lady threatened to bring everything crashing down upon him. The worst part was that Octavio knew next to nothing about her, and he should. He should have paid attention to her over the past fourteen years, but he never imagined that little girl could be a danger with both of her parents dead.

Returning to the cauldron, Octavio watched Julianna tossing and turning in her bed. He'd arranged this entire night, this confrontation in Shadybrook, so that he could learn Julianna's true nature. If she survived, he'd have a better understanding of how to deal with her, either as an enemy or potentially as an ally.

ENEMY OF MY ENEMY

W hy should we fear our enemy's mind?
Tread not softly behind those who fear
our deep unknown. Light a candle just
bright enough for our enemy to see
those of us closest to them, step
    in time, matching rhythm. Pace for pace.
Step by step. Rather than watch our

enemy kill our siblings, guide his steps
with the slightest nudging — right or left.
It makes no difference. Just turn him
away from your blood toward another foe.
Let the flame of your enemy cauterize
old wounds caused by another with such
Finality they will never wound again.
— Shara vara'Dubhan

ONE

Symond suppressed a sigh and contemplated his current situation.

He'd led his fellow Nightbrothers and the Daemyn hound through the rain and the woods to intercept the wagon, an impressive feat even without being well on his way to drunkenness. His force all hid behind the treeline a short way from the road. Symond had opened his mouth to give the command to charge, but another person rode into sight from out of the rain. Only, this newcomer was heading *toward* the township. Being one for caution, Symond bit back the order. Symond refused to underestimate anyone out in the middle of a night like this.

So, they waited. The man came closer. A flash of lightning confirmed Symond's caution was not a wasted effort. In that brief flash of light, Symond recognized the golden glow of the breastplate of a House Floraen Inquisitor. More than a few Inquisitors had hunted Symond over the years.

Did the Inquisitor's presence change anything? On one side of the coin, Inquisitors could speak miracles and were usually armed with at least one faerii steel weapon. On the other side of the coin, the Nightbrothers were eighteen strong, and they had a Daemyn hound. With those odds, could Symond be confident that their numbers would see them to victory?

Many throughout the Kingdom of the Sun saw the House Floraen Inquisitors as noble and honorable warriors protecting them from the minions of Old Uncle Night. Symond knew that the Inquisitors were far from the pinnacle of virtue Kingdom propaganda made them out to be. Not only did they destroy women's lives by offering them up to be brood mothers for Aengylborne, such as Symond's mother, Inquisitors also tended to uphold the exact letter of Kingdom laws and decrees, and circumstances be damned. The only safety Symond had ever found was in the ranks of the Brotherhood of the Night. Well, he felt mostly safe with them. When he didn't need to soak his blood with spirits.

Symond decided his Nightbrothers would kill the poor, unfortunate man in the cart as well as the Inquisitor. Then,

Symond would send the brothers down into the township while he returned to make sure that neither Adept Hardin nor Adept Carmine used either of the girls to bargain with a Daemyn in order to gain a greater advantage in the skirmish to come.

Now, the Nightbrothers would wait for the proper moment to strike.

TWO

The wind and rain buffeted Damian, and Stamper trudged along the muddy road, pulling the wagon. The horse's squelching footsteps were barely audible above the sounds of the storm. Even with the slow progress, the growing distance between him and Shadybrook pleased Damian.

Faelin's words echoed: *I know you, Damian Adryck. That woman is more trouble than all your father's guns combined. As a friend, I suggest you be about your business and be away from Koma. Perhaps visit your sultans in the Lands of Endless Summer for a time. I think in a very short time, Koma is going to be a place none of us want to be. And don't ask. The less you know of it at this point, the better.*

A man remembered a warning like that, well, a man with half a mind to know his friends and enemies, at least. Though years had passed since Damian had seen Faelin, he'd never known his friend to aggrandize anything, whether good or bad, especially when trouble was concerned. Faelin spoke plainly and directly about such things, always. And so, if Faelin felt Damian wanted no part of this, and that it would be best to leave Koma, leaving Koma is what Damian would do. As it happened, Damian numbered several sultans among his acquaintances, at least two of whom would welcome him as an honored guest if he brought a shipment of firearms. The Summerfolk were fascinated by such weapons and had none of the skittishness about them as Kingdom Adepts.

Damian thoughts consumed his attention so completely that he almost didn't see the man standing in his path. Even as Damian pulled on Stamper's reins, he blinked several times to make sure he wasn't just seeing a trick of the darkness.

Sure enough, about a quarter mile from Shadybrook, a man blocked the road. The moonless, starless night had hidden the man from sight until Damian was near to running him down. If not for the mud sucking at the horse's hooves and at the wagon's wheels, Damian might have considered running him down. He definitely would not have stopped for anyone wearing the mantle and breastplate of an Inquisitor of the Kingdom of the Sun.

"Gods and goddesses," Damian muttered under his breath. Louder he said, "What service may I give to the Kingdom of the Sun?"

"Who do I address?" the Inquisitor asked. "And what business do you have traveling on such a night and hour as this?"

Damian would have to choose his words with care. "High Blood...er...Adept...ah...Lord Inquisitor? Honestly, I am uncertain as to...ah...the proper form of address...ah...sir?"

"Any will do, young man," the Inquisitor said. "Please answer the question."

"Well...yes then...ah Lord...Inquisitor" Damian continued stammering for effect. "Zephyr. Ah...the people of Shadybrook call me Zephyr. Have ever since they've known me. I'm traveling this late...ah...because of a family squabble. Bad tidings those. Not interested in getting drawn into that. I keep myself to myself. A little wind and rain is a fine price to stay out of trouble."

"Well spoken, man who the people of Shadybrook call Zephyr," the Inquisitor said. "Not a word specific enough to be a lie."

Damian could usually talk his way past Kingdom officials, but Inquisitors always proved more challenging. Most Inquisitors possessed enough wits and cunning to realize when someone sought to talk circles around them. More than that, in serving their god, All Father Sun, they received a blessing that gave them the ability to perceive outright lies.

The Inquisitor walked toward him. Stamper whinnied and strained against its tack. Damian pulled at the reins and made soothing noises.

The Inquisitor veered a bit around the horse. While Stamper's behavior frustrated Damian at first, now he felt the horse's behavior might prove helpful. A nervous horse sometimes received more empathy than a nervous person. Damian considered how he might use this to deflect the Inquisitor's attention.

"That's an interesting hat," the Inquisitor said, as he came up beside Damian. "I've never seen one so far from the Dosahan lands."

Stamper pulled against the reins, trying to move forward. The last thing Damian needed was for this Inquisitor to think that Damian was trying to escape. He leaned back, attempting to get Stamper under control. At that moment, a gust of wind blew the brim of his hat upward giving the Inquistitor a full view of Damian's face. In turn, the Inquisitor was now close enough for Damian to recognize.

"Oh…" Damian groaned, "damn."

Adept Luciano Salvatore, the man who had executed Damian's father for possession of firearms, returned his gaze.

Inquisitor Luciano smiled. "Good evening, Damian Adryck, what a pleasure to see your High—"

Damian released the reins and kicked Inquisitor Luciano in the face. The Inquisitor's head snapped back, and he stumbled away from the wagon.

Free from restraints, Stamper lurched forward. Only the mud sucking at the wagon's wheels kept the animal from charging off.

Damian reached under his seat for his scattergun. The two-shot pistol might be more accurate, but he couldn't guarantee a well-aimed shot quickly enough to incapacitate Luciano long enough to finish the job. With the scattergun, Damian only needed to point it toward Luciano. That should hurt the Adept enough for Damian to finish him with a blade.

By the time Damian brought the scattergun to bear on Luciano, the Inquisitor had already recovered, had drawn his sword with one hand, and held his amulet of All Father Sun in the other.

And then, Damian realized why Stamper had been so skittish. It wasn't Luciano.

"Damn. We have a problem, Inquisitor."

Damian gestured with the scattergun to the figures in black leather armor with bone-white skull masks. If being surrounded by Nightbrothers, while fighting an Inquisitor wasn't bad enough, one of the Nightbrothers held a leash which had the biggest, ugliest dog Damian had ever seen. The monstrous thing strained to get free.

A Daemyn hound.

Of. Bloody. Course.

Inquisitor Luciano began chanting in the language of All Father Sun.

"Kill the Inquisitor," said the Nightbrother holding the hound.

The Daemyn hound snarled.

Stamper screamed and snorted, reared, and kicked. The wagon shook with the horse's efforts to get free.

Well, that decided the matter.

Damian launched himself out of his seat, toward the rear of the wagon. The tarp covering his merchandise had been treated to resist water. Rain had collected in puddles all along the length, making the tarp slick. He gripped his two firearms as tightly as he could so as not to drop them. Damian slid easily along the entire length of the wagon and into open space, where he hung for a brief moment and dropped.

Hitting the ground wasn't as bad as Damian had anticipated. The wagon tracks gave way as he sunk into the mud. Still, it knocked the air out of his lungs a bit. Fortunately, Damian's survival instincts had taken over, and his body ignored his lack of breath.

Stamper screamed again, only to be cut short by a gurgling whimper. Damian's throat clenched. Stamper had been a fine companion and deserved better. Why couldn't the Daemyn hound have followed instructions and gone for the Inquisitor?

Swearing vengeance on all of them, yet unsure of how he would repay the Daemyn hound, Damian didn't bother to roll over. He craned his neck to ensure he had the scattergun pointed roughly in the direction of the group of Nightbrothers behind the wagon and fired. The weapon kicked. Flame erupted from the barrel. Screams and cries of anguish followed. If luck smiled on Damian tonight, unlikely given his current predicament, the shot would have sent one or two of the Nightbrothers to meet their god. Even still, if they all lived, he'd likely taken several out of the fight.

Damian rolled over and scrambled to his feet, no easy task due to the mud. At least the same mud would also work to hamper the Nightbrothers' movements as well.

A Nightbrother charged Damian. Two others seemed stunned by seeing the effects of the scattergun on their compatriots.

The one coming at Damian made a clumsy cut at his neck. Ducking, Damian slammed the butt of his scattergun into the Nightbrothe's stomach. The Nightbrother doubled over, coughing in pain. Damian brought the scattergun down on his head with a satisfying crunch.

When the fight had started, Damian had counted ten Nightbrothers, which meant at least two more—perhaps as many as eight—that he hadn't seen. Damian didn't think it was eight. That would have been a lot for these untrained oafs to hold back. Twelve was the safest estimate. Twelve Nightbrothers, three of which he'd taken out of the fight with the scattergun. Had Luciano managed to eliminate any of the Nightbrothers before having to contend with the Daemyn hound?

Stop thinking. Start acting.

A yelp of decidedly unhuman pain came from around the corner of the wagon. Of course, a House Floraen Inquisitor would have a faerii steel weapon capable of harming a Daemyn.

At that point, the remaining two Nightbrothers who had been sent against Damian recovered from the shock of the Scattergun.

"Gods and goddesses." Damian dodged another attack and swept the Nightbrother's feet underneath him. The black-armored man splashed into the mud, and Damian added, "You men are bloody sloppy."

It wasn't the wind, the mud, or the rain. They possessed all the skills of newly trained conscripts. And while that was fine for troops standing a line on a battlefield, fighting side by side, these men were acting in pairs at best. Damian could have handled three at a time, they were that bad.

"If any of you were women, I might be worried." Damian kicked the man in the mud in the head. "Women would at least be quick and graceful, unlike you clumsy oafs."

Damian took two steps toward Shadybrook and saw more Nightbrothers. Six coming up the road at a quick jog. Apparently, luck was not on his side. When luck failed, and the odds grew longer and longer, sometimes a man had to rely on the dramatic and insane.

Lifting the scattergun at the Nightbrothers coming up the street, Damian hoped they didn't know enough about firearms to know he only had one shot, or that they'd been too far away to see he hadn't reloaded. Luck decided to grant him one favor in this completely unlucky situation. The Nightbrothers coming up the road scattered. Some dove into the underbrush next to the road. Some just dropped into the mud.

"If this is the best the Brotherhood has to offer, it's no wonder you've never been able to hold the Zenith for more than a few decades," Damian yelled down the road, then added over his shoulder, "It's pathetic that the Daemyn can't even kill one little Inquisitor from House Floraen."

With that taunt, Damian dropped and scrambled underneath the wagon to reload the scattergun.

He almost collided with a woman sitting comfortably in the mud. In the darkness, he couldn't see her features too well, but her shock of white-blond hair was impossible to miss. She wore Dosahan leathers, though without any of the paintings of tribe or family. She carried a two-shot pistol in a holster at her hip.

"Damn it," Damian said. "You're one of them, aren't you?"

"One of who?" The woman's voice carried a soft echo beneath the wagon.

To his left, just next to the wagon, someone cried in pain, followed by a yelp of pain from the Daemyn hound.

"A goddess," Damian replied. "Like Kahddria."

The woman laughed a full, rolling laugh from deep within her belly. The force of that laugh shook the wagon above. When she stopped, all the sounds beyond the wagon had stopped, save for the patter of raindrops on the ground. Even the heavy snarl-like panting of the Daemyn hound had stopped.

"Even if I am, as you suggest, a goddess, I assure you, young man, I am nothing like Kahddria."

"What do you want?" Damian asked. "I'm sort of fighting for my life here."

"And that is why I am here, my boy, because you are fighting for your life."

The wind died. The rain stilled. A single blast of lightning flashed across the sky right overhead, illuminating everything for the briefest moment. Before blindness in the absence of that light overtook him, Damian saw another person under the wagon, wearing a gray cloak, sitting behind the woman.

In the place of thunder, a man's voice grumbled from all around them, "Leave off him. My claim is greater."

"Oh, shut it," the woman said. "Leave him be to make his own choices."

Thunder came, rattling Damian in his bones.

In the thunder's wake, Damian heard the Daemyn hound sniffing the air. The woman was gone, but the two-shot pistol lay on the ground, in its holster, protected from the mud. Damian grabbed the gun. By the weight of it, he could tell it was loaded. This changed his plan slightly.

Damian shoved the pistol into his belt. Then he reached out with both arms, grabbed Inquisitor Luciano's boots, yanked hard, and pulled him under the wagon. While the Inquisitor struggled, Damian crawled on top of him. In those close quarters, Luciano could not use his sword. Damian felt Luciano shift underneath him, and anticipated the two-handed strike. Twisting, Damian managed to keep Luciano from slamming the hilt of his sword into the side of his head. Instead, Luciano clipped Damian's shoulder. He'd be bruised, but he'd trade that for a pair of blows to the skull any day.

Damian pulled the gun out of the holster and pushed the barrel against the soft bit under Luciano's chin.

"Gun," Damian said. "Stop."

Luciano stopped struggling.

"If I go out there," Damian said. "Will the hound toy with me? Or try to eat me right away?"

"Probably toy with you," Luciano said.

"Grand. When I say, *Now*, light the wagon on fire. As big a fire as you can."

"What?"

"And when you do," Damian snapped, "run like Old Uncle Night was plucking at your hair."

Without waiting for a response, Damian rolled off of Luciano and out from under the wagon. Right next to the Daemyn hound.

The creature sniffed as it glared down at Damian. "*Urik zhak t'hall.*"

"It talks," Damian said. "of course it bloody talks."

The stench of sulfur from the Daemyn hound's breath filled Damian's nostrils. Damian chuckled.

Sulfur. This whole scheme might just work out far better than he'd originally planned.

Damian shoved the pistol up against where the Daemyn hound's neck and shoulder met. He squeezed the trigger. The hammer fell. Sparks shone against the night. Miracle of miracles, the gunpowder in the pan flared. The right barrel of the two-shot pistol roared, spitting fire and lead.

The Daemyn hound howled. The gunshot shredded a large chunk of the creature's shoulder. The creature scurried back away to lick at the wound—a wound which wasn't healing.

"I'll be damned."

Damian hadn't expected it to actually hurt the Daemyn, just get its attention away from Inquisitor Luciano. Well, he'd done that and more. With this knowledge, a new plan, a much better plan, formed. Later he'd cry over his merchandise, but he couldn't sell anything if a Daemyn hound ate his soul.

Damian rolled to his feet and kept the pistol pointed in the Daemyn Hound's general direction, just to keep it from getting too close. One of the Nightbrothers must have dropped a sword. If Damian could get a sword, he could even the odds.

THREE

Luciano crouched under the wagon, mud clung to his mantle, his skin, his boots, his hair, his everything.

Damian Adryck rolled away from the Daemyn hound and came to his feet. By the shocked look on the fugitive's face, Adryck appeared just as surprised as Luciano was that the firearm had injured the Daemyn hound in such a deep and lasting way. Seeing that validated why those hideous weapons were outlawed in the Kingdom of the Sun and all of its protectorates.

The Daemyn hound shook its head and bellowed in pain. A moment later, despite the injury, it turned to face Adryck, hind legs flexing, getting ready to strike.

Luciano struck first and thrust his Faerii steel blade deep into the Daemyn hound's hind leg.

Again, the dark creature bellowed.

Damian Adryck cackled a delighted laugh.

The Daemyn hound turned toward this new attacker. Luciano tried scrambling away, but the mud, his position, and the cramped quarters underneath the wagon made this, a futile effort.

Adryck's pistol roared again.

Luciano nearly jumped out of his skin. Not for the first time, gunfire made him think of thunder and lightning. Blasphemy that such power could rest in the hands of anyone at all. Power such as that must be tempered by the wisdom of faith, wisdom few possessed.

This time the Daemyn hound's cries came at a higher pitch, more of whining at the pain than of furious anger.

"You can go for the Adept with the sword," Adryck said. "Do me the favor of killing him and giving me time to reload."

A pair of Nightbrothers closed behind Adryck. Luciano nearly called out a warning, but even as he drew breath to speak, the hound leaped for the fugitive. Adryck dove forward, rolling under the creature. The Daemyn landed, slid through the mud, and collided with the two Nightbrothers.

"Gods bless the mud," Adryck muttered and came to his feet again with one of the fallen Nightbrother's short swords in his left hand. He gave the weapon a test swing.

"Why can't anyone live in the world as it is now?" Adryck asked. "What do they expect to accomplish with these terrible weapons?"

Luciano started to pull himself out from under the wagon.

"No," Damian snapped and shoved the pistol into his belt. "If you come out, we're both dead."

Luciano stopped. Not for the words Adrick said; rather, for the resonance they carried when he spoke them. Was this fugitive from the Sun King's Justice aware that he had just spoken a Fate?

Adryck rushed over, more sliding than anything in the mud, to where the Daemyn hound and the two Nightbrothers were attempting to untangle themselves.

The Daemyn hound sank its teeth into one of the Nightbrother's necks. The Nightbrother's scream softened to a coughing gurgle. The light of life faded from the Nightbrother's eyes. With each bite, which also took a bit of the Nightbrother's soul, the Daemyn hound's wounds healed.

"That's not anything I ever needed to see or hear," Adryck said.

Three more Nightbrothers came around the wagon.

In a move that Luciano considered equal parts bold and mad, Adryck went right over to the feasting Damyn hound and scooped up the dead man's sword. The Nightbrothers rushed him as best they could in the mud. Adryck spun to meet these three additional Nightbrothers. A pleasant smile spread on Adryck's mouth, the same smile someone might wear as they walked into a spring ball after a particularly long winter.

The Nightbrothers reached Adryck. Damian Adryck flowed through the Nightbrothers, dodging, weaving, parrying, slashing, stabbing, and killing. At no point did any of his enemies come close to striking a blow. With those two swords in his hands, Damian seemed to have become another person entirely.

Luciano had heard reports of Adryck's skill with a blade. Most nobles of any realm trained in the arts of defense, many getting quite good. However, Luciano had always thought that the tales surrounding Damian Adryck we exaggerations by High Blood who went looking for him to curry favor with the Sun King but could never manage to capture him. Between Adryck's skill with those swords and offering a Fate into the world, Luciano better understood why Damian Adryck, one of the most elusive fugitives in the Kingdom, managed to remain free.

As a boy, Luciano had trained with the finest Maestros of D'fence, and then as a young man within the temples of the Inquisitors of the Sun, home to some of the most skilled warriors in the world. Not a single one of those men could match Adryck's grace and skill. The damnedest part of it was that Luciano knew how to spot a man's skill with the sword by how he moved, even when not fighting. Damian Adryck had not given the faintest indication that he would be capable of this masterful display.

In the span of perhaps ten breaths, Adryck had killed the three Nightbrothers. But now the Daemyn hound had finished eating, and having feasted on the flesh and souls of the two Nightbrothers, it had completely healed its wounds.

"The gods hate me," Adryck growled and threw one of the swords at the hound.

The weapon sank into the creature's flank. Unfortunately, it was just a normal weapon, so it did not harm the Daemyn hound in the least.

The Daemyn hound roared in fury.

FOUR

Damian faced the last two Nightbrothers. His hands gripped, almost caressed the hilts of the two swords he'd taken from the Nightbrothers. Gods and goddesses, it's good to hold a sword again. Even swords as old-fashioned and shoddy as these.

Ever since becoming a fugitive, he'd refused to even carry a sword and had completely retrained his movements so as not to draw suspicion from people who might see him. Zephyr the smuggler and gun runner was a scrapper and a marksman, which meant he would carry himself much differently than Damian Adryck who had dedicated his life to the study of the art of D'fence.

He wasn't so worried about the Daemyn hound anymore. The thing was certainly strong. A dead horse – the screams had been terrible – two dead Nightbrothers – not including the two it had eaten to heal itself the first time – and a shattered wagon wheel had proven that. However, the infernal thing was neither quick of mind nor very much of body. Though Damian suspected it might have been more trouble without the mud. Still, Damian read its movements even more easily than those of the Nightbrothers and had managed to keep the wagon between him and the beast as he'd fought the men.

The last two Nightbrothers looked at Damian, then at each other. They seemed to come to some unspoken agreement, threw down their swords, and fled into the night, in separate directions.

"Slide me the scattergun," Damian shouted.

He didn't expect the Inquisitor to actually touch the weapon, but men could dream. Surprisingly, the weapon slid out from underneath the wagon. Mud clung to almost every part of it, and it would require some cleaning, but he'd still have the weapon. Damian dropped his borrowed swords and snatched up the scattergun. Once again, his movements once again became those of Zephyr the Smuggler. And truly, he needed those movements for this next part of his scheme.

The Daemyn hound rounded the corner of the wagon slowly, now stalking Damian rather than charging blindly. It seemed the thing could learn and adapt. Excellent. That's just what Damian had hoped.

"I know why you haven't gotten me yet." Damian backed away from the monster. "Your mother must have lain with an Aengyl, and you can sense the inherent righteousness of my heart. That part of you that is pure can't bring yourself to destroy me."

A disbelieving cough sounded under the wagon. Perfect. Damian wanted the Daemyn to remember Inquisitor Luciano was down there waiting with his Faerii steel sword.

Damian climbed onto the wagon, grabbed his leather cloak, and scrambled from the driver's bench to stand on the boxes of weapons, powder, and shot. He was careful not to step on any of the bags of gunpowder he had stacked in the center. While he hated the waste of it all and the loss of business, from the fires he saw flashing in Shadybrook's single street, Damian was fairly certain he wouldn't be seeing Parsh or Korrin for business any time soon.

A moment later, the Daemyn hound leaped onto the back of the wagon, right in the center where the canvas tarp covered the bags of gunpowder. It snarled in surprise and anger as it sank. In its struggles to escape Damian's trap, the creature's claws shredded both the tarp and the bags holding the gunpowder.

"Now!" Damian yelled, and flung himself from the wagon. "Light it now!"

He slipped in the mud after landing. Then, after a moment to steady himself, Damian raced away from the wagon as if Old Uncle Night was plucking at his hair.

FIVE

The moment Luciano heard the thump of something heavy landing in the wagon, He fished his seeing glass out of his pocket. While most Adepts of All Father Sun carried small circles of the round glass things, Inquisitors carried larger versions. They used these in their investigations in service to the Sun King, as the seeing glass made it possible to discern details that might otherwise escape notice. Another trait of the seeing glass was that it could focus light to a point, causing heat and fire nearly spontaneously.

"Now!" Damian yelled. "Light it now!"

Luciano sucked in a breath and drew on All Father Sun's Dominion of Light from his Adept's medallion.

"*Amhyr'Shoul fiasiato mahi donosum Lusias!*"

Light radiated from the medallion. The radiance pushed the night back as if it were noon on a cloudless day. Luciano tilted his seeing glass ever so slightly, focusing the light coming through it to hit the wagon. Normally, it would take a considerable amount of time to dry the wood of the wagon, let alone make it burn. However, the light shining through the glass was no ordinary light. It came from the pure blessing of All Father Sun. The beam created from the light radiated a heat no Earthly fire could produce.

During Luciano's next breath, the wagon smoked where All Father Sun's blessing touched it.

During his second breath, the wagon burst into flames.

Above the crackling of flames, Luciano heard The Daemyn hound snarling in its infernal language. It sounded as if the thing were on the wagon above him.

A sudden chill that had nothing to do with the rain and wind settled over Luciano. He had forgotten just how dangerous and wily Damian Adryck could be. He was the sort of man who would absolutely maneuver his enemies in hopes that they would destroy each other.

Disjointed thoughts rushed through Luciano's mind.

The injury Adryck's firearm had caused the Daemyn hound.

What Adryck was likely hauling in this wagon.

The Daemyn hound's mutterings and snarlings in the wagon above.

What fire would do to the wagon's cargo?

Luciano scrambled out from under the wagon. Getting to his feet, he too, turned and ran as if Old Uncle Night was plucking at his hair.

Six

"Stop them!" Symond yelled.

Both the Inquisitor and the man driving the wagon fled in opposite directions.

More than half of the Nightbrothers Symond had led on this mission lay injured or dead on the road. The Daemyn hound had been momentarily confined in the wagon. The more the creature struggled, the more grayish dirt or sand flew about from inside the wagon. While the Inquisitor and the firearms had surprised the Brotherhood, with their numbers and the Hound, they could still win this fight.

Since Adept Carmine had specifically ordered Symond to kill the man in the wagon, Symond would call a few of his brothers to aid him in that task. The rest and the hound could deal with the Inquisitor.

Flames rose from the wagon, and the darkness of night faded. The flames enveloped the Daemyn hound as a massive bonfire.

Symond laughed. He couldn't help it. Did they really think that a fire, even one that big, would harm the Daemyn hound?

Symond drew a breath to call out orders, and a light brighter than any fire filled Symond's vision. A roar filled his ears. A wave of force lifted him off his feet, as if some god had reached down from the sky and swatted him away.

The world faded to darkness, not so much of an absence of light, but rather an absence of awareness. At long last, after nearly three decades of life, Symond waited to hear the Uncle whispering a welcome.

Seven

Grandfather Shadow watched Damian Adryck, the man would would proclaim the next Emperor of the Seven Mountains, and the Inquisitor who continued to hound the Lord Morigahn flee from the burning wagon. He felt Morag's presence behind him.

"Please, Grandfather," Morag asked, almost pleading, "let me take the hound?"

Morag was one of the few Stormseekers who had returned when Grandfather Shadow had called. That evening, Morag wore her human form, with her dark hair blowing free in the wind, crouched and ready to spring at his command.

A moment later, three more forms appeared next to Grandfather Shadow. He did not start or jump. He'd been expecting these three goddesses, in their varied outfits, wearing the skin of young women.

Morag growled.

"Calm your pet," one of the goddesses said.

"Watch," said another, "and learn."

"The world has changed," said the third.

A moment later, the wagon erupted in a blaze of light and sound. Flaming splinters flew in all directions. Most of the men wearing skull-shaped helmets died. Most amazingly, the Daemyn hound which had stood atop the wagon now lay scattered over a radius of about forty paces around the fiery remains of the wagon.

"How is it the firearm harmed the Daemyn?" Grandfather Shadow asked. "Can they be enchanted? Can bullets be fashioned from Faerii steel?"

The three goddesses sighed. If Grandfather Shadow hadn't determined who those goddesses truly were, he would have taken steps to correct their flippancy.

"Did you not imagine the world would change in a thousand years?" asked the goddess wearing a formal ball gown.

"Indeed," said the one wearing Dosahan leathers. "Even looking through the eyes of your high priests, you should have seen the workings of what defines faith and ritual can and has changed."

"I am well aware of this," Grandfather Shadow said. "What are your intentions with Damian Adryck? That young man is important to me."

"We know exactly who he is," the three goddesses said, "and what he means to you."

"We promise you," said a goddess dressed as a peasant, "we are as concerned for that one as you are."

"Yes," said the other two.

"We have far more invested in him," said the one in the ball gown.

"Than you could possibly dream of," said the goddess in Dosahan leathers.

Morag barked a quick laugh. Grandfather Shadow sighed at the poor attempt at humor.

The goddesses spoke in rapid succession, so quickly that Grandfather Shadow wasn't sure where one stopped and another began. Sometimes they spoke as individuals, in pairs, or all at once.

"Watch."

"Learn."

"Your precious Morigahnti and Komati will be fine."

"Or they won't."

"But it is time for you to start trusting mortals to handle themselves."

"They've been doing just fine without you for a thousand years."

Grandfather Shadow laughed. "Like you did, in giving Ardyck the pistol?"

"Ah," they said together. "Sometimes we still have to save them from themselves."

"And, when do you know exactly which moments are the moments when we should intercede?" Grandfather Shadow asked.

"As the god of knowledge."

"You should be able to determine quite easily."

"Now, excuse us."

"We must make ourselves hypocrites."

"We must see a young lady about a dream."

"More meddling with my followers?" Grandfather Shadow asked.

"I never meddle," the goddesses said. "I inform and nudge. Meddling is what got the five of you trapped away in the first place."

And with that, the goddesses vanished.

Grandfather Shadow sighed and turned his attention back to his Morigahnti.

EIGHT

Damian pulled himself out of the mud, wiped as much mud off his face as he could, and worked his jaw back and forth to open his ears and relieve some of the pressure from the blast of the explosion. The gunpowder had gone off sooner than he'd expected, and the blast had knocked him to the ground. Luckily, his thick leather cloak was designed to protect him from flying wood and stone that occasionally became a risk in the transportation and sale of firearms and gunpowder. Even so, something sharp stung his right arm.

Gingerly, Damian winced and grimaced the whole while he pulled the shard of wood out from a few inches below his shoulder. He tore the sleeve open and let rainwater wash the mud out as best it could. This led to more wincing and grimacing. He'd have to see a barber-surgeon at some point to ensure he hadn't left any slivers behind.

Damian looked around. He couldn't see Luciano anywhere. Fires still burned in Shadybrook's street, and Damian heard the shouts and cries of fighting. Likely, the Morigahnti and the Brotherhood of the Night were fighting. Faelin was down in the center of that, Faelin and that woman that Faelin had told Damian he didn't want to know about.

Shaking his head, Damian sighed. He couldn't leave Faelin to his fate in all that mess down there. Faelin didn't really know how to fight; he had too kind a heart for it. He, and the lady, would need Damian's help.

"Discretion, Inquisitor," Damian called out. "Heed it in this moment. If you place yourself into a battle between the Brotherhood of the Night and the Morigahnti, it could very well be the end of you."

Hoping that his bluff was enough to keep Inquisitor Luciano from following him, Damian jogged back toward Shadybrook. He had a muddy scattergun with no ammunition, a two-shot pistol with shot and powder for five loads, his boot knife, and his stiletto. That should be enough to get him through the battle long enough to collect a real sword.

The next time Damian happened to cross paths with Faelin vara'Traejyn, they would have to discuss the accuracy of Faelin's warnings. At this point, *That woman is more trouble than all your father's guns combined*, just didn't seem like an honest evaluation of the nature of the trouble surrounding her.

NINE

Octavio paced next to the table, occasionally stopping to adjust the figures on the map as the Night Adepts updated him on the movements and actions of the people in Shadybrook.

"First Adept," Tamaz said, almost stammering. "Uh. Your Darkness. I've discovered something that you need to know."

"Yes?" Octavio asked, not bothering to stop his pacing.

"An Inquisitor stopped the wagon," Tamaz said. "Luciano Salvatore."

Octavio stopped mid-stride. "My cousin?"

"Indeed, First Adept," Tamaz said. "But there's more. And I think it's worse."

"I'll be the judge of that," Octavio said.

"The man in the wagon is Damian Adryck," Tamaz said.

"Prince Damian?" Dante asked.

"The one who has evaded the Floraen Inquisitors for two years?" Rosella asked. "Are you sure?"

"Well," Tamaz said, "I don't know how many Damian Adrycks there are running around the Continent, but seeing as how Princess Josephine, Prince Xander, and Prince Damian are the only Adrycks in the world, it's a solid wager that's him."

"I can't imagine anyone taking that name as an alias," Ulfric said.

"The Inquisitor almost called Damian, 'Your Highness'," Tamaz said.

"Almost?" Octavio asked.

"Adryck interrupted him by kicking him in the face," Tamaz said.

Dante roared with laughter.

"What?" Dante asked when everyone glared at him.

"That's your cousin," Rosella said. "A High Blood of the Kingdom of the Sun."

Dante snorted. "And he's an insufferable bore who could use getting kicked in the face a few more times. Not that he's going to be alive long enough for that to make much of a difference.

Maybe Prince Damian will do us the courtesy of killing Luciano so we don't have to hunt him down when we ascend to the Zenith."

"First Adept?" Cadenza said.

"He's right," Octavio said. "I'd like to kick Luciano in the face myself. Repeatedly. And, if Adryck kills him, that's one less High Blood of House Floraen we have to worry about later, as I doubt Luciano will take the Night Oath."

"One last thing," Tamaz said. "And it's the worst bit."

"Seeing as we want both Luciano and Damian Adryck to die," Octavio said, "this hasn't been exactly bad news yet."

Tamaz swallowed. "It seems firearms can hurt Deamyn Hounds."

"What?" asked everyone else in the Temple of Night.

Tamaz nodded. "I saw Adryck shoot the Daemyn hound, and it bled. Then, he made a wagon loaded with firearms and gunpowder explode. The Daemyn Hound exploded with it."

Octavio stared at the map of Shadybrook. The stakes of this battle just grew exponentially.

"We must kill Damian Adryck and Inquisito Luciano," Octavio said. "At any cost. That knowledge cannot spread. If it does, the Brotherhood of the Night may never see the Zenith again."

MORIGAHNTI

The Morigahnti Fist is one of the most versatile combat units on this side of the world. Every member besides the leader is considered equal, and all are able to perform multiple tasks in both fighting and supporting roles. However, while equal, the whole Fist knows who will take charge should the leader fall. If two or more Fists meet and have less than seven Morigahnti, the Fists will adjust to make it so that each one has as close to seven as possible. This practice is so ingrained into their tactics that it seems to happen instinctively on the battlefield. They adapt to the loss of personnel almost instantly and lose very little of their effectiveness for it. The only way to weaken them is to strike at the head, at the Lord Morigahn or someone close to him.

–An excerpt from a letter by Grandmaster Myrs Byltaen to the Taekuri Council.

Gather round Morigahnti
Can't you hear the call?
The low dull roar of battle
That beckons to us all!
- Komati Battle Chant

ONE

Julianna couldn't sleep. She had tried, but between the wind, rain, and occasional thunder, she couldn't keep her eyes closed long enough to even begin to settle down. As much as she hated to admit it, the storm called to Julianna. As long as it raged outside the walls of the manner house, rest would elude her. She had lit a lantern and sat down to comb and braid her hair, just for something to do other than just lay in bed, when she noticed the hand mirror amongst the other toiletries she'd been given by Mistress Dressel.

With the mirror in one hand and the pitcher of wine in the other, Julianna sat at the table seeking the courage to look at her face. She wasn't drunk yet, but a pleasant and warm fog spread out from her stomach, and she chewed on her lower lip. Time moved slowly on. She lost track of how long she stared at the silver rosework etched into the back of the mirror, all to avoid looking at her face.

Julianna knew that Grandfather Shadow had scarred and disfigured her.

That knowledge didn't make it any easier to accept looking at the truth, and she had tried, tried to turn that mirror around and witness what her face had become. That's where the wine came into play. Julianna had seen her share of men spurred to acts of overconfident stupidity because of the spirit's ability to drown out fear. After taking several healthy swallows, Julianna felt ready.

She turned the mirror around.

Julianna's reflection stared back at her in the lantern light.

The sight pierced through the wine's warmth, chilling her to the core in an instant. The scar was a canyon down her face, glistening, as if a river of blood might burst forth at any moment. Closing her eyes, Julianna breathed deeply, in and out, in and out. She held out hope that her weariness and anticipation had tricked her imagination into making her believe that the scar looked worse than it actually was.

She opened her eyes again. Nothing had changed.

For a long while, Julianna stared at her reflection, taking it in. A scream of outrage formed in her chest, but her throat closed off, causing the sound to come out as nothing more than an anguished growl.

Again, she drew in a deep breath. This time, Julianna held her breath until her chest, sides, and throat burned. Releasing the breath, she placed the mirror on the table, and using the pitcher like a hammer, she smashed the glass. Her deformed reflection vanished as a shower of glass and wine rained down on the table. Several glass shards cut into her hands. Her breath came in ragged gasps. She flung the pitcher and the remains of the mirror to opposite sides of the room. Her eyes refused to focus anywhere as if her reflection had damaged them beyond her ability to control. She tried to stand, but her legs betrayed her and she slumped back into the chair. Her hands balled into fists and pounded on the table. Each time she struck, the glass cut into her hands even more, leaving small puddles of blood and shredded skin behind.

Julianna became vaguely aware of someone calling her from far away. She tried to stop, but the horror that had taken over her body refused to relinquish its control.

A pair of hands latched onto her wrists and stopped her from striking the table. The hands gripping Julianna pulled to her feet, and she found herself facing Faelin.

"What. Are. You. Doing?" he demanded.

Julianna jerked out of his grip. He grabbed at her again, but she danced out of his reach and went to the broken mirror. She picked it up. With one hand she held the mirror out to Faelin, and pointed to her face with the other.

She forced a single word past her lips. "Scar."

Faelin's eyes softened, and he rubbed his hand through his hair. "Oh, Julianna."

Something in Faelin's voice penetrated her panic. She flung herself at him, wrapped her arms around his neck, and hung on his shoulders. He held her and stroked her hair as she sobbed. Just when she thought she'd recovered from one horror, another took its place.

"I know this is hard for you," Faelin said, "but you have to be strong. The Morigahnti are here."

"I," the words, "don't," came between, "care," sobs. "Let. Them. Rot."

"We can't, Julianna." Faelin sounded as if he was trying to soothe a horse. "You can't afford to appear weak, nor can you offend them. You must at least meet Count Allifar." Faelin untangled himself from her embrace. "I remember Allifar Thaedus being a decent, honorable man, and loyal to the old ways. If any Morigahnti will accept you, he will. He may also sway many others to your side who would otherwise remain neutral."

"I thought we were going to flee Koma," Julianna said.

"It might be too late now that the Morigahnti have found us," he replied. "I wish we had time for you to recover from your ordeals, but we do not. We may be able to escape in the morning, but tonight you must play the part of the Lord Morigahn."

She turned her back on him.

"*Galad'Ysoysa tasta varten mina vihata sina*," she growled through clenched teeth. If she was going to insult Grandfather Shadow, she wanted to do so in his own language.

When the last word left her lips, the room changed. The walls seemed to close in as the light dimmed.

"*Siksi ola sita*," a voice whispered from every shadow in the room. "I am not overly fond of you either, Duchess Julianna Taraen of House Kolmonen, daughter of Maxian Taraen and Sorka, daughter of Razka. You are the last surviving blood of the Taraen family. You are not quite so strong as I had hoped, but by ancient celestial laws, now that I have marked you and named you, our destinies are entwined. I still see greatness in you, if only you will open yourself to the true strength within your heart. Now go. Become the leader I know you can be."

The light returned to normal, and the god's voice had purged all but the last remnants of her near-drunken haze from her mind.

Faelin's face paled, and his lips pressed together, as if he was trying to keep from vomiting. Julianna walked over to the window, opened it, and put her head out into the storm. The feeling of being trapped left as the wind drove the raindrops into her skin, stinging her, but it also drove away the very last of the wine fog.

She brought her head back inside. "You truly think I must do this thing now." It wasn't a question.

"Yes," Faelin replied. "I can't see anything good coming from avoiding this."

"Very well. I will meet the Morigahnti. Bring them up in a few minutes."

"He's not alone," Faelin said. "He has a full Fist with him."

Julianna thought for a moment. A Fist was seven Morigahnti. She'd learned that from reading in the *Galad'parma*.

"Bring them all up. If they wished me harm, I don't think they would have asked to see me."

He gave a slight nod and started for the door.

"Wait," she said. "Give me your gloves."

Faelin glanced at her still-bloody hands, pulled his gloves out of his belt, and handed them to her. "I'll have one of the servants bring up some bandages."

"No," Julianna said. "That will give them cause to wonder. Get them yourself while I'm speaking with the Morigahnti."

"You should change clothes," Faelin said.

She looked at the night dress she wore, yet another gift from Mistress Dressel. The corners of Julianna's mouth curved upward in a faint smile.

"I think I'll remain as I am."

Let them wonder why she chose to remain in her bedclothes. Julianna pulled the gloves on and wrapped the *Galad'fana* around her head.

"They might find the combination of bedclothes and riding gloves a bit odd."

Julianna sighed and looked about the room. She went over to the coat rack and took Khellan's frock coat. Putting it on was easy despite the gloves. Her hands slid through the sleeves that were slightly too large for her. Putting the coat on gave her at least a small semblance of modesty. Though all the niceties of polite society seemed trivial, others might not view her situation in the same light. It also diminished the oddity of her wearing gloves.

Faelin looked her over, shrugged, and left. Even though Julianna could only see the back of her friend's head, she was fairly certain he was rolling his eyes at her.

Shaking her head, Julianna went into the bathing room, collected the washing cloths, went back to her own room, and used the cloths to clean up the blood, glass, and spilled wine as best she could. She took Khellan's rapier and belted it to her waist. As the high priest of Grandfather Shadow, the Lord

Morigahn was a warrior. She should try to look the part. Julianna was used to keeping up appearances. In court life, she was required to play the game of status. Now, losing status was the least of her worries.

"Brother Stone," Julianna started, and then remembered what happened when she had offered a prayer to Sister Wind. Instead, she prayed to another god. "Grandfather Shadow, give me the strength I need."

No burst of energy came. No flash of insight appeared in her mind. However, a small bit of the tension left her shoulders. That was enough for now.

A knock on the door brought Julianna from her thoughts.

"Enter."

The door opened, and a man in middle years, perhaps forty winters or so, entered. He stood more than a full head taller than Julianna, and he had broad shoulders. He walked like a man used to people moving aside. He stopped just past the door and looked her up and down. After his green eyes finished inspecting her, he met her gaze and did not waver for a moment.

He opened his mouth, but she held up a hand.

"Once we were like wolves," Julianna said.

"Our time can come again," he replied in a deep voice.

The man's eyes sparkled with amusement, as if this was a game. Julianna could not afford to think that way. This might be her only chance to win his loyalty.

"If you truly deserve that veil," Julianna said, "you will tell me the First Law of *Galad'Ysoysa*." Then she added, "In *Galad'laman*."

He nodded slightly, and said, "*Kostota na aen paras kostota.*"

"And it means?"

"Revenge is the best revenge."

"Good. This is the closest of the laws to my heart. Do you take my meaning?"

"I do," he answered. "All Morigahnti seek revenge for Saent Khellan's death. Yet first, we seek out the heir to his title. We have all heard her name whispered in the shadows of our dreams and spoken by the Stormcrows."

"*Minas aen Morigahnti'uljas*," Julianna said. There. She said the words proclaiming herself as Lord Morigahn to a captain of a Morigahnti Fist. Deep in her heart, Julianna knew there was no turning back now.

"I am Count Allifar Thaedus," he said. "My Fist and I are your servants."

"Please, bring them in."

Allifar stepped aside and introduced each of the Morigahnti as they entered.

Parsh, Allifar's younger brother, was shorter, though no less muscled. The years seemed to have taken a greater toll on him than his older brother. He carried himself with less confidence, and he slouched a bit, as if tired.

Aurell Palment was perhaps a few years older than Julianna. She stood up to Julianna's chin, and her body was as wide as Allifar's shoulders, though she wasn't so much fat, but rather dense. Her face was neither homely nor pretty, just plain.

Korrin and Nathan Sontam were brothers, perhaps twins. While not identical, they were close enough. Each stood a slight bit shorter than Allifar, but where he was broad-shouldered, those two were thin as saplings. They moved with a fluid grace, but with an underlying sense that a rush of quick power could come at any moment. When Allifar named them, both saluted with right fists over their hearts and left hands on the hilts of their rapiers.

Wynd Sontam was Nathan's wife. She was nearly as tall as her husband and just as thin. Her face might be pretty, but Julianna couldn't quite tell from the mass of wild and unkempt hair that hung low to her chin. She could see Wynd's thin-lipped mouth, the edges turned upward in a slight smile as she curtsied when introduced.

Julianna judged them to be about her age.

Taebor was the last through the door. Younger than any of the others by a few years, he was a plain youth. He had long sandy hair that stuck out in odd places as if it had recently been short and he was trying to grow it out.

All of them except Taebor wore a *Galad'fana*.

"May we see the mark?" Allifar asked.

It was an honest request. They had the right to look upon the marred face of the Lord Morigahn. With only a slight hesitation, Julianna reached up and moved the part of her veil that covered her face.

As one, the Morigahnti dropped to their knees. "We serve Shadow's voice on earth."

Julianna looked at them, those seven kneeling warrior-priests of Grandfather Shadow. At the very least Allifar and Parsh had likely been worshipping the old ways all their lives. The others had worshipped for at least a few years. But Julianna had moments where she doubted all of this. Could this be a dream where she still might wake? Now she must make a choice that would likely dictate the rest of her life.

"I accept your service," Julianna replied. "Rise, Morigahnti."

The Morigahnti stood, each face before her somber.

"What tidings from the Grandfather?" Parsh asked.

"He has not spoken of anything other than gathering the Morigahnti to recognize me."

"Perhaps you should be more forthcoming with those who serve you," Aurell muttered under her breath, just loudly enough for Julianna to hear.

Julianna looked at Aurell. The stout Morigahnti woman's face tightened as she lowered her head. Still, her eyes flicked between Julianna's eyes and the floor. Julianna opened her mouth, but before she could respond, Allifar's arm snapped out. The back of his fist caught the girl just below the eye. Aurell stumbled backward into Korrin. The other Morigahnti suddenly found interesting things to examine in the far corners of the room. Nathan raised a hand and placed it on Wynd's shoulder. The left side of Wynd's mouth curled upward, turning the smile into a smirk.

Aurell recovered from the blow. She glared at Allifar. Allifar seemed to grow even larger as he stared Aurell down.

"Watch your tone," Allifar said. "The Lord Morigahn is not just any other pretty woman that you need to prove something against. I tolerate this behavior most of the time, but you overstep yourself too far this time."

Julianna went to Aurell. How she dealt with Aurell would define what kind of leader she was going to be. Julianna needed to choose whether she would lead by fear, or with strength.

"Aurell," Julianna said. "Why do you care about how you look as compared to somebody else? You have the gift of channeling *Galad'laman* into miracles. Aunt Moon might indeed have gifted some women more than others. But the gift of beauty comes only once and fades with age." Julianna pointed at the scar on her face.

"This is proof of how fleeting beauty can be. I will always use this as a reminder of where my true gifts come from."

Aurell dropped to her knee before Julianna.

"Forgive me, Lord Morigahn," Aurell said. "I misspoke myself."

"I will forgive you," Julianna said. "But do not expect me to suffer this foolishness again."

Aurell nodded. Julianna pulled the girl to her feet and glanced at Wynd. Wynd's smile was gone, her lips now pursed and twisted slightly to the right. Gods and goddesses, Julianna wished she could see Wynd's eyes, but her dark hair continued to hide most of her face.

"What are your orders, Lord Morigahn?" Allifar asked.

"I do not have any yet," Julianna said. "Leave me to pray." She wasn't going to pray, but it seemed like a plausible way to end the conversation without insulting them. "I will choose our path in the morning."

The Morigahnti bowed and filed to the door. A thought came to Julianna.

"Allifar," she said, "stay a moment."

The large Morigahnti stopped just inside the doorway. "Yes, Lord Morigahn?"

"I ask that you keep your Morigahnti ready," Julianna said. "We are being pursued."

"By who?" Allifar asked.

"The Brotherhood of the Night," she replied.

Allifar's face tightened. His eyes seemed to smolder.

"They will be dealt with. All the Morigahnti seek vengeance for Saent Khellan's death."

"They had Daemyn hounds," she said. "And will likely outnumber you two or three to one, even without the hounds."

"They can bring their possessed pets," Allifar said. "We will bring our Stormcrows and make them fear us again."

"This is not the time to show ourselves," Julianna said. "We do not have the strength to stand against the Kingdom."

That much was true. The Morigahnti had not been strong enough to repel the Kingdom a century and a half ago and hadn't managed to free themselves in the time since. Most Komati believed the Morigahnti were nothing more than a legend. If it came to open conflict, most of Koma's noble houses would probably side with the Kingdom of the Sun, as the Kingdom seemed to hold all the power.

"It is time," Allifar said. "Grandfather Shadow is speaking to the Stormcrows again. If ever the time came to free ourselves, it is now."

"It is true," Julianna said. "Grandfather Shadow is among us again. He looked into my eyes as he marked me, and I saw only endless twilight in his gaze. But we must be subtle. Do you think that all the Morigahnti will accept me because of a scar and a story?"

"You speak wisdom beyond your youth," Allifar replied. "Many of the others will be suspicious. You will need to undergo the rite of acceptance."

"What is that?" Julianna wanted to see how he would answer her.

"It is a test to see if a man is ready to lead us."

"A man?" Julianna asked.

Allifar coughed. "You are the first woman to bear the title, Lord Morigahn."

"Ah." This fact did not help her chances of acceptance. Most people were suspicious of change. "I think that is the first step before all others. Before anything else, we must have the Morigahnti united."

"Yes, Lord Morigahn."

Allifar bowed and left.

Just after, Faelin entered and shut the door behind him. He placed a bundle on the table and unwrapped it, revealing dressings for Julianna's injured hands.

She pulled off the gloves. Her hands were starting to stiffen. She winced and tossed the gloves on the table. With a deep breath, Julianna slumped into the chair. How was she going to lead these people? They were harder than granite, each of them ready to fight and kill. They were also fanatics. She saw that in the way their eyes lit at any mention of Grandfather Shadow.

"Are you alright?" Faelin asked, and tended to her wounds.

Julianna looked up and laughed. Grandfather Shadow had given her nothing but a life of pain and sorrow.

"How do you know so much about the Morigahnti ways?" Julianna asked. The thought had been nagging at the back of her mind.

"I told you that the Kingdom killed my family."

"For worshiping Grandfather Shadow," Julianna said.

"For being Morigahnti. My father sent me away just before the Kingdom attacked. I am the only surviving Traejyn."

"Why did they send you away?"

"Because I was the only one of my father's sons not to become Morigahnti." Tears welled in Faelin's eyes. "They said I was not fit to fight and die with the rest of my family."

She got up and pulled him into her arms, comforting him as he had just comforted her. How long had he borne this pain alone?

"If you wish," she said, "I will think of you as my brother."

Faelin stiffened, sucked in a deep breath, and broke from her embrace.

"What is it?" Julianna asked

"If you will excuse me, Lord Morigahn," he said with a formal bow, "I should see if there is anything I can do to repay Count Allifar or Mistress Dressel for their kindness."

He was out the door before she could respond, leaving her alone. It took Julianna only a few minutes to understand why. With the Morigahnti around them, Faelin and she could not appear too close. Some Morigahnti might find both suspicion and insult if they observed too much familiarity between them. Grandfather Shadow's influence had removed all her bonds of friendship. Faelin was the only person she could have any kind of relationship with. Love was denied her. She'd learned what love could bring the Lord Morigahn from Khellan. As much as her heart still ached for Khellan, he'd been irresponsible. He should not have acted on his love while he was the Lord Morigahn in a Koma still ruled by the Kingdom of the Sun.

Friendship was another matter. Friends had always surrounded her. Julianna had only ever had a small handful of friends, but those few companions shared everything with each other. Perrine was gone. Sophya was also likely dead as well, carried off by the Brotherhood of the Night and subjected to Shadow only knew what vicious rituals.

She couldn't trust any Morigahnti enough to be friends. She couldn't bring any of her few friends from court into her new life for the same reason Khellan shouldn't have pursued his love for her. Faelin was her only friend, the only one she could now count on to be a friend, and now being the Lord Morigahn had robbed her of even that luxury.

Throwing herself on her bed, Julianna choked back tears. She bit her lip, hoping the pain would overshadow the emptiness in her chest. It did not.

Two

Walking out of Julianna's room and closing the door was the hardest thing Faelin had ever done. It was even harder than leaving his family on the day they all died. Julianna needed him, had reached out to him, but if anyone discovered that a close bond had formed between them, it could be used as a weapon against her.

The Lord Morigahn could not afford luxuries such as friendship. Julianna had to learn that. If Faelin told her as much, she would have argued the point, which would have taken time they didn't have. The treacheries within the Morigahnti were a brutal web of lies, half-truths, machinations, and rivalries. If the Morigahnti of today still held onto the traditions of old, Julianna and Faelin might have been able to maintain their friendship. However, those days were gone.

It took Faelin a few moments to get his feet moving and walk away from Julianna's door. When he finally took a step toward the stairs, Faelin thought he saw Parsh's head descending to the first floor. Had the baron been listening?

Three

Wynd sat with her back to the hearth on the north wall breathing in the warmth from the fire. Nathan sat on one side of her, Korrin on the other. Aurell and Taebor had been sent to see to the horses. Count Allifar had ordered Baron Parsh to take most of the Fist away from Shadybrook. Only the Count and Korrin would remain with the Lord Morigahn. The other Morigahnti would travel as quickly as they could, occasionally speaking miracles to draw potential pursuers away from the township, and more importantly, the Lord Morigahn.

Now, Count Allifar and Baron Parsh spoke in hushed voices near the bottom of the stairs. Parsh expressed reservations about that plan, hence the conversation that had begun the moment he'd come downstairs.

Wynd couldn't hear anything the nobles said, but they interrupted each other with increasing frequency. Parsh, always the more volatile of the two, stood with his hands balled into fists. His shoulders shook as he leaned in toward his older brother's face. Allifar took a step back and raised his finger—a bad sign. Once the finger came up, it meant that *Count* Allifar had reminded *Baron* Parsh of their respective places in the order of precedence.

Footsteps came from the stairs. That would likely be Faelin, the man who wasn't Morigahnti, yet who seemed to hold the confidence of the Lord Morigahn. Both Parsh and Allifar seemed to know this Faelin.

Parsh turned toward the three sitting by the fire.

"Find something to do. His Excellency, the Count, and I have several private matters to discuss." Parsh spoke with the perfect edge of grating civility. That's how it was when he got angry. His voice was that of a reasonable man. His eyes, on the other hand, squinted a bit and his cheeks were so tense they appeared chiseled out of granite.

Hauling themselves to their feet, Wynd, Nathan, and Korrin headed for the kitchen. Wynd's back cooled as she moved away from the fire, and the coolness of her still-damp clothes settled back onto her skin. At least it would still be warm in the kitchen. Normally when she rode in the rain, she had a dry set of clothes and a warm husband waiting for her.

The kitchen was warmer than the manor's main room. The ovens were fully stoked, and the smell of baking bread permeated the air. Other odors lingered in the kitchen – honey and butter were almost, but not quite, smothered by the bread. The Dressels' cook, who was busy barking orders at her two assistants, turned on them, her eyes squinting and her mouth formed into a tight frown. After she recognized them, the cook's expression softened, and she dropped into a curtsy.

"May I get something for you, Morigahnti?" she asked.

"Some warm cider and a bit of that bread would do nicely," Korrin said. "And don't bow. We're servants ourselves."

The cook made some overly polite mutterings and busied herself with providing bread and cider. A few moments later while both men were washing mouthfuls of bread down with a spiced cider, Wynd looked around.

"Shouldn't Taebor and Aurell be done with the horses by now?" she asked.

"They both saw Parsh and Allifar starting up," Korrin said. "Perhaps Aurell is exhibiting a sense of discretion and Taebor a bit of insight…for once."

"I wouldn't go back in there if I didn't have to," Nathan said. "Nor do I relish the thought of riding out with Parsh after that conversation ends, but you'd think they'd at least come in the kitchen and get some food."

"Maybe Aurell decided to make Taebor into a real man," Korrin said. "You ever see the way she looks at him? It's the same look she has when looking at a full plate of food."

"She's not fat." Wynd punched her brother-in-law in the shoulder. "You should know better than anyone that her bulk is muscle."

"But you have to admit she does like her food," Korrin replied. "She's got to fuel her temper somehow."

Nathan, who had just placed his mug to his lips, sprayed cider into the air. Wynd fixed him with a look of displeasure, and her husband's laughter died before it left his throat. Korrin kept chuckling until Nathan kicked his shin. Korrin looked ready to lay into Nathan, but Nathan gestured with his eyes toward Wynd. Korrin glanced at her, and she fixed him with that same stare. Korrin didn't stop laughing quite as quickly as Nathan did, but then he wasn't married to her.

"Might be trouble," Wynd said.

"In Shadybrook?" Korrin said. "In this storm? In the middle of the night?"

"Normally, I'd think the same thing," Wynd said, "but the Lord Morigahn is here."

"Everything is fine," Nathan said.

"What does Parsh always say?" Wynd asked.

Korrin looked ready to retort, but Wynd fixed her displeased look on them again. Both squirmed under her gaze. Neither of them wanted to go outside before was absolutely necessary, but when neither met her eyes, she knew that they knew she was right.

Nathan and Korrin glanced at each other and recited in an exasperated tone, "If you suspect something amiss, better to check and be safe than die and not get the chance to regret it."

"Well?" Wynd asked.

"Fine," Nathan said. "Let's go check."

Wynd led the way outside. The storm had abated to a steady gentle rain, and the wind had died down almost completely. Still, she pulled her frock coat tight around herself. They all wrapped their *Galad'fana* around their faces, attempting to retain some of the warmth from inside the manor house. Even before taking three steps, Wynd knew something was wrong. The stable was dark. No light shone between the cracks of the door or from the small vent windows up in the hayloft.

"Nathan…" she started.

"I see," Nathan said.

Allifar and Parsh's training immediately took over. They formed a triangle, shoulders about one arm's span apart so they could draw their swords and fight without worrying about accidentally striking the others, and so their peripheral vision overlapped. They increased their pace toward the stable until Korrin stopped them with a whispered, "Listen."

All three froze.

Wynd strained her ears. From downwind she thought she heard horse hooves *squelching* in the mud. She glanced in that direction, but with the clouds covering the sky, even with the enchantments of her *galad'fana* and the fires of that hateful shrine to the lesser gods, she couldn't see that far. Leaning forward, she turned her head, hoping to help her discern what was coming. The noise grew more distinct, but she still couldn't see anything. A few moments later, the sound of footsteps joined the horse hooves, all of them moving at a steady cadence. There had to be more than just a few for her to hear them and still not see them. Even though the storm clouds covered the moon and stars, the lights from the manor house and the shrine gave enough illumination so that the night was not completely black.

"My wager is on Draqons," Korrin whispered. "They are the only ones who would march with such precision in weather like this."

"Draqons," Wynd whispered.

They'd fought with the Brotherhood of the Night twice before and once with a group of Kingdom nobles they'd ambushed on a hunt, but they had never faced the Kingdom's deadliest troops.

"The manner or stable?" Nathan asked.

"Split apart," Wynd said. "Stable, manor, and shrine."

Not giving either of them a chance to respond, Wynd darted for the stable. When she reached it, the door hung open just wide enough for her to fit through. She whispered thanks to Grandfather Shadow and slid halfway inside, hoping that the shadows would conceal her.

Looking back to the road, Nathan dashed behind the shrine.

Korrin retreated toward the manor, but before he made it out of the street, a voice called, "You there! Stand to be questioned in the name of His Radiance the King!"

Wynd looked toward the voice. Now she saw two people on horseback, flanked by maybe ten or a dozen figures, too tall to be human. One stood nearly as tall as the smaller of the horses. It could only be Kingdom Adepts with a squad of Draqons. Her thoughts returned: *the Kingdom's deadliest troops.*

Korrin turned and fled toward the shadows of the general store, crying out as he ran, "So long as the sun shines, there will be shadow!"

Please Shadow, Wynd prayed, *let them be Reds and not Whites.*

FOUR

Faelin reached the bottom of the stairs. The main room of the manor was empty except for Count Allifar and Baron Parsh. Only a few logs, surrounded by a bed of glowing coals, burn fitfully in each fireplace. Allifar gave Faelin a nod, picked up a mug from the mantle, and walked over to him. Parsh folded his arms across his chest, leaned against the wall next to the fireplace, and stared out the window into the storm.

"Will you speak with me, Faelin vara'Traejyn?" Allifar handed the mug to him.

"Yes, Excellency." Faelin took the mug. "I'm sure you have questions."

"First, call me Allifar," the Count said. "Second, I only wish to know more about this lady we serve."

Faelin understood. Julianna was an outsider, and the Morigahnti were suspicious of anyone not of their order. Faelin knew the truth of that barrier all too well.

Faelin took a sip from the mug, mostly for a moment to think. He tasted fresh geleva, brewed to near perfection. The perfect cup of geleva likely only existed in the world of dreams, for each man and woman had differing tastes when it came to the drink. And while Faelin normally added cream, honey, and a pinch or two of sugar, this was excellent without those, obviously from Inis O'lean. For some reason, the islands of Inis O'lean produced sweeter beans than anywhere else in the known lands.

"Thank you," Faelin said.

"You are welcome," Allifar said. "What manner of woman is the Lord Morigahn?"

Faelin considered for a moment. "I cannot give you a sufficient answer to that. I know what manner of girl she was, and what manner of young lady. As for knowing her as a woman, I have only traveled with her a few days."

"What can you tell me of her being marked the Lord Morigahn?" Allifar asked.

"Again, I can tell you little. She was already marked when I found her, and everyone around her was dead. I knew Khellan in his youth, also. He was dead when I arrived. From his injuries, I do not think that he could have passed the title on."

"Shades and damnation," Parsh muttered by the fireplace. "Do you know anything?"

"I'm sorry, my lords," Faelin said. "I cannot give you the answers you seek if I don't know them myself."

"A new Lord Morigahn is upstairs," Allifar began to pace, "and we are sworn to her. If I am to die for her, I want to know something about the woman before I do."

Faelin noticed that neither Allifar nor Parsh corrected Faelin's use of an honorific. He also saw that Allifar had the same fanatical look that Faelin's father and grandfather had had when they spoke of the Morigahnti and Grandfather Shadow. Faelin needed to give them something, anything to appease them, or they might decide to ask Julianna herself, and she needed rest.

"She has strength," Faelin said. "She is a survivor. She has just suffered greatly and will need time to heal from her wounds to both her body and spirit. Once she does, and given time, you will find her different than any other Lord Morigahn."

"What is your relationship with the Lord Morigahn?" Parsh asked.

Faelin drank and considered how best to respond. "You want to know if we are lovers."

Parsh grunted. Allifar nodded.

"We were friends through childhood and adolescence. Even if she were inclined to take a lover, which I doubt very much that she is, she would not choose me."

"Why?"

"I am too much like a brother to her. And even if she expressed interest in me, I have no interest in her."

"She is lovely," Parsh said. "And a duchess. And the Lord Morigahn.

Faelin shrugged and savored more of the geleva.

Parsh said, "You are still not Morigahnti." It was more of an accusation than a question.

"No. I do follow Grandfather Shadow; however, I do so in my own ways."

"If you worship Grandfather Shadow, why are you not Morigahnti?" Parsh asked.

"There are many ways to worship the gods. Even at the height of the Empire of the Seven Mountains, not even one in seventy Komati was a Morigahnti."

Allifar nodded. "What you say is wise and true. It's a shame your father and grandfather couldn't see that. Some of my Fist wonder if you are an enemy. I don't believe so. You protect the Lord Morigahn too well. You have a good strong heart. I can tell it is full of faith, more faith than some Morigahnti I know. I hope that one day we can come to trust each other as brothers, Faelin vara'Traejyn, the way your father and I did."

Faelin smiled, and having nothing to say to such high praise, offered his hand. Allifar took it in his. Faelin found himself warming to Allifar. The man might be a fanatic, but he didn't require everyone else to follow blindly behind him. That was different from Faelin's family. They had dreamed of a Koma free from the Kingdom of the Sun, where every citizen was a Morigahnti.

As Faelin and Allifar let go of each other's grip, the manor's front door burst open. Taebor rushed in and came right up to Allifar, gasping for breath.

"Adepts. Coming." Taebor gasped between breaths. "Draqons."

"Shades!" Allifar and Parsh swore.

The mug of geleva shook in Faelin's hand. Some of the warm drink splashed on his fingers. Escaping the Brotherhood of the Night with their Daemyn hounds was bad enough, and he had no doubt they were still hunting Julianna, but now they had to try and escape at least one squad of Draqons, creatures bred centuries ago through miracle and magic to be the backbone of the Kingdom's armies.

"Take a moment and breathe, boy," Allifar said.

"Aurell and I were with the horses," Taebor said, still trying to talk faster than he could get breath. "One got out. I went after it on Sotilas. Couldn't catch it. Saw Adepts and Draqons. Came back to warn."

Parsh dashed to the door leading to the kitchen and looked into the other room. "Korrin, Nathan, and Wynd are gone."

"After them," Allifar said. "Be ready to kill, even if it means speaking miracles." Allifar turned to Faelin as Parsh headed into the kitchen. "The Lord Morigahn must flee. Take her to Johki City. We will follow."

"Bastian's Inn," Faelin said. "He doesn't follow the old ways, but he is a good man, discreet, and has no love for the Kingdom. We'll await you there."

Allifar nodded. "Go."

Faelin sprinted up the stairs. Damn, but they absolutely *had* to put Julianna on the third floor of the manor.

FIVE

Wynd crouched in the shadows of the stable's doorway and watched Korrin turn and sprint toward the mercantile, shouting, "So long as the sun shines, there will be shadow!"

Korrin disappeared from view around the back of the shop. Wynd held her breath, fearing that the figures coming into view might hear her breathing and discover her.

The group came to a stop between the buildings, and Wynd could make out the riders. One rider wore the bright yellow and red mantle of an Adept of House Floraen, a servant to All Father Sun. Short and rotund, she looked enormous on a horse so small it was almost a pony. Wynd's heart went out to the poor beast having to carry such a burden as that. The other rider, tall and thin, wore the dark gray mantle and mask of an Adept of House Kaesiak, pretenders who claimed to serve Grandfather Shadow for the Kingdom. Like most Morigahnti, Wynd knew the difference between gray and black—even if to tell the difference between Kaesiak Adepts and Adepts of Old Uncle Night.

Then Wynd realized that she was specifically *not* looking at the twin columns of Red Draqons that flanked the riders. Words from Grandfather Shadow's Fourth Law came to her: *The weak and gullible are meant to serve the strong and wise.* By giving in to the fear of the myths that the Kingdom had created about these creatures, she was giving them unnecessary power over her. Wyndolen Sontam was a Morigahnti, a warrior priest of Grandfather Shadow, capable of channeling his divine power into the world as miracles. She would look upon the face of her enemy.

She looked upon these Red Draqons with their blood-colored breastplates and the slashed leather sleeves and trousers in the firelight of the shrine. They stood at attention in the rain, with spears resting on their shoulders and those strange, long, curved swords belted on their waists. The smallest of them stood a head taller than any human Wynd had ever known. Their faces were elongated, and just human-like enough to read the contemptuous sneers they wore while looking over the buildings of Shadybrook with slanted eyes. Elongated nostrils flared as several sniffed at the air with their snubbed noses. Each Red had its hair pulled back in dozens upon dozens of tiny braids, with each braid representing a battle the Red had fought for the Kingdom of the Sun.

"You two in the lead," said the Adept of House Floraen, "bring him to me alive for questioning."

The first Draqon at the head of each column handed its pike to the Draqon behind it and headed after Korrin.

Wynd gave thanks to Grandfather Shadow for sending this storm. Had it been a clear night, the Draqons' extraordinary senses would have likely alerted them to Nathan and Wynd. However, the rain masked their scents and allowed them to execute one of the few tactics that allowed a single Fist of Morigahnti to survive against a squad of Draqons. But Nathan and Taebor were normally the decoys because they were the only ones who could outdistance the Draqons for very long. Wynd recalled Parsh and Allifar had left their firearms at home. Firearms and miracles were the only reliable weapons the Morigahnti had against Draqons.

"You four search that house," the voice said. "And you two, off to that stable."

"Damn," Wynd cursed under her breath.

Wynd watched in terror as four Draqons headed for the house and two approached her. She feared not for herself or any member of her Fist. She feared for the Lord Morigahn and the people of Shadybrook. They would surely be punished for harboring traitors to the Sun Crown.

"Are you ready to die for the Lord Morigahn?" Aurell whispered into Wynd's ear.

Wynd bit her lip to keep from crying out. Pulling back into the stable, Wynd drew her rapier and faced Aurell. The other woman had a grim smile and held up four lanterns, likely the ones that normally lit the stable. A bit of cloth, probably taken from a saddle blanket, had been stuffed into the oil well of each one. Each cloth burned just at the tips.

"I rigged them," Aurell said, offering two of them to Wynd.

Wynd returned her rapier to its sheath and took the two incendiaries. As soon as she took them, her *Galad'fana* tingled from the Dominions of Shadows, Illusions, and Balance. That's why she couldn't see them when she first came into the stable. She shook her head. Few Morigahnti possessed Aurell's talent for subtly manipulating divine energy. Only Aurell's strongest or most quickly spoken miracles were detectable from a distance.

"How much fire is in each one?" Wynd asked.

"Enough," Aurell replied. Her smile grew wider. "I borrowed some from the shrine. You should be able to roast two of them with one of those if they're close enough, maybe three."

This was not the first time they'd rigged oil lamps to use as weapons. Once Wynd threw these two, Aurell would hand over the other two. Though Aurell had the stronger arm, Wynd had better aim. While Aurell's jealousy might show its ugly head in any peaceful moment, there would be no quarreling among them now.

Wynd looked out the door. The Draqons stood less than twenty paces away. They approached cautiously, swords drawn, sniffing at the air. Far behind those two, the four sent to the manor had almost arrived.

"Once we were like wolves!" Nathan shouted from over by the shrine.

Damned fool man, Wynd thought.

"After him!" the Adept of All Father Sun screamed. Her shrill voice raked through the air and at Wynd's ears. "All of you! Bring me that Morigahnti!"

The two Draqons approaching the stable turned and headed toward Nathan.

You may be a fool, Wynd thought, *but I love you.*

Wynd kicked open the stable door.

"Our time can come again!" she yelled, and flung the first lamp.

The makeshift grenado sailed through the air, and before it struck she had the second lamp flying toward the further group.

Shadow be praised these were Red Draqons and not Whites. Reds were brutal on the battlefield, but they weren't very creative. By catching them by surprise, the Morigahnti could reduce their numbers quickly, hopefully evening out the odds.

The first lamp hit, and fire erupted, spilling out all over both creatures.

The second lamp flew a bit wide of the far group. It only caught one of the Reds. However, the wall of flame it created forced the others to alter their course, giving Nathan a few more moments to run.

Wynd's heart quickened, and her blood raced. This was what she lived for, fighting against the Kingdom at any opportunity.

Six

Faelin passed the great window that looked out from the landing on the second floor and saw a huge light flash—the yellow light of fire rather than the white light of lightning. He stopped and looked out the window. A way out of Shadybrook, a pillar of fire rose into the air.

Please let that not be a miracle, Faelin thought.

A miracle of that size would require several Adepts together, or it would kill any single Adept, save for perhaps the First Adept of All Father Sun. Perhaps.

In the street, several other fires burned around Red Draqons squirming on the cobbles.

"Shades and damnation!" Allifar cursed from downstairs.

Steel ringing on steel echoed below.

A door slammed, and Allifar cried, "*Galad pita aen Draqonti viela!*"

Faelin knew that miracle. Eddryck had used it on him every chance he got once he earned his *Galad'fana*. The miracle called all the shadows in an area to bind a specified victim. In this case, it would be the Draqons.

Allifar laughed, deep and loud.

"This is what you get for hunting Morigahnti unprepared, Kingdom dogs!" Allifar yelled, then he spoke, "*Anta voima kansa mina ani.*" Allifar's next words boomed so loud, the manor house shook. "To arms, to arms! Komati and Morigahnti to arms! Shadybrook rise! Fight for your lord Thaedus, the Lord Morigahn, and Grandfather Shadow!"

Faelin shook his head and dashed upstairs. He and Julianna had to flee. The Adepts would not let anyone leave this village alive. If Allifar was determined to fight these Draqons, Faelin would do nothing to stand in his way. The Morigahnti might be formidable warriors, but they were outnumbered. Only death could come from fighting here and now. Faelin would hate himself later, but for tonight, he planned to use that fighting as a distraction while he led Julianna away to safety.

Seven

"Those idiots!" Carmine snarled through his grinding teeth.

He didn't even want to think about that fire on the far side of the village, except that if any of the Nightbrothers he'd sent that way still lived, he would consider that a surprise blessing. Aside from that, he wanted to ride down and kill Cadenza and Vycktor.

He watched the farce through his Nightbat's eyes. The spirit animal had hatched at nightfall the same day that Roma had given it to him. Carmine had spent all the time since then that he could get away from Cadenza and Vycktor bonding with the creature. He'd learned that first night that Nightbats possessed the ability to share sight with the human it was bonded to. Adepts of Old Uncle Night used that ability to great advantage against Adepts of the other gods.

Carmine now understood how Adepts of Old Uncle Night learned many of their enemies' secrets.

The only things he learned from the Nightbat tonight made Carmine want to scream.

Cadenza and Vycktor had the Morigahnti outnumbered and outmatched, but somehow the Morigahnti had gained the upper hand in a matter of moments. Like most Adepts, Cadenza and Vycktor thought their mantles made them invulnerable and undefeatable. Now a task that should have been completed without any Draqon casualties had turned into a pitched battle, and Carmine suspected it was only going to get worse.

"What now?" Hardin asked.

"Two Morigahnti in the stable possess some sort of incendiary weapons," Carmine answered. "Two others are trying to separate the Reds with misdirection and cunning. I think the rest of the Morigahnti are inside the manor. Three Reds are down, four are neutralized, two protect Cadenza and Vycktor, and the other three are scattered but are returning to the Adepts."

"Anything else?" Hardin asked.

"No," Carmine replied. "Wait. I see dozens of townsfolk sneaking out of their homes armed with crossbows and hand weapons, mostly spears and axes, but I see at least two swords. They're forming columns behind the buildings on either side of the main thoroughfare. Now they're loading crossbows. The center road is about to become a killing field."

"Damn those two and drown them in their own feces!"

Carmine flinched. Hardin seldom resorted to base language. He prided himself on remaining refined and dignified at all times.

"I will not fail again," Hardin said. "Go down there. Kill every living thing you find. Have your Nightbat return here so that you and I can continue to communicate. I will work on a contingency."

Carmine shook his head, bringing his vision back to himself. He turned and strode to the Bothers gathered under a small grove of trees. They huddled near the trunk, trying to escape the rain as best they could. They watched his approach with weary apprehension. They were cold, wet, and hungry. As Carmine came closer, he felt the tension like a physical weight.

Sylvie, who sat in the wagon wrapped in Carmine's best cloak, looked at him with a little less hate than usual. He hoped it was due to his charms and the time they spent together, but he knew it was more likely due to the cold.

"Up, lads," Carmine said. "Adept Hardin orders us to the village. We're to send anyone we find to Old Uncle Night."

It took a moment for them to comprehend his words, but when they did, they smiled, one and all. People joined the Brotherhood of the Night for any number of reasons, but there was one reason common to all: They wanted to serve Old Uncle Night, the God of Death. The best way to serve him was to kill. Killing was an intoxicating drug. The more a man tasted the power of taking another person's life, the more they wanted it. Hardin gave the men who served him many opportunities to kill. Carmine would do the same, but he would do something more. He would teach them to make a game of it, to toy with their prey. Carmine believed killing was best done quickly and efficiently, but he understood how prolonging a victim's death could heighten a man's bloodlust, and he meant to own Hardin's men before this night was through.

Carmine walked over to Jorgen and placed a hand on the Brother's shoulder.

"I need you to watch the Countess for me," Carmine said. When Jorgen looked longingly at the other Nightbrothers, Carmine gripped his shoulder and gave it a friendly shake.

"Do this for me, keep her safe, and I'll speak to the First Adept of your dedication and loyalty to the Brotherhood."

"Yes, Adept Carmine!" Jorgen saluted and bowed.

Carmine turned back to the rest of the Nightbrothers.

"Jump, lads," Carmine cried. "There's an enchanted weapon to the man with the most kills."

The Brothers cheered. Greed was also a strong motivator.

EIGHT

Julianna dreamed.

A plague swept over Koma, affecting anyone with the smallest drop of Komati blood. This plague did not kill them. It broke their courage, making them easy prey for the men to be carried away to foreign lands, one and all, to become slaves. The land of Koma itself became a homeland for Daemyn spawn, birthed by all the women who stayed. While her homeland fell into a reflection of the Realm of the Godless Dead, Julianna sat in a Dosahan round tent, far from these worries. She sat cross-legged, in the way of the Dosahan. The *Galad'parma* lay in her lap. She read what it meant to be the Lord Morigahn. Her dark hair was streaked with white; her skin was cracked and wrinkled. Even her eyes had changed: The sharp steel gray had softened to dull clay. The only thing that remained of her youth was the scar; it still looked as fresh as the day Grandfather Shadow had marked her.

How much of this is real? Julianna wondered, looking down on her future self.

Dreams are always real while you are in them, a voice whispered.

Galad'Ysoysa? Julianna asked, but even before she received a response Julianna knew it wasn't.

The voice chuckled. *No child. I have been with you much longer than he has.*

But he has been in my dreams since I can remember, Julianna said.

More laughter followed. *Indeed, has he? Interesting, since he was held prisoner, trapped in the mind of each successive Lord Morigahn since the end of the Second War of the Gods.*

Julianna shook her head. *But those eyes, I kept seeing eyes in my dreams.*

And here we are, in your dreams. What an odd coincidence.

Why haven't you spoken to me before? Helped me? Shown me things like you are doing now?

The laughter stopped. *And you're assuming I haven't been, why?* Julianna considered this.

Since Grandfather Shadow had marked her, she realized she had assumed that all these strange dreams had come from him, that he was obviously trying to teach her and guide her into being the Lord Morigahn he wanted. A myriad of questions came into Julianna's mind, but she bit them back. Even in the short time since she had become a piece on whatever game board the gods played on, she had learned the gods, well Grandfather Shadow at least, gave out information and answered questions when they saw fit. Considering that this goddess – yes, it was a goddess, not a god – had taken this long to reveal herself, Julianna concluded that she was cut from the same cloth as Grandfather Shadow. If that were so, asking questions about the goddess's intentions and motivations was futile at best.

Perhaps. However, she would answer questions about this specific dream.

Will this be real after I wake up? Julianna asked.

It might be, the goddess replied. *Like so much of life, it depends on the choices you make.*

What choice did I make here? Julianna asked.

What do you think?

Julianna considered for a moment.

I chose to flee, Julianna replied. *This is what comes from my choosing to hide and learn what it means to be the Lord Morigahn from the* Galad'parma.

And why do you think that is a poor choice?

This time Julianna laughed, laughed at her naiveté. She said, *you can never learn to be the Lord Morigahn by reading about it. One can only learn what it is to be the Lord Morigahn by* being *the Lord Morigahn.* Julianna considered this for a moment and then asked, *Can you show me what will happen if I make a different choice?*

No, the voice responded. *You haven't made any other choice yet.*

Julianna woke with a start. Somewhere below, Allifar's deep voice called the people to arms somewhere in the house below her.

Getting out of bed, she pulled the frock coat and trousers on over her night robe. Then she reached for Khellan's rapier and *Galad'fana*. Julianna wrapped the cloth around her neck and shoulders as she burst out of her room and rushed toward the stairs.

Others heard the call as well. People staying in rooms on this floor poked their heads out of their doors, eyes blinking awake. Their eyes flew open when Julianna hurried past with the *Galad'fana* on her shoulders and the rapier in her hand. Shocked gasps followed in her wake, and she heard footsteps trailing behind her.

Someone said, "The Morigahnti are fighting."

She didn't want to think about what that meant.

At the top of the stairs, she nearly collided with Faelin.

"We have to go," he said. "We can sneak away in the confusion."

"No." Julianna spoke softly in hopes that the people behind her could not hear. "I spoke the words and accepted this title. If the Morigahnti are fighting, then my place is here. I will not leave these people to suffer a fate similar to Kaelyb and Isnia."

Faelin opened his mouth to protest. Julianna cocked her head to the side, folded her arms, and stared at him, daring him to contradict her. Faelin sighed, then nodded. They headed down the stairs together, the crowd growing behind them as they went.

When they reached the bottom, Allifar stood with Parsh and Taebor as if waiting for her.

"What are your orders, Lord Morigahn?" Allifar asked.

Several gasps came from the crowd behind her.

Julianna had no idea what to say.

NINE

Amid the cries and gasps of surprise, Jenise forced herself to breathe and remember not to squeeze the babe in her arms too tightly.

Had she heard Count Allifar correctly? Had he truly referred to the young woman, this stranger who had come in the middle of autumn's first storm, *the Lord Morigahn?*

Jenise's skin pricked with the same excitement she always felt in anticipation of a dance or visiting storyteller. Her stomach clenched in the terror she felt at the thought of speaking to the handsome Zephyr. Her mouth went dry as if she'd just awakened from a nightmare. Her heart raced in a way she'd never experienced.

The Lord Morigahn.

Jenise had never dreamed of seeing the Lord Morigahn in the flesh, much less serving her. Her? A female Lord Morigahn? After a moment's consideration, Jenise accepted that a woman now bore that mantle. Since Kaeldyr the Grey first brought the blessing of Grandfather Shadow to the Komati, how many men had been marked as the Lord Morigahn? How many women? Strange that the god of balance would allow such a state of imbalance with those who were first chosen among his followers. Not that Jenise meant to question Grandfather Shadow's wisdom in this. Perhaps for the next few centuries, only women would be named.

All of these thoughts flew through Jenise's mind in between a pair of heartbeats as she came to embrace that she stood in the presence of the Lord Morigahn.

Jenise looked down at the babe. The little thing had been fussing all night, never quite settling down. Now, she looked up at Jenise with that awkward, almost-smile that only infants could manage.

"That's right, Little One," Jenise said. The Lord Morigahn is here. She will save us."

At those words, the baby cooed and her tiny mouth curved up into a smirk, the kind of smirk older children got when they were hiding some secret. Jenise's mouth grew even drier, and her stomach clenched tighter. Jenise took a deep breath and shook her apprehension away. It must have been a reaction to the babe being in the presence of the Lord Morigahn. What else could be the cause?

No matter what happened, Jenise knew that they would all be safe with the Lord Morigahn watching over them. She joined the crowd of servants and guests as they followed the Lord Morigahn downstairs, waiting to hear her commands.

TEN

Sylvie shivered on the driver's bench of the wagon. She pulled Carmine's cloak as tight around her as she could, but the cold still seeped into her. Next to the wagon, Jorgen paced back and forth, wrapped in a blanket. His teeth chattered, and he alternated between muttering curses at the weather and listing all the things he would have once he was raised to the High Blood when the Brotherhood of the Night rose to the Zenith.

"You two," Adept Hardin barked from where he sat on his horse a short way away. "Come over here." He had a guard of six men. Sylvie noticed that they almost always had six men, or some multiple of six for important tasks and duties.

Sylvie climbed down from the wagon and did her best not to walk through any deep puddles. When she stood in front of Harden, the ancient and bent Adept of the Night God appraised her as if he were a farmer or craftsman looking at a new tool he'd never seen before, attempting to ascertain whether it would actually be as useful a tool as the merchant claimed it would be.

"Brother Jorgen," Adept Hardin said. "Take some of the dried meat from the wagon and these brothers. Go out to the three farmhouses nearby and gather any dogs you might find there. We may need more Daemyn hounds."

"Yes, Adept Hardin," Jorgen said, though his voice cracked, and not from the cold. He sounded trepidatious at best.

Hardin twitched and squirmed in his saddle. At first, Sylvie thought he was having a fit of coughing, but then she realized Hardin was laughing.

"You're wondering why I'm trusting you with this?" Hardin said when his fit of laughter ended. "Since you are becoming Carmine's creature, and he desires you to keep this one," he gestured to Sylvie, "safe and from running away."

Jorgen nodded.

"Keep wondering," Hardin said. "If you determine it on your own, hold that reason to yourself, for then you will gain an insight into humanity that few ever do, and it will serve you well when we reach the Zenith."

Jorgen led the Nightbrothers off.

"And what of you?" Hardin asked Sylvie. "Do you know why I'm trusting Carmine's creature with this?"

"I know I'm cold," Sylvie said. "And hungry. What do I care about the schemes each of you has against each other? If the gods decide to smile upon me, perhaps you and Carmine will manage to kill each other."

Hardin laughed again, almost falling off of his horse.

ELEVEN

Wynd held the last of her grenados in one hand and her rapier in the other. Aurell stood next to her, armed in the same manner. The two Adepts were obviously lacking in their faith, for if they truly believed, their gods would have blessed them as Grandfather Shadow blessed the Morigahnti. The Draqons had retreated to protect the Adepts, forming a ring in the middle of the street, pikes sticking out in every direction. Wynd had been ready to throw the last lamp when Allifar had made his call to arms. Now she and Aurell held them in reserve knowing the townsfolk were preparing to strike.

Waiting for an attack, Wynd knew this battle was theirs. Reds were better suited to open warfare rather than the strike-and-hide tactics the Morigahnti used. The White Draqons, who mostly protected the cities, were better suited for this sort of combat. Because of that, the Kingdom had far less influence over country communities like Shadybrook than it had over the larger towns and cities.

Then Wynd heard a strange sound. It started as a whisper, then grew until it became like a strong wind through a large grove of trees. Wynd's heart raced. She couldn't help but smile.

As the sound grew, the Draqons pulled the Adepts off their horses and pushed them underneath the animals. An instant later, crossbow bolts rained down on the Adepts and Draqons. Each Draqon got hit several times, but because of their armor and breeding, each one remained standing. The horses screamed as each took bolts in the rump and neck, however neither animal panicked. They stomped in place, eyes rolling back into their heads, but they stayed in place, shielding the Adepts. Whoever had trained those horses must have been a master at his trade to instill such discipline.

The sound of a second volley rose, and Wynd's *Galad'fana* tingled with the Dominion of Shadows. Her smile faded. This time, not a single bolt struck a Draqon or a horse. Dozens of shadows lashed out at the sky, destroying any bolt that came close.

No third volley came. A few individual bolts flew, but that was all. The townsfolk had enough ammunition for four volleys, but the Morigahnti had trained them not to waste their shots.

Now they were at an impasse. The rain had limited the effectiveness of Allifar's power. Now the Adepts could counter Morigahnti miracles with miracles of their own. But they couldn't move for fear of getting too scattered, or without knowing where their enemy might lie waiting to ambush them. However, the Morigahnti could only finish them off by closing into a melee with the Draqons. More likely, the townsfolk would scatter and the Morigahnti would hound the Adepts as they made their way to a city. Having nowhere to go for aid and shelter, the Adepts and Draqons would fall, and Shadybrook would be safe. Wynd refused to consider any other alternative.

"Who drew on Shadows?" Aurell asked.

"One of the Adepts," Wynd replied.

"Kaesiak," Aurell growled. "We should go kill him. I'll unravel his miracles, and you kill all the Draqons."

All Morigahnti hated Adepts of House Kaesiak who claimed to serve Grandfather Shadow but in truth polluted Grandfather Shadow's message and had ground under heel every other people on this continent who worshipped the God of Shadows, except the Morigahnti.

Behind her, Wynd heard the hinges of the back door cry in protest. She spun around just as the door opened. Despite needing to protect the horses, Wynd raised the lantern and prepared to throw. Aurell crouched further into the shadows, preparing to strike from hiding.

Nathan entered. The moment his eyes met Wynd's, he smiled, rushed across the room, and kissed her. She let herself drown in that kiss, reveling in knowing that he was alive.

"We don't have time for that," Aurell said. "There's a Kaesiak out there that needs to die. Not to mention the other Adept and Draqons standing between us and the rest of the Fist."

Reluctantly, Wynd and Nathan pulled away from each other. Her lips still tingled from where they had touched his.

"Right," Nathan said. "You two see to the horses, I'll guard the door."

Saddling the horses would go faster with Aurell and Wynd working together. It was a task that could not be rushed, especially when they expected to do some hard riding. One of them might fall and be killed, or worse, captured.

A cacophony of screaming voices grew outside the township proper, getting louder and louder by the moment. Wynd had been in enough fights to know the sound of men lost to bloodlust. Aurell, Nathan, and Wynd looked out the door. A crowd of men charged toward Shadybrook with swords drawn and torches aloft. They all wore the black armor and white skull masks of the Brotherhood of the Night, except the one riding at their head. He rode a black horse and wore the Mantle of an Adept of Old Uncle Night.

"Damn," Wynd muttered through her teeth.

"At least they're charging the Draqons," Aurell said.

"But once the Brotherhood finishes with them, they'll come after us," Nathan said. "And they have the benefit of numbers and won't be nice enough to stand in lines while we kill them."

"If only we'd maintained the towns in the old ways," Aurell said. "Then this would be much different."

Nathan grunted. "Get the horses ready. I'll hold the door."

TWELVE

"Wheel right!" Carmine yelled when he and the Nightbrothers were fifty paces from Cadenza and Vycktor.

His plan had worked out just as he had hoped. By charging the Adepts, the Morigahnti had let the Nightbrothers come straight up the main road unmolested. In truth, it's likely what he would have done in their place. If he had two enemies bent on killing each other, he would have let them cut each other to ribbons and then dealt with the weakened victor once they finished. However, Carmine had no intention of sacrificing more men than necessary against those Red Draqons. Besides, as long as the Reds still stood, the Morigahnti might consider them the greater threat, at least until it was too late.

Now the Brothers charged three columns of Komati bearing crossbows. Several Komati on the flank closest to them shouted a warning, but the calls came too late for them to adjust to the attack. A few Komati brought their weapons to bear, but their formation was better suited to firing in full volleys at the Adepts and Draqons on the other side of the stable rather than individually at a force of charging men.

Bolts flew.

Carmine lowered himself behind Midnight's neck. Though he loved his horse, Carmine would rather the horse be injured than him. He did not fear death. He feared being shot and not dying. He'd seen men suffer from crossbow wounds before, and he had no wish to experience that firsthand.

Once the bolts passed, Carmine came up. Several Nightbrothers suffered minor injuries, and one had fallen, a bolt lodged in his eye socket. The Brothers would praise his passing once this battle was ended.

The Komati didn't have a chance to reload before the Nightbrothers fell on them. Carmine cleaved left and right with his saber, and Midnight stomped and kicked. Carmine had the traditional Brotherhood short sword belted at his waist, but such a weapon was impractical on horseback. The Brothers had cleared well away from him knowing that the horse would take an active part in this battle.

Peasants screamed. In a matter of moments, the Komati lines broke. More than half of them lay dead or dying, the rest fled for their lives.

Some of the Nightrothers broke off to pursue them, but Carmine yelled, "Stand your ground. If we separate, we die!"

Only one man ignored the order. Other Adepts of Old Uncle Night would have struck that man down for such insolence. Carmine admired the man's ability to lose himself in the need to kill. Either Old Uncle Night would grant him an early death for his insolence, or reward him with a longer life so he could kill again.

"You six," Carmine said, "secure that house as a staging area in case the Komati or Draqons manage to rally and counterattack. You six come with me. The rest of you, take the stable. No creature in this township lives to see dawn."

The Nightbrothers yelled their battle lust and ran to carry out his orders. The six he'd called to remain approached him. He led them into the darkness between two of the houses.

"You have all proven your devotion to Old Uncle Night time and again," Carmine said. In truth, none of them had done anything outstanding, but they would be more receptive to his orders if they thought themselves special. "Tonight you will be rewarded for that devotion. I have a special task for you. You will capture a woman. You may kill anyone who stands between you and her, but she is to be unharmed. Do you understand?"

"Yes, Adept," they said.

"Kneel and prepare to accept the blessing of Old Uncle Night," Carmine said.

All six dropped to their knees. In the deep eye holes of their skull helms, their eyes widened and teared up a bit. Few Adepts granted blessings to mere Nightbrothers, so this was a rare honor for them.

Carmine drew on the Dominions of Night and of Lies through his Adept's mantle, and spoke, "*Tzizma nachorte grys uchnas. Klaglen roosh eeriss mar.*"

The six Brothers faded from his sight as part of his strength fled. He forced himself to stay steady. Weakness of any kind could never be shown to the Brothers.

"So long as you remain under the night sky, no mortal eye besides your own will be able to see you. Now go and find her. She is my age. You will know her by her long, dark hair, gray eyes, and a deep scar running down the length of her face."

"The Lord Morigahn?" one of the Brothers asked.

"Yes," Carmine said. "Do not kill or take sport with her. If she is delivered to me unharmed, you may play with her all you wish once a Daemyn is done with her. Do this task, and I will hold all of you in my favor, especially when I have the opportunity to speak with the First Adept."

"Yes, Adept," the six of them said.

Carmine heard them moving away and saw their footsteps splashing through the mud. That might be problematic for them at some point, but likely not in the confusion of battle. Having done his best to ensure that Julianna would be his by night's end, Carmine turned Midnight around to rejoin the Nightbrothers who remained with him. Like them, he had not yet had his fill of killing. He yearned to send at least one Morigahnti to the Uncle's dark embrace. He'd developed a taste for it when he'd seen Khellan twitching at the end of his own *Galad'fana.*

Thirteen

Julianna watched from the window. The Morigahnti and the Shadybrook townsfolk dominated and controlled the battle. She couldn't help but wonder why the Morigahnti had not freed Koma from Kingdom rule long ago. They seemed two or three steps ahead of their enemies, and that was after being taken by surprise.

Then she saw the Brotherhood of the Night charging. With Khellan's *Galad'fana* wrapped around her head like a shawl, she saw as clearly at night as she could at dusk. The Brotherhood in their black armor charged toward the town on the main road, brandishing swords and torches. At first, it looked like they were going to attack the Kingdom force, but at the last moment, the Nightbrothers veered off and disappeared behind the buildings on the other side of the road.

Julianna turned back to the others. Allifar and Parsh leaned toward her a bit, waiting for her to speak. Faelin's expression was neutral, but his eyes darted back and forth, assessing everyone in the room. Other than the Morigahnti, the Dressels' household staff and guests stood together in the far corner of the room.

"Even with the power of miracle, can we defeat these odds?" Taebor asked.

"We can win," Korrin said, entering through the kitchen.

An overly large crow rode on his shoulder. The bird nodded at Julianna. She blinked back. She wanted to think she had imagined the gesture, but no – this couldn't be anything but one of the Stormcrows she'd heard and read about.

"Nathan, Wynd, and Aurell are in the stable saddling horses," Korrin continued. "The *kansati* are willing to fight." A *kansa* was any Komati who was not a Morigahnti or noble.

A broad-shouldered man in his middle years with thinning hair followed Korrin. He held a boar spear in one hand and a crude buckler in the other. A long hunting knife and a studded cudgel rode each of his hips.

"Are my people ready for this, Master Dressel?" Allifar asked the man on Korrin's heels.

"Yes, Your Excellency," Dressel said. "I've been ready ever since I learned to use the spear on a horse rather than a boar."

"I know your heart is strong and pure," Allifar said. "What of the rest?"

"All of Shadybrook has prepared since the betrayal at Kyrtigaen Pass."

Allifar turned to Julianna. "We await your commands, Lord Morigahn."

Julianna felt the weight of all eyes on her. How could she command these people? Some of them might die if she made the wrong choice. No. Some *would* die, no matter the choice. All of them would die if she led them poorly. Her earlier thoughts of sacrificing anyone so that she could be safe returned. These were good people. She had no right to order them to their deaths.

Then a solution came to her. She didn't know how to lead troops into battle, but she did understand how to run a household since she had been doing that for the last few years at her Aunt and Uncle's estate. Until she learned to be a leader in battle, she would use commanding a household as her model of leadership. In running the staff and servants, she never tried to give specific duties to every servant. That would have been idiocy.

"I do not know these people as well as you, nor do I know their strengths, nor how to make the best use of them. Deploy your people as you best see fit." Then, thinking of Kaelyb and Isnia, she added. "But, before we engage, we must see to the safety of those who won't be fighting."

Allifar regarded her for a long moment, considering. "Yes, Lord Morigahn." He turned to his people.

Julianna couldn't be sure, but she thought she detected a hint of disappointment in Allifar's voice. What did he want from her? She knew nothing of leading people into battle. Did he expect her to go off, charging the Brotherhood or the Kingdom with a sword in hand, destroying their enemies through the power of miracles? Then Julianna understood that Allifar, like most Morigahnti, had likely been waiting, dreaming, and longing, for a Lord Morigahn to come with all the answers and to give commands leading to immediate freedom from the Kingdom of the Sun. Now that Grandfather Shadow was free, they likely expected Julianna to be that Lord Morigahn.

"You." Allifar pointed at the young woman who had helped Julianna to her bath earlier that evening. "What is your name?"

The girl curtsied as best she could while holding a baby. "Jenise, excellency."

"Jenise," Allifar said. "Take the children and elders and..." he looked at Dressel. "Which is more secure, the attic or your basement?"

"Basement, my Lord," Dressel replied. "Especially with a guard with any kind of competence. The attic has two doors, the basement only one."

Allifar nodded. "Good. Good." He looked the crowd over again, more slowly this time, as if appraising them. "Jenise, take the folk who cannot fight to the basement. Taebor, you will go and guard the door."

"What? Why?" Taebor stamped his foot. "I want to fight."

"Patience, lad," Parsh said. "You'll likely see all the fighting you want and more before this night is done."

"Indeed," Allifar said. "Also, the true purpose of the Morigahnti is to defend those Komati from the enemies that would harm and oppress us. Should the rest of us fall, you must ensure that those who cannot fight see safety and shelter elsewhere. Do you understand?"

Taebor's face tightened, but he nodded and said, "Yes, Count Allifar."

"Dressel." Allifar turned to Master Dressel. "Your people will harry the Brotherhood. We need time to saddle the horses and retreat."

Dressel gave a slight bow. "Yes, excellency."

Allifar faced the Morigahnti. "Parsh and Korrin will deal with the Draqons. Don't kill them."

"Wait," Korrin interjected. "Don't kill the Draqons? Let the creatures the Kingdom bred to be the ultimate soldiers wander about?"

"Yes," Parsh said. "I understand. If we kill them, the Adepts might panic and do something unpredictably stupid."

"Indeed," Allifar said. "Keep them in check as best you can. If it comes to a choice between their life or yours, choose yours. However, as long as the Adepts think they can survive, they won't try to destroy the entire township before they die. If they think they can survive, they'll try to take as many of us alive as they can so they can put us on trial, to make examples of us. We can use that."

"Ah, yes." A wide grin split Korrin's face. "We can definitely use that."

"See to my commands," Allifar said.

As the room became a flurry of movement, Faelin stepped next to Julianna.

"I'll go with them," Faelin said. "If Vendyr is in one of his moods, they'll have no chance of saddling him. Also, the more hands we put to the task, the faster we can retreat."

"Wise," Julianna said.

As people left the room, Julianna recalled that the Tome of Shadows was still in its pack in her room.

"Taebor," she called, speaking with the voice of a duchess to a servant. "I need you to get something from my room. You'll find a leather satchel next to the bed. It has symbols in *Galad'laman* written on it. Bring it to me and then attend to those in the basement.

Julianna looked about the room, thinking of the discussion of defensible rooms. With All the entrances and exits, not to mention the number of windows that were large enough for a man to easily climb through, this was likely the least defensible room in the whole manor.

"Bring it to me in the kitchen."

There she would have fewer doors to watch, and likely no windows to worry about.

Taebor gave a deep bow, a little deeper than necessary to be polite, and headed up the stairs. Julianna sighed. She had spoken with haste and frustration. The lad deserved better than to be treated like a servant. Even though the Morigahnti were handling her like a porcelain teacup, each one of them would likely die for her. She made up her mind to apologize when he returned.

FOURTEEN

Wynd spun when she heard the stable's back door crash open. Three men in black armor rushed through the opening. They needed to stop the Brothers from flooding in before they had enough numbers to overwhelm the Morigahnti. She stepped away from the horse she was saddling, raised her finger at the man in the door, and drew on the Dominions of Shadows and Vengeance.

"*Tuska!*" Wynd cried.

A bolt of dark energy flew from her finger and struck the fourth Nightbrother in the abdomen. The man's stomach erupted. He gaped in disbelief at the entrails spilling out of his stomach. He dropped, and his eyes rolled into the back of his head as he tried to scoop his innards back inside. That was enough to give the other Nightbrothers pause.

"*Galad'seina rima aen ovi,*" Nathan spoke.

Wynd's *Galad'fana* tingled with the Dominions of Shadow and Balance. The shadows in the back of the stable obeyed Nathan's miracle and formed a barrier across the back door.

The three Nightbrothers faced off against the three Morigahnti

Wynd unbuckled her sword belt with her left hand and drew her fighting knife with her right. It was too cramped in the stable to try and fight with rapiers.

Aurell was the closest to the door, and two of the Brothers stalked toward her. The third was going for Nathan. Unfortunately for the Nightbrothers, Aurell was bridling her gelding, Dusk.

The Nightbrothers stalked toward her.

Aurell jerked on the reins and said, "Kick."

Dusk's back legs shot out and caught a Nightbrother full in the face. The skull-faced helm caved in. Bones crunched. The Nightbrother crumpled to the floor. He probably wasn't dead, at least not yet, but if he survived, he might very well wish his god had embraced him tonight.

Seeing this, the other Brother going toward Aurell veered to the side. It was unlikely that he was going to pose any threat to her so long as she hid behind Dusk, so Wynd turned her attention toward the Brother facing her husband.

Nathan held his rapier at arm's length, the blade pointed straight at the Nightbrother's eyes, and gripped his fighting knife backward, hiding the blade behind his forearm. Although the Brother's short sword would serve him better in these cramped quarters, he had to get past the rapier first. He seemed to realize that and shifted back and forth from foot to foot gauging for a weakness in Nathan's defense.

After countless hours of training with each of her fist mates, Wynd knew their strengths and their weaknesses fairly well. While Nathan was an accomplished swordsman, his knife-fighting skills left much to be desired. She wasn't about to let this Brother discover that. She judged the distance, flipped her knife over, caught the blade between her thumb and first two fingers, took a breath, and threw the knife.

The Nightbrother must have caught her movement out of the corner of his eye because he turned in that brief moment between when the knife left her hand and when it struck. Instead of catching him in the throat, her knife hit his shoulder, sinking halfway to the hilt. While it wasn't a killing blow, it distracted him long enough for Nathan to execute a leaping lunge and thrust his rapier into the Brother's chest.

The final surviving Brother threw down his sword, and cried, "Mercy! Gods and goddesses, please take mercy on me."

By this time Aurell had come out from behind Dusk, her own dagger in hand.

"Would you have granted mercy to me?" she asked. "Or would you and your fellows have raped me before killing me?"

The Nightbrother stammered assurances that he would not, while his eyes fell on Wynd. Wynd sighed and shook her head. Looking at her was the worst thing he could have done. Aurell ripped his skull-shaped helm from his head, grabbed him by the hair, and dragged him to the one empty stall. Wynd retrieved her knife, doing her best to ignore his screams.

While Aurell tortured him, something crashed against the front door of the stable. Wynd and Nathan looked at each other.

"Fun time is over," Nathan said, launching himself against the door to help hold it closed. "Aurell, get Dusk over here and turn his backside toward this door. Wynd, you get Shade."

Wynd rushed over to Parsh's horse, Shade, as another blow struck the door. Parsh helped the whole Fist train their horses to execute tricks in fighting. Dusk was second only to Shade. With those two horses filling the door, the Brothers were unlikely to make it inside unscathed—if they made it in at all.

They could have used shadows to wall off that door too, if they worked together; however, at least one of them would have been too tired to do anything else afterward. Both Allifar and

Parsh had taught them to expect any fight to grow from a minor skirmish to a prolonged battle at any moment, and to use miracles sparingly and only as an aid to tactics rather than as a crutch for weak ones because they never knew when they might need that energy later.

When Wynd and Aurell had the horses positioned, Nathan looked to the loft and called, "Thyr, tell Raze we need help."

Wynd heard the flutter of wings in the hayloft. She sent thanks to Grandfather Shadow for blessing the Morigahnti with the Stormcrows so many years ago. Thyr and Raze had allowed them to turn disaster into victory on more than one occasion.

"Ready?" Nathan asked when another blow hit the door.

"Ready," Wynd and Aurell said together.

Nathan lifted the wooden beam barring the door. It crashed open as he dove between the two horses.

Nightbrothers rushed in. Wynd thrust Shade's reigns to Aurell and scooped up one of the grenades. As Aurell spoke commands and the horses attacked the Brothers, Wynd threw the lamp over the animals and into the middle of the crowd pushing to get in. Fire exploded and screams echoed in the night as Brothers burned. That slowed their attack, giving the Morigahnti a fighting chance.

FIFTEEN

Faelin followed Allifar out of the manor house to the sight of Nightbrothers swarming the stable. The wide, double doors had just crashed inward, and the Brothers began to press inside. Something flew out of the door and landed in the center of the amassing Brothers. A bonfire exploded in the midst of them.

"We must help." Allifar drew his sword. It was as long as a rapier, but the blade was nearly as thick as a broad sword. Only someone with Allifar's build could wield such a weapon with one hand gracefully. "Escape is lost without the horses."

Without waiting for Faelin, Allifar charged toward the Nightbrothers.

Faelin hesitated. He'd seen enough fighting and bloodshed to last him for the rest of his life. Part of him wanted to turn back around, get Julianna, and flee, but they would never be able to flee from these numbers on foot. Well, as a portion of Grandfather Shadow's Sixth Law said: *The Morigahnti were born to fight and conquer.* And while Faelin wasn't a Morigahnti, Julianna was; she was the most important Morigahnti, and he wasn't about to leave her to face this life alone.

Drawing his sword, Faelin followed Allifar into the fray. To his right, Faelin saw other forms running out of the darkness. When he got closer to the light from the fire, Faelin saw Korrin leading a handful of men armed mostly with spears and axes. At least now the Brotherhood couldn't just turn and slaughter them once they realized they were being attacked from behind. Faelin killed two Nightbrothers before the others realized that they were being attacked.

The Nightbrothers turned and met the attack. While the townsfolk had the advantage of numbers, the Nightbrothers were armored and their swords were better suited to fighting than the Komati's hunting spears and woodsman's axes. Even Faelin's rapier wasn't an advantage in this kind of fighting. Had he been facing one Nightbrother, or perhaps two, the rapier would have given him the distinct advantage, but their short swords allowed three of them to swarm him at once. The rain-slick cobblestones kept him from backing away as quickly as he would have liked. He kept his rapier at throat level, flicking it back and forth at each of them. Thankfully, none of them wanted to be the one to try and make it past his guard. The first one that came at him was likely going to die, and their trepidation showed that they knew it.

Faelin drew the three facing him away from their fellows and prayed that Allifar had taught the people of Shadybrook to fight as well in close combat as he had with ranged attacks. If not, Faelin might survive, but he would likely take a wound that would make him easy prey.

The three Brothers followed Faelin. Korrin broke off from his line and lunged for the Brother threatening Faelin's right. Even before Korrin's blade sank into his target, Faelin slapped the center Nightbrother's sword with his own, knocking it out of line. The Brother on his left lunged, which Faelin had anticipated. With a twist of his wrist and torso, Faelin skewered his attacker.

In killing the right-most one, Korrin had left himself open. A Nightbrother broke from the crowd and rushed him, only to catch an axe blade in the face from one of the *kansa*. His leather mask did nothing to stop the heavy blade.

The center Nightrother recovered from Faelin's feint and lunged at him. Faelin pulled his sword free and parried. Rather than try and retreat so his rapier would be useful, Faelin stepped in close and slammed his elbow into the man's throat. The Nightbrother stumbled back from Faelin, gagging and coughing. This gave Korrin a chance to slip in and finish him.

"Once we were like wolves," Korrin said to Faelin, a wild grin splitting his face.

"Our time can come again," Faelin replied.

Now that he was a bit away from the fighting, Faelin quickly observed the situation. Dressel and more of the townsfolk had joined the fray.

"Shades!" one of the townsfolk cursed next to Faelin.

Faelin turned around, and his bowls turned to ice. Coming at them from one end of the street was another group of Brothers led by an Adept on horseback. From the other direction came the other two Adepts and the Draqons. With a quick count, it appeared that someone had freed the few Red's from Allifar's miracle.

"So much for winning the day," Faelin said to himself.

He turned to help cut a path through the Brothers and into the stable. Now their only hope was to get out of the street and into someplace defensible.

SIXTEEN

The worst part about returning with the dogs was that Sylvie knew she was going to be cold again. She didn't want to give up the three puppies she carried under her cloak that were warming her hands and torso.

When Sylvie and Jorgen approached Hardin with the dogs, the Adept had a fire burning in a raised brazier. Hardin was dropping things into the flame—were those sausages? —that popped and sizzled when they hit the coals. The two Daemyn hounds sat on either side of the fire. The creatures leaned forward, whispering to the flames.

"Well done," Hardin said, and craned his neck to look at the four dogs that followed Sylvie and Jorgen. "You're back much sooner than I expected."

Gathering the dogs had been so much easier than Sylvie had expected it to be. Dogs on her father's estates had been trained to discourage strangers from getting too close to the house. Out here, the animals had greeted them with wagging tails and lolling tongues, especially when Sylvie and Jorgen had offered them the dried meat.

"We did better than you see." Jorgen showed Hardin the bundle of three puppies in his arms. "And her Excellency has three more."

"Really?" Hardin smiled, though it held none of the warmth and comfort Sylvia usually associated with that expression.

Sylvie stepped forward and pushed her arms out of her cloak, showing the three puppies she also carried. The little animals squirmed and whined when she exposed them to the night air.

"Six puppies," Hardin tossed one of the sausage-like things into the fire and clapped his hands. "Well done indeed!" He held his hand back toward the Nightbrothers. "It looks like we'll need another few."

One of the Brothers sucked in a deep breath, the kind that Sylvie heard men do before performing some feat of strength or something that was going to foolishly cause them pain – all to show off for some lady, to prove he was greater than the other men around him, or both. The same Brother handed something to Hardin, which Hardin dropped in the fire as the Nightbrother wrapped a cloth around his hand.

"Fingers?" Sylvie asked. "You're burning their fingers?"

"Of course," Hardin replied. "How else are we to get the Daemyns' attention so we can bargain with them to possess the dogs?"

Flames danced around the fingers in the coals. The three puppies yipped when Sylvie dropped them before running away to vomit behind the wagon.

SEVENTEEN

Julianna paced in the kitchen. In those moments when the wind died and no thunder sounded, she heard shouts, screams of pain, and ringing weapons. In one such moment, she stopped and listened, wanting to rush out and fight. This wasn't a group of nobles fighting duels to first blood; people were killing each other, both for and against her. The thought that people were dying for her while she stayed safe burned in Julianna's chest. Her heart and breathing quickened as she recalled the sensation of Nicco's blood washing over her fingers when she killed him. She imagined how she would feel washing Carmine's blood from her hands.

Maxian's words echoed from the shadows of her mind: *Murder is only an easy way to exchange one problem for another.*

She would gladly exchange the problems that came with murdering Carmine with the problem of him still hunting her.

She resumed her journey back and forth across the kitchen. When she reached the halfway point next to the great table and overhead rack of pots and pans, the door leading to the front room swung open. Taebor stood there, holding the satchel with the *Galad'parma*.

"Lord Morigahn…" the young man's voice trailed off.

At first, Julianna thought it was due to nervousness, but his silence continued a moment too long. He made another sound, partway between a cough and a gasp. Blood spilled from his mouth and ran down his chin. He fell face-first to the floor, revealing two Nightbrothers. Their skull-headed masks glared at her, expressionless. Each held a short sword. Blood dripped from both weapons. Behind them lay four bodies, presumably the men Master Dressel had set to guard her.

Julianna's jaw tightened. Her excitement faded and turned to fury. Presented with this proof that people were dying for her, she decided then and there that every Nightbrother who trespassed in Shadybrook would die. These two would be the first.

Marcus's words came back through the years. *You're not as strong as a man*, her cousin would say, *but smarter than most, and even the smart ones will likely underestimate you. Use that and your environment to your advantage.* After that, Grandfather Shadow's Second Law came to the front of her mind: *A sharp sword is nothing without a sharp eye. Miracles are nothing unless tempered by faith. True power is found in the heart and mind.*

Julianna shrieked, imitating her cousin Raechel when the two of them discovered a mouse in Raechel's closet. Julianna had feared Raechel might shatter a window in her terror of the little rodent. The scream would let the Morigahnti know she was in danger, and she wanted the Nightbrothers to believe she was too afraid to put up a fight.

As the Nightbrothers stalked toward her, Julianna took in her surroundings and noted things she could use. The Brothers might have been less eager had they seen the rapier on her hip, but the table between them hid the sword from their sight.

Reaching up to a rack above the table, Julianna took a good-sized pot down and ducked behind the table. Cupboards built into the bottom hid her from view, and she scurried to the oven and scooped up some embers in the pot. The handle grew warm, but she wouldn't have it long enough to burn her.

Julianna drew her rapier as she stood. As she hoped, each man had gone to one side of the table to trap her.

She lunged at the closest man.

It was an obvious, clumsy lunge, the kind of thing that actors did because some of the audience was too far away to see the subtleties of true swordplay. He went to parry. As soon as she saw his wrist flick into the defensive maneuver, Julianna swung the pot in a large overhand arch. To his credit, the man managed to parry her lunge while catching her other arm with his free hand, keeping her from smashing his head with the pot. She didn't mind. She'd never intended the pot to hit him. Glowing embers rained down on him. He screamed, dropped his sword, and peddling backward, clawed at his eyes.

Julianna spun and threw the pot. The other man ducked. Again, the pot was only meant as a distraction. Julianna never expected to hit him. While that one recovered, Julianna spun to face the man she'd blinded. She leaped after him, executed a perfect ballestra lunge that covered the space in a heartbeat, and caught the Nightbrother between his fourth and fifth ribs. The blade slid smoothly through the man's body, so much more smoothly than Julianna ever expected. His hands flopped as if he were trying to swat away a biting insect. His breath came in gurgling, bloody gasps.

Julianna didn't try to pull her rapier free. Instead, she picked up the dying man's short sword and rushed toward the door leading to the common room.

Halfway to the door, two more Brothers stepped into the doorway. Julianna turned to flee, only to find two more blocking the door leading outside. The surviving member of the first pair pulled Khellan's rapier out of his comrade's chest and started toward her.

"He was my friend." The mask gave the Nightbrother's voice an ominous echo. "Your death is going to be long and painful, Morigahnti whore."

"No," another said. "The Adepts want her alive. Remember our orders."

The five of them stalked toward her, spreading out to surround her.

Her mind raced. A miracle, she needed a miracle.

Dozens floated in the back of her mind, all in *Galad'laman*, but she didn't have time to think about what they might do. She could only think of one thing to do.

"*Galad'Ysoysa, hivya mina sasta,*" Julianna said.

At those words, every shadow in the room seemed to stretch toward her.

Speak this one, Grandfather Shadow whispered in her mind. His voice echoed with the Dominion of Knowledge.

The words appeared to her with perfect clarity.

Julianna dropped the short sword, and drawing on all seven of Grandfather Shadow's Dominions, slapped her hands together, shouting, "*Galad'thanya kuiva aen eva ruth!*"

A thunderclap erupted from her hands, lifting the Nightbrothers from their feet and flinging them away. Their bodies slammed against the walls and crumpled to the floor. The walls of the kitchen bent outward, and in some places holes appeared, blown into the stormy night.

Julianna dropped to her knees. Exhaustion crashed down on her. She tried to cry for help, but she'd used her breath for that miracle and she didn't have the strength to draw enough breath for a whisper.

EIGHTEEN

Jenise paced back and forth in the small room where the children hid. Now and then, muffled gunshots and screams reached them, but mostly, they waited in quiet. The quiet bothered Jenice more than the sounds that startled her and made the children jump. Some of them whined and sniveled, but for the most part, they held themselves bravely.

"Your parents will be proud of your strength," Jenice said. She reminded them that fear was no cause for shame. As the old laws told them, Morigahnti did not suffer trouble alone—or something to that effect. "And just like the Morigahnti fighting outside, we are facing our fears together."

At long last, the baby went to sleep. Jenise ever-so-gingerly lowered herself into a rocking chair. Her legs and lower back ached. Jenise sat in a chair and gently rocked the adorable newcomer to the Township, thankful to be off her feet.

The baby wailed in Jenise's arms. One moment, the infant slipped peacefully. The next moment, the infant's eyes snapped open, and it wailed as if Jenice had dropped it.

Jenice sighed, stood, and rocked and bounced the baby, making hushing and shushing sounds. The other children were getting upset. The baby kicked and flailed its arms.

A thunderclap shuddered the building. The floor shook.

Jenise could not keep her feet and toppled sideways. Her mind and body screamed at her to protect the baby. Whatever else happened, she had to protect the baby. Jenise managed to twist as she fell. Instead of falling on her side, she fell almost straight backward. Her arms held the baby as tightly as they could. The baby was safe as Jenise could make the poor fragile thing.

The baby screamed louder.

The floor and Jenise's head collided. Spots and flashes stabbed Jenise's eyes. Instinctively her body tried to get up, but she only managed to lift her head a slight bit. Her muscles gave out, and her head dropped again. The *thunk* of that impact worked its way through Jenise's skull and blinded her. She would have thought that odd, the idea that a sound could blind her, if only her mind hadn't given out as well.

The baby screamed and screamed. The other children whimpered and cried.

NINETEEN

The charging Nightbrothers collided with the Draqons. Some of the worry weighing on Faelin's guts lessened as his enemies fought each other. If the gods were kind, they would kill each other. His head turned of its own volition to the manor house. A group of dark figures crowding the kitchen door. He abandoned the Morigahnti and townsfolk and danced his way back through the fighting, the need to protect Julianna forced him back toward the manor.

The tide of battle shifted. The three clashing forces swarmed between Faelin and the manor house. For a moment, it seemed the battle would sweep him up, but then Faelin's skin tingled. His head swam. A thunderclap echoed. The manor's walls creaked and bowed. The windows shattered outward, and several large tufts of thatching blew free of the roof. A moment later, the wave of force hit. It did not affect him any more than ruffling his clothes, but everyone else went sprawling—Komati, Nightbrothers, Adepts, and Draqons.

Faelin took only a moment to notice this. Part of him thought of killing the Nightbrothers and Draqons as they lay helpless, but that would slow him down. The need to be close to Julianna overtook him. Faeling rushed to her and prayed the Morigahnti recovered first.

TWENTY

Wynd and Nathan had just about gotten the stable doors closed when her *Galad'fana* burned with all seven of Grandfather Shadow's Dominions: Shadows, Storms, Balance, Vengeance, Illusions, Knowledge, and Secrets. Only one miracle used all seven Dominions, and Grandfather Shadow only allowed three people the privilege of speaking it.

Nathan looked up. "Could that be?"

Wynd didn't answer. She was too busy jumping away from the door.

The stable shook as if kicked by a giant foot. The doors blew inward, flinging Nathan across the room like a straw before the gale. The horses went into a frenzy, kicking and screaming. In her rush to get away from the door, Wynd had gotten too close to Shade. The stallion reared, and she barely avoided having her head crushed.

She dashed to her husband, knowing that she could do nothing to calm the horses. They would calm themselves in their own time. Nathan had a bump on his head from where the stable door had struck him, but he would recover. His eyes focused on her face and he smiled.

"Was that what I think it was?" Aurell asked, coming out of one of the stalls.

"I think so," Nathan said.

"The miracle of Shadow's Thunder?" Aurell asked.

Nathan sighed. "Again, I think so."

"She is the Lord Morigahn," Wynd said.

Nathan nodded.

All around them, the stable seemed to groan in protest as if the building was ready to come down around them.

"We have to calm the horses," Aurell said, "and then get them out."

Nathan gestured at the doors. Wynd looked. Both were too damaged to close completely. Outside, Komati and Brotherhood alike lay sprawled in the mud. Some moved, but most lay as still as corpses. Many of them likely were, but others were only stunned by the Lord Morigahn's miracle.

Then someone stood up.

"Shades!" Nathan said.

"Damn," Wynd said.

The figure was too tall to be human. There was no mistaking the silhouette of a Draqon. Another stood next to it.

Wynd's *Galad'fana* tingled ever so slightly with the Dominions of Illusions and Secrets.

Aurell spoke in a whisper, "*Galad'Ysoysa jata heita havaeta mikan uhkava tasta.*" When she completed the miracle, she swayed on her feet. That was likely the last miracle Aurell would speak in this battle.

Wynd looked at the Draqons. Aurell's quick thinking might have saved them all, especially by using *havaeta*, meaning detect, rather than *aestia*, meaning see. The Draqons didn't need to see them in order to find them, but her miracle would hide the three Morigahnti from all senses. One of the Draqons looked at the stable, but his gaze passed right over Wynd. She had no way of knowing what the Draqon saw, not even Aurell could tell that. The exact nature of the hiding miracle was for Grandfather Shadow to decide.

"Now we have some free time to work," Aurell said.

"What do we do about the horses?" Wynd asked.

Though the animals had stopped rearing and kicking, they still stamped their feet and whinnied, eyes wide and showing mostly white from their panic.

"We can use Balance to transfer all the panic into one horse and then put that one down. We'll never calm them down another way. If you and I work together, love, we won't tire out too much and will still be able to fight."

"I'm going to sneak out and find the others," Aurell said. "You keep getting the horses ready."

Wynd helped Nathan to his feet. With one miracle, the Lord Morigahn had changed the face of this battle. It was no longer about who had the best tactics, the strongest warriors, or the greatest numbers. Now it was about who recovered first and took advantage of that. Wynd wanted nothing more than to start slitting Kingdom throats, but the Morigahnti needed to retreat, and to do that, they needed horses saddled and ready to ride.

TWENTY-ONE

When the thunderclap sounded, Carmine reacted on pure instinct. Drawing on the Dominions of Lies and Corruption, he yelled, "*Tuznak maaish protsna nal!*"

He spoke the miracle only a moment before the wave of force carried him off Midnight. He whirled through the air for a few moments before slamming into the ground. Carmine lay there for a few moments, listening. He heard only the crackle of flames and the cries of the wounded and dying. He quickly flexed all the muscles in his arms, legs, and torso to determine that nothing was broken. Once he decided that he hadn't suffered anything more than heavy bruising, Carmine stood. His body groaned in protest, but only because of the fall. Luckily he'd managed to avert most of the effects of the attacking miracle with a miracle of his own.

As he rose, Carmine's vision spun for a moment, and then he found himself gazing at Hardin. A new pack of Daemyn hounds sniffed at the ground and the air behind the Swaenmarch Adept.

"What just happened?" Hardin asked.

"A miracle," Carmine responded. "I don't think I've seen one stronger."

"I'm sending the hounds."

"Not yet," Carmine said. "I'll tell you when."

Carmine shook his head, and when his vision returned to his surroundings, he scanned the area for any immediate threats. Few people moved, and the ones that did were not a threat. The miracle had flattened everyone indiscriminately, Komati and Kingdom alike. He'd never witnessed something with such unbridled power. How were he and Hardin going to face someone that strong?

Pushing that worry aside for later, Carmine slogged through the mud over to Cadenza and Vycktor. The rain was gone, and as cold as the wind was, it couldn't freeze out the warmth in Carmine's heart. Carmine liked killing, but he liked killing other Adepts most of all, especially from his own House. By rights, he should be an Adept of All Father Sun. His father's family had been Sun Adepts for as long as the four Great Houses had ruled the Kingdom. But Father had married a Komati for love, making Carmine's polluted blood unfit to wear the golden mantle of All Father Sun. Despite the bitter cold of that biting wind, Carmine smiled. There would soon be one less Adept of House Floraen.

Vycktor's head twisted at an unnatural angle from his shoulders. Cadenza lay in the mud, gasping for air and struggling to rise. She looked at Carmine, her gaze wandering over his black Adept's mantle. Eyes widening, she tried to scurry away, but she only managed to make small splashes in the mud with her hands.

"The Zenith is changing, Cadenza," Carmine said.

Cadenza pushed into the mud, as if Mother Earth would embrace her to safety. Carmine chuckled. She served the wrong god for that kind of rescue. All Father Sun might have done something, had he been watching, but it would be hours before he entered the sky.

"*Mishrak Amhyr'Shoul,*" Cadenza spoke, "*aevidho som vaso mirso Lusias.*"

Even as she began the miracle, Carmine raised his saber to strike. The instant before he struck, Cadenza vanished in a flash. She'd asked All Father Sun to transport her to the light, and that could potentially be anywhere a light shown. Even in all the centuries, Adepts had been speaking miracles, it was still not anywhere close to being entirely exact or predictable in all cases.

Now that she knew he was an Adept of Old Uncle Night, he would have to find her and kill her as soon as he could, or he would find himself hunted by the House Floraen Inquisitors.

Leaving his worries for Cadenza behind for the moment, Carmine went over to the nearest Red Draqon. This Red was from a line bred closer to humanity than any Carmine had seen in some time. Its scales were so faint he couldn't see them in the darkness. Unlike most Draqons, its hair looked more like human hair than like a horse's main. The creature had more braids than Carmine could count at a glance.

The Draqon looked up at Carmine with slitted eyes the color of blood. It couldn't take in his clothes because it didn't have the strength to move its head. Divinity had powered whatever force hit them, and Draqons were more susceptible to miracles than humans were. On the other hand, they were especially resilient to the powers of Daemyns.

"I have just come from Adept Cadenza," Carmine said. Carmine pulled a vial out of one of his belt pouches. "She gave me this to help revive you."

The Draqon's eyes softened a bit and it drank.

It wasn't completely a lie. The potion was something he'd developed several years before, a modification of a potion that would turn any human into a willing slave. He had changed it to affect Draqons instead, though he'd never gotten a chance to test it. He would be one of the few Adepts of Old Uncle Night to command a squad of Draqons. Now, hunting Julianna would prove no difficulty at all. The Draqons would cut down any

Morigahnti standing in the way.

TWENTY-TWO

Novan's mind stirred in that hazy place where men wallowed
between sleep, unconsciousness, and drunken stupor. Every time
he rolled over, his joints protested the wooden floor beneath him.
Another shift. Again his hips and shoulders cried out for the
perfectly good bed waiting for him upstairs.

Someone groaned.

Who was here with him?

Novan opened his eyes and lifted his head. He groaned. He
sounded just like the person who had grown first. Oh, that had
been him.

With his eyes open, he looked at the stairs.

His bed waited for him up there, but he hadn't handled the
stairs so well the last time he tried them.

Truth be revealed, Novan didn't think he could walk. Crawling
might be possible. He was on his side. Get into his hands and
knees shouldn't be too much trouble. Staying on them the whole
way up the stairs might be a challenge, but he could rest when he
got to the stairs. Then he could rest again when he got to the top.
He felt like if he could get to the top of the stairs, he could climb
into his bed. The bed waiting for him. The bed that was so much
more comfortable than this floor. At least, he had vague
recollections his bed was more comfortable than this floor.

Something buzzed around Novan's head. The fury of a storm
tugged at his hair. A *boom* from somewhere in the distance
thumped against Novan's eardrums. Something pushed him along
the floor, something he felt but could not see, something both
similar and wholly different than whatever had laid him down
instead of allowing him to break his life on the stairs. The cloth
around his head hummed with the battle hymns of ancient
Morigahnti heroes. They called for him to rise, to take up his
arms, and to fight for the Lord Morigahn against Grandfather
Shadow's enemies. Novan imagined his father's voice in that
chorus, singing to him from wherever his bones lay in Kyrtigaen
pass.

"Father," Novan said. "I will fight."

After all, Novan owed the Brotherhood of the Night a debt of blood compounded with many years' interest.

"*Kostota.*"

Novan rolled to his hands and knees.

"*Kostota na aen paras kostota.*"

Novan got to his feet. He wobbled. He took a deep breath. The next moment he took an even deeper breath.

The weapons he had gotten earlier from his father's chest lay at the bottom of the stairs.

Novan took a step. His body wobbled and swayed. He almost fell. He took a breath, steadied himself, and stepped again. With each step closer to Father's weapons, Novan's body gained more a surety in its movements.

When Novan reached the weapons, he crouched down and picked up his father's sword and firearm. He sheathed the sword and shoved the two-shot pistol into his belt next to the sword. He rewrapped the *Galad'fana* around his head so that only his eyes showed.

TWENTY-THREE

Wynd gripped her rapier so hard her fingers ached. She watched as the Adept of Old Uncle Night led Faelin away, surrounded by Red Draqons. From all she could tell, Faelin was a good man and didn't deserve this, but his capture wasn't the reason for the cold terror piercing her heart like an icicle. Until this moment, Draqons did not knowingly serve any Adept of High Blood who had pledged themselves to Old Uncle Night. A new dark time loomed ahead if the Brotherhood could openly command Draqons.

The last grenade rested at her feet, but she couldn't justify using it to save Faelin. He wasn't a Morigahnti, and if Wynd attacked, it might shatter Aurell's illusion and bring those Draqons charging.

The only thing to turn in their favor was the horses had settled once Aurell spoke her miracle. Grandfather Shadow must have wanted his Morigahnti to escape and fight the Kingdom another day.

Moments after Faelin, the Adept, and the Draqons faded from sight into the night, Wynd heard an eerie howl above the rain pounding on the stable's roof. Daemyn hounds. She heaved a sigh of defeat. Hounds were hard enough to escape even if all circumstances were favorable.

Allifar and Aurell stumbled out of the rain.

Allifar gave commands. "Nathan, get out there and lead those Daemyn hounds on a trail so confusing that they'll believe their own tails are made of divine power. Take Shade. Have Thyr tell Raze and Korrin to do the same."

"Shade?" Nathan asked. "But…"

"Yes, Shade!" Allifar snapped. "He's the fastest horse saddled and bridled. Parsh can whine about it *if* we survive the night, which we won't if we don't do something to confound those hounds."

"Yes, m'lord." Nathan saluted and went over to the monstrous gray gelding.

Wynd couldn't miss how her husband chewed on his lower lip as he approached Shade. She didn't blame him or envy him Parsh's future wrath. Nobody rode Shade except Parsh. He was known to cuff people on the ear for even touching the stallion without permission. Allifar might think that he could intercede on Nathan's behalf, but eventually, Parsh would arrange for the two of them to be alone.

"Nathan," Wynd said to her husband. "Would you rather suffer Parsh's anger or have your soul eaten by a Daemyn hound?"

"Right." Nathan mounted and kicked Shade into a canter.

"Aurell," Allifar said. "Find the Lord Morigahn and make sure she stays safe. The Shrine is likely the most secure structure after her miracle. Take her there and wait for us."

Aurell nodded and ran out into the rain.

"What about me?" Wynd asked.

"We're going to find Parsh, slit some Nightbrother throats, and then finish with the horses. As soon as we have enough saddled for Lord Morigahn and the Fist, we ride."

"I saw Faelin captured," Wynd said.

For a brief moment, Allifar's eyes looked far away. The last time Wynd had seen Allifar looking melancholy was after his wife died. He'd allowed himself one night of grief and tears. His grief for Faelin was much shorter.

"Nothing to be done about it tonight," Allifar replied, the hardness returning to his voice. "We can't stand against Draqons and Daemyn hounds together."

TWENTY-FOUR

Faelin slid to his knees next to Julianna. She was breathing, and her eyes were open, though they stared off to nothing somewhere above the ceiling.

"Julianna, can you hear me?" Faelin asked.

"Fae..." Julianna blinked. "in..."

"I'm here. Everything will be all right." He prayed it wouldn't turn into a lie.

Faelin left her and took one of the kitchen cleavers from a large rack of knives and spoons. It was heavy, as long as his forearm, and meant for cutting through bone. He used it to decapitate the Nightbrothers. Sometimes removing the head was the only way to keep a man who served the God of Death from getting up, even after he suffered injuries that should have killed him.

Next, Faelin went to Taebor. The youth lay in a large pool of his blood, and he was only barely alive. His breath came in short, watery gasps. By the glossy look in his eyes, Taebor had only a few moments of life remaining.

"No dying tonight, lad," Faelin said. "The Lord Morigahn needs you."

He pulled Taebor's shirt open and placed a hand over the young Morigahnti's heart. A small bit of that need to protect Julianna flowed out of Faelin, through his arm, then his hand, and finally into Taebor.

Faelin removed his hand. A gray handprint marked where he had touched Taebor. The gray color spread, covering Taebor and the pool of blood. Once every bit of him and his blood were the color of ash, the gray pool started to pull in on itself, as if being sucked back inside Taebor's body. Moments later, Taebor's color returned and all his wounds were gone. The gray handprint remained. Faelin hurried to lace the shirt back up. Explanations could come later, after Faelin figured out what he'd just done.

Taebor groaned as Faelin helped him to his feet.

"What happened?" Taebor asked.

"I don't know," Faelin said. "I found you lying here."

"I thought I'd been stabbed from behind. I thought I was dying."

Faelin shrugged. "Maybe you got hit in the back of the head."

"Maybe." Taebor's eyes said that he didn't believe Faelin.

"It's no matter right now," Faelin said. "We have to get the Lord Morigahn out of here."

Taebor looked around. He paled when saw the decapitated Nightbrothers.

"It had to be done," Faelin said. "Help me carry the Lord Morigahn."

They went to Julianna and picked her up. At first, Faelin thought that they would share the burden, but then gave her completely over to Taebor.

"Aren't you going to help me?" Taebor asked.

"One of us has to be ready to fight, and I'm pretty certain that between us, I've seen more fighting than you."

"Can you make that claim for me as well?" asked a voice from the door leading to the main room of the manor.

Faelin spun. Korrin stood there, a Stormcrow rode his shoulder.

"Why didn't Shadow's Thunder affect you?" Faelin asked.

"It did," Korrin replied, "but not as much as everyone else. I have a talent for unraveling miracles around me. It's a secondary benefit to one of my other talents. I could ask the same question of you."

"Honestly, I don't know," Faelin said. "And right now, I don't care. I care about getting her out of here alive. Will you help me?"

"Yes," Korrin replied, and went to help to reduce Taebor's burden.

Faelin went to the kitchen's side door, opened it, and looked into the face of a Red Draqon. Its eyes narrowed. Faelin tried to slam the door shut, but a second Red shoved back against the door. The first Red grabbed Faelin by the throat with blinding speed.

"Don't kill him," a voice behind the Draqons ordered.

"*Suorita hana ja ajo*," Faelin said. *Take her and run.*

The clawed hand shot out, grabbed him by the throat, and yanked him outside. Faelin managed to hold onto the door so that it shut behind him. He prayed that none of the Reds had seen inside.

One of the Reds tried the door, but it would not open. It braced one hand against the manor wall and pulled on the door with the other. Korrin must have heeded Faelin's warning and spoken a miracle to keep the door closed; otherwise, the Red would have easily ripped it free of the frame.

"What did you say?" Carmine demanded, rising in pitch.

Faelin did his best to imitate Damian's wild grin.

"Your mother is a traitorous whore," Faelin replied. Then he added. "How is Nicco?"

"What did you do to that door?" Carmine's pitch rose even more.

"I just locked it," Faelin replied. "I guess the Red breed is losing its potency. I'd suggest intermixing some White blood in there, but the Whites would never stand for that. You'll have to settle for mating your females with Greens."

All the Reds snarled. He didn't think Carmine would kill him. Any of the Great Houses would want to try and learn the Traejyn secrets from Faelin. Faelin didn't know any, but the Kingdom didn't know that, and Faelin would use anything as far as he could.

"Knock him out and bring him," Carmine said. "He won't tell us anything right now, but soon he'll beg tell us to everything we want to know."

Faelin didn't resist when the Draqon hit him in the side of the head. Black spots danced across his vision. Gods and goddesses, the blow hurt, and he had no idea how he remained conscious. He should have crumpled to the ground.

"You expected me to go down after that?" Faelin said. He had to give Korrin and Taebor time to escape. "Next time send a White."

The Red hit him again. Again it hurt, so much that Faelin couldn't form words. So he laughed instead.

"How noble of you to sacrifice yourself for her," Carmine said. "But it won't make a difference. Her soul will reek with the stench of miracle." Carmine's eyes rolled into the back of his head. "Send the hounds."

Faelin felt more than heard a chorus of unearthly bellows far in the distance. He prayed that Korrin and Taebor managed to get Julianna away and that they didn't do something stupid like try to rescue him.

Lightning flashed in the sky, and thunder followed a few moments later. This time it was just from the storm.

"Don't worry," Carmine sneered. "If Julianna truly is the chosen of Grandfather Shadow, she has no need to fear a few Daemyn hounds." Carmine glared at the Draqon. "I said, knock him out."

A torrent of rain began to pour from the sky.

The Red hit Faelin a third time.

The world went black.

OUR TIME CAN COME AGAIN

*A*en Morigahnti ala ansa veliti kashvoth vaara ykson.
Aen Morigahnti surata kimpas surempan kokonaetsin.
Sina olet valitos vartija.

The Morigahnti do not let brothers face danger alone.
The Morigahnti succeed together as a greater whole.
You are your brother's keeper.

The Third Law of Grandfather Shadow

Grandfather Shadow still stood on that hill overlooking Shadybrook, with Morag at his side, now in her wolf form. It pleased his heart to see his Morigahnti had not softened overly much during his imprisonment. Even more so, the doubts he'd harbored about naming Julianna the Lord Morigahn were fading. She had called to him when needed and spoken the Miracle of Shadow's Thunder correctly on her first attempt. She was his, and he expected great things from the Morigahnti under her leadership.

A sliver of lightning flashed two paces in front of the greater god, followed by a small thunderclap, and Razka stood in his human form.

"Good ev—" Grandfather Shadow began.

"You idiot," Razka snapped.

The God of Shadows blinked at the Stormseeker.

"Did you learn nothing in all those years when you had nothing better to do than think? Why would you have the girl speak that miracle when she's had no time for her body to become accustomed to the rigors of channeling divine power?"

Grandfather Shadow smiled. "Questioning me now, Razka?"

The Stormseeker alpha stepped forward.

Morag moved to place herself between her alpha and the god. Grandfather Shadow placed his hand upon her shoulder. Her reaction was completely a product of her nature. If this grew into a conflict where Grandfather Shadow needed Razka dealt with, the issue would be dealt with before Morag drew in her breath for the first warning growl. Still, it pleased him to see that Stormseekers remained, deep in their core, Stormseekers.

"I do when you are being an idiot," Razka said. "Either involve yourself completely or remove yourself from the game and let things play out as they will. It is unlike you to allow fear of the King of Order or the Lords of Judgment to sway your choices. Even this cub is showing more bravery and honor than you."

"Truly, Razka?" Grandfather Shadow asked. "You admonish me for my caution when I had a thousand years to consider the world through mortal eyes, always seeing and never acting. You, who has removed himself from the world due to grief when your people wish nothing more than to strike back? You, who stalks after your granddaughter, watching her attackers, offering only cryptic advice to her protector—a protector I gave her?"

Grandfather Shadow laughed. It was a quick blast of sound, lasting only a moment, but in that moment he allowed the full force of his divinity to come into the mortal world. His laughter was like thunder and knocked both Razka and Morag away from him. It seemed that Razka needed a reminder of where they both stood in the celestial order of precedence.

When both Stormseekers recovered, Grandfather Shadow wiped all humor from himself as he stepped toward the Stormseeker alpha.

"Razka, since the Battle of Kyrtigaen Pass, I have watched you become the most cowardly, self-serving creature I have known. Do not approach me again until you rediscover who you are."

With that, Grandfather Shadow turned his back on the Stormseeker. He felt Razka leave even before he heard the thunderclap.

"Did you mean that?" Morag asked.

"About being a coward and self-serving?" Grandfather Shadow asked.

Morag nodded.

"Every word," Grandfather Shadow replied, "and Razka needed to hear it. He should have heard it a long time ago, but I suppose the only Stormseekers with the courage to stand up to their alpha while I was imprisoned died at Kyrtigaen Pass."

A deep growl rumbled back in Morag's throat.

"Spare me your posturing, cub. Because I know you weren't born until after I was imprisoned, and you don't understand what a foolish thing you just did, I will not reprimand you this time. Razka has earned my tolerance and leniency with over a millennium of loyal service. You have earned nothing. Do not test me again."

Grandfather Shadow opened himself to the storm above. Or, did he draw the storm into himself? After so many centuries upon centuries, he wasn't exactly sure whether he served his Dominions or they served him—or even if a difference between them existed any longer. Grandfather Shadow looked over Shadybrook and its environs. Razka was wrong about one thing above all others. Grandfather Shadow had learned much in all those years when he had nothing better to do than think; he had learned that mortals didn't need Grandfather Shadow, or any god for that matter, to get directly involved in minor squabbles like this. On the other side of the coin, that didn't mean the God of Storms planned on leaving this encounter entirely to chance.

Grandfather Shadow drew in a deep breath and released it skyward toward the storm.

Rain began falling harder.

Two

Taebor was no stranger to rain. His fondest dream as a Morigahnti was that Koma would win its freedom from the Kingdom of the Sun and take the fighting to the Floraen Lands where it rained far less, or perhaps even across the sea to the Lands of Endless Summer where it rained almost not at all. Rain plagued Koma, and every season seemed to own its own particular brand of rain. However, the rain that had come with the Lord Morigahn's miracle was something entirely new. Unlike the usual gale-driven rain of the autumn storms, this was like the deluges that came at the beginning of spring. Unfortunately, the water pouring down on Taebor as he and Korrin carried the Lord Morigahn out of the manor wasn't warm like the spring rains—it pounded on his head with the biting cold of raindrops that weren't quite sleet yet.

Taebor's hood had fallen back and the water ran down the back of his shirt. Since he supported the Lord Morigahn with his right arm and held his rapier with his left, he couldn't get his hood back into place. Being right-handed, he didn't trust himself to manage it without hurting himself or the Lord Morigahn.

Taebor tasted blood from where his teeth cut into his lower lip. He'd bitten it to keep from crying in front of Korrin and the Lord Morigahn, even though she probably wasn't in any state to notice—it was principle. He hated the rain, the wind, and the cold, but most of all, he hated being a Morigahnti. True, he had grand dreams of the places he would go, but deep down he knew the truth. Koma would not be free, and Taebor would spend his life fighting a useless battle until he died on the sword of some Nightbrother, Draqon, or Floraen Inquisitor—again. Unfortunately, he never had a choice in the matter. His family had served the Thaedus family for generations, and even if they did not become Morigahnti, they all worshiped the God of Shadows. Taebor's father had been Morigahnti, and because he was the kind of father who demanded his sons follow in his footsteps, Taebor became a Morigahnti as well.

The rain pelted them, but something else weighed on Taebor. He couldn't shake the feeling of those swords piercing his back. He'd stood, helpless, feeling drained from his arms and legs.

Taebor glanced at Korrin, who trudged along, never losing that mischievous smirk. Now that man loved being a Morigahnti. Taebor knew others who embraced being Morigahnti. Some who enjoyed it. Others, like Allifar and Parsh, *lived* for being Morigahnti. Korrin, more than anyone Taebor had ever met, reveled in being Morigahnti. Korrin's passion was the opposite of Taebor's desire to run and hide from this life. Or, at least, that was how Taebor had felt before tonight, before he'd met the Lord Morigahn.

Now Taebor found himself caring. He didn't want to, but something about this woman made things different. Before meeting her, he likely would have fled at the first signs of battle, consequences be damned. His heart betrayed him by beating with excitement when Allifar had given Taebor the order to guard the Lord Morigahn. For the first time since becoming a Morigahnti, he was honored. Now he wanted to see her to safety. He wanted to see her make all the self-absorbed Morigahnti cry in shame at the mockery they made of Grandfather Shadow's faith. More than that, she made him want to believe. Something about her made Taebor want to revel in being Morigahnti the same way Korrin did.

"There," Korrin said, gesturing to the shrine dedicated to the eight lesser gods.

"But won't the lesser gods be angry with us for desecrating their shrine?" Taebor asked.

People were only supposed to enter shrines or temples if they intended to worship or beseech the gods for some favor. Those who entered the gods' house always incurred the gods' wrath, or so the priests said.

"It's where Allifar would want us to go," Korrin said. "Besides, you and I don't matter enough to the lesser gods to care."

"But what about her?" Taebor said. "She is important enough."

Korrin actually laughed. "Grandfather Shadow has returned, marked her with his own hand, if we are to believe the Stormcrows, and I believe Raze. If he's not going to protect her from the lesser gods and goddesses, then I guess she isn't really the Lord Morigahn, and we deserve whatever punishment the lesser gods cast down upon us for falling for her ruse."

Taebor sighed.

Korrin talked too much sometimes. Occasionally, Korrin used that trait for the good of the Fist, like the time when some House Floraen Inquisitors had found them preparing to perform a ritual to honor Grandfather Shadow. Korrin convinced them all that the Fist was rehearsing a play in which they were all going to die at the end, struck down by the wrath of the gods for stepping too far above their station. But mostly, Korrin's overzealous need to prattle on made Taebor's head swim in confusion.

"Shades!" Korrin's smile faded.

Taebor swallowed. Seeing Korrin without his smile chilled Taebor more completely than this near-freezing rain.

"What is it?" Taebor turned his head to and fro, searching for whatever had panicked Korrin.

"Somebody, no, several somebodies are drawing on Grandfather Shadow's Dominions, and being very obvious about it," Korrin said. "Blatantly obvious. Stupidly obvious. One of them is likely a Stormcrow because it's only drawing on Storms. The other is drawing mostly on Illusions and Secrets. I didn't catch them at first because of the residual traces of the Lord Morigahn's speaking of Shadow's Thunder."

"Can you tell where they are?" Taebor asked.

"Both are moving away from us, but not in a straight line. Oh bloody damn!"

"What?"

"That howling we heard before we came outside," Korrin replied.

"You mean the howling you told me was just the wind?" Taebor asked, not looking forward to the answer. "It wasn't the wind, was it?" Deep down he already knew what it was.

"It must be Daemyn hounds. We've got to get into the shrine, and I need to find Raze."

They made their way as quickly as they could, but the way behind the manor house to the shrine was a mix of mud and moss-covered stones that used to be part of the wall. Footing here was treacherous, and the way was mostly hidden between the manor and the wall.

When they entered the shrine and got out of the rain, Taebor thanked all of the lesser gods at once. He didn't care if it might be considered blasphemy by the other Morigahnti. This was the lesser gods' home, and their home allowed him to get out of the rain and mostly out of the wind.

He and Korrin placed the Lord Morigahn against a wall and gently slid her down into a sitting position. She kept muttering about Faelin, Faelin, where was Faelin. Her eyes flitted back and forth, not focusing on any one spot for very long, and sometimes she kept them closed as if getting ready to sleep. Each time her eyes would snap open, and she would begin her futile search again.

"Can we do anything for her?" Taebor asked, hating himself for not having a *Galad'fana* and not being able to speak a miracle to take some of this burden from her.

"No," came a voice from the far side of the shrine, "but I can."

Taebor shrieked and dropped his sword. The clattering of it striking the stone floor echoed in the shrine, and he hated himself even more for his cowardice.

When Taebor turned around, he saw Korrin facing off with a man in what could only be Dosahan leathers. Taebor had never seen a Dosahan, but he'd heard stories. They weren't always to be trusted, the Dosahan in those stories, and this one went so far as to cover his face with a mask. As he took in the sight, Taebor wondered how the man saw anything without holes in the mask for his eyes. Likely the only thing that had saved the man's life was that he had no obvious weapons aside from a silly stick with a long strand of braided leather.

"Name yourself," Korrin said, his smile had returned as he stared down the end of his sword at the stranger. "And name your business."

"Call me Smoke."

Korrin's smile widened. "I didn't ask what you were called. I told you to name yourself."

"On a night like this," a new voice said, from behind Smoke, "I'm inclined to agree."

A man came in, pointing a two-shot pistol at the Dosahan stranger. Taebor couldn't quite tell because of the mud covering this newcomer, but he looked to be in his early twenties, about the same age as Korrin.

"I thought you were leaving, Zephyr," Korrin said.

The newcomer sighed. "I *wanted* to leave. I *was* leaving. I *did* leave, really. I managed to get quite a ways down the series of muddy patches you call a road, and then I had to light my wagon on fire so I could get away from the Brotherhood of the Night, a Daemyn hound, and an Inquisitor of House Floraen. Oh, and could you please *not* use my name in front of strangers?"

"Sorry," Korrin said.

"I'm sure." Zephyr's tone indicated how little he believed the sincerity of Korrin's apology. "You look rather sorry. But back to the matter at hand. Take the mask down."

"No," the first stranger who had called himself Smoke replied. "You don't have time for this. The hounds cannot harm me, but the same cannot be said for you and the Lord Morigahn."

A boy of nearly ten years came in from the entrance Taebor and Korrin had just used.

"Silly people," the boy said. "You have no need to fear from Smoke. He won't harm her."

"And you know this from?" Korrin asked.

"A Stormseeker told me," the boy replied.

"Truly?" Korrin said.

"Truly." The boy crossed his arms over his chest and nodded. "Allifar said we have to," his face scrunched in concentration, which was silly—the boy wouldn't ever forget anything he heard or saw, "get out there and lead those Daemyn hounds on a trail so confusing that they'll believe their own tails are made of divine power."

"I'm not sure about leaving her with just Taebor and these two," Korrin waved his sword at both Smoke and Zephyr.

"Right," Taebor said. "Leaving me alone with these two is not a good idea."

At that, Zephyr shook his head and lowered his gun. He muttered something under his breath.

"You won't have to," Aurell's husky voice said just behind the boy.

Drenched with water, she looked even less pleasant than normal.

"Where are the others?" Korrin asked.

"The stable," Aurell replied. "Allifar and Parsh and Wynd are getting the horses ready to flee. You help lead those hounds away from Shadybrook. I'll handle things here."

Korrin sheathed his sword and said to the boy, "Always wondered what a game of hunt and hide with some Daemyn hounds would be like."

"Fun," the boy said. Then he looked at Aurell and pointed at Smoke. "He's here to help."

And with that, Korrin and the boy ran into the rainy night.

"Damn and bloody damn," Zephyr said. "More Daemyn hounds."

"We'll handle it," Aurell said.

"Yes," Zephyr replied. "By the look of things around Shadybrook, I can tell you've got everything well in hand."

Aurell put her hand on the hilt of her rapier.

"Truly?" Zephyr said, and then as if he couldn't quite comprehend her threat. "Truly?"

"If need be."

Zephyr snorted a laugh and leaned against the wall of the shrine.

"Stop it," Taebor said. "Just stop. It's not like we haven't enough problems without your pride getting in the way, Aurell." Part of him couldn't believe he was confronting her like that, and he knew he might pay the price later, but gods and goddesses, she could be so stupid sometimes. Taebor looked at Smoke, who had not moved at all throughout the exchange. "If you can help her, then help her."

"Indeed," Smoke said.

He produced a leather flask from one of the pouches on his belt, went to the Lord Morigahn, and made her drink from it. She struggled against it for a moment, but Smoke whispered to her in gentle tones and she drank.

Smoke stood. "She will recover shortly." He faced Zephyr. "I knew your father. We were not friends as such, only acquaintances, but he was a good man. He deserved better than he received at the hands of the Kingdom."

Zephyr shrugged. "Most men deserve better than they get. That seems to be life's great struggle. Everyone's running about, trying to deserve better than what they've got. Trouble is, the ones who do get it, well, they aren't usually the ones who deserve it."

"Well said," Smoke replied. "I would ask a favor, son of a good man."

"I'm eager to hear it." Zephyr's tone indicated he would rather wait a long while before hearing this favor.

"Just give her this when she revives," Smoke said, and held out a leather bag with symbols of *Galad'laman* painted all over it. "She'll need it, and it will be better if it comes from you."

"Why me?" Zephyr asked.

"So she'll trust you," Smoke said, "and then she may help you with what you have planned."

"How do you know what I have planned?"

Smoke laughed. "I know what it is like to have few friends. Men like us cannot afford to squander the friends we have."

Zephyr eyed the bag for a few moments, clicking his teeth, shrugged, and held out his hand. Smoke handed the bag over, and with no further word, Smoke walked back into the rain and the night.

It wasn't until a few moments after Smoke left, quiet moments those, that Taebor had enough time to reflect and realize that Smoke's leathers hadn't been drenched in rain. He suddenly became very glad that Korrin had decided not to fight Smoke.

"Is she really the Lord Morigahn?" Zephyr asked.

"Yes," Aurell said at the same time Taebor nodded.

"Faelin was right." Zephyr shook his head. "I didn't want to know."

"Seems you're getting more than you deserve," Taebor said. "I know exactly where you stand."

Zephyr laughed at that. "We are well met, then. What is your name?"

"Taebor."

"Well, Taebor," Zephyr said. "I think I like you. Once she wakes, I have an errand to run. Will you help me?"

"What's the errand?" Aurell asked. "We Morigahnti are not in the habit of assisting strangers."

"Calm yourself," Zephyr said. "I know Parsh and Korrin. I'm willing to wager that you have at least one gun hidden somewhere in the place you call home that you didn't bring with you tonight because of the wet and the damp. I'm also willing to wager that those weapons have a design like this."

He showed her the butt of his two-shot. Taebor squinted, and even in the dim light of the shrine's fires, he could see the craftsman's mark matching the mark of every single firearm Allifar's Fist possessed.

"What's the errand?" Taebor asked.

"I'm going to save my friend from the Brotherhood of the Night," Zephyr said. "And I'm fairly certain he's the Lord Morigahn's friend too."

"Colette," the Lord Morigahn said. "Are you there, Colette?"

THREE

Jenise returned to consciousness and slow, steady stages. Pain came first. The steady throbbing in the back of her head pulled her from a darkness that was anything but restful. Once Jenise shed that blanket over her mind, other pains came. The stiffness in her back from wine on the floor for shadow knowing how many hours spasmed and twitched. Pinpricks of cold covered her skin. The whimpering and wailing of a baby poked Jenise's ears. Together, all of that kept Jenise from sliding back into the darkness. It wasn't peaceful there. Not at all. Nor restful. But, that darkness provided a kind of distance and ignorance from all these sensations, especially that whaling baby.

Opening her eyes didn't change much in the way of darkness. Whatever had happened to knock everything about had also snuffed the candles. Jenise blinked. She blinked again. She took a breath full of dust, faint smoke, sawdust, and human waste. Please gods and goddesses let it not be hers. Better Uncle Night took her soul than suffered that. But no. Had she soiled herself, Jenise felt that would have been one of the first pains she would have noticed. Her pride would not have allowed her to ignore that aspect of her current situation.

Jenise rolled to her knees. The longer her eyes stayed open, the more she grew accustomed to the faint moonlight coming in from the shattered windows. And, all the windows were shattered. Thankfully, Jenise couldn't make out the glint of glass on the floor. The windows must have shattered outward. Jenise crawled over to the baby and picked it up. The moment she cradled the baby, it stopped whaling.

"Shadows be praised for small blessings," Jenise said.

"And pray tell me," Ida groaned, her voice sallow and strained, from the other side of the nursery, "what blessings do we have from this mess?"

Jenise peered around. The old woman lay against the far wall. Chunks of the ceiling had fallen and lay across her legs. Her breath came in shallow gasps. They were alone, Ida, the babe, and Jenise.

Jenise's face tightened to keep from wincing. How much pain must the old nurse feel right now? The last thing Ida would want is some simpering young woman sobbing over her.

Instead, Jenise asked, "Where are the children?"

"Sent them away," Ida said. "Sneak somewhere else. Somewhere that's not falling in on itself."

"Not this baby?" Jenise asked. "She couldn't help herself."

The nurse fixed Jenise with a harsh glare. "Our children know how to sneak and hide. That poor thing doesn't know when best to hush up. Even for a babe, its moods rage too fast and too loud. I couldn't risk all our little ones for one stray babe abandoned in a storm.

Jenise hated herself for agreeing with the nurse.

"Well, I can care for it now," Jenise said. "You and I, once I get your legs free."

The nurse shook her head. "My legs are gone. Even if you could manage to move this, she waved at the wreckage of Timbers on her legs, I'll never walk again. Go leave the baby and go."

Jenise opened her mouth.

Ida raised the hand and hissed Jenise quiet. "Don't be a daft fool. Go. Sneak the way we taught you. Keep hidden. Tell the story of what happened here. Tell those you meet of the Lord Morgan.

Jenise sighed. I don't remember which law it is but aren't we supposed to not let each other face danger alone? I'm not leaving you like this. I'm not leaving a baby here to die. We don't do that."

"We survive," the nurse snapped. "It's what we've done since night and day broke the world and grandfather was born. We survive. I'm dead. Uncle Night is just taking his time getting to me. He knows I'm not going anywhere. I'm sure he has other souls to collect out there that might wriggle out of his grasp if he dallies too much in finding them. With the draqons and Night Brothers wandering about, that babe will eventually call Uncle Night to you. You're still young and spry and lovely, but don't think for a moment you can dance or charm your way into Uncle Night leaving you be once he takes notice of you. Give me the babe. Do what shadows do. Survive. Whisper of this to other shadows.

Jenise made to argue. "But..." Her voice whimpered out under the nurse's unflinching gaze.

The nurse held her arms out to Jenise. "The child. Then go."

Jenise nodded, handed the baby to the nurse, and left. She didn't look back. If she had looked back, she would have stayed. Neither staying nor going was the right choice; However, and going, Jenise could honor the memory of those fallen. At least that's the lie she told herself. Just like the lie she told herself about how her tears were of grief for the two she was leaving behind and not tears of relief that she didn't have to care for Ida or the babe. Relief that she might not die tonight after all.

FOUR

Julianna blinked away the blurry haze covering her mind. For some odd reason, she recalled her fourteenth birthday. She'd been sick, and a stranger had come and made her drink something. It was the day Colette had become her maid and their friendship had begun. Only it hadn't been a real friendship. Real friendship is a bond between equals, and no matter how much they might have pretended otherwise, they had never been, nor would they ever be equals. That inequality eventually led to Colette being taken by Carmine and the Brotherhood of the Night.

These thoughts scratched new wounds into old memories. Exhaustion crushed her from speaking that terrible and wonderful miracle. Her whole body ached, and she groaned as she sat up. She found herself in the shrine of the eight lesser gods.

Next to Julianna, a deep, but distinctly feminine, voice said, "Easy."

Julianna squinted to focus her vision. Aurell knelt next to Julianna, holding a wineskin. "Drink this."

Julianna nodded and took the skin, anything to soothe her throat. She felt as if she had swallowed hot sand.

"Take as big a drink as you can," Aurell said.

Julianna put the skin to her lips and tossed it back with one big gulp. The next moment, she gasped. The liquid set her raging throat aflame.

"Breathe in through your nose," Aurell said, "and then out through your mouth."

Julianna gained enough control to do that. When the air passed out of her throat, the burning sensation faded. As it passed, a friendly warmth filled her stomach and the ache permeating her muscles and head faded. The pain didn't recede completely, but she didn't seem to care about it as much.

"What was that?" Julianna gasped.

"Aernacht whiskey," Aurell replied, "mixed with a bit of sugar and honey. It'll take the edge off the pain and cold."

"How did you know I was in pain?"

"You spoke the miracle of Shadow's Thunder. You're lucky that you can move at all."

"Where is my pack?" Julianna snapped, remembering the Tome of Shadows.

"It's here," Taebor said. He turned slightly, showing her the pack that held the *Galad'parma* on his back.

Julianna blinked at him. How could Taebor be here? She'd seen him die. Even if his wounds hadn't been fatal, Taebor shouldn't be standing here, much less have managed to make it out of the manor.

"What happened?" Questions about what had happened to Taebor could wait for later. Julianna needed to know their situation.

"Korrin and Taebor brought you here after you spoke the miracle. Now Korrin, Nathan, and the Stormcrows are leading the Daemyn hounds astray. Allifar and Wynd should have the horses ready for us to retreat soon."

"What about Faelin?" Julianna asked.

Aurell's shoulders slumped, and she would not meet Julianna's gaze.

"Taebor?"

The young man flinched as if she had slapped him, but he would not answer. He shuffled a little further away.

"Where is Faelin?" Julianna demanded.

"He was captured," a new, somewhat familiar, voice replied. Faelin's odd friend Zephyr leaned against the wall.

"How?" Julianna asked.

"He gave himself over to the Brotherhood so Korrin and I could get you to safety," Taebor said, unable to meet her gaze.

Without hesitation, Julianna said, "We have to go after him."

"That's exactly what they want," Aurell replied. "If we go after him, we're as good as delivering you into their hands. Faelin gave himself up so you could escape. You're too important to risk for anyone."

Upon first consideration, Aurell was right. Julianna was the Lord Morigahn. That meant she had the full support of the Morigahnti. What was one man compared to that? Thus far, she'd only met seven Morigahnti. Were they loyal to her? Were any of them? She could not know. Not for certain. *If* she had the full support of the Morigahnti, her title might mean something. Thus far, even with the supposed power of the Lord Morigahn at her command, she felt helpless. She'd only come this far with Faelin's help.

"No," Julianna whispered to herself. "I'm going after him."

She possessed power. The miracle she'd spoken in the kitchen confirmed that. When she first met Allifar, she demanded that he answer her questions, and he'd done so without question. He'd submitted himself to Julianna's orders when the fighting first started. She may have made mistakes, but she was alive and could learn from anything that did not kill her. It was time for her to begin acting like a Lord Morigahn. Faelin could have abandoned her, but instead, he'd cared for her and kept her safe. She owed him *kostota*.

"The Morigahnti do not flee from battle," Julianna said, quoting Grandfather Shadow's Seventh Law. "If you are afraid to die, you are already dead. Nothing is more honorable than victory."

"Excuse me," Zephyr said. "Not that I'm a believer of your ways, but doesn't achieving a victory sort of rely on understanding your enemy's desires?"

Julianna looked at Zephyer. "What?"

"He's right, Lord Morigahn," Taebor said. "In studying the chronicles, I learned that many previous Lords Morigahn avoided battle just to thwart their enemy's plans. If they are trying to get to you by using Faelin as bait, fleeing will rob them of the opportunity to capture you. That is how we achieve victory here."

"A Morigahnti does not let a brother face danger alone," Julianna quoted from the Third Law. "The Morigahnti succeed together in a greater whole. You are your brother's keeper."

"Faelin is not a Morigahnti," Aurell said.

"Truly?" Zephyr asked. "You're going to make that distinction?" He faced Julianna. "We're not going to leave Faelin to his fate. I'll go after him. I'm better suited. You stay here and command your Morigahnti. I'll have Faelin back by morning."

"I'm going too," Taebor said.

"Are you insane?" Aurell growled.

Taebor turned on her. The fear Julianna remembered seeing in his eyes was gone. Now he met Aurell's fierce gaze with a steady, unblinking confidence. Julianna considered intervening but decided to let them play this out.

"No." Taebor spoke with a soft tone that sounded almost at peace. "I owe him *kostota*, more than you can understand."

"You are sworn to Allifar and the Thaedus family."

"I am Morigahnti, sworn to Grandfather Shadow and the Lord Morigahn. And once, in the time of stories and legends we hope to become, the Morigahnti defended the *kansati* from threats like the Brotherhood of the Night. Faelin is a *kansa* with a truer heart than any three Morigahnti I know, and that includes Allifar, Parsh, and Korrin."

Aurell's mouth hung open. Julianna glanced between them. Taebor carried himself as if he were another man. He stood tall, his eyes unflinching. Aurell seemed unsure of herself; she leaned back on her heels, looking at Taebor as if judging this sudden display of backbone.

Julianna looked at Zephyr. "Why should I allow you to take one of my Morigahnti in my place?"

"Because rescuing Faelin is going to be a lot harder for me if I have to face the Daemyn hounds and a few Night Adepts by myself," Zephyr said. "Oh, and because I have this."

He tossed a leather bag at her. Dark symbols of *Galad'laman* covered the thing. The symbols indicated enchantments of secrets and knowledge. Julianna closed her eyes and sifted through her knowledge of *Galad'laman* to see what those symbols meant. After a moment, she decided someone had been trying to keep whatever was inside hidden from prying miracles.

She opened it. A black cloth lay within. She touched it. It wasn't cloth, but rather it was finely woven metal. Grandfather Shadow's Dominions sang within it at her touch. She drew the thing out of the bag. It was a *Galad'fana* charged with power, true divine power, as if this strange metal cloth was a conduit directly to Grandfather Shadow's celestial realm. Khellan's *Galad'fana*, which had called to her to speak miracles, seemed such a bland and plain thing now.

"Where did you get this?" Julianna asked.

"A man called Smoke gave it to him to give to you," Taebor said.

Again, Julianna's mind harkened back to her fourteenth birthday, only more clearly this time. A man dressed in Dosahan leathers had come and made her drink something, just as he had a few moments ago. It seemed Smoke had been watching and aiding Julianna for much longer than she realized.

Julianna stood and removed Khellan's *Galad'fana* from her shoulders. Then she draped this new *Galad'fana*, this one felt truer and more real than anything she'd ever touched in her life, over her head and shoulders like a hood. She left her face uncovered. True, it was tradition for Morigahnti to cover their faces when going into battle, but tradition had not gained the Morigahnti any ground in freeing Koma from the Kingdom of the Sun. The only way Julianna was going to truly survive as the Lord Morigahn was to free Koma. To do that, they were all going to have to break from tradition.

"Taebor," Julianna said, "come here."

Taebor stepped in front of Julianna. She wrapped Khellan's *Galad'fana* around his head and shoulders, masking his face.

"If you are to serve Grandfather Shadow," Julianna said, "you shall do it as a true Morigahnti, with the ability to speak miracles. Do not be foolish with your power, but it might mean the difference between victory and defeat."

"Yes, Lord Morigahn," Taebor said, saluting her.

"Go," Julianna said. "Rescue Faelin and return."

"Our place is by your side," Aurell said, "not running off after a *kansa* who may already be dead."

"It is not your place to command the Lord Morigahn, Aurell," Taebor said. "It is her place to command you."

Aurell opened her mouth, then closed it and turned away from them. She sighed.

"You're right," she spoke softly, just loud enough to be heard over the beating rain and howling wind. "I have spoken out of place. Please forgive me, Lord Morigahn. I will follow whatever orders you command."

"Good," Julianna said. "We do not have time for bickering and infighting. I understand your desire to defend and protect me, but every moment you waste is a moment Faelin nears death or worse. Please trust me to make it halfway across Shadybrook to Allifar and the others."

"She speaks sense," Zephyr said. "Except Faelin's not going to be dead yet, not for a good long while. I'm sure they plan to use him against this sweet lady here, to see how far she'll put herself out for him. Oh, and they'll torture him to see what secrets he remembers from his Morigahnti family."

Both Taebor and Aurell stiffened at Zephyr's flippant familiarity.

"Peace," Julianna said. "He's testing you, as many people will. Do not let them bait you."

"Yes, Lord Morigahn," Aurell and Taebor said together.

"Now," Zephyr said. "If we're going to do this, you must follow me. I may not be a Morigahnti, but I'm a smuggler by trade, and I've lived free selling guns to the Kingdom's enemies for some time. You may think you know best from whatever special things being a Morigahnti gives you. You don't. Listen to me, and we will all make it back with Faelin alive. The moment you start thinking you know more about this than I do and ignore me is the moment people start dying. And I *will* absolutely let you die in my place if you do something stupid. Understood?"

Aurell and Taebor nodded.

"Good," Zephyr said. "Then we'd best be off before Allifar or Parsh come and stop us." Then he added with a wild grin, "One more grand adventure with Faelin vara"Traejyn at the center of it."

"What do you mean by that?" Julianna asked.

Zephyr's smile widened. "Ask Faelin about it. It's more his story than mine. Like tonight, oh who am I kidding, like most of my life, once again I'm caught up in events so far beyond me that all I can do is laugh."

Was the man mad? He was leading a group of three against an unknown number of Nightbrothers, Draqons, Daemyn hounds, and at least two Adepts of Old Uncle Night. Well, if Zephyr was mad, Julianna must be even crazier. She was the one letting them go, knowing that some of them might not return. But she had to trust in Zephyr's expertise. If he was the smuggler he claimed to be, they at least had a chance.

"Do you have any ideas about what to do once we get there?" Julianna heard Aurell ask as the three left the shrine.

"Not in the faintest," she heard Zephyr say. "But I'll think of something. I always do."

"Taebor," Julianna said.

"Lord Morigahn?" the young man responded, face lighting up.

"Leave my pack," Julianna said. "I should keep the *Galad'parma* with me."

Taebor saluted, slid the pack off his shoulders, and handed it to Julianna. Aurell saluted as well. Zephyr just winked at her. Winked. At the Lord Morigahn. And then the three of them left.

Julianna shook her head at that thought. Amongst all this death and chaos, he'd been either flippant or flirtatious with a woman who, for all intents, was the First Adept of Grandfather Shadow for the Komati. She didn't know whether to be flattered or outraged. As it was, Zephyr certainly was lucky that neither Aurell nor Taebor had seen that, especially Aurell.

She looked into the pack and saw not only the *Galad'parma* but also the hilt of the Faerii steel dagger Faelin had taken from the Inquisitor they'd fought just before the Lords of Judgment had remade her soul.

A few moments after they left, Julianna left the shrine herself. She headed to the manor house first, to attend to anyone she might have injured when she spoke her miracle. Oddly, the wind and the rain did not cut into her with the same biting cold that seemed to affect everyone else, and Julianna allowed herself the faintest wisp of a smile. For the first time since Grandfather Shadow marked her, she was directing the course of her life.

FIVE

Novan stood at the back door of his family's cottage. Outside, the sounds of fighting had fallen quiet. Only the patter of rain against the windows and roof broke the silence. Even the wind had died down.

Who had the upper hand?

Surely with the Lord Morigahn here unspeaking miracles, the Brotherhood of the Night stood no chance at all. Novan didn't need a Galad'fana to tell him all the miracles being spoken in Shadybrook that night. Not with that thunderclap shaking the cottage in the ground. Still, shadow knew how many of the Morgahnti's enemies might still be working in the dark of the moonless night. The Brotherhood of the Night was even more insidious than the Morgahnti. Also, some Morgahnti might be injured and in need of aid—the townsfolk too. What better way to be taken into count Allifar's household than to offer aid before anyone asked for it?

Novan squeezed his shoulders up to his ears and rolled them back until his shoulder blades were almost touching. This was his ritual for calming himself before undertaking a difficult task. He released his shoulder blades drew his father's rapier and opened the door.

Even without a fire in the hearth or stove, the cottage was snug and warm compared to the cold and wet that blasted noven. He stood at the threshold. Cold and wet before him. Warm and dry behind. It would be so easy to step back, close the door, and wait out the night. Safe. Safe, dry, and warm. After all, what difference could a youth, hardly old enough to be called a young man, like him make on a night like this? This was the night of miracles, gunfire, Morigahnti, Adapts, the Brotherhood of the Night, and shadow only knew what else might be lurking out there in the dark. But then, a thought tugged on the strings and Novan's mind. He should be dead, or at the very least dying, after that fall from the stairs. Whatever a difference he might make, it wouldn't be from staying safe, warm, dry, and hidden.

Novan stepped into the night and pulled the door shut after him. The wind gusted at that moment, and the door shut harder than Novan had intended. The *thunk* filled the quiet following the gust of wind.

"What was that?" some voice asked out in the darkness.

Novan looked for a place to hide. With the storm clouds still covering the sky, shadows and darkness covered Shadybrook. He took seven side steps to his right into the shadow underneath the small bit of his parents' room that formed a sitting nook facing West. Father liked to drink tea at sunset and watch the shadows from the tree line grow and grow as the sun sank behind them. To counter his quickening heart, Novan deliberately steadied his breath with the way Baron Parsh and Korrin had taught him during fighting classes.

"Breath, more than anything, can decide who wins and who dies," the baron always said.

So, Novan slowed his breath. Seven counts in. Seven counts out. Don't move until you have the perfect opportunity to attack or if you are certain an enemy has spotted you. Several breaths later, two pale somethings appeared around the corner of the neighbor's house.

Seven in. Seven out.

The forms came closer. The closer they came, even in this darkness, Novan made out the overly large skulls that leered at him, seemingly floating, bobbing slightly.

His throat closed a bit, but he regained control of himself and his breath. Seven in. Seven out.

He'd seen the like of those skulls before. Now and then during practice, Baron Parsh or Korrin would wear the skull helmets of the Brotherhood of the Night so the villagers who hoped to one day become Morgahnti could become accustomed to that site. Still, seeing it during practice sessions and seeing two here in the lull of a battle seemingly floating out there in the darkness was an entirely different matter altogether.

Novan's stomach churned. Novan's everything churned. But still, he continued what he'd been taught. Seven in. Seven out.

"Where are we going?" one of the Nightbrothers asked.

"I told you," the other replied. "I heard something."

"That doesn't mean we have to find out what it is."

"I think," said the first, "it might be an injured Morgahnti. If we find one of them, the Adepts will reward us. We might even be raised."

"If it was a Morgahnti, it wouldn't have made a noise."

"It might if it was an injured Morgahnti."

Seven in. Seven out.

"You're an idiot. I swear if—"

One of the skull heads lurched to the side and fell to the ground with the *oomph* of wind blasting out of a person's chest due to a sudden impact with the ground.

"You damn and bloody idiot," the first sneered in a hiss.

The suddenness of the Nightbrother, one of the greatest terrors that, teen mothers used to get Komati children to behave, had just slipped in the mud and flattened himself against the earth struck Novan deep in his churning stomach with such a sense of buffoonery that all his tension left for just a moment, and he let out a snort of laughter.

"What was that?" asked the Nightbrother who still stood.

"That was me slipping and falling bloody fool," the other said. "Now help me up."

Novan didn't allow the first Nightbrother to respond. The young man lunged forward and let the slick mud carry the attack further than he might have otherwise reached. Korrin and Parsh regularly had the townsfolk practice in muddy terrain in the rain. After all, they served the god of storms. Foul weather was one of their subtlest weapons.

The rapier slid into the Nightbrother as easily as it did the pig corpses the Morgahnti tied to practice pells. Warriors should know the feeling of stabbing flesh, and more importantly, what it felt like to pull the blade back out again. Especially around the heart. Ribs can be tricky things, corn always told Novan after each time he had twisted the blade a bit and wedged it between two ribs. Just as he had now. He'd turned to deal with the Nightbrother in the mud just a breath too soon. The blade caught because the knight brother he'd stabbed fell at an angle away from Novan.

Practice and training took over. Novan released the rapier, completed turning, dropped to his knees, and pummeled the fallen Nightbrother with the butt of his father's two-shot pistol. Blow after blow smashed that skull face leering up at him.

"Give your god my greetings." Nova wanted so very much to sound like one of the Morgahnti—Korrin and Wynd being his favorites. However, even Novan could tell he sounded like a scared boy rather than a battle-tested warrior.

When he returned to the first Nightbrother to retrieve the rapier, Novan's hands shook. When he finally got his father's sword free, feeling the blade scraping the bones and his foot cracking the enemy's chest, Novan choked down the last bit of spirits in his stomach from earlier that evening. While he was not Morgahnti yet, one day he would be. One day he would wear a Galad'fana. He needed to teach himself, train himself, and master himself so that he would never vomit inside a Galad'fana.

Having retrieved his blade, Novan stopped and listened. Nothing. Just the wind.

Where to go? He didn't know.

The wind picked up around him, biting cold against his hands, Nose, ears, and eyelids. It might have been the wind. It might have been chance. It might have been Providence. Whatever might have been, a light flickered in one of the Manor house windows just as Novan turned to see it. The next moment, the light went out.

There. The manor house. People would need help. They would need a morganti. No fun would have to do. He headed toward the Manor and whoever might be in need. If it happened to be Kingdom forces, well, *Kostota na aen paras kostota*. Novan could vomit tomorrow.

Six

Wynd placed her hand on a Nightbrother's forehead. His eyes fluttered open. She let him regain just enough consciousness to see her leaning over him wearing a *Galad'fana*. The Nightbrother struggled, trying to pull away from her by sinking into the earth. Wynd slid her knife under his leather helm and yanked the blade across his throat. She left him, twitching as his blood soaked into the ground around him.

This was Wynd's fourth murder since Allifar had commanded her to gather all the townsfolk she could find and dispatch any Nightbrothers they found. Wynd knew the difference between killing in the heat of battle and murder. This was murder, and when it came to the Brotherhood of the Night and Kingdom Adepts, Wynd had long since made her peace with that. They deserved death for the suffering they had inflicted on Koma and its people.

She found another Nightbrother writhing in the mud, both his legs twisted at unnatural angles. Wynd deliberately stepped in a puddle, drawing his attention. The moment he saw her, she saw tears well in his eyes even behind his skull mask. Wynd pulled the Nightbrother's helmet off. His fine, smooth features suggested he was a few years younger than Wynd—perhaps an adult by Kingdom traditions, but he'd be barely two years into his apprenticeship if he had been Komati.

The Nightbrother lifted a knife. Wynd easily kicked it away.

"Please," he sobbed.

Wynd butchered his throat the same as she had the others. She wished that she didn't have to, but the Morigahnti and the Brotherhood were at war. If their roles had been reversed, she would have been offered over to a Daemyn to bear its dark spawn. The boy had made his choice, earning himself death.

"Wynd," Allifar called from the stable. "We are ready. Leave that work to the townsfolk and fetch the Lord Morigahn."

Allifar and Parsh were outside the stable, each astride a horse. They had four other animals in tow, one was Wynd's horse Kina, and the others must be for Aurell, Taebor, and the Lord Morigahn. Nathan and Korrin were still somewhere in the night, leading the Daemyn hounds astray.

Wynd jogged over to the shrine. When she stepped inside, she stopped short. Her breath caught in her throat, her stomach tied up in knots, and it felt like a hot branding iron pierced her heart.

The shrine was empty. She blinked several times to make sure that her eyes were not playing tricks on her. It was still empty. Her head turned back and forth as if trying to see where she had missed the Lord Morigahn, but the Lord Morigahn, Aurell, and Taebor were gone.

"Damn," Wynd said. "Damn, and bloody damn."

Her mind raced. She dashed to the other entrance at the back of the shrine and looked out over the fields stretching off behind Shadybrook. Wynd didn't know what she expected to see. If the Lord Morigahn wished to be hidden, the shadows would hide her, even from the Morigahnti. It didn't matter; Wynd suspected she knew where the Lord Morigahn had gone. If she had learned of Faelin's capture, the Lord Morigahn had likely convinced the others to go after him.

Wynd's chest felt hollow and a despairing panic rose within her, but before it could overwhelm her, two Nightbrothers came at her out of the darkness. Wynd drew her rapier and charged. Just before they clashed, she raised her finger, pointed at the one on her left, drew on the Dominions of Shadow and Vengeance, and screamed, "*Tuska!*"

A blast of dark energy flew from her finger and struck the Nightbrother in the face. The time for subtlety with miracles was over. His head exploded like an overripe melon. The headless body stumbled forward two more paces before pitching forward and collapsing into the mud, blood spilling out of the corpse. Wynd had intended to kill them both with miracles, but in her frustration, she channeled too much energy through her *Galad'fana.* Exhaustion crashed down on her, and only her momentum kept her charging the second Nightbrother.

Wynd shifted her balance forward a bit and raised her rapier. They were only a few paces from each other, and it was too late for him to stop. Unfortunately for him, that gave Wynd the advantage. Like most Komati who hated the Kingdom rule, Wynd carried a Bestrian rapier, making it half an arm longer than Kingdom Floraen-style rapiers and twice as long as the Brotherhood's short swords. She caught him in the center of the throat before he was anywhere close to threatening her. They slammed together with such force that Wynd's rapier sank up to the hilt.

Blood sprayed. His eyes widened with surprise then drooped to the half-open, drunken gaze of those who died of blood loss.

Wynd paused long enough to pry her blade out of his neck and turned back to find Allifar and the others riding around the shrine, rapiers drawn.

They rode up to her, and Wynd said, "The Lord Morigahn is gone,"

"What?" Allifar's shock showed on his face.

"Everyone's gone," Wynd said. "The Lord Morigahn, Aurell, or Taebor.

Allifar shook his head. "They've gone after Faelin."

"Of course they have," Parsh growled. "We should have gone after Faelin with our full strength. Now that fool girl will get herself and good Morigahnti killed."

"Well," Allifar said. "They're on foot, so they can't have gotten too far. We'll search for them."

Wynd pulled herself into Kina's saddle. All four Morigahnti kicked their heels into their horses' flanks, heading into the night after the Lord Morigahn and the others.

SEVEN

Luciano sat on his horse overlooking Shadybrook. Cadenza sat next to him astride Santo's old horse. As soon as they came to this rise, Cadenza had wanted to ride down and excommunicate everyone in the township, and by that, she meant slaughter any commoners she found and take as many nobles into custody for trial so they could suffer the Ritual of Undoing. Thank All Father Sun the rotund beast of a lady had stopped to argue with him or she would have ridden to her death. As much as Luciano despised the choices Cadenza D'Mario made as a person, she was still an Adept and Inquisitor of All Father Sun. And while her position likely came due to her proximity in relation to the Sun King, Luciano was still a man of honor. She was correct about the nobility and those who had taken up the *Galad'fana* as Morigahnti, but the common folk here should be given a chance to repent and return to their proper place in the order of precedence.

While they didn't agree on who should be excommunicated, both agreed that All Father Sun had obviously intended for them to work together in this, as he'd sent Cadenza to Luciano after she spoke a miracle to escape murder at the hands of her cousin, Carmine. They just didn't know what exactly they were supposed to do until they saw three figures leave the shrine of the lesser gods, heading for the orchards at the far edge of the community. Then, the Lord Morigahn went from the shrine to the manor house, alone. Shortly after that, the few remaining Morigahnti rode away as well.

"The All Father wants us to capture the Lord Morigahn," Luciano said.

"Are you certain we would even find the Lord Morigahn in such a place as this?" Cadenza asked, waving her hand dismissively over the town.

"As I said before, I have been tracking her."

"Your opinion," Cadenza interrupted. "Not a truth offered by the All Father. We've never heard the whisper of a rumor or a lie that a woman has ever held that title."

"Things change," Luciano said, "else we need never defend the Zenith from the Brotherhood of the Night. I assure you that girl is the Lord Morigahn, and now she is alone. Taking her will be no easy feat, even with the both of us. She is as clever and cunning as any Morigahnti you might ever face, and she commands the Dominions of Grandfather Shadow better than I've seen from many Kaesiak Adepts. If we are careful and we work together, we will be able to take her."

"Very well," Cadenza said. "Let us get down there before any of the other Morigahnti return. Once we have her, they will more than quickly fall into line."

"I doubt this notion will survive its collision with reality," Luciano said. Cadenza snorted, which Luciano ignored. "You need to spend more time hunting true Morigahnti and less time reading about them. Once we have her, we should be away as quickly as possible. These lands are not friendly to us. We cannot match a Fist for strength, never mind that we may also be facing Carmine D'Mario and his Nightbrothers."

"Very well," Cadenza said. "Let's fetch her and be away."

Luciano let out a long, slow breath and prayed to All Father Sun for the strength to endure whatever tests were coming before dawn.

EIGHT

Carmine stood with Hardin under the partial shelter of the grove of trees, huddled in their cloaks, and waiting for acknowledgment from the First Adept. A few of the tents had been hastily erected to form makeshift walls to give them some protection from the biting wind.

"What is taking him so long?" Hardin asked.

Carmine bit the inside of his cheek to keep from turning on Hardin and lashing out. The First Adept was a busy man, and he lived a highly public life. Many times he might find himself in a situation where he could not easily excuse himself quickly without drawing attention and raising questions. Hardin was too selfish to recognize anyone else's hardships or difficulties. Carmine was less than eager to speak to the First Adept. Having Cadenza learn that Carmine was an Adept of Old Uncle Night and then escape would not please the First Adept. Carmine was confident his Draqons would locate and kill her; once that happened, Carmine could report the deaths of two Adepts, leaving out the portion of Cadenza's temporary escape.

After a few more moments, the First Adept's face coalesced in the rune-marked circle.

"This had better be important," the First Adept said. "Otherwise I'm going to send you to convert the Dosahan, Hardin. By yourself."

Hardin swallowed and bowed.

That was the worst punishment any Adept could face. The Dosahan worshipped spirits and the Faerii people who had long ago departed from this world, and they had no tolerance for any gods, lesser or greater, or those who followed them. Any Adept sent into Dosahan lands either came back horribly maimed or was never heard from again.

"There are many important details I have to report, First Adept," Hardin said. "I will leave you to judge their worth. We have captured the infidel Faelin vara'Traejyn."

"Really?" The First Adept sounded hungry. "Excellent. There are many secrets the Traejyn family took to their graves. I know it will be somewhat problematic, but I want you to bring him back with you. The information he may have should prove useful once we attain the Zenith. What of this new Lord Morigahn?"

"She has met with some Morigahnti," Hardin said. "At least a full Fist, likely more, considering how easily they matched us on the field. The peasants of this area are fighting with them. We are outnumbered and outmatched by the power of miracles. We must retreat and strike another day."

"No," the First Adept commanded. "The Whisperer of Lies tells me the Komati have two heirs of their primary line. If Julianna Taraen were to join with them, it could bring all our plans to ruin. She must die. Find her and kill her."

"Your Darkness," Carmine said. "I have an idea. We could retreat just enough so that they will think we have given up. Then as they travel, we can harry them with the Brothers, Draqons, and Daemyn hounds. Eventually, they will grow too tired to speak miracles or defend themselves properly. Then we can strike."

"The Draqons follow you even with the Daemyn hounds?"

"Yes, First Adept," Carmine said. "I developed a potion that puts them completely at my command."

"Can you make more of it?" the First Adept asked.

"Of course, Your Darkness."

"Excellent," the First Adept's eyes smiled with malevolent joy. "Deal with the Morigahnti and keep a lookout for Roma. I'm sending him back to you. You will give him the recipe. I want to make as much of that potion as we can before we make our play for the Zenith. I want all the Whites here under the Brotherhood's command. Until then, kill her. I don't care how. She just needs to die before she can speak to either of the Komati heirs. If she finds them, we might as well give up Koma as we secure the Zenith."

Nine

Julianna sent silent thanks to Grandfather Shadow for the *Galad'fana* granting her the ability to see in the near darkness of the manor house. If she had to traverse this place in darkness and silence, she might not have been able to continue much beyond the kitchen and pantry. The quiet of the Dressels' manor house unsettled Julianna more than she had expected. Even in her bath and while she had been trying to sleep, noise from the celebrants had drifted up to her. Then, as the fighting with the Brotherhood of the Night erupted, Julianna was unable to remain open to her surroundings as she struggled with being kept out of the battle as well as how she might save as many people as possible. Now, as she made her way through the rooms and hallways, her vision enhanced from this *Galad'fana* Smoke had given her, by way of Zephyr, the silence seemed a physical thing, pressing down and snuffing out any noise that might dare attempt to be heard within these walls.

Thus far, Julianna had found nothing but death. Most of the rooms were empty, but in a few, she found corpses of members of the household and the elderly and young guests. The only small comfort was that none of them appeared to have died by her miracle. Rather it seemed that the Nightbrothers who had attacked her in the kitchens had served their god well before they found Julianna.

Julianna decided to brave the stairs to the third level, hoping, praying that the Nightbrothers had not come so high. These stairs were not nearly as precarious as the stairs leading to the second floor. She supposed the second floor had suffered more damage because it had been closer to where she'd spoken the miracle. Julianna did not fear that she would fall through the steps here.

At the top of the stairs, she listened. She thought she heard something from the room Mistress Dressel had given her. Julianna drew her rapier and crept down the hall.

When she reached the door, she heard someone crying. A few days ago, Julianna might have mistaken that sound for the wind, understanding that it would mostly have been her mind not wanting to accept the truth. Really, other people's tears would not have concerned her, but now these people had looked to her to protect them. She had failed. It didn't matter that she had no idea how to lead battles, all these people were still dead. She owed any survivors whatever aid she could give them.

Julianna pushed the door open. The crying stopped.

"I am the Lord Morigahn," Julianna said. "I am here to help you. The Nightbrothers and the Draqons are gone. We're going to try and evacuate the township and find you safe homes elsewhere."

No answer. Julianna closed the door but left it open just a crack. A moment after the door appeared to close, someone started sniveling. It came from under the bed.

Julianna pushed the door open again. The sniveling stopped. Julianna sheathed her sword, walked over to the bed, and knelt. The young servant girl who had helped prepare her bath huddled under the bed, curled into a ball, face buried in her arms.

"Please let me help you," Julianna said.

The girl let out a screech and hit her head on the bottom of the bed as she jumped in fright.

"You helped me earlier tonight," Julianna said. "Look at my face and know me. This house was celebrating in honor of Grandfather Shadow. I am his first chosen. I am the Lord Morigahn. I will protect you."

The girl looked at Julianna. Her hair was a mess and tears streaked her face.

"What's your name?" Julianna asked.

"Jenise."

"Well Jenise," Julianna offered her hand to the girl. "When I was seven, I watched the Brotherhood of the Night murder my mother while I escaped."

"Wha…what did you do?" Jenise asked.

Julianna smiled at the memory, not in fondness as most people do when they think of childhood memories. She smiled because she could actually recall that night now.

"I looked the Adept leading the Nightbrothers in the eye, and I told him that my father's god was going to eat his soul. My father was the Lord Morigahn. The Brotherhood of the Night killed him the same night. I couldn't do anything to save him either."

"But you're the Lord Morigahn," Jenise said.

"I am now, but even as the Lord Morigahn I don't have the power to save everyone. We must accept who we are and what we are capable of. Come with me, so that one day maybe you can become strong."

Jenise took Julianna's hand. Julianna helped pull her out from under the bed. When they stood, Jenise wrapped her arms around Julianna and buried her face in Julianna's shoulder. Julianna stroked her hair and couldn't help but smile. Of all the men who had held the title, of Lord Morigahn, how many of them had played the part of older sister pushing the horrors of the world away by stroking hair? She imagined she would bring even more change to the title of Lord Morigahn and to the Morigahnti.

"Jenise," Julianna said. "Quiet. Just for a moment."

Jenise stopped breathing. It seemed the girl was only capable of sniveling, crying, or not breathing.

In the quiet, Julianna heard it again. Something sounded like a door closing below. Jenise must have heard it too, because she gave a frightened squeak and buried her face deeper in Julianna's shoulder.

"It's all right," Julianna said. "The Nightbrothers are gone. Someone else likely needs aid. Even so, stay behind me. If it is a danger, I'll protect you."

"But, but."

The time for softness had gone. Julianna pried the girl off her.

"You have a black eye and a broken nose. Consider yourself fortunate. Many people have died tonight. More still might. Be as brave and strong as you can. You are Komati, one of the chosen people of Grandfather Shadow, born to fight and conquer. Show me something of that courage."

While Jenise did not suddenly transform into an equal of Aurell or Wynd, she did stop blubbering, mostly. It was enough. Julianna left the room, heading downstairs.

She hadn't checked all the rooms on the second floor because she'd heard Jenise and gone to investigate. Now, Julianna heard soft sounds coming from the second door on the right. She couldn't make them out so she crept closer, signaling Jenise to stay at the stairs and to stay quiet.

When she reached the door, Julianna listened and still couldn't make out what the noise was. Julianna gritted her teeth as she slowly turned the knob and pushed the door open just enough to peek into the room.

Six tiny creatures that might have once been dogs chewed at various parts of Mistress Dressel. Dressel's face looked right at the doorway, lifeless eyes staring at Julianna, devoid of any color. Only a short time ago, those eyes had been full of life and love and laughter. Now, not only was Gillaen Dressel dead, but the soul that was so full of the joy of existence would never again pass through the cycle of Life, Death, and Rebirth.

Julianna's stomach churned at the sight, and she had to tighten every muscle in her throat, chest, and stomach to keep from vomiting.

"Shades and damnation."

Two of the vile little beasts eating Mistress Dressel looked up from their meal with eyes burning a sickly greenish-yellow color. They barked, which got the attention of the others. All six looked at Julianna and growled. The floor seemed to vibrate in time with that rumble.

Faster than Julianna would have even dreamed possible, one of the things leaped at the door. Startled, Julianna stumbled back and the door opened a bit more, just enough for the beast to wedge its clawed paw between the door and the frame.

Julianna recovered from her fright—she and Faelin had faced one of these before, one much larger and much more frightening. She grabbed the doorknob and pulled the door shut. Or, at least she tried to. Before closing, the door met resistance from the Daemyn hound's tiny leg. The sound of bones snapping on impact crawled over Julianna's skin as if it had become a physical thing trying to get inside her. The thing yelped and snarled in pain, but its leg was too sturdy. A simple door wouldn't be able to rip through its flesh and muscle. In a few moments, even the bones would knit back together.

The other Daemyn hounds were scratching at the door, barking and growling.

Struggling to keep the door closed as tight as she could with her right hand, Julianna reached under her frock coat with her left and drew her mother's knife. She sliced down the door with the red-bladed weapon, cutting two legs and severing one completely. A chorus of pained howling and yelping came from the other side of the door. Julianna smiled and closed the door.

For a moment, they had a reprieve.

Julianna heard running footsteps scratching the floor beyond the door. Something hit the door so that it shook in the frame. Well, it would take them quite a while to break through the door.

Julianna turned to Jenise. "We should go."

Jenise wasn't looking at Julianna. She was staring at the door, mouth hanging open.

Julianna turned. The doorknob was lowering. Of course, the vile little things weren't trying to break through the door. As much as they might resemble dogs, Daemyn hounds possessed the intellect and cunning of the Daemyns that possessed them.

"Jenise," Julianna said, "we need to run."

Jenise fled *up* the stairs, her scream making it obvious where she was going.

"Shades of damnation," Julianna swore and followed.

Hopefully, the Morigahnti would hear the wailing and come to help.

TEN

Wind howled and whistled through the manor. Now and then, something clacked or banged in some distant room. Each time, Novan spun around or his head whipped to one side or the other so his ears could strain and try and discern whether the sound came from someone else carelessly moving through the manner, or if it was just another noise brought on by the power of the Lord Morgan's miracle.

Room by room, Novan crept through the first floor and found it empty. The stairs beckoned, but he hesitated—only for a few moments though. Between two staircases and the soaked earth beneath most windows, Novan felt he wouldn't be trapped on the second floor, even if he met a whole squad of knight brothers. The third floor was a different matter altogether.

"So, I won't go on the third floor," Novan said to himself.

He made his way to the kitchen and went up the stairs next to the pantry. If the enemy had anyone guarding the back stairs, they likely wouldn't be guarding them as heavily. Servants weren't soldiers, nobles, or Morgahnti, at least not usually. If anything, a Nightbrother guard would be waiting for stragglers leaving rather than anyone returning. Novan's feet made hardly a sound going up the stairs. The one time a step groaned under his weight, the noise fit right in with all the sounds resonating randomly through the walls and rooms. At the top of the stairs, no one was waiting for Novan or anyone else, so he continued along the upstairs servants' hall. Each door in the servants' hall, hidden on the opposite side, had a single eye hole looking into the room beyond and not so as not to interrupt the occupants in a private or intimate moment. The dark of night made it near impossible to discern if anyone was hiding in any of the rooms, until Novan looked into the fourth room. Faint light from the window showed a man, well someone somewhat broad-shouldered like a man, kneeling over another body.

Novan pushed the servants' door open. He stopped breathing and prayed the door remained silent and as such were intended, the better to give the illusion of nonexistence. Instead of drawing his rapier Novan pulled the two-shot pistol from his belt, pointed at the stranger's head, and cocked back the hammer for the left barrel. In the near silence of that small sitting room, the click might as well have been a full gunshot.

And the man in front of Novan flinched but otherwise did not immediately move. Novan kept the gun aimed at the man's head and allowed himself to breathe again. His hands steadied, and Novan shifted his feet for a bit more balanced position. A moment later, the man raised his hands but otherwise remained kneeling.

"This poor soul was dead when I got here," the man whispered. "I take it that since you haven't shot me, you have a reason for keeping me alive."

"Answers," Novan said. "Who are you? And no lies." To emphasize this, Novan cocked the hammer for the two shots right barrel.

"No lies is it?" The stranger didn't laugh, but his tone of voice suggested he found this turn of events rather humorous. "Very well. Call me Symond. I am currently suffering the abysmal fate of traveling and fighting with a troop of the Brotherhood of the Night. Even though I have ample opportunities to walk different paths, they have a young lady with them. I am biding my time so as to help her escape before they force her into breeding with the daemyn. So, you can shoot me if you want, but you'll be condemning that girl to a fate worse than excommunication.

Oddly, Novan believed him.

"So what do we do?" Novan's voice did not crack as it had with the Nightbrothers he had killed earlier.

"I suppose that depends on you," the stranger said.

"How many people have you killed?" Novan asked.

"Many," the stranger replied. "I tried to keep count when I was younger, but that number grows beyond the mind's capacity to contain. However, I speak true when I say I've killed no one this night."

Novan took in the man's words. The stranger moved not at all and spoke softly and evenly. Opposite desires waged a war in Novan's mind.

"What are you doing in the manor house?" Novan asked.

The stranger's right arm moved ever so slowly toward a dark lump on the floor, a lump Novan hadn't noticed before. When the stranger's hand reached this lump, the stranger lifted a bottle out of a satchel. Now that Novan saw them both, his mind connected them.

"You're stealing our spirits?" Novan asked

"I am forced into the Brotherhood of Night by birth and circumstances," the stranger said. "I've got to keep my spirits up anyway I can."

Novan stood behind the stranger and looked between the bottle, the satchel, and back to the back of the stranger's head. The lad who hoped to become a Morigahnti had not a single notion of what to do with this situation. The moment lingered on and on.

"Look," the stranger said at last. "Either shoot me and be about your business, or just go about your business and let me be about mine. And remember, the Nightbrothers have a Komati lady with no one to care after her but me."

Novan clenched his teeth so he wouldn't clench his fists and squeeze the trigger.

The stranger went back to rummaging about the body on the floor.

"Stop," Novan hissed.

"Alright," the stranger replied. "I found what I was looking for." He held up a flask and shook it so the contents inside swished about.

At the absurdity of this situation, Novan could not even incredulously stammer out a question about this obsession with stealing spirits.

Somewhere off in another part of the manor house, a scream erupted.

"Oh my." The stranger's tone didn't shift at all. "Someone is in trouble." How could anyone be so insufferably calm in a situation like this? "Sounded like a lady. She might need help. But at least you're stopping me from stealing a dead man's spirits."

Novan struggled to keep from squeezing the trigger. Was this man purposely trying to goad Novan into killing him? Should Novan oblige him? But that would alert everyone in the house that Novan was here with a firearm. Could Novan murder a man with his back turned? He knew what Korrin and Baron Parsh would say.

"Bah," Novan snapped, turned, and headed in search of whoever had screamed.

ELEVEN

Faelin closed his eyes and slowed his breathing, removing the discomfort of the ropes cutting into his wrists and the throbbing on the side of his head where Carmine's Red Draqon had struck him. He hadn't practiced this technique in over a year, not since he'd stopped fighting in Heidenmarch, and so it had taken him quite a while to relax enough to focus his hearing in one direction. Luckily, Carmine and the other Night Adept had waited even longer for the First Adept of Old Uncle Night to acknowledge and speak to them. Still pretending to be unconscious, Faelin overheard everything Carmine and his master had shared with the First Adept, including their plans for himself, Julianna, and the two heirs.

Faelin's heart raced with the joy of knowing that there were two living heirs to the Throne of the Seven Mountains, something even his Father hadn't known for certain. If Julianna could find those two siblings and bring them forward, the Morigahnti, all of the Morigahnti, just might rally behind them, along with enough of the nobles to throw off the yoke of Kingdom tyranny. But having this information was useless as long as he remained Carmine's prisoner or they killed him.

Faelin opened his eyes and took stock of the situation. Two Reds stood guard over him, and two more patrolled through the trees. Two Daemyn hounds were chained to a tree perhaps thirty paces away. He couldn't get an exact count on the Nightbrothers, but he suspected at least a dozen in the camp.

One of the Daemyn hounds started barking. Nightbrothers jumped up, alert and looking for a threat. Faelin also scanned the area; any threat to the Brotherhood might be a friend to him.

"There it is." One of the Brothers pointed to a Stormcrow on a branch far out of reach.

Seeing this Stormcrow made escape less urgent. If the Stormcrows had overheard everything the Adepts had said. Then again, maybe The Stormcraw didn't need to have heard. They hadn't gagged Faelin.

"*Galad Setseman'Vuori aen Keisari ja aen Tsumari'osa ovat'sa varhata,*" Faelin yelled. "*Aen Tzizma'Veljekset tunists. Varoita aen Morigahnti.*"

Several Brothers took aim with their crossbows. The Stormcrow flapped its wings and rose from the branch. Bolts sailed past the Stormcrow as it wove through the air.

Carmine stomped over to Faelin. "What did you tell it?"

Faelin smiled and considered what Damian might say right now. "I didn't tell it anything. I said I can't believe you Nightbrothers haven't begun to violate each other's backsides yet. Isn't that how you pay homage to the god of *darkness*?"

Carmine slammed the back of Faelin's head into the tree six times. Black spots of pain danced across Faelin's vision. He felt blood trickling down the back of his neck, and he was fairly certain he'd felt his skull crack a bit.

"Untie me and see how easy that is," Faelin groaned.

He wasn't sure he formed all the words completely, but when Carmine snarled, "Bastard!" Faelin knew he'd gotten the point across.

Time to rub salt on the wound. Faelin managed the best grin he could.

"Bastard? Is that supposed to hurt me? My grandfather, uncles, and brothers called me that every day. At least my blood is pure Komati and not polluted with Floraen filth. My mother knew the love of a true-born Lord of the Shadows, while your mother was a whore who tried to sell herself for the tiniest climb in precedence, and only got two unmarriageable sons for her trouble. Oh, I'm sorry. It's *one* unmarriageable son now, isn't it?"

Carmine stomped between Faelin's legs so hard that Faelin vomited all over himself and on Carmine's boots. Faelin gasped for breath. Carmine stalked away, shouting orders. Pain fogged over Faelin's head so much that he couldn't hear what the orders were—likely something to do with the Stormcrow, not that they had any hope of catching it.

Faelin prayed that he'd made Carmine mad enough to slip up with the other Adept. It was plain to see that the other one was Carmine's superior and that Carmine didn't like him at all. Faelin wanted to add to the tension and perhaps put the two Night Adepts even more at odds, giving the Morigahnti a chance to escape.

Later, Faelin wasn't sure how much later, something pulled on the ropes that bound him to the tree.

"Don't worry," a gruff voice whispered. "Help is here."

"Who?" Faelin groaned.

"It seems that you did not heed my warning," the voice answered.

"Razka?"

"Yes. Now hold still while I untie you."

Hope rose in Faelin's heart. Razka's presence meant the tide might shift in Julianna's favor.

"Will you help—"

"Absolutely not," Razka said with a low growl. "I will not help the Morigahnti."

"But—"

"You are not Morigahnti. Now be quiet. You'll be free in a moment."

Now that's a comfort, Faelin thought. *I'm in no condition to make use of that.*

TWELVE

Symond let himself relax, that was, really relax. Keeping up the masque of careless nonchalance was exhausting. His arms sagged. His neck ached even after it slumped forward. His breath quickened, as if to make up for all the breaths Symond didn't take when the committee youth had that firearm pointed at the back of his head.

Before this night, Symond wouldn't have needed to pretend to be at ease. He would have trusted in the protection offered by his celestial and infernal bloodlines. Of all the copious injuries inflicted upon his person by others in his life, Symond had never been shot by a firearm. Crossbows and bows aplenty. Firearm, never. Still, he never felt any greater concern for them other than that he disliked pain. However, he'd always assumed that an injury caused by a firearm would just heal just like any other wound. But then...

Symond pulled the cork from the flask and swallowed a generous helping of decent Brandy.

But then... that man in the wagon shot a daemyn hound and actually injured the creature. Seriously injured the creature. For all Symond knew, the exploding wagon destroyed the creature. If a firearm could injure a daemyn hound, what might a firearm do to him?

Symond decided to settle his churning guts with another swallow of decent brandy. It did a job of settling his stomach and also soothing his frayed nerves.

Elsewhere in the manor, Symond heard crashes and screams. They sounded as if they were on this floor, over by the main staircase out the door that Symond had used to enter this room. The same door the Komati youth had used to leave the room. And now Symond saw another door opposite the first, a door he would have never noticed if not for the lad. Well, never one to waste a gift, Symond tucked the flask into his coat pocket, hefted the sack of bottles onto his shoulder, and left with the servants' door the youth had used to sneak up on him so unexpectedly.

At the end of the thin passage, Symond took the stairs up. The third floor had a few more rooms. He didn't expect to find anyone still alive, but the revelers might have left some drink behind once the fighting had started. When he reached the top of the stairs, some strange sensation crawled across his skin. His leather armor felt too constricting. It was like being close to a daemyn hound but worse, so much worse.

Symond emptied the brandy in the flask into his stomach. It would take a bit to spread into his body, but better a little late than not at all.

Somewhere down the hall, a baby fussed. Not crying as much

as not happy, possibly on the verge of crying. Then, someone made hushing and comforting coups at the baby.

Symond took each step down the hallway timidly and gingerly. The baby continued to fuss. The other voice continued to try and comfort the child. The closer Symond got to the door at the end of the hall, the more he could make out the words.

"It's all right. I know you're cold, but it will be over soon. I don't have milk. No. No. This Tavern has been dry many years." A soft chuckle came after that, but not the kind that comes from someone thinking something is actually funny. This was someone in a hopeless moment trying to grasp onto any small sliver of light or joy.

Symond went to the door at the end of the hall and pushed it open. An old woman sat against a wall. A fallen timber from the ceiling had crushed both her legs. A baby—

"Lords and Princess," Symond spat when he saw the thing.

It was not a thing, not a baby. Oh, it wore the form of a baby, but something far more vile and sinister lurked beneath the surface of that deceiving shell.

The old woman took her gaze from the baby and placed it upon Symond.

"Curse you," the woman said. "May the grandfather give you all the knowledge you keep hidden from yourself and force you to know yourself."

"Dear lady," Symond said. Your grandfather cannot give me much more than I already know. Where did the child come from?"

May the Stormcrews flay your mind, and the Stormseekers rend your corpse, all while the Lord Morigahn keeps you alive as long as she can keep you suffering.

Symond had always admired the way Komati and Morigahnti phrased a curse or an insult.

From the look of her, the lady might live as long as one more day, perhaps a bit longer. But her journey to death would be a painful one. And, that is, if the child didn't affect her or one of the hounds found her. Then, she would suffer a fate so much worse than merely dying.

Somewhere else in the house, someone or something was fighting someone or something else, but Symond couldn't bring himself to either care or worry about that. This thing, whatever might be in that shell, was worse than anything Symond had ever known.

The old woman continued making hushing noises. Each time her comforting the child stopped, the child thing would whimper again. Each time the old woman took longer and longer to respond, and her comforting grew shorter and shorter. Each time she stopped, she looked older and older. She seemed to have completely forgotten about Symond.

With only the hesitation of getting closer to the child thing, Symond crossed the room with purposeful strides and killed the old woman with a swift knife thrust to the eye and into her brain. It might be considered gruesome by many, but truly, it was so quick that she wouldn't suffer—not like the lingering wasting with the timber across her legs and the child thing draining away what little life she had left.

"May your next life end better than this one," Symond said.

When the old woman died, the child went silent. Its eyes opened fully, and it looked directly at Symond, drew in a deep breath, opened its mouth wide, and...

Symond shoved a cork from the now-empty flask into the creature's mouth. Deep into the creature's mouth. So deep, the whale couldn't escape as anything louder than a whimpering wine.

Thank all the gods and goddesses that Symond now knew about the servant stairs. He could escape with the spirits and be away from this thing, this creature, this abomination that rankled at his skin. He did not believe for a second that it would perish, but maybe, just maybe one of the inquisitors would find it when they came to investigate what had happened in this Township. In the meantime, Symond planned to sneak out of this town and get rather drunk on his way back to the Nightbrothers camp.

THIRTEEN

The trouble with Daemyn hounds, Julianna decided, was that they could think their way around problems that would confound normal dogs—things like doors. She had no idea how they'd done it, but that pack of Daemyn puppies had managed to get the door open, and snarling and growling, were coming for her and Jenise.

It didn't help that once the Daemyn hounds escaped the room Jenise had panicked to the point of hysteria and retreated upstairs rather than the wiser choice of going downstairs where she wouldn't be trapped.

Julianna chased Jenise up the stairs and back into the room where she'd first found the girl. Jenise wept hysterically as she tried to scramble back underneath the bed.

For just a moment, Julianna considered using her mother's dagger on Jenise, just to give the girl a quick death and a chance to be reborn. She suppressed the urge. Instead, Julianna shut the door and looked at the wardrobe on the far side of the room.

"*Galadti laeta aen kaepin ovean aen vast*," Julianna spoke, channeling the Dominions of Shadows and Balance through the *Galad'fana.*

Her new *Galad'fana* hummed the power of Shadows and Balance. It seemed every shadow in the room, created from the fires still burning in the street outside, replied with a quiet, almost silent, "*Ji, Morigahn'uljas*," before reaching out, picking up the wardrobe, and placing it in front of the door.

Julianna smiled, and not a small smile that she'd become accustomed to in the days since being marked; a wide, pleased grin split her face. While Julianna felt slightly more tired than she'd been before speaking the miracle, she did not suffer the crushing exhaustion that she expected. This changed her calculations. Even though miracles would not touch the Daemyn hounds, they could prove useful in other ways.

The Daemyns howled and barked once she spoke the miracle, as she suspected they would, smelling the divine energy. It didn't matter overly much; if Faelin was correct, the hounds should be able to smell the *Galad'fana* at this range. Now was the time to do anything she could to survive.

Now that the door was secure, Julianna grabbed a handful of cloth where Jenise's skirt and bodice met and pulled the girl to her feet.

"Stop!" Julianna snapped. "I swore to protect you, but if you keep acting the idiot, I'll leave you to die. This is your last chance. Do you understand?"

Had Faelin felt like this only a few short hours ago while he had admonished Julianna in this very room for her own foolish choices?

"Ye...ye...yes," Jenise said.

"Good." Julianna spoke softer now, though maintaining a tone of firm command. "You're going to need to be brave." Julianna turned to face the door and knelt. She raised her dagger, waiting for the Daemyn hounds to come through the door. "Look in my pack."

Julianna felt Janice open the pack.

"Do you see the knife?"

"Yes," Jenise answered.

The hounds started scratching and barking at the door. Jenise yelped.

"It's special. Iit can hurt those creatures coming after us."

"I can't. I don't know how to fight."

"Take the knife," Julianna ordered. "The Daemyn hounds will know what it is. They will be afraid of it. I don't plan on having you fight them, but they will hesitate if you have it. That will give me time to help you."

Jenise sniffed. "Alright"

Julianna stood and turned to Janise. Seeing the tear-stained face, cheeks, and forehead tense with worry, Julianna realized that she was still making foolish choices. She imagined Faelin berating her if Zephyr and the Morigahnti managed to save him. What had she been thinking, exploring by herself without any kind of guard?

"Stupid girl," Julianna said.

Jenise stepped away from Julianna, mouth hanging open. "But—"

"Not you," Julianna said. "I'm speaking about myself."

Jenise opened her mouth again, but Julianna waved her quiet

"I need to start thinking more clearly." Julianna rubbed her free hand through her hair and pressed at the side of her head, rubbing her temple. The first thing they had to do was get away from those hounds, and that meant first getting off this floor. "Is there another stairway?"

Jenise nodded. "For the servants. At the far end of the floor."

"Is there another way to get there from here?"

"We can go through the bathing room and sneak around those things."

"Good. Let's go, but quietly."

They crept to the door that led into the bathing room.

Julianna peeked in.

The way was clear, though the door was off one of its hinges, likely due to her speaking the miracle of Shadow's Thunder. On the far side of the room, a narrow door tucked into a corner and beckoned to Julianna. This door was normally hidden behind a screen, but the screen had been knocked over. Most rooms in manors, palaces, and country homes had a myriad of doors and passageways that lay beyond doors like this one. It was how servants moved through the house quickly without disturbing guests.

If they could make it to that hallway, it would lead them right to the stairs Jenise had mentioned.

"Let's go," Julianna whispered, and pointed to the servants' door.

Quietly as they could, they tiptoed across the bathing room. Julianna held her breath for fear of being heard. To her amazement, Jenise kept her sniveling and whimpering under control. Even if the girl was still acting up behind Julianna, she was quiet enough for the winds outside to mask her.

When they reached halfway across the room, the scratching on the door behind them stopped. Julianna froze. For a brief moment, she considered jumping out the window, but at this height that would only serve to shatter their legs at best, making them easy prey for the hounds.

In the quiet moment that followed, Julianna realized that the most foolish thing to do at that moment was to stop moving. The Daemyn hounds weren't tracking her like dogs; they would be tracking her *Galad'fana*, especially now that she'd recently spoken a miracle through it.

"Go," Julianna hissed, as she reached back and grabbed Jenise. "Now."

Julianna pulled Jenise past her and shoved the servant girl toward the door leading to their escape.

As they sprinted toward the door, the scurry of claws scraping wood came from the hall outside. Just as Jenise pulled the door open, two of the Daemyn hounds came through the door.

Hardly thinking, Julianna reached through the *Galad'fana* for Shadows and Balance, *"Keira aen amae yh!"*

Just as they had when she'd wished the wardrobe moved, the shadows in this room reached out and grabbed the bathtub and flipped it over onto the two Daemyn hounds. The room echoed with the *clang* of the tub crashing to the floor. Two smaller *thuds* followed as the Daemyn hounds collided with the wall of their new prison.

Julianna didn't have time to rejoice in her success. A third hound hopped onto the overturned tub and leaped at Julianna. Jenise screamed. Julianna took a breath and judged its flight as she would an incoming rapier thrust. Her cousin Marcus's words bubbled up from her memory: *It's not enough to know the attack is coming, you must know the angle of your opponent's attack. Then, and only then, should you consider countering.* And so she waited. Compared to a rapier thrust, the thing came at her with clumsy slowness.

At the last moment, when it would be too late for the Daemyn hound to twist, Julianna sidestepped. The hound only managed to crane its neck to watch her stab it. She thrust the dagger like a rapier. The blade slid easily into the hound's side, piercing it completely. The Daemyn's body went limp on the blade.

More growling came from the door. The last three Daemyn hounds stalked into the bathing room. They split apart, one coming through the center of the room while the other two flanked them. The two under the bathtub sounded as if they were trying to claw through the floor.

Flicking her arm and wrist, Julianna dislodged the one she'd just killed. She moved the tip back and forth at each of the three hounds coming toward her.

"Get in the hall," Julianna said.

"I am," Jenise wailed from further back than Julianna expected.

Well, that was something at least. Good sense seemed to be breaking through the girl's panic.

Julianna bolted for the door. She heard the scramble of claws on the floor. When she made it to the servants' passage, Julianna grabbed the doorknob.

"Tuo aen amae," she spoke, *"onyt!"*

The bathtub lurched and slid past the charging Daemyn hound. The instant after Julianna closed the door, the bathtub crashed into it. The Daemyn hounds might be able to open doorknobs, but Julianna expected those small things might have some difficulty getting that heavy metal tub out of the way.

Safe for the moment, Julianna blinked, waiting for the *Galad'fana* to adjust her vision. The darkness did not fade. It seemed there was no light in this passageway. Where there was no light, there could be no shadows.

Julianna reached forward to where she heard Jenise. The girl screeched again when Julianna took hold of her shoulder. Gods and goddesses, that was really beginning to grate. Julianna had to remind herself that Jenise was barely out of childhood. Not everyone could be strong when faced with circumstances such as these.

"What do we do?" Jenise whimpered.

"You've been in these passages before," Julianna said. "You've been up and down them countless times, I'm sure. I'm trusting you to get us to the stairs. Just pretend your candle or lamp went out and you have to go down and fetch a new one."

"I'll try," Jenise said.

"Grandfather Shadow, bless this girl with the knowledge she needs to lead us, your loyal servants, to safety."

With those words, Jenise stood a little straighter and started walking into the darkness, away from the scratching and snarling Daemyn hounds behind them.

FOURTEEN

Damian hid in the shadows of a thicket just on the edge of the Brotherhood of the Night's encampment. Aurell lay on Damian's right, keeping a crossbow aimed at the Nightbrothers on sentry. Taebor was scouting to see if their enemy had any patrols. The rain, which had softened while they had sought the camp, had picked up again. Finding the camp had been relatively easy. A shift in the wind had carried the sounds of it to them. Now, the patter of rain on leaves and the moaning wind through the branches hid their whispered conversation from the Nightbrothers.

A twig snapped to Damian's left. He spun. A pair of Nightbrothers were slinking through the thicket toward them.

Damian's heart hammered like a blacksmith, and he reached for his two-shot. The Nightbrothers lifted their helmets, showing the faces of Korrin and Taebor.

"Look what Taebor and I found lying around," Korrin whispered.

"What are you doing here?" Aurell asked, "and not following Allifar's orders."

Korrin grinned. "Raze told me that you were headed out this way, and it didn't take me more than half a moment to figure out what you were up to. Now Zephyr here is pretty clever, but you and Taebor are surely going to need my help if you're going to make it out of this little endeavor alive."

Damian didn't have to look back at Aurell to know she was rolling her eyes; the disgusted sigh that he'd learned came with that expression told him well enough what she was doing.

"Welcome," Damian said. "Getting those uniforms was a great thought. But Taebor hasn't been gone that long."

"I knew you needed them before you got out here," Korrin said.

"How?" Damian asked.

"He can speak prophecy," Taebor said.

"Really?"

Korrin grinned and nodded. "Sometimes I speak in a strange language, and writing comes out of my mouth and hangs in the air. Only I seem to be able to read the writing."

"Did it tell you anything about how to free Faelin without any of us getting killed or eaten by a Daemyn hound?" Damian asked.

Korrin shook his head. "You're the smart one. I thought you'd have this all planned out by now."

"Unfortunately, I don't know enough about what you can do with those things," Damian waved at the *Galad'fana* Korrin had tied around his waist. "Or them, either." He craned his neck toward the Brotherhood camp.

"Saent Kaeldyr wrote that we should make our enemy's greatest strength into their greatest liability," Taebor said.

"Not every answer in the world is found in a book," Aurell said.

"More often than you think," Damian replied. "And this time Taebor might be correct. If only we could figure out some way to turn the Daemyn hounds against the Brotherhood."

"Why can't we?" Korrin asked.

"Because whichever Night Adept summoned them controls them," Aurell said. "The hounds won't go against their master's orders."

"What does the Brotherhood use the hounds for?" Damian asked. "Aside from scaring people and eating their souls?"

"The Daemyn hounds track divine energy," Korrin replied. "Usually spoken as miracles."

"According to several texts about the Second War of the Gods, Daemyn hounds can sense the different Dominions," Taebor said. "They'll likely be sniffing for any Dominions other than Old Uncle Night's."

A plan bubbled up from the back of Damian's mind.

"Do Night Adepts channel divine power the same way you Morigahnti do?" Damian asked.

"Yes." Taebor's face brightened more and more with each question he answered. "They have different foci and Dominions, but the process is essentially the same. They channel the divine power from their god through their foci, and using Old Uncle Night's divine language, they bring the miracle into the world."

"Can the Daemyn hounds sense the Dominions in a divine foci?" Damian asked. The answer to that question might give them a way to rescue Faelin and cause a host of problems for the Night Adepts.

"What kind of question is that?" Aurell asked. "The only Dominions that can be channeled through a divine focus are the Dominions of the god that the focus is dedicated to."

"Ignore her," Damian said, waving Aurell to silence. "Just tell me."

"Maybe?" Taebor's shoulders slumped a little, and he looked at the ground. "This is where my specific knowledge has some holes. I'm extrapolating from second and third-hand sources, but I think if a miracle has been channeled through any foci recently enough, or if the Daemyn hound is close enough, it might be able to sense the difference. Of course, the more powerful the miracle, the easier it is for Daemyn hounds to sense it."

"Perfect," Damian said. "Well, maybe it's perfect if this is possible. Can one of you use Balance to transfer some of Grandfather Shadow's Dominions into their divine foci? If the

Daemyn hounds suddenly turned on their masters that would probably cause enough confusion for us to get Faelin and get away."

Taebor looked from Aurell to Korrin. "Is that even possible?"

"Of course, it's not possible," Aurell replied. "If it were, Morigahnti would be doing it all the time. Besides, miracles don't affect Daemyns and Aengyls."

"It might be possible," Korrin said, "even on Daemyns."

Damian turned to her, "Might?"

"Might." Korrin looked at someplace far away for a few moments. "If we're switching the Dominions as you suggest, the Miracle isn't against the Daemyns, it's against the foci. The Daemyns should perceive that change, just like they would perceive it if I created a wall of shadows. I don't know why, but Daemyns can perceive the effects of miracles."

"These divine, celestial, and infernal laws give me a headache," Damian said. "How possible is it?"

Korrin was still staring off into whatever faraway thing had caught his attention.

Aurell sighed again and looked at Taebor. "All right. Supposing this is truly possible. Let's put your book learning to the test. Would we use *fana* to speak of the Night Adepts' foci as well?"

"I think so," Taebor said.

"*Think?*" Aurell asked. "We're talking about a miracle no one has ever spoken before, as in *ever before*, and you *think* so?"

"I can't see why we wouldn't," Taebor said. "It's the only word we use for the *Galad'fana* and I don't know of a word we use for the foci of the other gods. So, that should be the word for them, too."

Korrin snapped back into the discussion. "Aurell, pretend it's possible and think on the wording. You're better at so many miracles than the rest of us because you adhere rigidly to the structures of *Galad'laman* as we understand it in training. Just, let yourself be a little freer with it than you usually are."

Aurell glared, but said, "I'll try. Give me a moment."

"This is brilliant," Taebor said. "If this works, it will change the way we fight the Kingdom forever. How did you even think of something like this without any understanding of how miracles work?"

"Sometimes ignorance can lead to genius," Damian replied. "I don't have all the preconceptions that you all do from your teachers forcing tradition down your throats and stifling your creativity. That's the problem with tradition: It doesn't like innovation."

"I've got it," Aurell said, and spoke a long stream of words in *Galad'laman*. Taebor and Korrin recited them back. Aurell corrected their pronunciation.

Korrin grinned wider than Damian had ever seen. "I can't decide who is crazier: Zephyr for concocting this scheme in the first place, you two for being excited about trying this, or me for even considering being a part of it."

"Now, as for—" Damian started, but Korrin's eyes rolled into the back of his head, and he spoke words in some strange tongue that made less sense to Damian than *Galad'laman*. Words formed in the air in some strange script. The worst part was that Korrin was speaking in a loud, clear voice.

"You three," a voice said in the Nightbrothers' camp, "Check on that noise."

Korrin's eyes returned to normal. He shook his head and looked at the words.

"We have to do this now," Korrin hissed. "Faelin is already free. The Brotherhood knows we're here. Daemyn hounds are attacking the Lord Morigahn."

"We're doomed," Aurell said.

"No," Damian spoke in a voice that didn't sound like either his normal voice or Zephyr's. "This will work. Go."

Damian's head swam a bit in the silence that followed him speaking. The air around them hung with the weight of an echo of the words.

Korrin stared at Damian hard. "Who are you really?"

A voice called from the camp, "I heard something else over there."

Damian bit off a retort as he scrambled through the thicket. "One of you get that miracle spoken and get those Daemyn hounds taken care of. I'm going for Faelin."

FIFTEEN

Octavio Salvatore gripped the edges of the cauldron, despite the heat giving his fingers and palms slight burns. Dante had suggested he placed the cauldron's viewing upon the thicket near Harden's camp. There, the Night adepts in the Temple of Night watching the battle of Shadybrook saw several Morgahnti and Damian Adryck concoct a scheme to rescue Faelin vara'Trajan. More to the point, Damian AdrycK had spoken a Fate.

"First Adept?" Tamez said in that voice people used when they didn't really have anything to say, but wanted to fill an awkward silence with some kind of sound, any kind of sound.

Ignoring the Kaesiak Adept, Octavio pulled his hands from the cauldron, and said, "Find me Julianna Taraejn. I want to see the Lord Morigahn.

The waters in the cauldron bubbled and steamed.

"Shall we not watch and see if the Morgahnti succeed in Harden's camp?" Ulfric asked. "After all, did not the Whisperer suggest that we watch it?"

Octavio made a sound not unlike an erratic, irritated horse. "Dante, explain it to Ulfric. Explain it as if his cousin isn't the Singer of the Moon.

The waters within the cauldron now showed the manor house. Julianna had faced Damyn hounds before and survived. Now that one of the true heirs was coming into his true mantle, Octavio wondered if he should beseech Uncle Night to turn his gaze away from her. With this new wrinkle, would it be better to know where the Lord Morigahn was and what she was about, rather than have to discover who Grandfather Shadow might mark next?

And still, his mind returned to the truth that Damian Adryck had proclaimed a fate. Had he even realized what he'd done? Was he aware that he could do so? Each possibility led to adjustments in the Brotherhood's stratagems. Did the Inquisitors know the man's significance? So many new threads to either weave into or pluck from the tapestry Octavio had spent the better part of a decade creating.

"Patience," Octavio whispered to himself.

Patience had been his greatest weapon in all of this. His predecessor and mentor had not possessed patience, at least, not as much as necessary as the brotherhood had needed at the time.

"Patience." Then, louder, to bring his mind back to a more practical reaction over Adrick and the Morgahnti's scheme, he said, "Rosella, if any of those Morigahnti survive to walk or ride away from Shadybrook, spread the word that the Night Adepts need to transfer their divine foci from their mantles and into their small clothes.".

Sixteen

Grandfather Shadow sat on the very top of the manor house and looked out through the storms and shadows all throughout Shadybrook and its surroundings. He saw the brilliance of Damian Adryck, whom he had seen occasionally through the eyes of two Lords Morigahn. The only disappointment about Damian was his lack of faith in the old traditions, something the young man's father should have done more about during his upbringing.

Morag paced back and forth on the roof.

"Patience," Grandfather Shadow said. "You will have ample opportunity to fight and hunt Daemyns in the coming weeks, months, and years."

"Only if she survives," Morag countered. "Why have you not allowed the other Morigahnti to feel her channeling the miracles?"

"She has an important lesson to learn," Grandfather Shadow replied. "Especially considering that she now has the first *Galad'fana.*"

Grandfather Shadow wasn't exactly sure how Damian had gotten it in order to give it to Julianna, but the god had a very good educated guess. Damian had referred to someone known as Smoke and had apparently had a conversation with this individual, a conversation that turned out to be very one-sided for Grandfather Shadow.

Razka appeared in a flash of lightning and thunder. "Even if the lesson kills her?"

The God of Shadows stood and pulled his senses back to himself. He rounded on the two Stormseekers.

"I seem to recall a time when my followers were born to fight and conquer, when they did not lie down with their prey, and when they knew that by fearing death, they were dead already." In the distance, thunder rumbled matching his displeasure. "You shame your heritage, Razka. Who came to me with his father and grandfather wanting to break ties with the Queen of Passion because you saw in me the road to freedom from her madness? You were strong then, proud and strong. Now you are afraid. Afraid because some humans found a way to hurt you, and you are scared they might be the end of you." Grandfather Shadow pointed downward. "In this very house, the woman I marked is fighting. She is surviving. She becomes what it means to be Morigahnti." Grandfather Shadow waved into the distance. "Look beyond that treeline. Even Damian Adryck, who does not truly believe, proves his worthiness as *aen Tsumari'osa* more than most who have received that honor as an accident of birth. He leads a handful of Morigahnti into the heart of the enemy because they will not allow a brother to face danger alone. Damian and Faelin are not Morigahnti; they are Komati brothers—brothers who bear my laws in their hearts and souls for no other reason than they are Komati. They are the wolves whose time has come again."

"And you," said a voice behind him, "should show more understanding for those left to muddle about in your absence."

Grandfather Shadow turned and saw the goddess many people had associated as his counterpart.

"Bah," Grandfather Shadow sneered. "I will not argue with you. You were always too good at making whatever point you wished to make sound reasonable. You say you have laid claim to Damian Adryck, yet I'm sure you know of his birthright."

"I am aware of his lineage," the goddess said. "My plans for him do not conflict with you. In fact, you might actually be pleased with what he will bring to the world."

"Like that gun you gave him that injured the Daemyn?"

"Like that," the goddess said. "I predict exciting changes for humanity in the coming years. Part of me is pleased to have you back to witness them with me."

"Truly?" Grandfather Shadow asked.

"Indeed. Though I would prefer it if you could stop lecturing and pontificating all the time."

"It's what I am."

"It doesn't have to be. The world has changed. You, and the other Greater Eldar as they become free, will have to change with it, or you may very well find yourselves back in the King of Order's prison, or perhaps worse."

Grandfather Shadow considered this. "I am trying. I have taken no direct hand."

"It's not enough." She offered him her arm. "Watch how I guide Damian. Perhaps you will learn a thing or two."

"Very well." Grandfather turned to the Stormseekers. "Please excuse us."

The Stormseekers left, to when and where, Grandfather Shadow was uncertain, and nor did he care overly much as long as they weren't here. It was entirely possible that she might show some weakness in him that he would rather not share with others.

As they settled in together, Grandfather Shadow couldn't help but hope that he could adapt to this new, modern world he'd awakened into. "You're doing it."

"Only insomuch as it's in my nature," the goddess said, "it would prove me wrong if I did otherwise."

SEVENTEEN

Julianna and Jenise came to the bottom of the spiral stairs and burst into the kitchen.

She didn't have even time to thank Grandfather Shadow's blessing before Jenise screamed, yet again. Julianna pulled the girl back and scanned the room.

A Daemyn hound puppy dropped from a hole in the ceiling. It landed on the center table, snarling at her. A cloud of fresh dust and splinters followed it. Julianna glanced up and saw two fresh holes had been clawed through the ceiling from above. A Daemyn hound looked down at her from each one, eyes glowing reddish-orange and lips pulled back around low growls.

Julianna wanted to scream, *You're puppies! Go romp and play somewhere!* But for all she knew, this was how Daemyn hound puppies played. Instead, she first made sure the horrid little creatures saw her Faerii steel knife and then began pushing Jenise back the way they'd come.

One of the Daemyn hounds hopped off the counter and out of view.

"Back to the hall," Julianna said.

This worked fine for two steps, and then Jenise wouldn't budge. Julianna looked back. Another pair of glowing eyes stared back from between the grated steps of the spiral staircase they'd just come down.

One of the Daemyn hounds above dropped onto the counter, and another took its place glaring at Julianna from the hole in the ceiling. Jenise gripped Julianna's shoulder hard enough to actually hurt. Glancing back, the Daemyn hound in the stairwell had begun to descend.

"We're going to fight our way to the door to the manor proper," Julianna whispered. "Be brave as you can."

"I'll try," Jenise said. Her voice lost a bit of its panic.

Had she given up, or did she truly mean to fight to the end with Julianna? They would both know when the Daemyn hounds attacked.

EIGHTEEN

Taebor walked through the camp toward the two Night Adepts. One was hunched and ancient. The other looked barely older than Taebor. Both wore the mantles of Adepts of Old Uncle Night. With each step, Taebor kept repeating this new miracle over and over in his mind and tried not to think about the magnitude that his first spoken miracle may very well change how the Morigahinti fought the Brotherhood of the Night.

Heart pounding and throat dry, nobody challenged Taebor. In between repetitions of the miracle, Taebor considered Grandfather Shadow's fourth law. The weak and gullible are meant to serve the strong and wise. Play upon their frailties and fears, or their hopes and dreams, and they will follow you heart, body, and soul. With the Brotherhood so easy to infiltrate, why didn't every Morigahnti possess a suit of Nightbrother armor?

When Taebor stood within ten paces of the Adepts, he touched his *Galad'fana* where it wrapped around his waist, and spoke, "*Pasasta kaki aen johtoasema muta sadela sa hinan Galad'fanati ja vahida hinan kansa aen Oinen'fanati li Ahk Tzizma'Uthra.*"

The miracle pushed through Taebor's *Galad'fana*. The next moment, all of the Dominions bound into the cloth, save for Balance, faded and were replaced by six new Dominions. Each one squirmed within the *Galad'fana* as if they were living things, like fish trapped in a net, trying to escape.

Exhaustion crashed down on him, crushing his lungs, and making breath come in shallow gasps. Taebor barely managed to keep his feet. Nothing in the world, no amount of explanation from the other Morigahnti of his Fist had prepared him for the toll speaking that miracle took on his body.

Outside, Taebor thought, *focus on things outside myself.*

The two Adepts of Old Uncle Night stiffened, as if an icy wind caressed their rain-soaked bodies. A moment later, they looked around frantically.

A moment later, a blast of lightning struck the midst of the Nightbrothers' camp. The thunderclap that followed it shook Taebor's bones. The effect was not nearly as devastating as the miracle of Shadow's Thunder, but the effect on the Brotherhood was better than they could have hoped for. The lightning only put down two Brothers, but the rest descended into chaos.

"Release the hounds," one of the Adepts screamed. He was an ancient man, hunched over a walking cane, but his voice carried clearly. "Release the hounds, damn you all."

The other Adept spoke words Taebor assumed were Old Uncle Night's divine language. Taebor smiled at the shock that came over the younger Adept's face when nothing happened.

Wrong language you Daemyn buggering bastard, Taebor thought.

Korrin dashed across the camp—Taebor recognized him in the black armor because he also had his *Galad'fana* wrapped around his waist. Eventually, the Nightbrothers might pick up on that little difference, but for now, too much was happening too quickly, and the disguises had worked well enough for the moment. None of the Nightbrothers moved to stop either Taebor or Korrin. Even the Adepts also failed to notice Korrin's presence until he was right next to them, reaching for their heads. By the time the younger Adept started to react, turning toward Korrin, it was too late.

Grabbing each Adept by an ear, Korrin slammed their heads together. Then he did it again. Neither Adept fell, so Korrin slammed their heads together twice more. The older Adept crumpled like a sack of dirty laundry. The younger dropped to his knees, eyes staring blankly at nothing.

By that time, the Reds had noticed Korrin and rushed toward him, swords drawn.

"Mind the Draqons!" Taebor called.

Korrin dropped to his knees, grabbed the Night Adept's mantles, and spoke, "*Galadti'Draqonti eneta ja sanata aen Draqonti*."

Taebor had never considered that he might use the Night Adepts' mantles to speak miracles from Grandfather Shadow.

A moment after Korrin spoke the miracle, the Draqons' shadows leaped to life. One Draqon fell immediately, its shadow cutting halfway through its neck and its head lolling to the side as it crumpled to the mud. The other shadows injured their Draqons but did not drop them. Now alert to this new danger, the Draqons fought against their own shadows. The living shadows were not invincible, but they were hardy things and would likely keep the Draqons out of this fight.

Not far away, the Daemyn hounds bellowed. The otherworldly howl chilled Taebor's blood. The hounds cried out again, this time closer.

The Nightbrothers recovered from their panic, drew their swords, and stalked toward Korrin, who had not yet risen. It seemed that the last miracle had been too much for him. The Nightbrothers seemed to sense this and rushed him. The first Nightbrother fell as a crossbow bolt hit him in the head. The other two dropped low and scampered for cover in nearby trees.

Two Stormcrows screamed all the fury of a storm as they dove out of the night, adding to the chaos as lightning sparked from their talons.

Hoofbeats splashed in the mud as the Stormcrows rose into the air. Nathan galloped into the camp astride a huge black horse, and stopping next to Korrin, Nathan pulled his brother onto the saddle behind him, kicked the horse's flanks, and the brothers rode off into the night. Several Nightbrothers leaped onto their horses to follow. One of the Reds had broken away from his shadow and also charged after the retreating Morigahnti. The thing was fast.

Taebor looked around and couldn't see Zephyr or Faelin in all the chaos. The Daemyn hounds howled, coming even closer. Taebor decided that this was the time to exercise discretion and fled the camp.

Nineteen

Yrgaeshkil didn't want to admit it to herself, but she was actually impressed by the innovative miracle they had used to call the Daemyn hounds back upon their masters. Neither of the Night Adepts was her creature, so she didn't care overly much if the Daemyns ripped them to shreds and feasted on their souls. Still, she saw no reason to allow Grandfather Shadow's first chosen puppet to escape so easily – not when she could easily corrupt the miracle or end the deception that fueled it.

The Daemyn Goddess and Mother of Lies reached out toward the miracle with her mind, ready to snap it to turn the five Daemyn hound cubs. Before she could, twin flashes of lightning and claps of thunder sounded behind her. Yrgaeshkil froze, ignoring the miracle for a moment and wrapping the Lie that hid her with all the strength she could. One Stormseeker, she could potentially deal with, even if that Stormseeker was Razka; two, on the other hand, would be a challenge she might not overcome, worse if one was Razka.

"I warned you," Razka growled behind her.

"How, this time?" Yrgaeshkil asked. She had wrapped a lie around her scent as well.

"Tell her, Morag," Razka said.

A second voice, this one feminine, or as feminine as a Stormseeker female could sound, replied, "The grass she's standing on. It looks like it's not being stood on, but it's not wet enough and the raindrops aren't touching it."

"Do you not believe me?" Razka asked, "Do you wish war with us? Consider carefully before you proceed."

Another two flashes of lightning, followed an imperceptible instant later by claps of thunder, and Yrgaeshkil felt herself alone again. She did not change the miracle. It could not be a fixed point in time, or Razka would not have bothered warning her. She had a choice, which meant that Razka was allowing her to choose continued peace, as tenuous as that peace was, or war. She could not afford any more enemies, yet. She surmised that Razka was of the same mind. When his mind changed, then Yrgaeshkil suspected the Stormseeker Alpha would no longer tell her about the mistakes she made in her Lies.

TWENTY

Novan had dashed out of the room and down the hall for three steps. His feet pounded on the floor and made it impossible for him to hear anything else in the house and might very well give him away. So now, Novan returned to his creeping. He heard movement in other parts of the house—footsteps and voices above, scurrying about and more voices down below. The stairs before him went up and down into darkness. Novan took a deep breath to try and decide which way he should go. Who might need more help more., or who might be the biggest threat to Shadybrook and the Morgahnti?

In a moment when all the sounds died down, even the wind, Novan heard a horse whinny outside the front of the manor. Would that be friend or foe? Either way, knowing the answer to that question would change any other course Novan might take.

Novan half tiptoed, half scurried to the nearest room off the upstairs hall. The desire to not give himself away warred with his need to know who was outside. Who did they serve? How many were they?

The darkness of a stormy night stretched on and on, making the horizon impossible to detect. Other buildings in the township were only discernible as slightly darker patches against the night. Still, even with that, Novan recognized the two Floraine Inquisitors riding toward the manner. Their mantels didn't exactly glow as much as the darkness refused to get close for fear of being burned away. One was a man who carried himself warrior-like, almost as a Morgahnti might. The other, a woman, was no warrior. Her stature was so large, so rotund, that she struggled to remain in the saddle.

The firearm in Novan's belt seemed to weigh a slight bit more than it had before he spied these enemies. Truth be told, ask any Morigahnti who was the greater threat to those who followed the old ways, and more often than not, they would say the Inquisitors. Yes, Morgahnti acknowledged the Brotherhood of the Night destroyed more lives, spread greater sorrow, and did so largely indiscriminately. However, the House Floraine Inquisitors relentlessly hunted any who worshipped too high above their station, which included every traditional, Komati.

Novan remained in the shadow just to the side of the window and drew his father's firearm. Two shots. One for each Inquisitor. He didn't dare imagine that he could kill either of them with one shot. But, he could wound them enough to drop down and finish them with a blade. Two Inquisitors. Two shots. He just needed to wait for them to get close enough so that he wouldn't miss. Surely, Count Allifar and Baron Parsh would make Novan a Morgahnti if he presented them with two Inquisitor corpses.

TWENTY ONE

Damian hadn't considered that they might have begun torturing Faelin already. Faelin clutched at his stomach and moved with staggering steps through the trees. Even with the camp in chaos, a few Brothers noticed, and one of the Reds noticed and hurried after him. Faelin had no hope of making it away.

"Think, damn you," Damian cursed at himself. "Think." A thought came, nearly as foolish a thought as his scheme with the wagon had been. Then again, as foolish as it had been, it had worked.

Damian pulled the pistol out of its holster and raced forward, pointing the gun at his enemies and screaming at the top of his lungs. The Nightbrothers and the Red turned to face him. The Brothers scattered when they saw the two-shot pistol, the Red did not. It veered toward Damian, sword ready to strike. The problem with swords was they didn't do very well against a gun, which was probably the reason the Kingdom outlawed them because guns also came closer to putting the common man on equal footing with an Adept. Damian slid to his knees, aimed carefully, and fired his first barrel.

The pistol cracked. Flame spewed from the barrel. The Draqon's head pitched back, braids fluttering prettily in the spray of blood. This wasn't the first time Damian had killed a Draqon, but it was the first time he'd actually done it with a gun.

Before the Red hit the ground, Damian was back on his feet. He shoved the gun into his belt, not having time to holster it properly, and picked up the Draqon's sword. Now this was a real weapon. The Kingdom spared no expense in arming their Red and White Draqons. The curved-bladed sword was a bit tip-heavy for Damian's taste, but he didn't have the raw strength that the Reds did. In the time it took to take a single breath, Damian's body adjusted to the necessary changes of technique required to use the weapon at maximum efficiency.

The Nightbrothers recovered and came at Damian: three of them, short swords in one hand, daggers in the other.

"What a joke," Damian said.

Four cuts later, the brothers were dead. The first cut disemboweled the forward-most brother and shifted into a parry of the one behind him. Moving past the second Brother, and easily dodging a clumsy attack from the last, Damian's second cut hamstrung the last Nightbrother. Spinning for the third cut, Damian slid the blade halfway through the second Brother's neck. The final cut was actually a thrust, as Damian pinned the last Brother to the earth.

The combat finished, Damian let go of the sword and his movements became those of Zephyr the smuggler again.

Faelin stumbled over to him.

"You are the last person I would expect to see here," Faelin said.

"You're welcome," Damian replied. "And you look like you're gripping hands with Old Uncle Night."

"I'll be fine," Faelin said. "Does this," Faelin gestured at the bodies of the Nightbrothers and the Red, "mean you've joined us?"

"Not hardly," Damian laughed. "I came to help a friend, a friend I owe a very large favor. Debt repaid, *kostota*, as you fanatics like to say. Enjoy your war. I'm going to take your advice and visit some friends who live very far away."

In the distance, horse hooves beat the ground, growing closer and closer. Damian scooped the Red's sword from the ground, and his body went into a fighting stance meant for men on horseback. Luckily, he had a nearly perfect blade for turning horsemen into footmen.

The men who rode two monstrous black Saifreni horses were not wearing the armor of the Brotherhood of the Night; rather, *Galad'fana* covered their faces. The riders reigned in and uncovered their faces. Damian recognized Parsh immediately, but it took him a moment to recall the other man. It had been years since he had seen Count Allifar Thaedus at court. Apparently, Allifar was also having problems placing Damian in his memories, but then the Count's eyes widened.

"You're—"

"Don't," Damian interrupted Allifar. "Just don't." He dropped the sword, and his body shifted back to Zephyr's. "I'm not who you think I am, and I don't need any rumors associating me with him. So don't."

Allifar took a long moment looking at Damian. Finally, he nodded, and Damian released a breath he hadn't realized he was holding.

"The Lord Morigahn," Allifar said. "Where is she?"

"Please tell me she didn't come with you?" Faelin asked.

"I may be foolish and an idiot at times," Damian said, "but I'm not stupid. She's back in Shadybrook… looking… for… you. Oh, damn. Well, you'd best be after her."

"You're not coming?" Allifar asked.

"No," Damian replied. "You'll never see me again. Parsh, I think our business relationship is at an end. I'll recommend you to one of my colleagues. Find him in Koma city by the name of Gareth. I'll tell him to expect you. Goodbye, Faelin. Take good care of that beauty."

Before anyone could say another word, Damian ran into the night. He should have left this continent and never returned a long time ago. Thankfully, he had one storehouse of weapons left, enough for one last sale in Koma City. That should earn him more than enough to book a passage to the Lands of Endless Summer.

TWENTY TWO

Julianna stood in the kitchen wondering what had just happened. One moment the Daemyn hounds were coming at them, even the one with a severed foreleg. Then, Julianna's *Galad'fana* tingled and the next moment, the hounds let out an eerie howl and fled from the room.

"Shadow be praised," Jenise said, falling to her knees and muttering thanks over and over to *Galad'Ysoysa*.

"Indeed," Julianna said, hoisting the girl to her feet. While Julianna felt very much the same thanks in her heart for whatever had called the Daemyn hounds away, she could pray later. "Let's not squander the gift. Let's get to the stable and get out of here."

Jenise nodded.

Together, they rushed out of the kitchen and through the house. Julianna considered taking the Faerii steel knife from Jenise, but the hounds might return before they reached the stable.

They met no more trouble as they went, but when Julianna pushed open the manor's front door, she felt like taking her mother's dagger and shoving it into her own eye again and again and again. Julianna had expected to see perhaps a few of the townsfolk and the Morigahnti at the stable, all preparing to leave. Instead, she saw two Inquisitors of House Floraen dismounting their horses in the middle of the street. One was a fat, bulbous woman who looked at Julianna with a disdainful sneer. Julianna recognized the other. She'd seen him before and was amazed he'd managed to survive when she had left him to face the Brotherhood of the Night and the Daemyn hound alone.

"Lord Morigahn," the male Inquisitor said.

"Stay back," Julianna whispered and stepped between Jenise and the Inquisitors.

"You again," Julianna said.

"Indeed." The Inquisitor nodded. "Your god has yet to eat my soul."

"Perhaps you are beneath his notice." Julianna shrugged, as she drew on the Dominion of Storms. Then, she pushed her hand outward and spoke a miracle, "*Mina kehia turvata!*"

TWENTY THREE

Luciano recognized the words of the Lord Morigahn's miracle even before she finished speaking it. Luciano pitched himself out of his saddle just as the Lord Morigahn completed speaking. He felt winds rush by him even as the cobbled street rushed up to meet him. Cadenza's cry of surprised outrage echoed across Shadybrook as those divine winds carried her away. Luciano hit the cobbles, and something snapped in his left arm. Pain flared, but he ignored it and scrambled away. He doubted he would need his swords in this fight anyway.

TWENTY FOUR

Novan waited and aimed until the Inquisitors were almost just below him. He only had two shots. No room for mistakes. He aimed for the man's head at first. No telling what kind of armor he might be wearing under that mantle. But with one shot per Inquisitor, Novan shifted his aim toward the Inquisitor's body. Even with the armor, Novan had a gun. In practice firing, Novan had seen bullets go through brigandine, chain, and even breastplates on occasion. He would take the biggest target and trust Grandfather Shadow to guide the bullet.

He had taken a breath and steadied to pull the trigger when the male inquisitor addressed the Lord Morgan. They spoke, the Lord Morgan and the Inquisitor. Novan convinced himself that he was now waiting on the Lord Morgan to act so he could follow. His hesitation had nothing to do with the shock at standing almost directly above Grandfather Shadow's voice in the world. Novan kept aim on the Inquisitor and waited for the Lord Morgan's guidance.

The Lord Morgan spoke a miracle.

The male Inquisitor flung himself from his horse.

The miracle summoned a gale force, and then some, of wind. Grandfather Shadw's divine power flung the horses a ways down the road between the buildings. The woman Inquisitor flew out of sight into the darkness.

Novan adjusted his aim to the now-prone Inquisitor and squeezed the trigger. The right-hand pan flared, but the gun did not fire.

"Shades and damnation," Novan growled and pulled back the second hammer. "Please, Shadow. Please."

He squeezed the trigger.

The gun fired.

Novan couldn't tell if he hit the inquisitor or not. It didn't matter. He needed to reload.

TWENTY FIVE

Carmine inched backward, putting Hardin between him and the Daemyn hounds. The decrepit Adept stood screaming at the hounds in Old Uncle Night's language. Though Hardin's panicked orders kept them from tearing into the two Night Adepts, the hounds continued stalking forward. All four creatures' eyes glowed like embers in a dying fire, indicating they were tracking the scent of miracles. With these four here, it meant eight others were still out there, two large, and the six that had possessed the puppies, and those might arrive at any moment.

Continuing to creep away from the hounds, Carmine slowly removed his Adept's mantle. He didn't know how the Morigahnti had stolen his Dominions and replaced them with others, but that had to be the reason why the hounds came at them despite Hardin's commands. Once Carmine had shed his mantle he would tell Hardin his theory, but not until then. At this point, Hardin drew all four hounds' attention, having spoken the most recent miracle—or at least that was what it seemed like from what that Morigahnti had done. If the hounds ate their master, the Daemyns possessing the hounds would depart the mortal realm upon Hardin's death, and command of the Nightbrothers would fall upon Carmine. The only reason that he would save Hardin was because one of the hounds might come after Carmine before Hardin was dead.

Unfastening the final bone button of his mantle, Carmine shed the garment and tossed it into the fire. He had no idea if the change of Dominions was permanent or not, but he hoped that by destroying his mantle he brought some harm to the divine foci of the Morigahnti as well.

The garment first smoked and burst into flames. Carmine struggled with whether or not to warn Harding. In the end, Carmine cried, "The hounds are after your mantle."

Hardin continued screaming frantic orders as his fingers struggled with his buttons. Carmine snickered to himself. He imagined Hardin inwardly regretting whatever power, gift, or favor the decrepit Adept had received in exchange for his youth. Even with his unsteady hands, the old snake managed to slither his way out of his mantle. He stumbled a few steps toward the fire and dropped the mantle on top of Carmine's.

As soon as Hardin separated himself from the mantle, the hounds pounced, ripping the garment to shreds and scattering flaming logs across the camp. It took the hounds less than ten heartbeats to reduce the mantles to tatters. Still, the creatures seemed unsatisfied with that. They gnawed and tore at the remnants of the garments.

Hardin seemed to be content to let the creatures have their way. Luckily, the art of summoning and controlling Daemyns was completely removed from the Dominions and foci of Old Uncle Night. Once the hounds satiated their destructive urges, Hardin would be able to control them again. At least, Carmine hoped so.

Following the old Adept's example, Carmine stood patiently watching the hounds destroy what had taken Carmine months of grueling work to create. He did however, move a little closer to Hardin's back, dagger in hand, in case the hounds had somehow freed themselves from the Adept's control. No matter what else had changed, they would return to the Realm of the Godless Dead once Hardin died.

A few minutes later, the hounds looked up. All four bellowed to the sky. The sound was full of frustration and rage.

"Get after them, you mangy beasts!" Hardin shrieked. "Destroy them all!" All four Daemyn hounds bellowed and turned after the Morigahnti. Then Hardin turned toward the few Brothers who had not fled. "Follow them and kill any Komati you find."

In the distance, from the direction of Shadybrook, the direction the hounds were headed, a flash of light shone against the sky. The light faded from something nearly blinding to a soft glow.

"What was that?" Carmine asked.

"Someplace where we are glad not to be," Hardin asked. "That is an Inquisitor decisively ending a threat to the Kingdom. Trust me that we are more than pleased to let the hounds handle that."

TWENTY SIX

Gritting his teeth against the pain that slammed into his shoulder and burned, Luciano drew on the Dominion of Light through the medallion on his chest.

"*Mishrak Amhyr'Shoul clapious pyr Lusias!*"

Lights from the few fires elsewhere in the township surged out toward Luciano. The light flattened into a sheet of yellow, orange, and red, shimmering and waving above him. The Lord Morigahn winced as her eyes blinked at the sudden brightness in her direct field of vision.

"*Galadti eneta ja sanata aen Adept Floraen,*" The Lord Morigahn called.

Luciano was already scrambling to his feet and saw no reason to slow down long enough to discover the effect of the Lord Morigahn's miracle. His right arm hung limp at his side, the pain pulsing from the bullet lodged in his shoulder. He made it two steps when his shadow, which stretched out in front of him from the light at his back, rose and blocked his path.

"*Lusias bruiarce al ombrita!*" Luciano spoke.

The shield of flame and light spun with the fury of a typhoon and shredded his shadow as easily as any light pushed back the darkness.

The light and flames parted for him, and Luciano dashed away from the Lord Morigahn. His feet grew sluggish from the effort of channeling divine energy. Currently, the Lord Morigahn had the advantage, what with the sniper above and the girl with the faerii steel knife, and Luciano wouldn't be able to swing his sword, even if he managed to draw it. Even though he now commanded the fires, and thus the light, the Lord Morigahn had too many places to draw shadows from, and Luciano didn't have nearly the light he needed to counter them all. Well, that was easily changed.

"*Lusias bruiarce al aedifecta!*"

The whirlwind of flames that surrounded him exploded outward, assaulting the buildings. Nearly immediately, all four buildings burned brightly. Even though they were mostly stone, and wet at that from several days of rain, what started as steam and smoldering began to blaze in several places on each building.

"No!" he heard the Lord Morigahn scream. "Vendyr!"

While at first he thought her outrage might be due to this shift in the environmental advantage she's just lost, it seemed she had momentarily forgotten him. Instead, she stared, wide-eyed, at the stable.

She moved her lips, but Luciano could not hear her over the roar of flames the mercantile shop had become. It was the newest building here, and so was constructed more of wood than of stone. With this blaze behind him and the other buildings burning, light shone about the center of the township, light that had been absent from the first time they'd fought. Now they were on more equal footing when it came to miracles. He might just survive this, after all.

The flames from the stable leaped in one great rush to the mercantile shop. The building nearly exploded with the sudden rush of heat and fire. Warmth spread over Luciano's back growing hotter and hotter, to the point where he feared his breastplate might begin to cook him alive.

The Lord Morigahn turned toward him, her pale eyes shaded underneath the *Galad'fana* she had wrapped around her head as a hood. The scar that cut her face glistened in the firelight. Her chest rose and fell in a steady rhythm. Despite having spoken a miracle that would have burned many Adepts alive from the inside out, the Lord Morigahn looked as if she were only beginning this fight. Her face held none of the flippancy she'd shown before. For the first time since he'd seen her, Luciano Salvatore, Inquisitor of House Floraen, felt the Lord Morigahn meant to feed his soul to her god.

Ignoring the rising heat and pain in his shoulder, Luciano faced Julianna.

"*Mishrak Amhyr'Shoul,*" Luciano called to the sky, pulling on the Dominions of Light, Day, Duty, and Justice, "*benectos mhi milestor demanctium hoacus flagrios!*"

Luciano spoke the miracle out of desperation, and he would pay for it in short order once the miracle had run its course. Until then, he became the avatar of the Sun God.

Flames from all the buildings rushed toward him, swirling about him, lifting him into the air. It was unknown whether those who spoke this miracle became one with the flames, or if the flames merely became a massive suit of armor. To Luciano, it didn't matter. He'd spoken this miracle only twice before. He'd saved the lives of many High Blood, Adepts, and Draqons during the last uprising of the Brotherhood of the Night. He'd been desperate then as well.

With his newfound strength and power, Luciano reached out with his massive arms and grabbed the mercantile shop. He pulled the flaming building from its foundations and turned toward the manor house.

Luciano witnessed the fear the LordMorigahn had struck into his heart now reflected on her face. Gone was the confident, master of miracles. Now she was just a young woman struck with the realization that she wasn't prepared for this level of battle, not truly. Luciano would have loved for nothing more than to parade this woman through Koma City and publicly subject her to the Rite of Undoing, but she was too powerful to fight alone and capture. His only choice was to end this quickly and decisively.

He lifted the burning shop over his head. The Lord Morigahn fled into the manor. Luciano smashed the mercantile shop onto the manor house, crying, "*Bruiarce!*"

The flames erupted like a tiny sun, and for a moment, night became day. The flash of light faded, and Luciano's miracle ended.

He fell from the center of where the flaming armor had been. Not tired. Not fatigued. Not exhausted. These terms were too small for the numbness the miracle brought over Luciano. He could not even feel the gunshot wound. Even as darkness rolled over him, he managed one last miracle just before hitting the ground.

He spoke, if the choking noises he made could be called speaking, "*Mishrak Amhyr'Shoul, aevidho som vaso mirso aetirumes.*" Rain fell suddenly, a cloudburst that drenched him in the moment before he disappeared.

TWENTY SEVEN

Novan's hands hurried to reload the two-shot pistol.

Below, the Inquisitor and the Lord Morigahn spoke their miracles.

Novan largely ignored them until the ceiling and walls burst into flame. Heat washed over him, but the powder horn in his hand caught all of his attention. He didn't know what might happen if even a tiny spark hit the gunpowder, but he didn't want to find out. Even without the gunpowder, going deeper into the manor would likely prove fatal.

Novan drew a deep breath of scorching air, coughed on the smoke, faced the window, dashed towards the flames, and left shoulder first, flung himself at the window. The glass shattered. Cool air rushed over Novan, and he dropped toward the earth.

His grand idea that the ground would be soft from the rain did not account for falling toward the hard-packed road leading to the manor. Yes, it was somewhat softer from the rain, but it had been a long, dry summer.

When he struck the ground, the road, though muddy, gave way very little. Air and a bit of smoke rushed out of Noman's lungs upon impact. Bright and dark spots flushed across his vision. He tried to groan but only managed a wheezing cough. His shoulder and hip ached as if someone had struck them with a mallet the size of a barrel. He rolled onto his back, stared upward, and settled into the sensation of rain pattering over his face and soaking into his clothes. With all the buildings on fire, Novan imagined he could see their light reflected on the clouds above.

Grandfather Shadow was up there. Somewhere.

Novan whispered prayers for Grandfather Shadow to aid the Lord Morgan, and give her miracle strength to defeat the inquisitor, or all of Shadybrook might suffer from kingdom justice.

"We are loyal," Novan whispered in between fighting for breath. "We have been," cough, "loyal since," gasp, "the conquest."

The raindrops fell faster. They struck with greater force.

"I know."

Novan blinked and cocked his head to the side. Had someone actually spoken those words, or had that been wishful thinking and a trick of the wind?

"I know, Novan from a family of no name. I know of your loyalty."

The rain continued to increase in strength and speed.

Novan imagined a slightly darker form moving through the dark clouds above him. The more rain that soaked him and ran down his body and into the earth, the more and more it seemed to wash his pain away.

"Clever," a second voice said, this one far more feminine, yet possessing as much authority as the first. "It seems even with all your knowledge, you can learn something new."

"Bah," the first voice said. "Now rise Novan. You are still needed in the world of men."

Novan sat up. The Inquisitor was gone, and the manor house was a ruined heap of wood and flames. Novan couldn't see the Lord Morigahn anywhere.

TWENTY EIGHT

Taebor came to the edge of the thicket and paused his progress. The trees were sparse beyond the brambles and thorns for ten or so paces. After that short distance, the trees grew closer together and would provide some greater cover for him to escape.

Twigs snapped nearby. Several people tromped through the brush. Taebor rolled further into the thicket, causing himself even more cuts and scrapes. He'd shed the Nightbrother armor at his first opportunity—the thick leather might blend in with the dark of night, but it didn't allow for the freedom of movement needed for stealth in a natural environment. Taebor bit the inside of his lower lip and cheek to keep from crying out. Three Nightbrothers passed two paces from him, arguing in whispered voices. They were so intent on their discussion that they paid no real attention to their surroundings. After they passed out of sight, Taebor waited for his heart to slow and counted another seventy beats before leaving the minor safety of the thicket.

The moment Taebor crawled free of his hiding place, he dashed toward where the trees thickened. He stopped after twenty paces and leaned against the trunk of a tree as wide as his shoulders, listening for any sign of pursuit. When he was finally satisfied that he'd remained undetected, Taebor started further into the trees. When he passed the second tree, an arm shot out, grabbed a fistful of his hair, and pulled him backward.

"I told you someone was hiding in that brush," a man's voice said, as the grip on his hair tightened.

Taebor fought past the fright rising in his chest. After tonight, he was finished letting pain and fear rule him. He had fought the Brotherhood of the Night, gained the Lord Morigahn's favor, received a *Galad'jana* by her hand, and he had spoken a miracle no other Morigahnti had ever spoken in their entire history.

He twisted and felt some of his hair pull loose from his scalp as he turned to face the three Nightbrothers who had just passed him.

"Calm down boy," said the one holding locks of Taebor's hair. "Stop struggling and we won't hurt—"

Balling his hand into a fist, Taebor punched the Nightbrother in the nose. The leather of his mask crumpled, his head snapped back, and he let go. Taebor backed away from him slowly, drawing his knife.

"You'll pay for that, Morigahnti," the Brother growled.

"Teach him a lesson," one of the other Brothers said.

Taebor knew the look in their eyes, even behind their skull masks. They saw a child. Allifar and Parsh had taught him to recognize that look, just as they had taught him to fight as a man.

Taebor anticipated as the first Brother lunged for him. He sidestepped and left his knife in place. The Nightbrother impaled himself on the blade. His eyes widened and he let out a pained gasp. Taebor twisted the weapon, wrenched it through the man's gut, and yanked it out of his side.

The Nightbrother dropped, and Taebor fled before the other two realized what had happened. Not letting fear rule him was one thing, but he wouldn't catch the other two by surprise like that. Taebor plotted a course through the trees and glanced back. The two remaining Brothers wove through the trees behind him.

"We have a Morigahnti!" one of his pursuers shouted. "He's heading north!"

Hearing that, Taebor immediately turned to his right, back toward Shadybrook. He only stayed free from the Brothers by weaving between the trees, using the trunks to shield himself from them, but he couldn't evade them forever. His legs screamed with fatigue, calling for him to stop and rest. Just a few moments would do, but in those moments the Nightbrothers would be on him.

Taebor caught hold of a sapling and used it to spin himself in a new direction, only to find himself face-to-face with one of the Brothers. Taebor tried to scramble, but the Nightbrother caught hold of his shoulder. Before Taebor could bring his knife up, a crossbow bolt sprouted from the side of the Nightbrother's head.

Turning to flee, Taebor saw another figure coming toward him out of the darkness, rapier drawn. He breathed a sigh of relief when he recognized Aurell.

The second Nightbrother decided that he didn't like these odds and fled back in the direction of the Nightbrother camp.

"Are you alright?" Aurell asked.

"I'm fine," Taebor replied. "But we should go. They called for help."

"We know," Aurell said. "That's how we found you."

"We?"

"Yes," Wynd said, stepping out from behind a tree. "We. Now come on, we have horses waiting."

After a few minutes, the three Morigahnti came to a break in the trees. Nathan and Korrin stood waiting, holding the horses as the animals grazed.

"Now," Korrin said, "let's find the others, get back to Shadybrook, and leave before anything worse happens."

As he said those words, they saw an explosion of daylight erupt at Shadybrook.

"That's not good at all," Wynd said.

"The Lord Morigahn," Aurell said. "She's there."

"Shades and damnation," Nathan and Korrin said together.

As if that strange light weren't enough, suddenly all of Grandfather Shadow's Dominions returned to Taebor's *Galad'fana*.

A chorus of howls echoed in the distance.

"Gods and goddesses," Taebor swore. "Not that, too."

"What?" Nathan asked.

"My Dominions have come back," Taebor replied. "We have to leave."

Without another word, the Morigahnti mounted and kicked their horses into motion. The Daemyn hounds were hunting the Morigahnti once again.

TWENTY NINE

"And where do you think you're going?" Sylvie asked.

Colette, Julianna's darling maid, had managed to sneak quite a ways away in the chaos and confusion during the attack on the camp. Unfortunately, Sylvie had only cared about the attackers enough to make sure they wouldn't harm her. For the briefest moment, Sylvie had considered calling out. Instead, she had remained hidden in the shadows beneath the wagon. However, the men rescuing the man Carmine had taken prisoner were Morigahnti, and Sylvie couldn't very well have gone with them. They would have had to kill her to keep their secrets from the Kingdom. Besides, if she went with them, she would lose her opportunity to become High Blood. She'd dreamed of marrying well, but never well enough to be High Blood. Even Carmine's Komati mother had not been named High Blood when she had married his father. Carmine had taken steps to ensure that he would be a powerful High Blood, and not just the joke most people considered him as being High Blood by accident. Sylvie wanted, desired, and yearned for people to call her High Blood. She imagined entering a ball and being introduced as Countess Sylvie D'Mario of the House of Night.

"Please, Miss," Colette whispered, "we can escape if we're quick and quiet."

"No we can't," Sylvie said. "They'll only send those dog things after us."

Sylvie grabbed a fistful of Colette's hair and pulled her back toward the Nightbrother's camp.

"And even if we could," Sylvie said, "I've no desire to escape anymore. I'm not about to let you run off and leave me to be the one to do all the cooking and cleaning. I didn't subject myself to the advances of that *common* brute to go back to doing the same amount of work as you, servant."

Colette tried to fight, when she did, Sylvie yanked her hair and pulled the servant off her feet. Gods and goddesses, did this girl have no respect for her place in precedence? Well, Sylvie would correct that oversight on Julianna's part, posthaste.

"What is this?" Jorgen said, coming through the trees.

"Don't just gape at us," Slyvie snapped. "Help me. She was trying to escape."

A few minutes later, Sylvie and Jorgen pulled Colette back into the camp. Carmine and Adept Hardin were there, speaking in low tones. They looked at Sylvie. Hardin frowned in confusion. Carmine just smiled.

"I told you," Carmine said. "She's becoming one of us."

"Oh, it's a little more than that," Sylvie said. "I've been listening when you two think I haven't been. I've figured out who the First Adept of Night is, and don't worry, I also learn fast enough to know that I'm not to speak his name. I've met him, the First Adept. He's going to be the Night King isn't he?"

"Yes," Hardin asked. "What is it you want?"

"I want to join the Brotherhood," Sylvie said. "I want to learn to not be afraid of death, to celebrate my sister in death rather than keep this empty spot in my heart, and to be named High Blood when we take the Zenith. Here is proof of my sincerity."

Sylvie pushed Colette toward Hardin. The servant girl began to cry, which was fine. She could cry for both of them. Sylvie was through with tears.

Thirty

Symond heard feminine voices through the trees and hurried toward them. Sylvia and Colette were quarreling. He almost stopped stepped forward and intervened, but then Jorgen approached from the other direction. Sylvie could have been dealt with, quickly, quietly, and most of all, unlethally. With her noble's arrogance, Symond was sure she wouldn't be able to describe him as anything other than one Nightbrother. Remembering the color of his hair would have been a miracle for her.

He could have gotten Colette far enough away by the time Sylvie reported them to make finding the runaways require more time and resources than the Adepts could spare.

Jorgen, on the other side of the coin... Jorgen was driven. Jorgen not only yearned for Carmine's favor, he wanted to remain in Sylvia's good graces for all the rewards she gave him. Symond would have to kill Jorgen. During the fight, Sylvie would likely raise such a racket as to alert the Nightbrothers and Adepts.

Symond sighed and turned away from the confrontation. He would return to camp, though, taking a long way around to come in from a different direction. He'd watch, listen, and wait for another chance to get Colette away. Oh, and he would drink. Yes. He would drink and drink and drink.

Thirty One

Jorgen followed Adept Carmine through the apple orchard south of the township. The Adept walked with Sylvie on his arm. One of the Red Draqons Carmine had come to control trailed behind them all as a guard might. Jorgen still couldn't be quite comfortable with the thought of that thing behind him knowing that Jorgen was a sworn Brother of the Night. They had followed Adept Carmine's Nightbat to this place, so he could truly test his control over the Red Draqon.

They found her underneath a tree, hanging onto life by a thread. The Inquisitor of House Floraen lay in a broken, mangled heap. Split branches lay all around her. Her arms and legs twisted at angles that made Jorgen's skin squirm. He enjoyed killing as much as the next Nightbrother, but seeing someone, anyone, having to suffer through this was, well wrong. Uncle Night taught that death was many times the threshold of relief from suffering.

"Hello, Cadenza."

At the sound of Adept Carmine's voice, the Inquisitor's eyes rolled back into her head. Her arms and legs twitched as she let out a wail that sounded more like an animal caught in a hunter's trap rather than anything a human might utter.

"I told you the Zenith was changing, and this is why." Carmine looked back over his shoulder at the Red Draqon. "Kill her."

The Red drew its sword as it stepped forward. One thrust and it was done. No other ceremony accompanied one of the most significant events in the history of the Kingdom of the Sun, a Draqon of any breed killing an Adept of any god other than Old Uncle Night upon the orders of an enemy of the Sun Crown.

Jorgen glanced at Sylvie. It surprised him to see her looking back at him. They both understood the truth of this moment. Adept Carmine had created the potion, and these Draqons were his. He had done something no other Night Adept had done in all the centuries the Kingdom had existed. He had taken the advantage of the Draqons away from the other Houses. A man like that might not actually sit on the Night Throne when the Zenith shifted, but he would be close to it.

At the same time, Jorgen and Sylvie nodded to each other—they understood they were firmly Carmine's creatures.

THIRTY TWO

The waiting was worse, by far, than the growing fatigue. Flames continued to burn around the sphere of wind and rain Julianna had created to shield Jenise and herself from the Inquisitor's attack – if that thing could still be called an Inquisitor after such a transformation. Even with the added power of her new *Galad'fana*, Julianna grew weary of pulling fresh wind and rain down through the cracks and crevices of the ruined buildings pressing down on her. The question that plagued her: *How long should she wait for the Inquisitor to think she was dead?* On the other side of the coin, Julianna didn't know if she could accurately judge the passage of time trapped down here. It seemed like quite a long time, but she couldn't really tell.

In the end, Jenise decided the matter. When Julianna couldn't take the girl's sniffling and tears anymore, she gathered on the Dominion of Storms, adding a touch of Vengeance this time, just on the chance the Inquisitor had remained waiting.

"Mina kehia turvata!"

The winds blasted outward, creating a wide hole in the debris. Rain beat down upon them from above, sizzling as it fell into the flames. A line of people stretched from the rubble and ruins to the well. Julianna recognized some of the people from the celebration earlier that night as they handed buckets of water down the line. As she and Jenise climbed out of the wreckage, a cheer went up.

Erik Dressel ran up to her. "Shadow be praised, you're alive."

A youth followed him, and said. "I told you she was in there."

"I know, boy," Erik said. "Many of us watched the fighting."

"You were wise to stay out of that fight," Julianna said.

"I didn't," the young man said. "I was in the manor house. I shot the Inquisitor with my father's pistol." He raised the weapon as if it were a holy relic."

The mayor of Shadybrook waved the boy silent, then craned his neck to look behind Julianna, into the rubble she'd just come from. "Are there any others?"

Mistress Dressel's face came unbidden to Julianna's mind. Those colorless eyes glared at Julianna, as if accusing and pleading with her all at the same time. *Why didn't you save me?*

"I'm sorry," Julianna said. "Only Jenise."

Dressel took in a slow, deep breath. Julianna's stomach churned, and she wanted to vomit. She placed a hand on the mayor's shoulder. He looked at her hand, and then at her, blinking, mouth moving as if to say something, but unable to form the words.

"I am truly sorry," Julianna said, "that I brought this upon your house."

Dressel's face tightened. His body stiffened under Julianna's hand, and he stood straight.

"Do not dare be sorry for what those outsiders do to us," Dressel said. "We are Komati, living in Komati lands. They are the ones who bring this strife to us, who tell us we cannot worship as we please. They are the ones who should be," he gripped his boar spear tight and shook it to the sky, "who *will* be sorry."

Dressel turned to the people of Shadybrook. Julianna could not see a single one without injury. Some had weapons, others buckets still full of water.

"*Kun vaen ovat kuten makaesti!*" Dressel shouted.

"*Medan kerta voida tas johta!*" the people shouted back, the young man behind the mayor being the loudest of all.

"Erik Dressel." Julianna looked past him to the youth with the two-shot pistol. "I think your people never stopped being wolves. The rest of Koma did."

The young man—how could she be thinking of someone barely a few years younger than she as a youth—stood a bit taller and beamed a smile.

"You'll be surprised how many wolves are waiting to rise and follow you," Dressel said.

Howls echoed in the distance. No creature born of the earthly realm would sound like that. A moment later, more howls echoed in on the night wind.

As if summoned by the approaching Daemyn hounds, two groups of riders galloped into the remains of Shadybrook. Allifar, Parsh, and Faelin were one group. Wynd, Nathan, Korrin, Aurell, and Taebor were the second. Faelin was riding a familiar black and white gelding.

"Vendyr!" Julianna flung her arms around her horse's neck. "Where did you find him?"

"He was the first we saddled," Taebor said, "but somehow he managed to get loose and out of the barn. It happened so fast during a thunderclap right before the Brotherhood of the Night attacked. I had his bridle in my hand for one minute. The lightning and thunder struck came the next, and he was running from the stable."

"We found him under an apple tree," Faelin said, "contentedly eating his fill."

"Thank the Grandfather that you are safe, Lord Morigahn," Allifar said. "When Faelin and Aurell told us you were still here, we returned for reinforcements against the Brotherhood. I'm sorry that we left you."

"I am never alone so long as a single loyal Komati is near me," Julianna said, looking at Erik Dressel.

"We can exchange pleasantries later," Parsh said. "The Daemyn hounds are coming."

"As are the Draqons," Korrin said, "as well as the last of the Nightbrothers."

"We will flee," Allifar said, and before anyone could protest, he lifted his hand. "I know you are eager to strike back. This is not the time. We are tired, and our miracles will not aid us against the hounds."

"But how can we outrun them?" Parsh asked. "Our horses are tired, too."

"We only need to speak one more miracle," Julianna said. "The Miracle of Seven Mirrors. Saent Julian used it to great effect in the Battle of Ykthae Wood. We will speak it together, and I will channel it through my *Galad'fana*. I have some strength left in me yet. The words are, *Galadti jatae smina ajota kansa aen toynenti. Galad kukin tae ol miten omata aemelian muta halinta essa mina maelisian.* When you speak the miracle, draw on Shadows, Illusion, Secrets, and Balance. Send the power to me, and I will channel the miracle into existence."

"How can you know so much about this?" Parsh asked. "You have been a Morigahnti less than a week."

"I am not merely a Morigahnti, Baron Thaedus," Julianna replied. "I am the Lord Morigahn, raised by the Shadow God to be his voice in the physical realm. He gave me knowledge lost to the Morigahnti for centuries. After the miracle takes effect, ride as hard and fast as you can. Once we escape, send the Stormcrows to find me, and I will tell them where and when we will rendezvous."

"Why not now?" Aurell asked.

"Because then the Brotherhood cannot torture the information out of anyone they capture," Allifar replied. The Morigahnti captain looked to Faelin. "The place you recommended to me earlier this evening."

Faelin nodded.

"Send the Stormcrows to me as well," Allifar said.

"We will cover your retreat, Lord Morigahn," Master Dressel said, stepping forward.

"No," Julianna replied. "You will flee as well. I will have no more innocent blood spilled for me this night."

"We have all lost loved ones to the Brotherhood," Dressel said. "We wish to make the Brotherhood pay."

"You cannot hope to defeat the hounds," Julianna said. "Do not throw away any more lives for me."

A short way off, two small flashes of lightning and claps of thunder exploded. A man and a wolf stood where they had hit. The man was old and grizzled, wearing mismatched leathers and furs. His near-white eyes surveyed the strange assembly here.

"They cannot defeat the hounds," the man said, "but we can."

Behind Julianna, people whispered the word *Stormseekers* again and again.

"I thought you didn't aid Morigahnti, Razka" Faelin said, as he dismounted Vendyr. One of the townsfolk had brought another horse for him.

The man in leathers, Razka, chuckled. "I do not." He pointed at Dressel first, and then at the other people of Shadybrook. "They are not Morigahnti."

"*Kun vaen ovat kuten makaesti,*" Razka said to Dressel.

"*Medan kerta voida tas johta,*" Dressel replied.

The two men shook hands, and Julianna felt that she had just witnessed something profound.

Howls sounded again, closer this time.

Julianna sighed. It seemed she was losing more than one battle this night. With everything, many of these people would still die, worse, they would die unremembered.

Faelin stepped next to her. "Even as the Lord Morigahn, you can only do so much, especially with being so new to the mantle and those who follow the old ways being scattered."

Julianna looked at the people around her preparing for battle.

"Jenise," Julianna said. Then, she pointed at the youth. "You, boy what is your name?"

"Novan, Lord Morigahn."

The two of them approached her. Julianna placed her right hand on Jenise's shoulder and her left hand on the lad's.

"Jenise, you are not a warrior," Julianna said. "Go. Live. Speak to other townships and villages of this night. Tell them of the Morigahnti. Tell them that we are wolves again." She looked at Novan. "You stood in the face of danger and fought as any Morigahnti. If not for your aid against the Inquisitor, he might have bested me. Take your father's weapons and protect Jenise. The Komati must know, our time is coming."

The two young Komati could only stare dumbfounded at the Lord Morigahn and nod.

"Komati attend me!" Julianna called and climbed into Vendyr's saddle. "Fight well, people of Shadybrook, with the blessing of Grandfather Shadow." She turned to Allifar and his Fist. "Morigahnti, speak your miracle."

As one, the Morigahnti chanted the miracle Julianna had taught them. The air around her resonated with Grandfather Shadow's Dominions. She brought their divine energy into her *Galad'fana*. She spoke the words herself, adding Faelin into the miracle. The words left Julianna's lips, and all the shadows around her and around the Morigahnti sprang to life. The shadows shifted, molded, and gained color until there were six more of Julianna, Faelin, and each Morigahnti and their horses.

"Now ride," Julianna ordered.

A chorus of howls bellowed from the far side of the township. Hulking shapes lurched forward in the dark. Eyes that glowed like embers fixed on Julianna. Other shadows, shadows like those of men, only taller, came behind the hounds.

Julianna turned Vendyr away and kicked him first into a canter and then a gallop. Faelin followed close behind her. They fled from the township, and shadow forms of all the Morigahnti surrounded them.

"Thaedus!" Allifar yelled.

"The strength of my sword!" Taebor's youthful voice called after him. "For the Lord Morigahn!"

And then the call went up. "Thaedus! Lord Morigahn! Thaedus!"

Julianna dared to glance back.

Allifar and Taebor road toward the Daemyn hounds. The shadow forms of the others rode with them. Dressel and the townsfolk charged after their lord, taking up his call. Flashes of lightning appeared here and there throughout the battlefield.

Julianna turned and buried her face in Vendyr's mane. Tears threatened to pour from her eyes, but she blinked them back. Tears were a luxury she could no longer afford. After some time had passed, she looked up. The shades of Allifar and Taebor no longer rode with them.

THIRTY THREE

Duke Octavio Salvatore, Governor of the Kingdom protectorate of Koma left the Temple of Night, walked through the Lies he'd woven around the place to keep it from being discovered, and headed to his favorite balcony where he would stare into the night sky and consider all he'd seen and learned throughout everything that had occurred in Shadybrook. Dante hurried up and fell into step next to Octavio.

"Please, dear brother," Octavio said, "if you don't have anything to offer by way of a Fate or prophesy, I'd rather you stay quiet. Or, better yet, leave me to my thoughts."

"Good night, brother," Dante said, and turned at the next intersection of hallways.

Octavio continued straight. His thoughts outpaced his footsteps. Unconsciously, he quickened his pace every so often with the intent to catch them. Then, when he'd reach the point just short of a jog, he slowed, took a breath, and reminded himself, "Patience."

In one such hurried moment, Octavio came around a corner and nearly collided with a pair of serving girls. Neither of them was native to the Kingdom of the Sun. One, Octavio was sure, was Komati, but he couldn't place the other. He never bothered to learn the features of the various people the Kingdom conquered, save for the Komati. He found the pale, creamy complexion of Komati women a fascinating change from the olive tone of Floraen skin. The other Great Houses were fairer of skin than Floraen, but none had the smooth, porcelain-like skin of the Komati.

Both girls curtsied when they saw him, casting their eyes toward the floor.

"Rise, and be about your duties," Octavio said.

They did so, but as they walked away, he saw the Komati girl glancing at him. When she noticed him looking back, she giggled a little.

"What is your name?" Octavio asked.

"Layla, my lord," the girl answered.

"How long have you been in my service?"

"A few months, my lord."

"You are a comely thing," Octavio said. "I'll have to speak to Roma about assigning you duties in my personal chambers."

"Your lordship is too kind." Layla gave him a deep curtsy, though her eyes met his and he saw a hint of passion behind her false meekness.

He watched them go. Once they were out of sight, Octavio continued toward his balcony. Only, now the first rays of dawn shone through the windows along this corridor. Octivio's stomach growled. Instead of going on to the balcony, he turned and headed for the dining room.

If he happened across the serving girls again, he'd spare a few more words with Layla. By the way she'd looked at him, Layla no doubt thought that Octavio intended to make her his mistress. However, Octavio would never dishonor his vows of marriage. His wife, Portia, was far too beautiful and, more importantly, dangerous for him to consider taking another woman into his bed. Besides, she held his heart firmly in her hand and they both knew it. It was well because Octavio had the same effect on her. They shared everything with each other, having no secrets.

Still, they didn't mind some rumors circulating through the staff that Octavio occasionally took lovers. It made it easier to explain why some of the young servant girls would be transferred away after turning up pregnant.

Entering the dining room, Octavio pushed aside his thoughts of matters that would best wait for later.

Portia rose from her seat and gave him a slight curtsy, due to his position as the governor and because his title of Duke slightly outranked her title of Countess. It was an unnecessary show of respect, but Portia did it just to be playful. She wore a red dress with wide hoops and a low-cut neckline. Her corset was tied in such a way as to make her small breasts look as if they were about to spill from her dress. Her curtsy only enhanced this effect.

Octavio drank in this view of his wife. She met his gaze with her deep, dark eyes. Her smile and the slight droop of her eyelids spoke volumes of what he could expect this evening when they were alone.

"You had a long night, my love," Portia said.

Octavio nodded. "I need tea. Lots of it. Strong tea."

"You should rest," Portia said, and poured him a cup.

"I should, but I cannot." Octavio swallowed the whole cup of near-scalding tea in one swallow. "I have to deal with some affairs of state, including a pack of Komati nobles who might be Morigahnti."

Portia poured another cup. "Why not kill them?"

"So many at once would be too challenging to keep quiet." Octavio sipped the tea this time. "And right now, considering what we have planned, we cannot afford to draw attention to ourselves."

"What will you do?" Portia asked.

Octavio didn't need to ask which situation Portia was asking about. The answer remained the same.

"Be patient." He sipped the tea again. "Trust that the answers will come, either from my mind or Dante's pronouncements."

MOMENTS BETWEEN UPHEAVALS

god will never comprehend
how a man's mind will split
at each of life's crossroads.

Which harp string will fate pluck next?
Which way shall we dance?

Gravestones are for the survivors.
Leave my body to rejoin the elements,
and get on with your business of living.

-Archer

ONE

Hours later, Julianna rode Vendyr and followed Faelin down a strip of semi-packed earth somewhere between a trail and a side road. The trees had thinned. Finally, hours after dawn the rain stopped, the clouds parted in places, and the sun peeked out from between them. Julianna tugged on Vendyr's reigns, closed her eyes, and reveled in the warmth of the sun on her face. For the briefest of moments, her body tensed for fear that Grandfather Shadow would admonish her for her enjoying another god's blessing, but then considered that he was the god of balance, and Julianna had suffered wind, rain, and cold for days and days, this could hardly be called the sin worthy of admonishment. Even that bit of warmth washed away a sliver of her exhaustion.

Up ahead, the sounds of Faelin's horse tromping through the mud ceased. Julianna imagined him turning in his saddle.

"Julianna?" Faelin asked.

Julianna held up a hand. They had been going and going and going, harder and faster, fighting, and all of it with little rest for days and days. She needed this moment. Thankfully, Faelin said nothing until Julianna gave Vendyr a slight tap with both her heels to get the horse moving again.

"We should be able to rest soon," Faelin said.

"Should?"

Julianna forced herself not to glance sidelong at him as she had when they were children. So many old habits she would have to overcome to keep people from knowing how close they truly were. The Brotherhood of the Night had exploited that once already.

"If memory serves," Faelin replied.

Julianna left that be for now.

They rode a bit longer. The clouds continued to clear. The sun continued to shine and warm them both.

Vendyr's steps became a bit more energetic. He loved rolling in mud and prancing and streams, but he hated rain. The continuous cold made him snappish and grumpy. With the sun soaking into his black hair, he'd be a bit more likely to test Julianna's patience. She kept a tight rein on him indeed, and when he behaved himself, she scratched behind his ears and rubbed his favorite spot on his neck.

A short time later, they came to a river so wide they couldn't possibly cross it anywhere nearby. More than that, a bridge was also unlikely. Julianna looked up and downstream. Some several dozen yards downstream, Julianna spied a large river barge. A man worked back and forth on the deck to make it ready for travel. After observing for a few moments, she recognized Faelin's friend Zephyr.

"That's your plan?" Julianna asked.

"Indeed it is," Faelin said. "It's a choice neither the Brotherhood nor the Inquisitors will expect. We'll get downriver to a city and hide among the masses until the Morigahnti join us."

"I thought you wanted to avoid the Morigahnti," Julianna said.

"Well, things changed quite a bit last night," Faelin replied

Julianna snorted at his understatement. Instead of pursuing that line of thought, she asked, "How did you know he would still be here?"

"I didn't," Faelin said. "I took a gamble."

"You trust him enough to gamble being alone on a boat with him for several days?"

"He helped free me from the Nightbrothers camp," Faelin said.

"He told me he was planning to," Julianna said. "I know he's your friend, but this is a little different."

"Perhaps," Faelin said. But he had left Shadybrook hours before the attack. He could have been well enough away, safe and clear, but he came back to help me. More than that, he has much more reason to fear the Kingdom as you do."

"I doubt that," Juliana said. "It's one thing to be a smuggler. It is ill-becoming to lie to your Lord Morigahn."

Faelin snickered through his nose. "I would never speak a falsehood to Grandfather Shadow's chosen voice. That one has been running years longer than you have."

"For guns?" Julianna asked.

Faelin shrugged. "Those, and other secrets that are his to tell or not tell."

By this time, the man on the boat had noticed them. Zephyr stood on the raised platform in the rear of the boat and regarded them with arms crossed.

"No," Zephyr called when they grew closer.

"As a favor to an old friend?" Faelin called back.

"No," Zephyr said. "I already did you several favors last night. You're already in debt to me more than you have a lifetime to repay me."

By that time, Faelin and Julianna had reached the boat.

"You are going to cast this lady and an old friend to the winds of chance and fate?" Failing asked.

Without so much as a glance at Julianna, Zephyr said, aren't you the one who told me I wanted nothing to do with that particular lady, and I should flee, post haste?"

Julianna drew a breath to retort but Faelin placed his hand on her forearm. She decided to remain silent.

"I was just explaining to her that much has changed since that conversation," Faelin said. "Much has changed for all of us last night."

"Yes." Zephyr made a point of rolling his eyes. "Over the course of the night the brotherhood of the night, Red Draqons, Floraen Inquisitors, Daemyn hounds, and the Morigahnti almost discovered who I truly am. That's quite a change since the sun last set."

"Who are you?" Julianna blurted before Faelin could stop her.

Zephyr looked at Faelin. "Didn't tell her?"

Faelin shook his head. "As I just told her, your secrets are not mine to share."

Zephyr groaned and turned around. "Damn you for your overly self-righteous sense of honor and friendship."

"May we please come aboard?" Faelin asked.

Zephyr gave an exaggerated sigh. "Damn you. Fine. But I can only accommodate one horse."

"Thank you," Faelin said. "We only plan on taking one with us anyway."

TWO

Yrgaeshkil strode through the remains of Shadybrook township. So many souls there had been returned to the cycle of life, death, and rebirth. More than that, the Daemyn hounds had consumed some souls completely. Unfortunately, the Stormseekers had joined the battle on the side of the townsfolk. Every Damyn hound save one had fallen, and not a single Stormseeker. The sole Daemyn hound that survived was now hunting the two that the Lord Morigahn had sent away from Shadybrook before the fighting began.

Razka was out there, somewhere or somewhen, waiting to appear and inform Yrgaeshkil how cleverly he had pierced her Lie. That is, he would have done so if Yrgaeshkil had chosen to do so. Instead, rather than give him the satisfaction once again, the Mother of Daemyns walked with no Lies about her, not even masking her true nature. Her right wing spread upward to shield herself from All Father Sun's light, and her hooves stomped through any of those on the field still clinging to life. Each time, she snatched the soul before it could escape into the spirit world and then enter the realm of whichever god it had held dear in this life. Instead, she flung those souls into the dark realm of the godless dead.

"You are a tricky one," Galad'Ysoysa spoke from behind her.

"Come to try again?" Yrgaeshkil asked, and stopped walking.

"No, Galad'Ysoysa said. "I can sense the second dominion on you. Congratulations. It's been a long while since I've fallen victim to any ruse."

Yrgaeshkil turned to face the god of shadows. He appeared as a late middle-aged man with salt and pepper through his dark beard and dark hair and dressed in the current heights of fashion in Koma City. If not for the battle around him, he might have looked as if he was heading to a ball or an evening at his gentlemen's club.

"If you aren't here to kill me what do you want?"

Galad'Ysoysa smiled. "I have two simple requests. First, spare the souls of my people on this field."

"Very well," Yrgaeshkil replied. "The other?"

"Second, we keep our distance. Meddle in each other's affairs through proxies and careful and subtle interventions. Anything too overt from any of the Greater Eldar will draw the King of Order's attention."

"You're scared of him," Yrgaeshkil scoffed.

"I'm realistic when it comes to him," Galad'Ysoysa countered. "You should be as well. He's already dragged me through the realms once for an audience and a warning. I don't relish the thought of too much of his attention on this world. You're clever, I'll give you that. However, I've been at this game longer. We can enjoy each other as distant adversaries, or we can both suffer his impatience."

Yrgaeshkil considered. "Fine. Agreed."

Galad'Ysoysa clapped his hands together as if he had just won a game of cards or a wager on some sport or other. "Excellent. I look forward to matching the Lord Morigahn against your high priest, once you name one. I'm also looking forward to your husband's freedom."

Yrgaeshkil merely offered a soft "Humph," in response.

Galad'Ysoysa chuckled and vanished.

Yrgaeshkil had hoped the Lie of her death would have lasted a bit longer, but she shouldn't have been surprised. Care and subtlety. She had tried. But... well... she'd remained free of the King of Order's exile due to her quick thinking and adaptability. Learn and change. Humans did it. How challenging could it be? Care and subtlety.

Yrgaeshkil resumed walking through the ruined township, reached the smoky remains of the manor house, and summoned several of her lesser children.

"Dig through the timbers and ash," Yrgaeshkil said. "Free Saent Muriel, bring her to me, then return to the realm of the godless dead. Do nothing else. I must attend to one of my priests."

For a moment, Yrgaeshkil considered stepping into the spirit realm, or perhaps finding an entrance to one of the faerii *ajorta* paths. Either one would take her to Koma City with the same quickness. Then, she disregarded either option. She was a Greater Elder now. She had proven her patience over the last thousand years. Instead, the mother of demons, the goddess of lies, stretched her wings out and took to the sky. What good was it to be Greater Eldar if she kept slinking about like some lesser creature?

In the center of a low floating cloud, Yrgaeshkil realized she should probably stop that last hound from hunting. It might not violate the letter of her agreement with Galad'Ysoysa, but it would do no harm to garner a bit of goodwill with him. Especially, since at some point, her husband would become free, and then allies would be her most precious commodity of all.

THREE

Jenice woke with a start and sat up. Something was coming towards them through the underbrush.

Novan had set a hard pace through the dawn and well into the morning until neither of them could continue without stumbling every few steps. They went a good way from the road, lay against a tree and a small clearing, and huddled together for warmth.

Jenice grabbed Novan's arm and shook it. "Wake up."

Novan bolted upright with the two-shot pistol in his hand. He aimed it in the direction of the rustling leaves and snapping twigs.

Moments later, a puppy came romping out of the brush. Novan lowered the gun and took a step toward it.

"No. Don't." Jenice grabbed his shoulder and pulled him back "That thing and others like it hunted the Lord Morigahn and me last night."

"That tiny thing?" Novan asked. "He didn't fight against Jenice, but didn't seem to grasp her urgency."

"Yes," Jenise hissed. "Shoot it, and flee."

The puppy's eyes glowed a sickly orange, and it rushed at them.

Mid-leap, something crashed through the tree branches above, dropped to the earth, and snapped the demon hound puppy out of the air.

Jenice might have screamed if her mind hadn't been so overwhelmed by the sight before her. A creature with a woman's body, a bat's head, horns like a ram's, hooves like a ram's, and leathery wings that filled the clearing looked at the puppy in its hand with a tender expression completely out of place on its inhuman features. The pup barked and snarled.

Now now. The creature's voice washed over Jenice like her old gran's when offering tea after a disappointment.

"No need for that. You had fun last night. Ate a few souls. It's time to go now."

The pups sniveled and whined.

"You'll get to come and play again soon, the monstrous thing said. I promise." She blew in the pup's face, and the thing went limp.

Then, in the midst of turning towards Novan and Jenice, the creature became a striking woman in a black and velvet ball gown. She circled around the two, the youths. Novan and Jenice leaned into each other under the woman's ancient gaze.

"So interesting that Galad'Ysoysa such places so much care of such upon such simple minuscule beings as such as you. Why? What makes you who can't even speak miracles so worthy of his care?"

The woman wasn't really talking to them, rather musing about them under examination as a farmer might muse over livestock at the spring fair.

"Oh well. I have centuries upon centuries to puzzle this out."

The massive wings burst from her back, flapped with such force as to kick up leaves, twigs, and clouds of mud, and she took to the sky once again.

Jenice and Novan held each other for several long moments more and looked up through the trees where the woman had gone.

"We should go," Novan said at last.

Jenice could only nod. If they quickened their pace, they could reach Count Allifar's estate, Duskwind, by sunset. Together they will tell everyone what had occurred what had occurred in Shadybrook..

FOUR

It had been a long time since Damian had thought deeply about what made this riverboat so easy to navigate and why he didn't need a crew. However, seeing Faelin and that woman with the scar—Julianna or the Lord Morigahn, he couldn't decide how to hold her in his mind—brought back so many memories and contemplations about the influence of gods and goddesses on the world. Did they often meddle in the affairs of humans, or were he and Faelin special?

About an hour down the river, Faelin was softly snoring, and the woman stood and joined him in the back. Julianna was far easier for Damian to accept rather than the Lord Morigahn. Damian nodded at her when she joined him. She looked haggard as any overworked guardsman he'd ever seen, and given his time smuggling over the last few years, he'd seen far many overworked guardsmen. Bribed a lot of them.

"How long have you known Faelin?" Julianna asked.

"Most of my life," Damian replied. "Our fathers were friends. Well, before my father died. Even after that, Faelin and I had our adventures."

"My uncle and his father were friends as well," Julianna said. "Well until the Kingdom killed all the Traejyns. Odd that we've never met before this."

Damian shrugged. He felt he should change the subject before it led them into uncomfortable questions he had no desire to dance around.

"That's quite an animal you have there'" Damian gestured with his chin toward the bow of the boat where they tethered the magnificent horse. The black and white monster happily chomped on the apples meant for Damian's horse, killed last night.

"I've had him even longer than I've known Faelin," Julianna said. "He has spirit, but he also knows when he's up against a futile battle."

"Like being tethered in a riverboat," Damian said.

Julianna nodded. "Like being tethered in a riverboat. The basket of apples doesn't hurt either."

Damian chuckled. "I'd noticed. Rather food motivated?"

Now Juliana chuckled. "More than any other horse I've ever known."

It was a nice chuckle. A natural chuckle. Damian hadn't expected to hear such a sound coming from someone who had obviously been through so much hardship so recently.

Damien decided he liked Julianna, this Lord Morigahn. A shame they'd never met at court before his father's scandal, execution, and Damian's self-imposed exile. However, that exile was preferable to death. The problem with liking Julianna was that Damian couldn't afford friends. Even Faelin had proven himself to be one friend too many over the last night and day.

Before the silence between them lapsed into questions from Julianna, Damian turned the subject to the mundane, "Shouldn't you take Faelin's example and get some rest?"

"Sleep and rest rarely offer me any comfort," Julianna replied. Besides, I'm enjoying the sun.

Well, perhaps Damian could deflect that into another way to get her to leave him be.

"Is that rest thing because you are the Lord Morigahn?" Damien asked.

"Yes." Julianna paused. "And no. Some of it is in remembering my parents and cousins. Some of it is in what led me to become the Lord Morigahn. Most of it is in questions I can't figure out the answers to."

Well, the gamble hadn't paid off. He'd expected her to leave him be once he started prying.

"Why share this with me?" Damian asked.

Julianna turned around, leaned on the rail, and watched the river pass for a time. Damian let her have her moment, content with the silence between them. Hopefully, the silence would last through most of the voyage over the next few days.

A short time later, she spoke. "Faelin trusts you. That speaks well for you. He wouldn't trust the Morgahnti, well not all of them. We were originally going to flee Koma entirely. But you? He trusts you enough to be on this boat alone for a few days." She looked around. "Where's your crew?"

"Don't need one," Damian said.

"Why not?" Julianna asked.

Her curiosity about the response was natural. Normally it would have been a far larger craft than Damien could manage on his own. How would he answer her other questions?

"I just don't."

"Who are you?" Julianna asked. "And don't say Zephyr the smuggler. We both know that's a fiction, a mask, your armor against the Kingdom and the people you do business with."

"Faelin didn't tell you?" Damian asked.

Julianna shook her head. "He told you so himself just before we got on your boat. It's your secret to tell."

"Good man, that Faelin vara'Traejyn," Damian said.

"One of the best," Julianna said. "I'd be dead many times over if it were not for him."

"At least two for me," Damian said. "As for who I am, I suppose it's only fair considering I know that you're the Lord Morigahn. I am Damian Adryk."

Julianna turned around to look at him again.

"The Unkilled Prince?" Julianna's voice grew higher in pitch with her surprise.

Damien couldn't help but smile. "I've liked that one since the moment I first heard it, but I'm slightly more partial to the Whirlwind Blade myself."

"That does have a certain sound of legend to it."

Julianna returned to watching the river. A few minutes later she barked a sudden, brief laugh. It was the kind of laugh someone gives when something isn't really funny, but they don't know what other expression or sounds to give it.

"What?" Damian asked.

"Two thoughts," Julianna replied. "One led to the other. If my aunt, my guardian, knew that I was on this boat with a prince of the realm, she'd be whispering in my ear to be more charming. She's very conscious of the Order of Precedence and how well I can marry. That thought, my station and yours, led me to thinking about how much any number of High Blood would pay to know that we are both on this boat, together, with no real chance for escape if they came for us with sufficient numbers."

Damian laughed in much the same way as Julianna had.

"I have some thoughts now."

Julianna continued to face the river. "Oh?"

"First," Damian said, "I noticed you tend not to face people when you speak to them. Is that about the scar?"

It took Julianna a few moments to reply, "Yes."

"Does it—" Damian stopped himself. "Sorry."

"You want to know if it hurts," Julianna said.

"I shouldn't have asked," Damien said.

"Only sometimes," Julianna replied. "And that's all I'll say about it. What other thoughts did you have?"

"One that you wouldn't know about. If the Kingdom attacked us here, they might not find it as easy as kiss my hand to assault the boat."

"Why is that?"

This time Julianna did turn around to face him. Her pale gray eyes fixed on his. He forced himself to maintain his gaze on her.

"For the same reason I don't need a crew," Damien replied. "I possess the blessings of Sister Wave. And no, I'm not ready to share all of that story. Part of it is mine to tell." He glanced at Faelin sleeping on sacks of gunpowder.

"Intriguing," Julianna said.

"Odd that you would use that word," Damian said. "It's at the heart of my final thought.

"And that is?" Juliana asked.

"Your aunt knows very little of men," Damien replied. "At least it seems so if she wants you to try and be charming. Men don't want a charming woman. We want a woman who intrigues us. A bit of mystery or intrigue will capture a man's heart faster than charm has any hope to. I predict you will capture many a man's heart. They will love you and break themselves for your love."

Julianna's eyes went hard. She glared at Damian for a long moment. Even before her gaze changed, he knew he'd overstepped as soon as he'd spoken. She turned her back to him.

"Loyalty is what I need, Zephyr." She used his smuggler's name in a way that told him they were done with any casual conversation. "I have no use for love."

Damian choked back a sigh. He was an idiot. It was going to be a long few days.

FIVE

Princess Josephine Adryck hated needlework more than anything else in the world. The tedium of the task represented everything she hated about the expectations of being a woman in court. A Komati woman was expected to be graceful, still, and be a perfect vision of aesthetic beauty; however, that was as much as she was permitted to become. Any true depth of character or intellect was frowned upon, if not outright scorned.

Because Josephine desired so much more than outward expectations, she had first mastered the ability to appear as the proper courtly lady. She had learned all the appropriate skills, needlework being the foremost of them. Needlework allowed her to better keep her emotions hidden. She had become an expert at stabbing her finger, dropping her project at just the right time, or feigning some mistake at just the right moment of a conversation when anyone came close to discovering her true cunning. The games she played at using her needlework while dealing with other nobles had become so enjoyable that she had come to detest it a little less, until six months ago.

Her fingers had begun to develop the tremor that sometimes came with old age. If she had been born of different parents, Josephine might have gone another two decades without a single tremor creeping into her hands. However, her father had developed this condition while he was very young, as had his father. Now it was her turn, and she had been forced to take up needlework in private again to maintain her skill. She prayed that this family trait passed over Xander and Damian—especially Damian. His life depended on him being able to hold a sword with a steady hand.

A soft gust of wind blew the curtains inward, bringing the scent of wet flowers into the sitting room. Josephine loved the smell of her flower garden just after a rain, though she took little pleasure in it this evening. There had been no breeze before, and this one died almost as soon as it arrived. This strange occurrence of wind only happened when one man came to call.

"What do you want?" Josephine asked.

Maxian stepped into the room. "I have news regarding your sons."

As always, he wore the leathers and furs of the Dosahan savages, and his nearly black eyes pierced deep into hers. Ever since they were young, Josephine found it difficult to breathe when she was the subject of Maxian's unwavering gaze. However, after knowing him for nearly three decades, she had finally managed to build a resistance to him.

Josephine set down her needlework, reached over to the table beside her, and turned over the small sandglass that she kept there. Shortly after Maxian first started making his unannounced and uninvited visits, Josephine placed a small sandglass within reach. At first, she reserved its use for Maxian alone, but now she used it for everyone who came to call. Any visitor had until the sand ran out to pique her interest or Josephine dismissed them. Having set the sand pouring, Josephine folded her hands together, placed them in her lap, and faced Maxian with her most practiced bored expression.

"Grandfather Shadow is free," Maxian said.

"You are lying," Josephine said, her voice flat.

"I have wronged you in many ways over our lives, but I've never lied to you. Why would I start now?"

Maxian lied to many people. Sometimes Josephine had wished that he could lie to her, if only to spare her feelings. However, in all the years they had known each other, Maxian had always been honest with her, sometimes brutally so.

More than half of the sand remained in the upper part of the sandglass. Josephine reached over and tipped the timepiece on its edge.

"And the other greater gods?" she asked.

Grandfather Shadow being free presented its own problems for Xander and Damian. If any of the other gods were also free, the world would be a very deadly place for Josephine's sons.

"As far as I know, they are still imprisoned," Maxian answered.

"Khellan and the Morigahnti must be overjoyed their god is finally free," Josephine said.

She wanted to know more about Xander and Damian, but didn't want to appear overanxious. Even though she and Maxian were usually allies, they each had goals independent of each other.

"Khellan is dead. The Brotherhood killed him the day Grandfather Shadow was freed."

Khellan's death meant the Morigahnti would begin squabbling amongst themselves trying to determine who would be the next Lord Morigahn. Then again, Grandfather Shadow would likely choose the strongest man among the Morigahnti and raise him to the title.

However, another far more pressing question plagued Josephine's mind. "How much do the Morigahnti know about my sons?"

"Of the few that know who your sons are, most are your late husband's friends and allies," Maxian replied. "The only two who know and were not in your husband's small circle of friends are Sandré Collaen and Jaesyn Thaems."

"Sandré will be my sons' enemy, and nobody truly knows where Duke Jaesyn's loyalties lie," Josephine said. "You have to kill them."

"No," Maxian replied with the emotionless, almost bored expression that Josephine despised.

"You would leave those two living and have them oppose Xander and Damian?"

"As much as I loathe Sandré Collaen, I cannot be sure he will oppose either the Lord Morigahn or Xander and Damian. Grandfather Shadow is speaking to the Stormcrows. They will tell the Morigahnti the truth about Julianna."

"But Sandré has always held the Stormcrows with a certain disdain. How often has he spoken of his feelings that the Morigahnti of old relied too much on the Stormcrows, and that if it weren't for that reliance, Koma would still be its own nation?"

"It will likely be different with Grandfather Shadow free. Sandré will either bring himself to heel, or Grandfather Shadow will ruin him. Even still, knowing Sandré, he will focus his attention on the new Lord Morigahn before everything else. He has known about your sons for years, and he is biding his time. He will likely wait and see what path Xander and Damian take before committing himself. Jaesyn is even more careful. Your sons are not in any immediate danger from the Morigahnti, and if I've heard correctly, all Koma might just rally behind Xander and Damian."

"How do you know all this?"

A thin smile crept onto Maxian's lips. "Razka and I still speak from time to time. He has been watching the Lord Morigahn, just as the Stormcrows have been watching your sons."

"Do you know the new Lord Morigahn?" Josephine asked.

Maxian nodded.

"Who?"

"Julianna Taraen."

That caught Josephine off guard. "But she hasn't followed Grandfather Shadow since—"

"She does now," Maxian replied. "Grandfather Shadow named her the Lord Morigahn, and she seems to be acclimating to the role rather quickly. She has gained a Fist of Morigahnti followers who seem loyal to her, and she speaks miracles as if she has been doing so for years. I have a feeling she will meet Sandré Collaen sooner rather than later, and then the first true test of her worthiness to lead the Morigahnti will begin."

"Why tell me all this?" Josephine asked.

"Your sons are being drawn into this, whether they or you like it or not," Maxian said. "You may not be able to aid either of your sons directly, but I think the time is coming when they will need your influence. You can walk in places and influence people that neither of them can access. Grandfather Shadow means to free Koma from the Kingdom. That means your sons will be called to rule. They will need you to teach them the tactics and strategies of court, Josephine."

"I will make the necessary arrangements," Josephine replied. "Is it truly time? Will Koma be free at last?"

"With Grandfather Shadow free, it would seem so. However, I imagine the outcome of present events will be something none of us, gods or men, can possibly imagine."

He bowed and turned to leave.

"Maxian, what of Julianna?" Josephine called after him. "Who will protect her from Sandré Collaen?"

"She is protected." Maxian's tone indicated that he was finished with the conversation.

Normally, Josephine would have left well enough alone, but this time she felt that Maxian could not afford to remain aloof from the situation. He'd already sacrificed too much of his humanity since his wife died. "You are the only man to bear the mantle of Lord Morigahn that she could trust. Will you help her?"

"I have been helping her. When the time is right, I will reveal myself to the Morigahnti."

He stepped back through the curtains, and, with a small gust of wind, he was gone.

Six

Octavio Salvatore and Portia entered the small dining room for his afternoon meeting with Dyrk, the leader of the Vara in Koma city. The Vara were a ragged and unruly group who acted as constables and guardsmen within many cities and large towns throughout Koma. They dealt with crimes that did not involve the High Blood. No need to waste the White Draqons on such petty matters. However, any High Blood with a modicum of intelligence sent to Koma did their best to gain some influence over the Vara. Personally, Octavio couldn't decide if he loathed or liked Dyrk. Politically, the Vara commander had become a distasteful necessity.

Dyrk sat with his feet on the table, a goblet of wine in one hand, and a leg of mutton in the other. His black hair was pulled back and spilled over the back of the chair. His black eyes sparkled with malicious humor. As usual, he wore all gray, including the gray hood that all of the Vara wore.

"Your hospitality lacks for nothing, as always, Governor Salvatore," Dyrk said.

The infuriating man never showed Octavio his due respect in private. However, when others were about, the ruffian's manners became impeccable. Dyrk's ability to display just the right amount of subservience in public settings had earned him the right to be a bit arrogant when he and Octavio were alone. That Dyrk was also incredibly useful and good at removing people *before* they became problems also played a part in Octavio's tolerance.

"I'm happy you approve," Octavio said.

"I'll leave you two to discuss your business," Portia said. "I'll be waiting in our chambers, my husband."

"Good night, my flame," Octavio said, and watched her depart.

"You have a beautiful woman there," Dyrk said.

"And that's just the least of the reasons that I love her." Octavio sat at the other end of the table.

A place had been set out for him, with wine already poured. He knew at a glance that a Komati servant, a new one at that, had laid out the utensils. Even though the placement of the utensils was perfectly aligned, they were silver. Being House Floraen, Octavio preferred to eat with goldware, at least publicly. Komati only used goldware for the most formal occasions.

"Thank you for accepting my invitation," Octavio continued. "I know what a busy man you are."

"Nonsense," Dyrk said. "I'm never too busy for the Governor, especially because your gifts are much more lavish than any of your countrymen."

"Indeed," Octavio said. "And that is why I've asked you here this evening. I wish to exchange gifts. Does the name Damian Adryck mean anything to you?"

Dyrk grinned. "The Unkilled Prince? The Whirlwind Blade? Though now just a common gun smuggler you Kingdom lot can't seem to capture?"

Octavio nodded.

Dyrk shook his head. "Can't say I've heard of him."

Octavio wasn't surprised Dyrk had heard of Adryck. Nearly every Komati had. Damian had been a fugitive for years and had become something of a folk hero to many Komati common folk, and an embarrassment to the Komati nobility.

"Well, now you have," Octavio said.

"What do you want with him?" Dyrk asked.

"My sources tell me that he's coming to Koma City," Octavio said.

"You want me to capture Damian Adryck so you can make an example of him?"

"No," Octavio said. "I want you to kill him, quietly, so that nobody knows and nobody mourns him, especially not his older brother."

SEVEN

At just past dawn two days after stepping on Damian's riverboat, Julianna and Faelin stood on the Bank of the Jokhi River and watched Damian Adryck float out of sight around a bend. Vendyr grazed on nearby grass, bright and green from the rains. Faelin and Damian had shared final waves a few minutes before. The wayward Prince and smuggler would pass Johki City hours before Julianna and Faelin, but he would not stop. Julianna had heard Damian telling Faelin how he wanted nothing to do with people or cities until Koma City where he could sell his firearms and get off this damn and bloody continent. For her part, Julianna kept her distance from Damian as the riverboat allowed for the duration of their voyage.

Once Damian was out of sight, Faelin coughed, and asked, "Are you going to tell me what happened between you two?"

"No," Julianna said.

Doing so would only lead to deeper thoughts about Kkellan. She could not afford love. Men were idiots enough on their own. The last thing any of them needed was to suffer the consequences of loving the Lord Morigahn.

"To Johki then?" Faelin asked.

"Yes," Julianna replied, and wrapped her *galad'fana* around her face to hide the scar. "When the Morigahnti join us, I want to make one change to our strategy."

"What's that?" Faelin asked.

Julianna drew her Mother's faerii steel dirk.

"I am the Lord Morigahn." Julianna thought about all those who had already died so that she could continue on. "I am done running."

About the Author

Recently, the #GallowglasArmy, the name M. Todd Gallowglas gave to his tiny, yet rabidly loyal fan club, have met with dismay and sorrow as their beloved storyteller and author was sentenced to a life sentence in Folsom Prison after he suffered a psychotic episode and decapitated four drunken hecklers at one of his storytelling shows. In the seventy-two hours following the incident, nearly half of the #GallowglasArmy attempted to take credit for the brutal slayings, but Todd would not have any of his devoted followers suffer in his stead. Rather than flee from his actions, Todd turned himself in and pleaded guilty. Still, so many members of the #GallowglasArmy tried to interrupt the trial with nearly-continuous shenanigans, the trial is now the longest murder trial in the history of the United States as well holds the most arrests for contempt of court in recorded history. So as not to be without their beloved storyteller, several members of the #GallowglasArmy, pulled their ingenuity, time, and resources together, to create a perfect facsimile of Todd in robot form. That robot performs at Renaissance Faires and attends comic cons while Todd uses the quiet of solitary confinement to constantly improve his writing craft. Really. It's the robot that shows up to all of Todd's appearances. REALLY.

Made in the USA
Columbia, SC
23 February 2025